130-82

D1499641

The Robot Novels

THE CAVES OF STEEL
THE NAKED SUN

ISAAC ASIMOV

The Robot Novels

THE CAVES OF STEEL
THE NAKED SUN

DOUBLEDAY & COMPANY, INC.
GARDEN CITY, NEW YORK

The Caves of Steel

To my wife, Gertrude,
and my son, David

Contents

1

Conversation With a Commissioner

LIJE BALEY had just reached his desk when he became aware of R. Sammy watching him expectantly.

The dour lines of his long face hardened. "What do you want?"

"The boss wants you, Lije. Right away. Soon as you come in."

"All right."

R. Sammy stood there blankly.

Baley said, "I said, all right. Go away!"

R. Sammy turned on his heel and left to go about his duties. Baley wondered irritably why those same duties couldn't be done by a man.

He paused to examine the contents of his tobacco pouch and make a mental calculation. At two pipefuls a day, he could stretch it to next quota day.

Then he stepped out from behind his railing (he'd rated a railed corner two years ago) and walked the length of the common room.

Simpson looked up from a merc-pool file as he passed. "Boss wants you, Lije."

"I know. R. Sammy told me."

A closely coded tape reeled out of the merc-pool's vitals as the small instrument searched and analyzed its "memory" for the desired information stored in the tiny vibration patterns of the gleaming mercury surface within.

"I'd kick R. Sammy's behind if I weren't afraid I'd break a leg," said Simpson. "I saw Vince Barrett the other day."

"Oh?"

"He was looking for his job back. Or any job in the Department. The poor kid's desperate, but what could *I* tell him. R. Sammy's doing his job and that's all. The kid has to work a delivery tread on the yeast farms now. He was a bright boy, too. Everyone liked him."

Baley shrugged and said in a manner stiffer than he intended or felt, "It's a thing we're all living through."

The boss rated a private office. It said JULIUS ENDERBY on the clouded glass. Nice letters. Carefully etched into the fabric of the glass. Underneath, it said COMMISSIONER OF POLICE, CITY OF NEW YORK.

Baley stepped in and said, "You want to see me, Commissioner?"

Enderby looked up. He wore spectacles because his eyes were sensitive and couldn't take the usual contact lenses. It was only after one got used to the sight of them that one could take in the rest of the face, which was quite undistinguished. Baley had a strong notion that the Commissioner valued his glasses for the personality they lent him and suspected that his eyeballs weren't as sensitive as all that.

The Commissioner looked definitely nervous. He straightened his cuffs, leaned back, and said, too heartily, "Sit down, Lije. Sit down."

Baley sat down stiffly and waited.

Enderby said, "How's Jessie? And the boy?"

"Fine," said Baley, hollowly. "Just fine. And your family?"

"Fine," echoed Enderby. "Just fine."

It had been a false start.

Baley thought: Something's wrong with his face.

Aloud, he said, "Commissioner, I wish you wouldn't send R. Sammy out after me."

"Well, you know how I feel about those things, Lije. But he's been put here and I've got to use him for something."

"It's uncomfortable, Commissioner. He tells me you want me and then he stands there. You know what I mean. I have to tell him to go or he just keeps on standing there."

"Oh, that's my fault, Lije. I gave him the message to deliver and forgot to tell him specifically to get back to his job when he was through."

Baley sighed. The fine wrinkles about his intensely brown eyes grew more pronounced. "Anyway, you wanted to see me."

"Yes, Lije," said the Commissioner, "but not for anything easy."

He stood up, turned away, and walked to the wall behind his desk. He touched an inconspicuous contact switch and a section of the wall grew transparent.

Baley blinked at the unexpected insurge of grayish light.

The Commissioner smiled. "I had this arranged specially last year, Lije. I don't think I've showed it to you before. Come over here and take a look. In the old days, all rooms had things like this. They were called 'windows.' Did you know that?"

Baley knew that very well, having viewed many historical novels. "I've heard of them," he said.

"Come here."

Baley squirmed a bit, but did as he was told. There was something indecent about the exposure of the privacy of a room to the outside world. Sometimes the Commissioner carried his affectation of Medievalism to a rather foolish extreme.

Like his glasses, Baley thought.

That was it! That was what made him look wrong!

Baley said, "Pardon me, Commissioner, but you're wearing new glasses, aren't you?"

The Commissioner stared at him in mild surprise, took off his glasses, looked at them and then at Baley. Without his glasses, his round face seemed rounder and his chin a trifle more pronounced. He looked vaguer, too, as his eyes failed to focus properly.

He said, "Yes."

He put his glasses back on his nose, then added with real anger, "I broke my old ones three days ago. What with one thing or another I wasn't able to replace them till this morning. Lije, those three days were hell."

"On account of the glasses?"

"And other things, too. I'm getting to that."

He turned to the window and so did Baley. With mild shock, Baley realized it was raining. For a minute, he was lost in the spectacle of water dropping from the sky, while the Commissioner exuded a kind of pride as though the phenomenon were a matter of his own arranging.

"This is the third time this month I've watched it rain. Quite a sight, don't you think?"

Against his will, Baley had to admit to himself that it was impressive. In his forty-two years he had rarely seen rain, or any of the phenomena of nature, for that matter.

He said, "It always seems a waste for all that water to come down on the city. It should restrict itself to the reservoirs."

"Lije," said the Commissioner, "you're a modernist. That's your trouble. In Medieval times, people lived in the open. I don't mean on the farms only. I mean in the cities, too. Even in New York. When it rained, they didn't think of it as waste. They gloried in it. They lived close to nature. It's healthier, better. The troubles of modern life come from being divorced from nature. Read up on the Coal Century, sometimes."

Baley had. He had heard many people moaning about the invention of the atomic pile. He moaned about it himself when things went wrong, or when he got tired. Moaning like that was a built-in facet of human nature. Back in the Coal Century, people moaned about the invention of the steam engine. In one of Shakespeare's plays, a character moaned about the invention of gunpowder. A thousand years in the future, they'd be moaning about the invention of the positronic brain.

The hell with it.

He said, grimly, "Look, Julius." (It wasn't his habit to get friendly with the Commissioner during office hours, however many 'Lijes' the Commissioner threw at him, but something special seemed called for here.) "Look, Julius, you're talking about everything except what I came in here for, and it's worrying me. What is it?"

The Commissioner said, "I'll get to it, Lije. Let me do it my way. It's—it's trouble."

"Sure. What isn't on this planet? More trouble with the R's?"

"In a way, yes, Lije. I stand here and wonder how much more trouble the old world can take. When I put in this window, I wasn't just letting in the sky once in a while. I let in the City. I look at it and I wonder what will become of it in another century."

Baley felt repelled by the other's sentimentality, but he found himself staring outward in fascination. Even dimmed by the weather, the City was a tremendous thing to see. The Police Department was in the upper levels of City Hall, and City Hall reached high. From the Commissioner's window, the neighboring towers fell short and the tops were visible. They were so many fingers, groping upward. Their walls were blank, featureless. They were the outer shells of human hives.

"In a way," said the Commissioner, "I'm sorry it's raining. We can't see Spacetown."

Baley looked westward, but it was as the Commissioner said. The horizon closed down. New York's towers grew misty and came to an end against blank whiteness.

"I know what Spacetown is like," said Baley.

"I like the picture from here," said the Commissioner. "It can just be made out in the gap between the two Brunswick Sectors. Low domes spread out. It's the difference between us and the Spacers. We reach high and crowd close. With them, each family has a dome for itself. One family: one house. And land between each dome. Have you ever spoken to any of the Spacers, Lije?"

"A few times. About a month ago, I spoke to one right here on your intercom," Baley said, patiently.

"Yes, I remember. But then, I'm just getting philosophical. We and they. Different ways of life."

Baley's stomach was beginning to constrict a little. The more devious the Commissioner's approach, the deadlier he thought might be the conclusion.

He said, "All right. But what's so surprising about it? You can't spread eight billion people over Earth in little domes. They've got space on their worlds, so let them live their way."

The Commissioner walked to his chair and sat down. His eyes looked unblinkingly at Baley, shrunken a bit by the concave lenses in his spectacles. He said, "Not everyone is that tolerant about differences in culture. Either among us or among the Spacers."

"All right. So what?"

"So three days ago, a Spacer died."

Now it was coming. The corners of Baley's thin lips raised a trifle, but the effect upon his long, sad face was unnoticeable. He said, "Too bad. Something contagious, I hope. A virus. A cold, perhaps."

The Commissioner looked startled, "What are you talking about?"

Baley didn't care to explain. The precision with which the Spacers had bred disease out of their societies was well known. The care with which they avoided, as far as possible, contact with disease-riddled Earthmen was even better known. But then, sarcasm was lost on the Commissioner.

Baley said, "I'm just talking. What did he die of?" He turned back to the window.

The Commissioner said, "He died of a missing chest. Someone had used a blaster on him."

Baley's back grew rigid. He said, without turning, "What are *you* talking about?"

"I'm talking about murder," said the Commissioner, softly. "You're a plain-clothes man. You know what murder is."

And now Baley turned. "But a Spacer! Three days ago?"

"Yes."

"But who did it? How?"

"The Spacers say it was an Earthman."

"It can't be."

"Why not? You don't like the Spacers. I don't. Who on Earth does? Someone didn't like them a little too much, that's all."

"Sure, but——"

"There was the fire at the Los Angeles factories. There was the Berlin R-smashing. There were the riots in Shanghai."

"All right."

"It all points to rising discontent. Maybe to some sort of organization."

Baley said, "Commissioner, I don't get this. Are you testing me for some reason?"

"What?" The Commissioner looked honestly bewildered.

Baley watched him. "Three days ago a Spacer was murdered and the Spacers think the murderer is an Earthman. Till now," his finger tapped the desk, "nothing's come out. Is that right? Commissioner, that's unbelievable. Jehoshaphat, Commissioner, a thing like this would blow New York off the face of the planet if it really happened."

The Commissioner shook his head. "It's not as simple as that. Look, Lije, I've been out three days. I've been in conference with the Mayor. I've been out to Spacetown. I've been down in Washington, talking to the Terrestrial Bureau of Investigation."

"Oh? And what do the Terries have to say?"

"They say it's our baby. It's inside city limits. Spacetown is under New York jurisdiction."

"But *with* extraterritorial rights."

"I know. I'm coming to that." The Commissioner's eyes fell away from Baley's flinty stare. He seemed to regard himself as having been suddenly demoted to the position of Baley's underling, and Baley behaved as though he accepted the fact.

"The Spacers can run the show," said Baley.

"Wait a minute, Lije," pleaded the Commissioner. "Don't rush me. I'm trying to talk this over, friend to friend. I want you to know my position. I was there when the news broke. I had an appointment with him—with Roj Nemennuh Sarton."

"The victim?"

"The victim." The Commissioner groaned. "Five minutes more and I, myself, would have discovered the body. What a shock that would have been. As it was, it was brutal, brutal. They met me and told me. It started a three-day nightmare, Lije. That on top of having everything blur on me and having no time to replace my glasses for days. *That* won't happen again, at least. I've ordered three pairs."

Baley considered the picture he conjured up of the event. He could see the tall, fair figures of the Spacers approaching the Commissioner with the news and breaking it to him in their unvarnished emotionless way. Julius would remove his glasses and polish them. Inevitably, under the impact of the event, he would drop them, then look down at the broken remnants with a quiver of his soft, full lips. Baley was quite certain that, for five minutes anyway, the Commissioner was much more disturbed over his glasses than over the murder.

The Commissioner was saying, "It's a devil of a position. As you say, the Spacers have extraterritorial rights. They *can* insist on their own investigation, make whatever report they wish to their home governments. The Outer Worlds could use this as an excuse to pile on indemnity charges. You know how *that* would sit with the population."

"It would be political suicide for the White House to agree to pay."

"And another kind of suicide not to pay."

"You don't have to draw me a picture," said Baley. He had been a small boy when the gleaming cruisers from outer space last sent down their soldiers into Washington, New York, and Moscow to collect what they claimed was theirs.

"Then you see. Pay or not pay, it's trouble. The only way out is to find the murderer on our own and hand him over to the Spacers. It's up to us."

"Why not give it to the TBI? Even if it is our jurisdiction from a legalistic viewpoint, there's the question of interstellar relations——"

"The TBI won't touch it. This is *hot* and it's in our lap." For a moment, he lifted his head and gazed keenly at his subordinate.

"And it's not good, Lije. Every one of us stands the chance of being out of a job."

Baley said, "Replace us all? Nuts. The trained men to do it with don't exist."

"R's," said the Commissioner. "*They* exist."

"What?"

"R. Sammy is just a beginning. He runs errands. Others can patrol the expressways. Damn it, man, I know the Spacers better than you do, and I know what they're doing. There are R's that can do your work and mine. We can be declassified. Don't think differently. And at our age, to hit the labor pool . . ."

Baley said, gruffly, "All right."

The Commissioner looked abashed. "Sorry, Lije."

Baley nodded and tried not to think of his father. The Commissioner knew the story, of course.

Baley said, "When did all this replacement business come up?"

"Look, you're being naïve, Lije. It's been happening all along. It's been happening for twenty-five years, ever since the Spacers came. You know that. It's just beginning to reach higher, that's all. If we muff this case, it's a big, long step toward the point where we can stop looking forward to collecting our pension-tab booklets. On the other hand, Lije, if we handle the matter well, it can shove that point far into the future. And it would be a particular break for you."

"For me?" said Baley.

"You'll be the operative in charge, Lije."

"I don't rate it, Commissioner. I'm a C-5, that's all."

"You want a C-6 rating, don't you?"

Did he? Baley knew the privileges a C-6 rating carried. A seat on the expressway in the rush hour, not just from ten to four. Higher up on the list-of-choice at the Section kitchens. Maybe even a chance at a better apartment and a quota ticket to the Solarium levels for Jessie.

"I want it," he said. "Sure. Why wouldn't I? But what would I get if I couldn't break the case?"

"Why wouldn't you break it, Lije?" the Commissioner wheedled. "You're a good man. You're one of the best we have."

"But there are half a dozen men with higher ratings in my department section. Why should they be passed over?"

Baley did not say out loud, though his bearing implied it strongly, that the Commissioner did not move outside protocol in this fashion except in cases of wild emergency.

The Commissioner folded his hands. "Two reasons. You're not just another detective to me, Lije. We're friends, too. I'm not forgetting we were in college together. Sometimes it may look as though I have forgotten, but that's the fault of rating. I'm Commissioner, and you know what that means. But I'm still your friend and this is a tremendous chance for the right person. I want you to have it."

"That's one reason," said Baley, without warmth.

"The second reason is that I think you're my friend. I need a favor."

"What sort of favor?"

"I want you to take on a Spacer partner in this deal. That was the condition the Spacers made. They've agreed not to report the murder; they've agreed to leave the investigation in our hands. In return, they insist one of their own agents be in on the deal, the whole deal."

"It sounds like they don't trust us altogether."

"Surely you see their point. If this is mishandled, a number of them will be in trouble with their own governments. I'll give them the benefit of the doubt, Lije. I'm willing to believe they mean well."

"I'm sure they do, Commissioner. That's the trouble with them."

The Commissioner looked blank at that, but went on. "Are you willing to take on a Spacer partner, Lije?"

"You're asking that as a favor?"

"Yes, I'm asking you to take the job with all the conditions the Spacers have set up."

"I'll take a Spacer partner, Commissioner."

"Thanks, Lije. He'll have to live with you."

"Oh, now, hold on."

"I know. I know. But you've got a large apartment, Lije. Three rooms. Only one child. You can put him up. He'll be no trouble. No trouble at all. And it's necessary."

"Jessie won't like it. I know that."

"You tell Jessie," the Commissioner was earnest, so earnest that his eyes seemed to bore holes through the glass discs blocking his stare, "that if you do this for me, I'll do what I can when this is all over to jump you a grade. C-7, Lije. C-7!"

"All right, Commissioner, it's a deal."

Baley half rose from his chair, caught the look on Enderby's face, and sat down again.

"There's something else?"

Slowly, the Commissioner nodded. "One more item."

"Which is?"

"The name of your partner."

"What difference does that make?"

"The Spacers," said the Commissioner, "have peculiar ways. The partner they're supplying isn't—isn't . . ."

Baley's eyes opened wide. "Just a minute!"

"You've got to, Lije. You've *got* to. There's no way out."

"Stay at my apartment? A thing like that?"

"As a friend, please!"

"No. *No!*"

"Lije, I can't trust anyone else in this. Do I have to spell it out for you? We've *got* to work with the Spacers. We've got to succeed, if we're to keep the indemnity ships away from Earth. But we can't succeed just any old way. You'll be partnered with one of their R's. If *he* breaks the case, if he can report that we're incompetent, we're ruined, anyway. We, as a department. You see that, don't you? So you've got a delicate job on your hands. You've got to work with him, but see to it that *you* solve the case and not he. Understand?"

"You mean co-operate with him 100 per cent, except that I cut his throat? Pat him on the back with a knife in my hand?"

"What else can we do? There's no other way out."

Lije Baley stood irresolute. "I don't know what Jessie will say."

"I'll talk to her, if you want me to."

"No, Commissioner." He drew a deep, sighing breath. "What's my partner's name?"

"R. Daneel Olivaw."

Baley said, sadly, "This isn't a time for euphemism, Commissioner. I'm taking the job, so let's use his full name. *Robot* Daneel Olivaw."

2

Round Trip on an Expressway

THERE WAS the usual, entirely normal crowd on the expressway: the standees on the lower level and those with seat privileges above. A continuous trickle of humanity filtered off the expressway, across the decelerating strips to localways or into the stationaries that led under arches or over bridges into the endless mazes of the City Sections. Another trickle, just as continuous, worked inward from the other side, across the accelerating strips and onto the expressway.

There were the infinite lights: the luminous walls and ceilings that seemed to drip cool, even phosphorescence; the flashing advertisements screaming for attention; the harsh, steady gleam of the "lightworms" that directed THIS WAY TO JERSEY SECTIONS, FOLLOW ARROWS TO EAST RIVER SHUTTLE, UPPER LEVEL FOR ALL WAYS TO LONG ISLAND SECTIONS.

Most of all there was the noise that was inseparable from life: the sound of millions talking, laughing, coughing, calling, humming, breathing.

No directions anywhere to Spacetown, thought Baley.

He stepped from strip to strip with the ease of a lifetime's practice. Children learned to "hop the strips" as soon as they learned to walk. Baley scarcely felt the jerk of acceleration as his velocity increased with each step. He was not even aware that he leaned forward against the force. In thirty seconds he had reached the final sixty-mile-an-hour strip and could step aboard the railed and glassed-in moving platform that was the expressway.

No directions to Spacetown, he thought.

No need for directions. If you've business there, you know the way. If you don't know the way, you've no business there. When Spacetown was first established some twenty-five years earlier, there was a strong tendency to make a showplace out of it. The hordes of the City herded in that direction.

The Spacers put a stop to that. Politely (they were always polite), but without any compromise with tact, they put up a force barrier between themselves and the City. They established a combination Immigration Service and Customs Inspection. If you had business, you identified yourself, allowed yourself to be searched, and submitted to a medical examination and a routine disinfection.

It gave rise to dissatisfaction. Naturally. More dissatisfaction than it deserved. Enough dissatisfaction to put a serious spoke in the program of modernization. Baley remembered the Barrier Riots. He had been part of the mob that had suspended itself from the rails of the expressways, crowded onto the seats in disregard of rating privileges, run recklessly along and across the strips at the risk of a broken body, and remained just outside the Spacetown barrier for two days, shouting slogans and destroying City property out of sheer frustration.

Baley could still sing the chants of the time if he put his mind to it. There was "Man Was Born on Mother Earth, Do You Hear?" to an old folk tune with the gibberish refrain, "Hinky-dinky-parley-voo."

"Man was born on Mother Earth, do you hear?
Earth's the world that gave him birth do you hear?
Spacer, get you off the face
Of Mother Earth and into space.
Dirty Spacer, do you hear?"

There were hundreds of verses. A few were witty, most were stupid, many were obscene. Every one, however, ended with "Dirty Spacer, do you hear?" Dirty, dirty. It was the futile throwing back in the face of the Spacers their most keenly felt insult: their insistence on considering the natives of Earth as disgustingly diseased.

The Spacers didn't leave, of course. It wasn't even necessary for them to bring any of their offensive weapons into play. Earth's outmoded fleet had long since learned that it was suicide to venture near any Outer World ship. Earth planes that had ventured over the Spacetown area in the very early days of its establishment had simply disappeared. At the most, a shredded wing tip might tumble down to Earth.

And no mob could be so maddened as to forget the effect of the subetheric hand disruptors used on Earthmen in the wars of a century ago.

So the Spacers sat behind their barrier, which itself was the product of their own advanced science, and that no method existed on Earth of breaking. They just waited stolidly on the other side of the barrier until the City quieted the mob with somno vapor and retch gas. The below-level penitentiaries rattled afterward with ringleaders, malcontents, and people who had been picked up simply because they were nearest at hand. After a while they were all set free.

After a proper interval, the Spacers eased their restrictions. The barrier was removed and the City Police entrusted with the protection of Spacetown's isolation. Most important of all, the medical examination was more unobtrusive.

Now, thought Baley, things might take a reverse trend. If the Spacers seriously thought that an Earthman had entered Spacetown and committed murder, the barrier might go up again. It would be bad.

He lifted himself onto the expressway platform, made his way through the standees to the tight spiral ramp that led to the upper level, and there sat down. He didn't put his rating ticket in his hatband till they passed the last of the Hudson Sections. A C-5 had no seat rights east of the Hudson and west of Long Island, and although there was ample seating available at the moment, one of the way guards would have automatically ousted him. People were increasingly petty about rating privileges and, in all honesty, Baley lumped himself in with "people."

The air made the characteristic whistling noise as it frictioned off the curved windshields set up above the back of every seat. It made talking a chore, but it was no bar to thinking when you were used to it.

Most Earthmen were Medievalists in one way or another. It was an easy thing to be when it meant looking back to a time when Earth was *the* world and not just one of fifty. The misfit one of fifty at that.

Baley's head snapped to the right at the sound of a female shriek.

A woman had dropped her handbag; he saw it for an instant, a pastel pink blob against the dull gray of the strips. A passenger hurrying from the expressway must inadvertently have kicked it in the direction of deceleration and now the owner was whirling away from her property.

A corner of Baley's mouth quirked. She might catch up with it, if she were clever enough to hurry to a strip that moved slower still and if other feet did not kick it this way or that. He would never know whether she would or not. The scene was half a mile to the rear, already.

Chances were she wouldn't. It had been calculated that, on the average, something was dropped on the strips every three minutes somewhere in the City and not recovered. The Lost and Found Department was a huge proposition. It was just one more complication of modern life.

Baley thought: It was simpler once. Everything was simpler. That's what makes Medievalists.

Medievalism took different forms. To the unimaginative Julius Enderby, it meant the adoption of archaisms. Spectacles! Windows!

To Baley, it was a study of history. Particularly the history of folkways.

The City now! New York City in which he lived and had his being. Larger than any City but Los Angeles. More populous than any but Shanghai. It was only three centuries old.

To be sure, something had existed in the same geographic area before then that had been *called* New York City. That primitive gathering of population had existed for three thousand years, not three hundred, but it hadn't been a *City*.

There were no Cities then. There were just huddles of dwelling places large and small, open to the air. They were something like the Spacer's Domes, only much different, of course. These huddles (the largest barely reached ten million in population and most never reached one million) were scattered all over Earth by the thousands. By modern standards, they had been completely inefficient, economically.

Efficiency had been forced on Earth with increasing population. Two billion people, three billion, even five billion could be supported by the planet by progressive lowering of the standard of living. When the population reaches eight billion, however, semistarvation becomes too much like the real thing. A radical change had to take place in man's culture, particularly when it turned out that the Outer Worlds (which had merely been Earth's colonies a thousand years before) were tremendously serious in their immigration restrictions.

The radical change had been the gradual formation of the Cities over a thousand years of Earth's history. Efficiency implied bigness. Even in Medieval times that had been realized, perhaps unconsciously. Home industry gave way to factories and factories to continental industries.

Think of the inefficiency of a hundred thousand houses for a hundred thousand families as compared with a hundred-thousand-unit Section; a book-film collection in each house as compared with a Section film concentrate; independent video for each family as compared with video-piping systems.

For that matter, take the simple folly of endless duplication of kitchens and bathrooms as compared with the thoroughly efficient diners and shower rooms made possible by City culture.

More and more the villages, towns, and "cities" of Earth died and were swallowed by the Cities. Even the early prospects of atomic war only slowed the trend. With the invention of the force shield, the trend became a headlong race.

City culture meant optimum distribution of food, increasing utilization of yeasts and hydroponics. New York City spread over two thousand square miles and at the last census its population was well over twenty million. There were some eight hundred Cities on Earth, average population, ten million.

Each City became a semiautonomous unit, economically all but self-sufficient. It could roof itself in, gird itself about, burrow itself under. It became a steel cave, a tremendous, self-contained cave of steel and concrete.

It could lay itself out scientifically. At the center was the enormous complex of administrative offices. In careful orientation to one another and to the whole were the large residential Sections connected and interlaced by the expressway and the localways. Toward the outskirts were the factories, the hydroponic plants, the yeast-culture vats, the power plants. Through all the melee were the water pipes and sewage ducts, schools, prisons and shops, power lines and communication beams.

There was no doubt about it: the City was the culmination of man's mastery over the environment. Not space travel, not the fifty colonized worlds that were now so haughtily independent, but the City.

Practically none of Earth's population lived outside the Cities. Outside was the wilderness, the open sky that few men could face with anything like equanimity. To be sure, the open space was necessary. It held the water that men must have, the coal and the wood that were the ultimate raw materials for plastics and for the eternally growing yeast. (Petroleum had long since gone, but oil-rich strains of yeast were an adequate substitute.) The land between the Cities still held the mines, and was still used to a larger extent than most men realized for growing food and grazing stock. It was inefficient, but beef, pork, and grain always found a luxury market and could be used for export purposes.

But few humans were required to run the mines and ranches, to exploit the farms and pipe the water, and these supervised at long distance. Robots did the work better and required less.

Robots! That was the one huge irony. It was on Earth that the positronic brain was invented and on Earth that robots had first been put to productive use.

Not on the Outer Worlds. Of course, the Outer Worlds always acted as though robots had been born of their culture.

In a way, of course, the culmination of robot economy had taken place on the Outer Worlds. Here on Earth, robots had always been restricted to the mines and farmlands. Only in the last quarter century, under the urgings of the Spacers, had robots filtered their slow way into the Cities.

The Cities were good. Everyone but the Medievalists knew that there was no substitute, no reasonable substitute. The only trouble was that they wouldn't stay good. Earth's population was still rising. Some day, with all that the Cities could do, the available calories per person would simply fall below basic subsistence level.

It was all the worse because of the existence of the Spacers, the descendants of the early emigrants from Earth, living in luxury on their underpopulated robot-ridden worlds out in space. They were coolly determined to keep the comfort that grew out of the emptiness of their worlds and for that purpose they kept their birth rate down and immigrants from teeming Earth out. And this——

Spacetown coming up!

A nudge at Baley's unconscious warned him that he was approaching the Newark Section. If he stayed where he was much longer, he'd find himself speeding southwestward to the Trenton Section turning of the way, through the heart of the warm and musty-odored yeast country.

It was a matter of timing. It took so long to shinny down the ramp, so long to squirm through the grunting standees, so long to slip along the railing and out an opening, so long to hop across the decelerating strips.

When he was done, he was precisely at the off-shooting of the proper stationary. At no time did he time his steps consciously. If he had, he would probably have missed.

Baley found himself in unusual semi-isolation. Only a policeman was with him inside the stationary and, except for the whirring of the expressway, there was an almost uncomfortable silence.

The policeman approached, and Baley flashed his badge impatiently. The policeman lifted his hand in permission to pass on.

The passage narrowed and curved sharply three or four times. That was obviously purposeful. Mobs of Earthmen couldn't gather in it with any degree of comfort and direct charges were impossible.

Baley was thankful that the arrangements were for him to meet his partner this side of Spacetown. He didn't like the thought of a medical examination any better for its reputed politeness.

A Spacer was standing at the point where a series of doors marked the openings to the open air and the domes of Spacetown. He was dressed in the Earth fashion, trousers tight at the waist, loose at the ankle, and color-striped down the seam of each leg. He wore an ordinary Textron shirt, open collar, seam-zipped, and ruffled at the wrist, but he was a Spacer. There was something about the way he stood, the way he held his head, the calm and unemotional lines of his broad, high-cheekboned face, the careful set of his short, bronze hair lying flatly backward and without a part, that marked him off from the native Earthman.

Baley approached woodenly and said in a monotone, "I am Plainclothes Man Elijah Baley, Police Department, City of New York, Rating C-5."

He showed his credentials and went on, "I have been instructed to meet R. Daneel Olivaw at Spacetown Approachway." He looked at his watch. "I am a little early. May I request the announcement of my presence?"

He felt more than a little cold inside. He was used, after a fashion, to the Earth-model robots. The Spacer models would be different. He had never met one, but there was nothing more common on Earth than the horrid whispered stories about the tremendous and formidable robots that worked in superhuman fashion on the far-off, glittering Outer Worlds. He found himself gritting his teeth.

The Spacer, who had listened politely, said, "It will not be necessary. I have been waiting for you."

Baley's hand went up automatically, then dropped. So did his long chin, looking longer in the process. He didn't quite manage to say anything. The words froze.

The Spacer said, "I shall introduce myself. I am R. Daneel Olivaw."

"Yes? Am I making a mistake? I thought the first initial——"

"Quite so. I am a robot. Were you not told?"

"I was told." Baley put a damp hand to his hair and smoothed it back unnecessarily. Then he held it out. "I'm sorry, Mr. Olivaw. I don't know what I was thinking of. Good day. I am Elijah Baley, your partner."

"Good." The robot's hand closed on his with a smoothly increasing pressure that reached a comfortably friendly peak, then declined. "Yet I seem to detect disturbance. May I ask that you be frank with me? It is best to have as many relevant facts as possible in a relationship such as ours. And it is customary on my world for partners to call one another by the familiar name. I trust that that is not counter to your own customs."

"It's just, you see, that you don't look like a robot," said Baley, desperately.

"And that disturbs you?"

"It shouldn't, I suppose, Da-Daneel. Are they all like you on your world?"

"There are individual differences, Elijah, as with men."

"Our own robots . . . Well, you can tell they're robots, you understand. You look like a Spacer."

"Oh, I see. You expected a rather crude model and were surprised. Yet it is only logical that our people use a robot of pronounced humanoid characteristics in this case if we expected to avoid unpleasantness. Is that not so?"

It was certainly so. An obvious robot roaming the City would be in quick trouble.

Baley said, "Yes."

"Then let us leave now, Elijah."

They made their way back to the expressway. R. Daneel caught the purpose of the accelerating strips and maneuvered along them with a quick proficiency. Baley, who had begun by moderating his speed, ended by hastening it in annoyance.

The robot kept pace. He showed no awareness of any difficulty. Baley wondered if R. Daneel were not deliberately moving slower than he might. He reached the endless cars of expressway and scrambled aboard with what amounted to outright recklessness. The robot followed easily.

Baley was red. He swallowed twice and said, "I'll stay down here with you."

"Down here?" The robot, apparently oblivious to both the noise and the rhythmic swaying of the platform said, "Is my information wrong? I was told that a rating of C-5 entitled one to a seat on the upper level under certain conditions."

"You're right. I can go up there, but you can't."

"Why can I not go up with you?"

"It takes a C-5, Daneel."

"I am aware of that."

"You're not a C-5." Talking was difficult. The hiss of frictioning air was louder on the less shielded lower level and Baley was understandably anxious to keep his voice low.

R. Daneel said, "Why should I not be a C-5? I am your partner and, consequently, of equal rank. I was given this."

From an inner shirt pocket he produced a rectangular credential card, quite genuine. The name given was Daneel Olivaw, without the all-important initial. The rating was C-5.

"Come on up," said Baley, woodenly.

Baley looked straight ahead, once seated, angry with himself, very conscious of the robot sitting next to him. He had been caught twice. First he had not recognized R. Daneel as a robot; secondly, he had not guessed the logic that demanded R. Daneel be given C-5 rating.

The trouble was, of course, that he was not the plain-clothes man of popular myth. He was not incapable of surprise, imperturbable of appearance, infinite of adaptability, and lightning of mental grasp. He had never supposed he was, but he had never regretted the lack before.

What made him regret it was that, to all appearances, R. Daneel Olivaw *was* that very myth, embodied.

He had to be. He was a robot.

Baley began to find excuses for himself. He was accustomed to the robots like R. Sammy at the office. He had expected a creature with a skin of a hard and glossy plastic, nearly dead white in color. He had expected an expression fixed at an unreal level of inane good humor. He had expected jerky, faintly uncertain motions.

R. Daneel was none of it.

Baley risked a quick side glance at the robot. R. Daneel turned simultaneously to meet his eye and nod gravely. His lips had moved naturally when he had spoken and did not simply remain parted as those of Earth robots did. There had been glimpses of an articulating tongue.

Baley thought: Why does he have to sit there so calmly? This must be something completely new to him. Noise, lights, crowds!

Baley got up, brushed past R. Daneel, and said, "Follow me!"

Off the expressway, down the decelerating strips.

Baley thought: Good Lord, what do I tell Jessie, anyway?

The coming of the robot had rattled that thought out of his head, but it was coming back with sickening urgency now that they were heading down the localway that led into the very jaws of the Lower Bronx Section.

He said, "This is all one building, you know, Daneel; everything you see, the whole City. Twenty million people live in it. The expressways go continuously, night and day, at sixty miles an hour. There are two hundred and fifty miles of it altogether and hundreds of miles of localways."

Any minute now, Baley thought, I'll be figuring out how many tons of yeast product New York eats per day and how many cubic feet of water we drink and how many megawatts of power the atomic piles deliver per hour.

Daneel said, "I was informed of this and other similar data in my briefing."

Baley thought: Well, that covers the food, drink, and power situation, too, I suppose. Why try to impress a robot?

They were at East 182nd Street and in not more than two hundred yards they would be at the elevator banks that fed those steel and concrete layers of apartments that included his own.

He was on the point of saying, "This way," when he was stopped by a knot of people gathering outside the brilliantly lighted force door of one of the many retail departments that lined the ground levels solidly in this Section.

He asked of the nearest person in an automatic tone of authority, "What's going on?"

The man he addressed, who was standing on tiptoe, said, "Damned if I know. I just got here."

Someone else said, excitedly, "They got those lousy R's in there. I think maybe they'll throw them out here. Boy, I'd like to take them apart."

Baley looked nervously at Daneel, but, if the latter caught the significance of the words or even heard them, he did not show it by any outward sign.

Baley plunged into the crowd. "Let me through. Let me through. Police!"

They made way. Baley caught words behind him.

". . . take them apart. Nut by nut. Split them down the seams slowlike . . ." And someone else laughed.

Baley turned a little cold. The City was the acme of efficiency, but it made demands of its inhabitants. It asked them to live in a tight routine and order their lives under a strict and scientific control. Occasionally, built-up inhibitions exploded.

He remembered the Barrier Riots.

Reasons for anti-robot rioting certainly existed. Men who found themselves faced with the prospect of the desperate minimum involved in declassification, after half a lifetime of effort, could not decide cold-bloodedly that individual robots were not to blame. Individual robots could at least be struck at.

One could not strike at something called "governmental policy" or at a slogan like "Higher production with robot labor."

The government called it growing pains. It shook its collective head sorrowfully and assured everyone that after a necessary period of adjustment, a new and better life would exist for all.

But the Medievalist movement expanded along with the declassification process. Men grew desperate and the border between bitter frustration and wild destruction is sometimes easily crossed.

At this moment, minutes could be separating the pent-up hostility of the crowd from a flashing orgy of blood and smash.

Baley writhed his way desperately to the force door.

3

Incident at a Shoe Counter

THE INTERIOR of the store was emptier than the street outside. The manager, with commendable foresight, had thrown the force door early in the game, preventing potential troublemakers from entering. It also kept the principals in the argument from leaving, but that was minor.

Baley got through the force door by using his officer's neutralizer. Unexpectedly, he found R. Daneel still behind him. The robot was pocketing a neutralizer of his own, a slim one, smaller and neater than the standard police model.

The manager ran to them instantly, talking loudly. "Officers, my clerks have been assigned me by the City. I am perfectly within my rights."

There were three robots standing rodlike at the rear of the department. Six humans were standing near the force door. They were all women.

"All right, now," said Baley, crisply. "What's going on? What's all the fuss about?"

One of the women said, shrilly, "I came in for shoes. Why can't I have a decent clerk? Ain't I respectable?" Her clothing, especially her hat, were just sufficiently extreme to make it more than a rhetorical question. The angry flush that covered her face masked imperfectly her overdone makeup.

The manager said, "I'll wait on her myself if I have to, but I can't wait on all of them, Officer. There's nothing wrong with my men. They're registered clerks. I have their spec charts and guarantee slips——"

"Spec charts," screamed the woman. She laughed shrilly, turning to the rest. "Listen to him. He calls them men! What's the matter with you anyway? They ain't men. They're ro-bots!" She stretched out the syllables. "And I tell you what they do, in case you don't know. They steal jobs from men. That's why the government always protects them. They work for nothin' and, on account o' that, families gotta live out in the barracks and eat raw yeast mush. Decent hard-working families. We'd smash up all the ro-bots, if *I* was boss. I tell you that!"

The others talked confusedly and there was always the growing rumble from the crowd just beyond the force door.

Baley was conscious, brutally conscious, of R. Daneel Olivaw standing at his elbow. He looked at the clerks. They were Earthmade, and even on that scale, relatively inexpensive models. They were just robots made to know a few simple things. They would know all the style numbers, their prices, the sizes available in each. They could keep track of stock fluctuations, probably better than humans could, since they would have no outside interests. They could compute the proper orders for the next week. They could measure the customer's foot.

In themselves, harmless. As a group, incredibly dangerous.

Baley could sympathize with the woman more deeply than he would have believed possible the day before. No, two hours before. He could feel R. Daneel's nearness and he wondered if R. Daneel could not replace an ordinary plain-clothes man C-5. He could see the barracks, as he thought that. He could taste the yeast mush. He could remember his father.

His father had been a nuclear physicist, with a rating that had put him in the top percentile of the City. There had been an accident at the power plant and his father had borne the blame. He had been declassified. Baley did not know the details; it had happened when he was a year old.

But he remembered the barracks of his childhood; the grinding communal existence just this side of the edge of bearability. He remembered his mother not at all; she had not survived long. His father he recalled well, a sodden man, morose and lost, speaking sometimes of the past in hoarse, broken sentences.

His father died, still declassified, when Lije was eight. Young Baley and his two older sisters moved into the Section orphanage.

Children's Level, they called it. His mother's brother, Uncle Boris, was himself too poor to prevent that.

So it continued hard. And it was hard going through school, with no father-derived status privileges to smooth the way.

And now he had to stand in the middle of a growing riot and beat down men and women who, after all, only feared declassification for themselves and those they loved, as he himself did.

Tonelessly, he said to the woman who had already spoken, "Let's not have any trouble, lady. The clerks aren't doing you any harm."

"Sure they ain't done me no harm," sopranoed the woman. "They ain't gonna, either. Think I'll let their cold, greasy fingers touch me? I came in here expecting to get treated like a human being. I'm a citizen. I got a right to have human beings wait on me. And listen, I got two kids waiting for supper. They can't go to the Section kitchen without me, like they was orphans. I gotta get out of here."

"Well, now," said Baley, feeling his temper slipping, "if you had let yourself be waited on, you'd have been out of here by now. You're just making trouble for nothing. Come on now."

"Well!" The woman registered shock. "Maybe you think you can talk to me like I was dirt. Maybe it's time the guv'min' reelized robots ain't the only things on Earth. I'm a hard-working woman and I've got rights." She went on and on and on.

Baley felt harassed and caught. The situation was out of hand. Even if the woman would consent to be waited on, the waiting crowd was ugly enough for anything.

There must be a hundred crammed outside the display window now. In the few minutes since the plain-clothes men had entered the store, the crowd had doubled.

"What is the usual procedure in such a case?" asked R. Daneel Olivaw, suddenly.

Baley nearly jumped. He said, "This is an unusual case in the first place."

"What is the law?"

"The R's have been duly assigned here. They're registered clerks. There's nothing illegal about that."

They were speaking in whispers. Baley tried to look official and threatening. Olivaw's expression, as always, meant nothing at all.

"In that case," said R. Daneel, "order the woman to let herself be waited on or to leave."

Baley lifted a corner of his lip briefly. "It's a mob we have to deal with, not a woman. There's nothing to do but call a riot squad."

"It should not be necessary for citizens to require more than one officer of the law to direct what should be done," said Daneel.

He turned his broad face to the store manager. "Open the force door, sir."

Baley's arm shot forward to seize R. Daneel's shoulder, swing him about. He arrested the motion. If, at this moment, two law men quarreled openly, it would mean the end of all chance for a peaceful solution.

The manager protested, looked at Baley. Baley did not meet his eye.

R. Daneel said, unmoved, "I order you with the authority of the law."

The manager bleated, "I'll hold the City responsible for any damage to the goods or fixtures. I serve notice that I'm doing this under orders."

The barrier went down; men and women crowded in. There was a happy roar from them. They sensed victory.

Baley had heard of similar riots. He had even witnessed one. He had seen robots being lifted by a dozen hands, their heavy unresisting bodies carried backward from straining arm to straining arm. Men yanked and twisted at the metal mimicry of men. They used hammers, force knives, needle guns. They finally reduced the miserable objects to shredded metal and wire. Expensive positronic brains, the most intricate creation of the human mind, were thrown from hand to hand like footballs and mashed to uselessness in a trifle of time.

Then, with the genius of destruction so merrily let loose, the mobs turned on anything else that could be taken apart.

The robot clerks could have no knowledge of any of this, but they squealed as the crowd flooded inward and lifted their arms before their faces as though in a primitive effort at hiding. The woman who had started the fuss, frightened at seeing it grow suddenly so far beyond what she had expected, gasped, "Here, now. Here, now."

Her hat was shoved down over her face and her voice became only a meaningless shrillness.

The manager was shrieking, "Stop them, Officer. Stop them!"

R. Daneel spoke. Without apparent effort, his voice was suddenly decibels higher than a human's voice had a right to be. Of course, thought Baley for the tenth time, he's not——

R. Daneel said, "The next man who moves will be shot."

Someone well in the back yelled, "Get him!"

But for a moment, no one moved.

R. Daneel stepped nimbly upon a chair and from that to the top of a Transtex display case. The colored fluorescence gleaming through the slits of polarized molecular film turned his cool, smooth face into something unearthly.

Unearthly, thought Baley.

The tableau held as R. Daneel waited, a quietly formidable person.

R. Daneel said crisply, "You are saying, This man is holding a neuronic whip, or a tickler. If we all rush forward, we will bear him down and at most one or two of us will be hurt and even they will recover. Meanwhile, we will do just as we wish and to space with law and order."

His voice was neither harsh nor angry, but it carried authority. It had the tone of confident command. He went on, "You are mistaken. What I hold is not a neuronic whip, nor is it a tickler. It is a blaster and very deadly. I will use it and I will not aim over your heads. I will kill many of you before you seize me, perhaps most of you. I am serious. I look serious, do I not?"

There was motion at the outskirts, but the crowd no longer grew. If newcomers still stopped out of curiosity, others were hurrying away. Those nearest R. Daneel were holding their breath, trying desperately not to sway forward in response to the mass pressure of the bodies behind them.

The woman with the hat broke the spell. In a sudden whirlpool of sobbing, she yelled, "He's gonna kill us. I ain't done nothing. Oh, lemme outta here."

She turned, but faced an immovable wall of crammed men and women. She sank to her knees. The backward motion in the silent crowd grew more pronounced.

R. Daneel jumped down from the display counter and said, "I will now walk to the door. I will shoot the man or woman who touches me. When I reach the door, I will shoot any man or woman who is not moving about his business. This woman here——"

"No, no," yelled the woman with the hat, "I tell ya I didn't do nothing. I didn't mean no harm. I don't want no shoes. I just wanta go home."

"This woman here," went on Daneel, "will remain. She will be waited on."

He stepped forward.

The mob faced him dumbly. Baley closed his eyes. It wasn't his fault, he thought desperately. There'll be murder done and the worst mess in the world, but *they* forced a robot on me as partner. *They* gave him equal status.

It wouldn't do. He didn't believe himself. He might have stopped R. Daneel at the start. He might at any moment have put in the call for a squad car. He had let R. Daneel take responsibility, instead, and had felt a cowardly relief. When he tried to tell himself that R. Daneel's personality simply dominated the situation, he was filled with a sudden self-loathing. A *robot* dominating . . .

There was no unusual noise, no shouting and cursing, no groans, no yells. He opened his eyes.

They were dispersing.

The manager of the store was cooling down, adjusting his twisted jacket, smoothing his hair, muttering angry threats at the vanishing crowd.

The smooth, fading whistle of a squad car came to a halt just outside. Baley thought: Sure, when it's all over.

The manager plucked his sleeve. "Let's have no more trouble, Officer."

Baley said, "There won't be any trouble."

It was easy to get rid of the squad-car police. They had come in response to reports of a crowd in the street. They knew no details and could see for themselves that the street was clear. R. Daneel stepped aside and showed no sign of interest as Baley explained to the men in the squad car, minimizing the event and completely burying R. Daneel's part in it.

Afterward, he pulled R. Daneel to one side, against the steel and concrete of one of the building shafts.

"Listen," he said, "I'm not trying to steal your show, you understand."

"Steal my show? Is it one of your Earth idioms?"

"I didn't report your part in this."

"I do not know all your customs. On my world, a complete report is usual, but perhaps it is not so on your world. In any case, civil rebellion was averted. That is the important thing, is it not?"

"Is it? Now you look here." Baley tried to sound as forceful as possible under the necessity of speaking in an angry whisper. "Don't you ever do it again."

"Never again insist on the observance of law? If I am not to do that, what then is my purpose?"

"Don't ever threaten a human being with a blaster again."

"I would not have fired under any circumstances, Elijah, as you know very well. I am incapable of hurting a human. But, as you see, I did not have to fire. I did not expect to have to."

"That was the purest luck, your not having to fire. Don't take that kind of chance again. I could have pulled the grandstand stunt you did——"

"Grandstand stunt? What is that?"

"Never mind. Get the sense from what I'm saying. I could have pulled a blaster on the crowd myself. I had the blaster to do it with. But it isn't the kind of gamble I am justified in taking, or you, either. It was safer to call squad cars to the scene than to try one-man heroics."

R. Daneel considered. He shook his head. "I think you are wrong, partner Elijah. My briefing on human characteristics here among the people of Earth includes the information that, unlike the men of the Outer Worlds, they are trained from birth to accept authority. Apparently this is the result of your way of living. One man, representing authority firmly enough, was quite sufficient, as I proved. Your own desire for a squad car was only an expression, really, of your almost instinctive wish for superior authority to take responsibility out of your hands. On my own world, I admit that what I did would have been most unjustified."

Baley's long face was red with anger. "If they had recognized you as a robot——"

"I was sure they wouldn't."

"In any case, remember that you *are* a robot. Nothing more than a robot. Just a robot. Like those clerks in the shoe store."

"But this is obvious."

"And you're *not* human." Baley felt himself being driven into cruelty against his will.

R. Daneel seemed to consider that. He said, "The division between human and robot is perhaps not as significant as that between intelligence and nonintelligence."

"Maybe on your world," said Baley, "but not on Earth."

He looked at his watch and could scarcely make out that he was an hour and a quarter late. His throat was dry and raw with the thought that R. Daneel had won the first round, had won when he himself had stood by helpless.

He thought of the youngster, Vince Barrett, the teen-ager whom R. Sammy had replaced. And of himself, Elijah Baley, whom R. Daneel *could* replace. Jehoshaphat, at least his father had been thrown out because of an accident that had done damage, that had killed people. Maybe it *was* his fault; Baley didn't know. Suppose he had been eased out to make room for a mechanical physicist. Just for that. For no other reason. Nothing he could do about it.

He said, curtly, "Let's go now. I've got to get you home."

R. Daneel said, "You see, it is not proper to make any distinction of lesser meaning than the fact of intel——"

Baley's voice rose. "All *right*. The subject is closed. Jessie is waiting for us." He walked in the direction of the nearest intrasection communo-tube. "I'd better call and tell her we're on our way up."

"Jessie?"

"My wife."

Jehoshaphat, thought Baley, I'm in a fine mood to face Jessie.

4

Introduction to a Family

IT HAD BEEN her name that had first made Elijah Baley really conscious of Jessie. He had met her at the Section Christmas party back in '02, over a bowl of punch. He had just finished his schooling, just taken his first job with the City, just moved into the Section. He was living in one of the bachelor alcoves of Common Room 122A. Not bad for a bachelor alcove.

She was handing out the punch. "I'm Jessie," she said. "Jessie Navodny. I don't know you."

"Baley," he said, "Lije Baley. I've just moved into the Section."

He took his glass of punch and smiled mechanically. She impressed him as a cheerful and friendly person, so he stayed near her. He was new and it is a lonely feeling to be at a party where you find yourself watching people standing about in cliques of which you aren't a part. Later, when enough alcohol had trickled down throats, it might be better.

Meanwhile, he remained at the punch bowl, watching the folks come and go and sipping thoughtfully.

"I helped make the punch." The girl's voice broke in upon him. "I can guarantee it. Do you want more?"

Baley realized his little glass was empty. He smiled and said, "Yes."

The girl's face was oval and not precisely pretty, mostly because of a slightly overlarge nose. Her dress was demure and she wore her light brown hair in a series of ringlets over her forehead.

She joined him in the next punch and he felt better.

"Jessie," he said, feeling the name with his tongue. "It's nice. Do you mind if I use it when I'm talking to you?"

"Certainly. If you want to. Do you know what it's short for?"

"Jessica?"

"You'll never guess."

"I can't think of anything else."

She laughed and said archly, "My full name is Jezebel."

That was when his interest flared. He put his punch glass down and said, intently, "No, really?"

"Honestly. I'm not kidding. Jezebel. It's my real-for-true name on all my records. My parents liked the sound of it."

She was quite proud of it, even though there was never a less likely Jezebel in the world.

Baley said, seriously, "My name is Elijah, you know. My full name, I mean."

It didn't register with her.

He said, "Elijah was Jezebel's great enemy."

"He was?"

"Why, sure. In the Bible."

"Oh? I didn't know that. Now isn't that *funny*? I hope that doesn't mean you'll have to be my enemy in real life."

From the very beginning there was no question of that. It was the coincidence of names at first that made her more than just a pleasant girl at the punch bowl. But afterward he had grown to find her cheerful, tender-hearted, and, finally, even pretty. He appreciated her cheerfulness particularly. His own sardonic view of life needed the antidote.

But Jessie never seemed to mind his long grave face.

"Oh, goodness," she said, "what if you do look like an awful lemon? I know you're not really, and I guess if you were always grinning away like clockwork, the way I do, we'd just explode when we got together. You stay the way you are, Lije, and keep me from floating away."

And she kept Lije Baley from sinking down. He applied for a small Couples apartment and got a contingent admission pending marriage. He showed it to her and said, "Will you fix it so I can get out of Bachelor's, Jessie? I don't like it there."

Maybe it wasn't the most romantic proposal in the world, but Jessie liked it.

Baley could only remember one occasion on which Jessie's habitual cheer deserted her completely and that, too, had involved her name.

It was in their first year of marriage, and their baby had not yet come. In fact, it had been the very month in which Bentley was conceived. (Their I.Q. rating, Genetic Values status, and his position in the Department entitled him to two children, of which the first might be conceived during the first year.) Maybe, as Baley thought back upon it, Bentley's beginnings might explain part of her unusual skittishness.

Jessie had been drooping a bit because of Baley's consistent overtime.

She said, "It's embarrassing to eat alone at the kitchen every night."

Baley was tired and out of sorts. He said, "Why should it be? You can meet some nice single fellows there."

And of course she promptly fired up. "Do you think I can't make an impression on them, Lije Baley?"

Maybe it was just because he was tired; maybe because Julius Enderby, a classmate of his, had moved up another notch on the C-scale rating while he himself had not. Maybe it was simply because he was a little tired of having her try to act up to the name she bore when she was nothing of the sort and never could be anything of the sort.

In any case, he said bitingly, "I suppose you can, but I don't think you'll try. I wish you'd forget your name and be yourself."

"I'll be just what I please."

"Trying to be Jezebel won't get you anywhere. If you must know the truth, the name doesn't mean what you think, anyway. The Jezebel of the Bible was a faithful wife and a good one according to her lights. She had no lovers that we know of, cut no high jinks, and took no moral liberties at all."

Jessie stared angrily at him. "That isn't so. I've heard the phrase, 'a painted Jezebel.' I know what that means."

"Maybe you think you do, but listen. After Jezebel's husband, King Ahab died, her son, Jehoram, became king. One of the captains of his army, Jehu, rebelled against him and assassinated him. Jehu then rode to Jezreel where the old queen-mother, Jezebel, was residing. Jezebel heard of his coming and knew that he could only mean to kill her. In her pride and courage, she painted her face and dressed herself in her best clothes so that she could meet him as a haughty and defiant queen. He had her thrown from the win-

dow of the palace and killed, but she made a good end, according
to my notions. And that's what people refer to when they speak of
'a painted Jezebel,' whether they know it or not."

The next evening Jessie said in a small voice, "I've been reading
the Bible, Lije."

"What?" For a moment, Baley was honestly bewildered.

"The parts about Jezebel."

"Oh! Jessie, I'm sorry if I hurt your feelings. I was being childish."

"No. No." She pushed his hand from her waist and sat on the
couch, cool and upright, with a definite space between them. "It's
good to know the truth. I don't want to be fooled by not knowing.
So I read about her. She *was* a wicked woman, Lije."

"Well, her enemies wrote those chapters. We don't know her
side."

"She killed all the prophets of the Lord she could lay her hands
on."

"So they say she did." Baley felt about in his pocket for a stick
of chewing gum. (In later years he abandoned that habit because
Jessie said that with his long face and sad, brown eyes, it made him
look like an old cow stuck with an unpleasant wad of grass it
couldn't swallow and wouldn't spit out.) He said, "If you want her
side, I could think of some arguments for you. She valued the religion of her ancestors who had been in the land long before the
Hebrews came. The Hebrews had their own God, and, what's more,
it was an exclusive God. They weren't content to worship Him
themselves; they wanted everyone in reach to worship Him as well.

"Jezebel was a conservative, sticking to the old beliefs against the
new ones. After all, if the new beliefs had a higher moral content,
the old ones were more emotionally satisfying. The fact that she
killed priests just marks her as a child of her times. It was the usual
method of proselytization in those days. If you read I Kings, you
must remember that Elijah (*my* namesake this time) had a contest
with 850 prophets of Baal to see which could bring down fire from
heaven. Elijah won and promptly ordered the crowd of onlookers to
kill the 850 Baalites. And they did."

Jessie bit her lip. "What about Naboth's vineyard, Lije. Here was
this Naboth not bothering anybody, except that he refused to sell
the King his vineyard. So Jezebel arranged to have people perjure

themselves and say that Naboth had committed blasphemy or something."

"He was supposed to have 'blasphemed God and the king,'" said Baley.

"Yes. So they confiscated his property after they executed him."

"That was wrong. Of course, in modern times, Naboth would have been handled quite easily. If the City wanted his property or even if one of the Medieval nations had wanted his property, the courts would have ordered him off, had him removed by force if necessary, and paid him whatever they considered a fair price. King Ahab didn't have that way out. Still, Jezebel's solution was wrong. The only excuse for her is that Ahab was sick and unhappy over the situation and she felt that her love for her husband came ahead of Naboth's welfare. I keep telling you, she was the model of a faithful wi——"

Jessie flung herself away from him, red-faced and angry. "I think you're mean and spiteful."

He looked at her with complete dismay. "What have I done? What's the matter with you?"

She left the apartment without answering and spent the evening and half the night at the subetheric video levels, traveling petulantly from showing to showing and using up a two-month supply of her quota allowance (and her husband's, to boot).

When she came back to a still wakeful Lije Baley, she had nothing further to say to him.

It occurred to Baley later, much later, that he had utterly smashed an important part of Jessie's life. Her name had signified something intriguingly wicked to her. It was a delightful makeweight for her prim, overrespectable past. It gave her an aroma of licentiousness, and she adored that.

But it was gone. She never mentioned her full name again, not to Lije, not to her friends, and maybe, for all Baley knew, not even to herself. She was Jessie and took to signing her name so.

As the days passed she began speaking to him again, and after a week or so their relationship was on the old footing and, with all subsequent quarrels, nothing ever reached that one bad spot of intensity.

Only once was there even an indirect reference to the matter. It was in her eighth month of pregnancy. She had left her own position as dietitian's assistant in Section Kitchen A-23 and with unaccustomed time on her hands was amusing herself in speculation and preparation for the baby's birth.

She said, one evening, "What about Bentley?"

"Pardon me, dear?" said Baley, looking up from a sheaf of work he had brought home with him. (With an additional mouth soon to feed and Jessie's pay stopped and his own promotions to the non-clerical levels as far off, seemingly, as ever, extra work was necessary.)

"I mean if the baby's a boy. What about Bentley as a name?"

Baley pulled down the corners of his mouth. "Bentley Baley? Don't you think the names are too similar?"

"I don't know. It has a swing, I think. Besides, the child can always pick out a middle name to suit himself when he gets older."

"Well, it's all right with me."

"Are you sure? I mean . . . Maybe you wanted him to be named Elijah?"

"And be called Junior? I don't think that's a good idea. He can name his son Elijah, if he wants to."

Then Jessie said, "There's just one thing," and stopped.

After an interval, he looked up. "What one thing?"

She did not quite meet his eye, but she said, forcefully enough, "Bentley isn't a Bible name, is it?"

"No," said Baley, "I'm quite sure it isn't."

"All right, then. I don't want any Bible names."

And that was the only harking back that took place from that time to the day when Elijah Baley was coming home with Robot Daneel Olivaw, when he had been married for more than eighteen years and when his son Bentley Baley (middle name still unchosen) was past sixteen.

Baley paused before the large double door on which there glowed in large letters PERSONAL—MEN. In smaller letters were written SUBSECTIONS 1A—1E. In still smaller letters, just above the key slit, it stated: "In case of loss of key, communicate at once with 27-101-51."

A man inched past them, inserted an aluminum sliver into the key slit, and walked in. He closed the door behind him, making no attempt to hold it open for Baley. Had he done so, Baley would have been seriously offended. By strong custom men disregarded one another's presence entirely either within or just outside the Personals. Baley remembered one of the more interesting marital confidences to have been Jessie's telling him that the situation was quite different at Women's Personals.

She was always saying, "I met Josephine Greely at Personal and she said . . ."

It was one of the penalties of civic advancement that when the Baleys were granted permission for the activation of the small washbowl in their bedroom, Jessie's social life suffered.

Baley said, without completely masking his embarrassment, "Please wait out here, Daneel."

"Do you intend washing?" asked R. Daneel.

Baley squirmed and thought: Damned robot! If they were briefing him on everything under steel, why didn't they teach him manners? I'll be responsible if he ever says anything like this to anyone else.

He said, "I'll shower. It gets crowded evenings. I'll lose time then. If I get it done now we'll have the whole evening before us."

R. Daneel's face maintained its repose. "Is it part of the social custom that I wait outside?"

Baley's embarrassment deepened. "Why need you go in for—for no purpose."

"Oh, I understand you. Yes, of course. Nevertheless, Elijah, my hands grow dirty, too, and I will wash them."

He indicated his palms, holding them out before him. They were pink and plump, with the proper creases. They bore every mark of excellent and meticulous workmanship and were as clean as need be.

Baley said, "We have a washbasin in the apartment, you know." He said it casually. Snobbery would be lost on a robot.

"Thank you for your kindness. On the whole, however, I think it would be preferable to make use of this place. If I am to live with you men of Earth, it is best that I adopt as many of your customs and attitudes as I can."

"Come on in, then."

The bright cheerfulness of the interior was a sharp contrast to the busy utilitarianism of most of the rest of the City, but this time the effect was lost on Baley's consciousness.

He whispered to Daneel, "I may take up to half an hour or so.

Wait for me." He started away, then returned to add, "And listen, don't talk to anybody and don't look at anybody. Not a word, not a glance! It's a custom."

He looked hurriedly about to make certain that his own small conversation had not been noted, was not being met by shocked glances. Nobody, fortunately, was in the antecorridor, and after all it *was* only the antecorridor.

He hurried down it, feeling vaguely dirty, past the common chambers to the private stalls. It had been five years now since he had been awarded one—large enough to contain a shower, a small laundry, and other necessities. It even had a small projector that could be keyed in for the news films.

"A home away from home," he had joked when it was first made available to him. But now, he often wondered how he would bear the adjustment back to the more Spartan existence of the common chambers if his stall privileges were ever canceled.

He pressed the button that activated the laundry and the smooth face of the meter lighted.

R. Daneel was waiting patiently when Baley returned with a scrubbed body, clean underwear, a freshened shirt, and, generally, a feeling of greater comfort.

"No trouble?" Baley asked, when they were well outside the door and able to talk.

"None at all, Elijah," said R. Daneel.

Jessie was at the door, smiling nervously. Baley kissed her.

"Jessie," he mumbled, "this is my new partner, Daneel Olivaw."

Jessie held out a hand, which R. Daneel took and released. She turned to her husband, then looked timidly at R. Daneel.

She said, "Won't you sit down, Mr. Olivaw? I must talk to my husband on family matters. It'll take just a minute. I hope you won't mind."

Her hand was on Baley's sleeve. He followed her into the next room.

She said, in a hurried whisper, "You aren't hurt, are you? I've been so worried ever since the broadcast?"

"What broadcast?"

"It came through nearly an hour ago. About the riot at the shoe counter. They said two plain-clothes men stopped it. I knew you

were coming home with a partner and this was right in our sub-
section and right when you were coming home and I thought they
were making it better than it was and you were——"

"*Please*, Jessie. You see I'm perfectly all right."

Jessie caught hold of herself with an effort. She said, shakily,
"Your partner isn't from your division, is he?"

"No," replied Baley miserably. "He's—a complete stranger."

"How do I treat him?"

"Like anybody else. He's just my partner, that's all."

He said it so unconvincingly, that Jessie's quick eyes narrowed.
"What's wrong?"

"Nothing. Come, let's go back into the living room. It'll begin to
look queer."

Lije Baley felt a little uncertain about the apartment now. Until
this very moment, he had felt no qualms. In fact, he had always
been proud of it. It had three large rooms; the living room, for instance, was an ample fifteen feet by eighteen. There was a closet
in each room. One of the main ventilation ducts passed directly by.
It meant a little rumbling noise on rare occasions, but, on the other
hand, assured first-rate temperature control and well-conditioned air.
Nor was it too far from either Personal, which was a prime convenience.

But with the creature from worlds beyond space sitting in the
midst of it, Baley was suddenly uncertain. The apartment seemed
mean and cramped.

Jessie said, with a gaiety that was slightly synthetic, "Have you
and Mr. Olivaw eaten, Lije?"

"As a matter of fact," said Baley, quickly, "Daneel will not be
eating with us. I'll eat, though."

Jessie accepted the situation without trouble. With food supplies
so narrowly controlled and rationing tighter than ever, it was good
form to refuse another's hospitality.

She said, "I hope you won't mind our eating, Mr. Olivaw. Lije,
Bentley, and I generally eat at the Community kitchen. It's much
more convenient and there's more variety, you see, and just between
you and me, bigger helpings, too. But then, Lije and I *do* have permission to eat in our apartment three times a week if we want to—
Lije is quite successful at the Bureau and we have very nice status—

and I thought that just for this occasion, if you wanted to join us, we would have a little private feast of our own, though I do think that people who overdo their privacy privileges are just a bit anti-social, you know."

R. Daneel listened politely.

Baley said, with an undercover "shushing" wiggle of his fingers, "Jessie, I'm hungry."

R. Daneel said, "Would I be breaking a custom, Mrs. Baley, if I addressed you by your given name?"

"Why, no, of course not." Jessie folded a table out of the wall and plugged the plate warmer into the central depression on the table top. "You just go right ahead and call me Jessie all you feel like—uh—Daneel." She giggled.

Baley felt savage. The situation was getting rapidly more uncomfortable. Jessie thought R. Daneel a man. The thing would be someone to boast of and talk about in Women's Personal. He was good-looking in a wooden way, too, and Jessie was pleased with his deference. Anyone could see that.

Baley wondered about R. Daneel's impression of Jessie. She hadn't changed much in eighteen years, or at least not to Lije Baley. She was heavier, of course, and her figure had lost much of its youthful vigor. There were lines at the angles of the mouth and a trace of heaviness about her cheeks. Her hair was more conservatively styled and a dimmer brown than it had once been.

But that's all beside the point, thought Baley, somberly. On the Outer Worlds the women were tall and as slim and regal as the men. Or, at least, the book-films had them so and that must be the kind of women R. Daneel was used to.

But R. Daneel seemed quite unperturbed by Jessie's conversation, her appearance, or her appropriation of his name. He said, "Are you sure that is proper? The name, Jessie, seems to be a diminutive. Perhaps its use is restricted to members of your immediate circle and I would be more proper if I used your full given name."

Jessie, who was breaking open the insulating wrapper surrounding the dinner ration, bent her head over the task in sudden concentration.

"Just Jessie," she said, tightly. "Everyone calls me that. There's nothing else."

"Very well, Jessie."

The door opened and a youngster entered cautiously. His eyes found R. Daneel almost at once.

"Dad?" said the boy, uncertainly.

"My son, Bentley," said Baley, in a low voice. "This is Mr. Olivaw, Ben."

"He's your partner, huh, Dad? How d'ya do, Mr. Olivaw." Ben's eyes grew large and luminous. "Say, Dad, what happened down in the shoe place? The newscast said——"

"Don't ask any questions now, Ben," interposed Baley sharply.

Bentley's face fell and he looked toward his mother, who motioned him to a seat.

"Did you do what I told you, Bentley?" she asked, when he sat down. Her hands moved caressingly over his hair. It was as dark as his father's and he was going to have his father's height, but all the rest of him was hers. He had Jessie's oval face, her hazel eyes, her light-hearted way of looking at life.

"Sure, Mom," said Bentley, hitching himself forward a bit to look into the double dish from which savory vapors were already rising. "What we got to eat? Not zymoveal again, Mom? Huh, Mom?"

"There's nothing wrong with zymoveal," said Jessie, her lips pressing together. "Now, you just eat what's put before you and let's not have any comments."

It was quite obvious they *were* having zymoveal.

Baley took his own seat. He himself would have preferred something other than zymoveal, with its sharp flavor and definite aftertaste, but Jessie had explained her problem before this.

"Well, I just can't, Lije," she had said. "I live right here on these levels all day and I can't make enemies or life wouldn't be bearable. They know I used to be assistant dietitian and if I just walked off with steak or chicken every other week when there's hardly anyone else on the floor that has private eating privileges even on Sunday, they'd say it was pull or friends in the prep room. It would be talk, talk, talk, and I wouldn't be able to put my nose out the door or visit Personal in peace. As it is, zymoveal and protoveg are very good. They're well-balanced nourishment with no waste and, as a matter of fact, they're full of vitamins and minerals and everything anyone needs and we can have all the chicken we want when we eat in Community on the chicken Tuesdays."

Baley gave in easily. It was as Jessie said; the first problem of living is to minimize friction with the crowds that surround you on all sides. Bentley was a little harder to convince.

On this occasion, he said, "Gee, Mom, why can't I use Dad's ticket and eat in Community myself? I'd just as soon."

Jessie shook her head in annoyance and said, "I'm surprised at you, Bentley. What would people say if they saw you eating by yourself as though your own family weren't good enough for you or had thrown you out of the apartment?"

"Well, gosh, it's none of people's business."

Baley said, with a nervous edge in his voice, "Do as your mother tells you, Bentley."

Bentley shrugged, unhappily.

R. Daneel said, suddenly, from the other side of the room, "Have I the family's permission to view these book-films during your meal?"

"Oh, sure," said Bentley, slipping away from the table, a look of instant interest upon his face. "They're mine. I got them from the library on special school permit. I'll get you my viewer. It's a pretty good one. Dad gave it to me for my last birthday."

He brought it to R. Daneel and said, "Are you interested in robots, Mr. Olivaw?"

Baley dropped his spoon and bent to pick it up.

R. Daneel said, "Yes, Bentley. I am quite interested."

"Then you'll like these. They're all about robots. I've got to write an essay on them for school, so I'm doing research. It's quite a complicated subject," he said importantly. "I'm against them myself."

"Sit down, Bentley," said Baley, desperately, "and don't bother Mr. Olivaw."

"He's not bothering me, Elijah. I'd like to talk to you about the problem, Bentley, another time. Your father and I will be very busy tonight."

"Thanks, Mr. Olivaw." Bentley took his seat and, with a look of distaste in his mother's direction, broke off a portion of the crumbly pink zymoveal with his fork.

Baley thought: Busy tonight?

Then, with a resounding shock, he remembered his job. He thought of a Spacer lying dead in Spacetown and realized that for hours he had been so involved with his own dilemma that he had forgotten the cold fact of murder.

5

Analysis of a Murder

JESSIE SAID good-by to them. She was wearing a formal hat and a little jacket of keratofiber as she said, "I hope you'll excuse me, Mr. Olivaw. I know you have a great deal to discuss with Lije."

She pushed her son ahead of her as she opened the door.

"When will you be back, Jessie?" asked Baley.

She paused. "When do you want me to be back?"

"Well . . . No use staying out all night. Why don't you come back your usual time? Midnight or so." He looked doubtfully at R. Daneel.

R. Daneel nodded. "I regret having to drive you from your home."

"Don't worry about *that*, Mr. Olivaw. You're not driving me out at all. This is my usual evening out with the girls anyway. Come on, Ben."

The youngster was rebellious. "Aw, why the dickens do I have to go, anyway. I'm not going to bother them. Nuts!"

"Now, do as I say."

"Well, why can't I go to the etherics along with you?"

"Because I'm going with some friends and you've got other things——" The door closed behind them.

And now the moment had come. Baley had put it off in his mind. He had thought: First let's meet the robot and see what he's like. Then it was: Let's get him home. And then: Let's eat.

But now it was all over and there was no room for further delay. It was down at last to the question of murder, of interstellar complications, of possible raises in ratings, of possible disgrace. And he had no way of even beginning except to turn to the robot for help.

His fingernails moved aimlessly on the table, which had not been returned to its wall recess.

R. Daneel said, "How secure are we against being overheard?"

Baley looked up, surprised. "No one would listen to what's proceeding in another man's apartment."

"It is not your custom to eavesdrop?"

"It just isn't done, Daneel. You might as well suppose they'd—I don't know—that they'd look in your plate while you're eating."

"Or that they would commit murder?"

"What?"

"It is against your customs to kill, is it not, Elijah?"

Baley felt anger rising. "See here, if we're going to be partners, don't try to imitate Spacer arrogance. There's no room for it in you, R. Daneel." He could not resist emphasizing the "R."

"I am sorry if I have hurt your feelings, Elijah. My intention was only to indicate that, since human beings are occasionally capable of murder in defiance of custom, they may be able to violate custom for the smaller impropriety of eavesdropping."

"The apartment is adequately insulated," said Baley, still frowning. "You haven't heard anything from the apartments on any side of us, have you? Well, they won't hear us, either. Besides, why should anyone think anything of importance is going on here?"

"Let us not underestimate the enemy."

Baley shrugged. "Let's get started. My information is sketchy, so I can spread out my hand without much trouble. I know that a man named Roj Nemennuh Sarton, a citizen of the planet Aurora, and a resident of Spacetown, has been murdered by person or persons unknown. I understand that it is the opinion of the Spacers that this is not an isolated event. Am I right?"

"You are quite right, Elijah."

"They tie it up with recent attempts to sabotage the Spacer-sponsored project of converting us to an integrated human/robot society on the model of the Outer Worlds, and assume the murder was the product of a well-organized terrorist group."

"Yes."

"All right. Then to begin with, is this Spacer assumption necessarily true? Why can't the murder have been the work of an isolated fanatic? There is strong anti-robot sentiment on Earth, but there are no organized parties advocating violence of this sort."

"Not openly, perhaps. No."

"Even a secret organization dedicated to the destruction of robots and robot factories would have the common sense to realize that the worst thing they could do would be to murder a Spacer. It seems much more likely to have been the work of an unbalanced mind."

R. Daneel listened carefully, then said, "I think the weight of probability is against the 'fanatic' theory. The person killed was too well chosen and the time of the murder too appropriate for anything but deliberate planning on the part of an organized group."

"Well, then, you've got more information than I have. Spill it!"

"Your phraseology is obscure, but I think I understand. I will have to explain some of the background to you. As seen from Spacetown, Elijah, relations with Earth are unsatisfactory."

"Tough," muttered Baley.

"I have been told that when Spacetown was first established, it was taken for granted by most of our people that Earth would be willing to adopt the integrated society that has worked so well on the Outer Worlds. Even after the first riots, we thought that it was only a matter of your people getting over the first shock of novelty.

"That has not proven to be the case. Even with the co-operation of the Terrestrial government and of most of the various City governments, resistance has been continuous and progress has been very slow. Naturally, this has been a matter of great concern to our people."

"Out of altruism, I suppose," said Baley.

"Not entirely," said R. Daneel, "although it is good of you to attribute worthy motives to them. It is our common belief that a healthy and modernized Earth would be of great benefit to the whole Galaxy. At least, it is the common belief among our people at Spacetown. I must admit that there are strong elements opposed to them on the Outer Worlds."

"What? Disagreement among the Spacers?"

"Certainly. There are some who think that a modernized Earth will be a dangerous and an imperialistic Earth. This is particularly true among the populations of those older worlds which are closer to Earth and have greater reason to remember the first few centuries of interstellar travel when their worlds were controlled, politically and economically, by Earth."

Baley sighed. "Ancient history. Are they really worried? Are they still kicking at us for things that happened a thousand years ago?"

"Humans," said R. Daneel, "have their own peculiar makeup. They are not as reasonable, in many ways, as we robots, since their circuits are not as preplanned. I am told that this, too, has its advantages."

"Perhaps it may," said Baley, dryly.

"You are in a better position to know," said R. Daneel. "In any case, continuing failure on Earth has strengthened the Nationalist parties on the Outer Worlds. They say that it is obvious that Earthmen are different from Spacers and cannot be fitted into the same traditions. They say that if we imposed robots on Earth by superior force, we would be loosing destruction on the Galaxy. One thing they never forget, you see, is that Earth's population is eight billions, while the total population of the fifty Outer Worlds combined is scarcely more than five and a half billions. Our people here, particularly Dr. Sarton——"

"He was a doctor?"

"A Doctor of Sociology, specializing in robotics, and a very brilliant man."

"I see. Go on."

"As I said, Dr. Sarton and the others realized that Spacetown and all it meant would not exist much longer if such sentiments on the Outer Worlds were allowed to grow by feeding on our continued failure. Dr. Sarton felt that the time had come to make a supreme effort to understand the psychology of the Earthman. It is easy to say that the Earth people are innately conservative and to speak tritely of 'the unchanging Earth' and 'the inscrutable Terrestrial mind,' but that is only evading the problem.

"Dr. Sarton said it was ignorance speaking and that we could not dismiss the Earthman with a proverb or a bromide. He said the Spacers who were trying to remake Earth must abandon the isolation of Spacetown and mingle with Earthmen. They must live as they, think as they, be as they."

Baley said, "The Spacers? Impossible."

"You are quite right," said R. Daneel. "Despite his views, Dr. Sarton himself could not have brought himself to enter any of the Cities, and he knew it. He would have been unable to bear the hugeness and the crowds. Even if he had been forced inside at the point of a blaster, the externals would have weighed him down so that he could never have penetrated the inner truths for which he sought."

"What about the way they're always worrying about disease?" demanded Baley. "Don't forget that. I don't think there's one of them that would risk entering a City on that account alone."

"There is that, too. Disease in the Earthly sense is unknown on the Outer Worlds and the fear of the unknown is always morbid. Dr. Sarton appreciated all of this, but, nevertheless, he insisted on the necessity of growing to know the Earthman and his way of life intimately."

"He seems to have worked himself into a corner."

"Not quite. The objections to entering the City hold for human Spacers. Robot Spacers are another thing entirely."

Baley thought: I keep forgetting, damn it. Aloud, he said, "Oh?"

"Yes," said R. Daneel. "We are more flexible, naturally. At least in this respect. We can be designed for adaptation to an Earthly life. By being built into a particularly close similarity to the human externals, we could be accepted by Earthmen and allowed a closer view of their life."

"And you yourself——" began Baley in sudden enlightenment.

"Am just such a robot. For a year, Dr. Sarton had been working upon the design and construction of such robots. I was the first of his robots and so far the only one. Unfortunately, my education is not yet complete. I have been hurried into my role prematurely as a result of the murder."

"Then not all Spacer robots are like you? I mean, some look more like robots and less like humans. Right?"

"Why, naturally. The outward appearance is dependent on a robot's function. My own function requires a very manlike appearance, and I have it. Others are different, although all are humanoid. Certainly they are more humanoid than the distressingly primitive models I saw at the shoe counter. Are all your robots like that?"

"More or less," said Baley. "You don't approve?"

"Of course not. It is difficult to accept a gross parody of the human form as an intellectual equal. Can your factories do no better?"

"I'm sure they can, Daneel. I think we just prefer to know when we're dealing with a robot and when we're not." He stared directly into the robot's eyes as he said that. They were bright and moist, as a human's would be, but it seemed to Baley that their gaze was steady and did not flicker slightly from point to point as a man's would.

R. Daneel said, "I am hopeful that in time I will grow to understand that point of view."

For a moment, Baley thought there was sarcasm in the sentence, then dismissed the possibility.

"In any case," said R. Daneel, "Dr. Sarton saw clearly the fact that it was a case for C/Fe."

"See fee? What's that?"

"Just the chemical symbols for the elements carbon and iron, Elijah. Carbon is the basis of human life and iron of robot life. It becomes easy to speak of C/Fe when you wish to express a culture that combines the best of the two on an equal but parallel basis."

"See fee. Do you write it with a hyphen? Or how?"

"No, Elijah. A diagonal line between the two is the accepted way. It symbolizes neither one nor the other, but a mixture of the two, without priority."

Against his will, Baley found himself interested. Formal education on Earth included virtually no information on Outer World history or sociology after the Great Rebellion that made them independent of the mother planet. The popular book-film romances, to be sure, had their stock Outer World characters: the visiting tycoon, choleric and eccentric; the beautiful heiress, invariably smitten by the Earthman's charms and drowning disdain in love; the arrogant Spacer rival, wicked and forever beaten. These were worthless pictures, since they denied even the most elementary and well-known truths: that Spacers never entered Cities and Spacer women virtually never visited Earth.

For the first time in his life, Baley was stirred by an odd curiosity. What was Spacer life really like?

He brought his mind back to the issue at hand with something of an effort. He said, "I think I get what you're driving at. Your Dr. Sarton was attacking the problem of Earth's conversion to C/Fe from a new and promising angle. Our conservative groups or Medievalists, as they call themselves, were perturbed. They were afraid he might succeed. So they killed him. That's the motivation that makes it an organized plot and not an isolated outrage. Right?"

"I would put it about like that, Elijah. Yes."

Baley whistled thoughtfully under his breath. His long fingers tapped lightly against the table. Then he shook his head. "It won't wash. It won't wash at all."

"Pardon me. I do not understand you."

"I'm trying to get the picture. An Earthman walks into Spacetown, walks up to Dr. Sarton, blasts him, and walks out. I just don't see it. Surely the entrance to Spacetown is guarded."

R. Daneel nodded. "I think it is safe to say that no Earthman can possibly have passed through the entrance illegally."

"Then where does that leave you?"

"It would leave us in a confusing position, Elijah, if the entrance were the only way of reaching Spacetown from New York City."

Baley watched his partner thoughtfully. "I don't get you. It's the only connection between the two."

"Directly between the two, yes." R. Daneel waited a moment, then said, "You do not follow me. Is that not so?"

"That *is* so. I don't get you at all."

"Well, if it will not offend you, I will try to explain myself. May I have a piece of paper and a writer? Thank you. Look here, partner Elijah. I will draw a big circle and label it 'New York City.' Now, tangent to it, I will draw a small circle and label it 'Spacetown.' Here, where they touch, I draw an arrowhead and label it 'Barrier.' Now do you see no other connection?"

Baley said, "Of course not. There is no other connection."

"In a way," said the robot, "I am glad to hear you say this. It is in accordance with what I have been taught about Terrestrial ways of thinking. The barrier is the only *direct* connection. But both the City and Spacetown are open to the countryside in all directions. It is possible for a Terrestrial to leave the City at any of numerous exits and strike out cross country to Spacetown, where no barrier will stop him."

The tip of Baley's tongue touched his upper lip and for a moment stayed there. Then he said, "Cross country?"

"Yes."

"Cross *country!* Alone?"

"Why not?"

"Walking?"

"Undoubtedly walking. Walking would offer the least chance of detection. The murder took place early in the working day and the trip was undoubtedly negotiated in the hours before dawn."

"Impossible! There isn't a man in the City who would do it. Leave the City? Alone?"

"Ordinarily, it would seem unlikely. Yes. We Spacers know that. It is why we guard only the entrance. Even in the Great Riot, your people attacked only at the barrier that then protected the entrance. Not one left the City."

"Well, then?"

"But now we are dealing with an unusual situation. It is not the blind attack of a mob following the line of least resistance, but the organized attempt of a small group to strike, deliberately, at the unguarded point. It explains why, as you say, a Terrestrial could enter Spacetown, walk up to his victim, kill him, and walk away. The man attacked through a complete blind spot on our part."

Baley shook his head. "It's too unlikely. Have your people done anything to check that theory?"

"Yes, we have. Your Commissioner of Police was present almost at the time of the murder——"

"I know. He told me so."

"That, Elijah, is another example of the timeliness of the murder. Your Commissioner has co-operated with Dr. Sarton in the past and he was the Earthman with whom Dr. Sarton planned to make initial arrangements concerning the infiltration of your city by R's such as myself. The appointment for that morning was to concern that. The murder, of course, stopped those plans, at least temporarily, and the fact that it happened when your own Commissioner of Police was actually within Spacetown made the entire situation more difficult and embarrassing for Earth, and for our own people, too.

"But that is not what I started to say. Your Commissioner was present. We said to him, 'The man must have come cross country.' Like you, he said, 'Impossible,' or perhaps, 'Unthinkable.' He was quite disturbed, of course, and perhaps that may have made it difficult for him to see the essential point. Nevertheless, we forced him to begin checking that possibility almost at once."

Baley thought of the Commissioner's broken glasses and, even in the middle of somber thoughts, a corner of his mouth twitched. Poor Julius! Yes, he *would* be disturbed. Of course, there would be no way for Enderby to have explained the situation to the lofty Spacers, who looked upon physical disability as a peculiarly disgusting attribute of the non-genetically selected Earthmen. At least, he couldn't without losing face, and face was valuable to Police Commissioner Julius Enderby. Well, Earthmen had to stick together in some respects. The robot would never find out about Enderby's nearsightedness from Baley.

R. Daneel continued, "One by one, the various exit points from the City were investigated. Do you know how many there are, Elijah?"

Baley shook his head, then hazarded, "Twenty?"

"Five hundred and two."

"What?"

"Originally, there were many more. Five hundred and two are all that remain functional. Your City represents a slow growth, Elijah. It was once open to the sky and people crossed from City to country freely."

"Of course. I know that."

"Well, when it was first enclosed, there were many exits left. Five hundred and two still remain. The rest are built over or blocked up. We are not counting, of course, the entrance points for air freight."

"Well, what of the exit points?"

"It was hopeless. They are unguarded. We could find no official who was in charge or who considered them under his jurisdiction. It seemed as though no one even knew they existed. A man could have walked out of any of them at any time and returned at will. He would never have been detected."

"Anything else? The weapon was gone, I suppose."

"Oh, yes."

"Any clues of any sort?"

"None. We have investigated the grounds surrounding Spacetown thoroughly. The robots on the truck farms were quite useless as possible witnesses. They are little more than automatic farm machinery, scarcely humanoid. And there were no humans."

"Uh-huh. What next?"

"Having failed, so far, at one end, Spacetown, we will work at the other, New York City. It will be our duty to track down all possible subversive groups, to sift all dissident organizations——"

"How much time do you intend to spend?" interrupted Baley.

"As little as possible, as much as necessary."

"Well," said Baley, thoughtfully, "I wish you had another partner in this mess."

"I do not," said R. Daneel. "The Commissioner spoke very highly of your loyalty and ability."

"It was nice of him," said Baley sardonically. He thought: Poor Julius. I'm on his conscience and he tries hard.

"We didn't rely entirely on him," said R. Daneel. "We checked your records. You have expressed yourself openly against the use of robots in your department."

"Oh? Do you object?"

"Not at all. Your opinions are, obviously, your own. But it made it necessary for us to check your psychological profile very closely. We know that, although you dislike R's intensely, you *will* work with one if you conceive it to be your duty. You have an extraordinarily high loyalty aptitude and a respect for legitimate authority. It is what we need. Commissioner Enderby judged you well."

"You have no personal resentment toward my anti-robot sentiments?"

R. Daneel said, "If they do not prevent you from working with me and helping me do what is required of me, how can they matter?"

Baley felt stopped. He said, belligerently, "Well, then, if I pass the test, how about you? What makes you a detective?"

"I do not understand you."

"You were designed as an information-gathering machine. A man-imitation to record the facts of human life for the Spacers."

"That is a good beginning for an investigator, is it not? To be an information-gathering machine?"

"A beginning, maybe. But it's not all there is, by a long shot."

"To be sure, there has been a final adjustment of my circuits."

"I'd be curious to hear the details of that, Daneel."

"That is easy enough. A particularly strong drive has been inserted into my motivation banks; a desire for justice."

"*Justice!*" cried Baley. The irony faded from his face and was replaced by a look of the most earnest distrust.

But R. Daneel turned swiftly in his chair and stared at the door. "Someone is out there."

Someone was. The door opened and Jessie, pale and thin-lipped, walked in.

Baley was startled. "Why, Jessie! Is anything wrong?"

She stood there, eyes not meeting his. "I'm sorry. I had to . . ." Her voice trailed off.

"Where's Bentley?"

"He's to stay the night in the Youth Hall."

Baley said, "Why? I didn't tell you to do that."

"You said your partner would stay the night. I felt he would need Bentley's room."

R. Daneel said, "There was no necessity, Jessie."

Jessie lifted her eyes to R. Daneel's face, staring at it earnestly.

Baley looked at his fingertips, sick at what might follow, somehow unable to interpose. The momentary silence pressed thickly on his eardrums and then, far away, as though through folds of plastex, he heard his wife say, "I think you are a robot, Daneel."

And R. Daneel replied, in a voice as calm as ever, "I am."

6

Whispers in a Bedroom

ON THE uppermost levels of some of the wealthiest subsections of
the City are the natural Solariums, where a partition of quartz with
a movable metal shield excludes the air but lets in the sunlight.
There the wives and daughters of the City's highest administrators
and executives may tan themselves. There a unique thing happens
every evening.

Night falls.

In the rest of the City (including the UV-Solariums, where the
millions, in strict sequence of allotted time, may occasionally expose
themselves to the artificial wavelengths of arc lights) there are only
the arbitrary cycles of hours.

The business of the City might easily continue in three eight-hour
or four six-hour shifts, by "day" and "night" alike. Light and work
could easily proceed endlessly. There are always civic reformers
who periodically suggest such a thing in the interests of economy
and efficiency.

The notion is never accepted.

Much of the earlier habits of Earthly society have been given
up in the interests of that same economy and efficiency: space, privacy, even much of free will. They are the products of civilization,
however, and not more than ten thousand years old.

The adjustment of sleep to night, however, is as old as man: a
million years. The habit is not easy to give up. Although the evening
is unseen, apartment lights dim as the hours of darkness pass and
the City's pulse sinks. Though no one can tell noon from midnight

by any cosmic phenomenon along the enclosed avenues of the City, mankind follows the mute partitionings of the hour hand.

The expressways empty, the noise of life sinks, the moving mob among the colossal alleys melts away; New York City lies in Earth's unnoticed shadow, and its population sleeps.

Elijah Baley did not sleep. He lay in bed and there was no light in his apartment, but that was as far as it went.

Jessie lay next to him, motionless in the darkness. He had not felt nor heard her move.

On the other side of the wall sat, stood, lay (Baley wondered which) R. Daneel Olivaw.

Baley whispered, "Jessie!" Then again, "Jessie!"

The dark figure beside him stirred slightly under the sheet. "What do you want?"

"Jessie, don't make it worse for me."

"You might have told me."

"How could I? I was planning to, when I could think of a way. Jehoshaphat, Jessie——"

"Sh!"

Baley's voice returned to its whisper. "How did you find out? Won't you tell me?"

Jessie turned toward him. He could sense her eyes looking through the darkness at him.

"Lije." Her voice was scarcely more than a stirring of air. "Can he hear us? That thing?"

"Not if we whisper."

"How do you know? Maybe he has special ears to pick up tiny sounds. Spacer robots can do all sorts of things."

Baley knew that. The prorobot propaganda was forever stressing the miraculous feats of the Spacer robots, their endurance, their extra senses, their service to humanity in a hundred novel ways. Personally, he thought that approach defeated itself. Earthmen hated the robots all the more for their superiority.

He whispered, "Not Daneel. They made him human-type on purpose. They wanted him to be accepted as a human being, so he must have only human senses."

"How do you know?"

"If he had extra senses, there would be too much danger of his giving himself away as non-human by accident. He would do too much, know too much."

"Well, maybe."

Silence fell again.

A minute passed and Baley tried a second time. "Jessie, if you'll just let things be until—until . . . Look, dear, it's unfair of you to be angry."

"Angry? Oh, Lije, you fool. I'm not angry. I'm scared; I'm scared clean to death."

She made a gulping sound and clutched at the neck of his pajamas. For a while, they clung together, and Baley's growing sense of injury evaporated into a troubled concern.

"Why, Jessie? There's nothing to be worried about. He's harmless. I swear he is."

"Can't you get rid of him, Lije?"

"You know I can't. It's Department business. How can I?"

"What kind of business, Lije? Tell me."

"Now, Jessie, I'm surprised at you." He groped for her cheek in the darkness and patted it. It was wet. Using his pajama sleeve, he carefully wiped her eyes.

"Now, look," he said tenderly, "you're being a baby."

"Tell them at the Department to have someone else do it, whatever it is. Please, Lije."

Baley's voice hardened a bit. "Jessie, you've been a policeman's wife long enough to know an assignment is an assignment."

"Well, why did it have to be you?"

"Julius Enderby——"

She stiffened in his arms. "I might have known. Why can't you tell Julius Enderby to have someone else do the dirty work just once. You stand for too much, Lije, and this is just——"

"All right, all right," he said, soothingly.

She subsided, quivering.

Baley thought: She'll never understand.

Julius Enderby had been a fighting word with them since their engagement. Enderby had been two classes ahead of Baley at the City School of Administrative Studies. They had been friends. When Baley had taken his battery of aptitude tests and neuroanalysis and found himself in line for the police force, he found Enderby there ahead of him. Enderby had already moved into the plain-clothes division.

Baley followed Enderby, but at a continually greater distance. It was no one's fault, precisely. Baley was capable enough, efficient enough, but he lacked something that Enderby had. Enderby fit the administrative machine perfectly. He was one of those persons who was born for a hierarchy, who was just naturally comfortable in a bureaucracy.

The Commissioner wasn't a great brain, and Baley knew it. He had his childish peculiarities, his intermittent rash of ostentatious Medievalism, for instance. But he was smooth with others; he offended no one; he took orders gracefully; he gave them with the proper mixture of gentleness and firmness. He even got along with the Spacers. He was perhaps overobsequious to them (Baley himself could never have dealt with them for half a day without getting into a state of bristle; he was sure of that, even though he had never really spoken to a Spacer), but they trusted him, and that made him extremely useful to the City.

So, in a Civil Service where smooth and sociable performance was more useful than an individualistic competence, Enderby went up the scale quickly, and was at the Commissioner level when Baley himself was nothing more than a C-5. Baley did not resent the contrast, though he was human enough to regret it. Enderby did not forget their earlier friendship and, in his queer way, tried to make up for his success by doing what he could for Baley.

The assignment of partnership with R. Daneel was an example of it. It was tough and unpleasant, but there was no question that it carried within it the germs of tremendous advance. The Commissioner might have given the chance to someone else. His own talk, that morning, of needing a favor masked but did not hide that fact.

Jessie never saw things that way. On similar occasions in the past, she had said, "It's your silly loyalty index. I'm so tired of hearing everyone praise you for being so full of a sense of duty. Think of yourself once in a while. I notice the ones on top don't bring up the topic of their *own* loyalty index."

Baley lay in bed in a state of stiff wakefulness, letting Jessie calm down. He had to *think*. He had to be certain of his suspicions.

Little things chased one another and fitted together in his mind. Slowly, they were building into a pattern.

He felt the mattress give as Jessie stirred.

"Lije?" Her lips were at his ear.

"What?"

"Why don't you resign?"

"Don't be crazy."

"Why not?" She was suddenly almost eager. "You can get rid of that horrible robot that way. Just walk in and tell Enderby you're through."

Baley said coldly, "I can't resign in the middle of an important case. I can't throw the whole thing down the disposal tube just any time I feel like it. A trick like that means declassification for cause."

"Even so. You can work your way up again. You can do it, Lije. There are a dozen places where you'd fit into Service."

"Civil Service doesn't take men who are declassified for cause. Manual labor is the only thing I can do; the only thing you could do. Bentley would lose all inherited status. For God's sake, Jessie, you don't know what it's like."

"I've read about it. I'm not afraid of it," she mumbled.

"You're crazy. You're plain crazy." Baley could feel himself trembling. There was a familiar, flashing picture of his father in his mind's eye. His father, moldering away toward death.

Jessie sighed heavily.

Baley's mind turned savagely away from her. In desperation, it returned to the pattern it was constructing.

He said, tightly, "Jessie, you've got to tell me. How did you find out Daneel was a robot? What made you decide that?"

She began, "Well . . ." and just ran down. It was the third time she had begun to explain and failed.

He crushed her hand in his, willing her to speak. "Please, Jessie. What's frightening you?"

She said, "I just guessed he was a robot, Lije."

He said, "There wasn't anything to make you guess that, Jessie. You didn't think he was a robot before you left, now did you?"

"No-o, but I got to thinking . . ."

"Come on, Jessie. What was it?"

"Well . . . Look, Lije, the girls were talking in the Personal. You know how they are. Just talking about everything."

Women! thought Baley.

"Anyway," said Jessie. "The rumor is all over town. It must be."

"All over town?" Baley felt a quick and savage touch of triumph, or nearly that. Another piece in place!

"It was the way they sounded. They said there was talk about a Spacer robot loose in the City. He was supposed to look just like a man and to be working with the police. They even asked *me* about it. They laughed and said, 'Does your Lije know anything about it, Jessie?' and I laughed, and said, 'Don't be silly!'

"Then we went to the etherics and I got to thinking about your new partner. Do you remember those pictures you brought home, the ones Julius Enderby took in Spacetown, to show me what Spacers looked like? Well, I got to thinking that's what your partner looked like. It just came to me that that's what he looked like and I said to myself, oh, my God, someone must've recognized him in the shoe department and he's with Lije and I just said I had a headache and I ran——"

Baley said, "Now, Jessie, stop, stop. Get hold of yourself. Now why are you afraid? You're not afraid of Daneel himself. You faced up to him when you came home. You faced up to him fine. So——"

He stopped speaking. He sat up in bed, eyes uselessly wide in the darkness.

He felt his wife move against his side. His hand leaped, found her lips and pressed against them. She heaved against his grip, her hands grasping his wrist and wrenching, but he leaned down against her the more heavily.

Then, suddenly, he released her. She whimpered.

He said, huskily, "Sorry, Jessie. I was listening."

He was getting out of bed, pulling warm Plastofilm over the soles of his feet.

"Lije, where are you going? Don't leave me."

"It's all right. I'm just going to the door."

The Plastofilm made a soft, shuffling noise as he circled the bed. He cracked the door to the living room and waited a long moment. Nothing happened. It was so quiet, he could hear the thin whistle of Jessie's breath from their bed. He could hear the dull rhythm of blood in his ears.

Baley's hand crept through the opening of the door, snaking out to the spot he needed no light to find. His fingers closed upon the knob that controlled the ceiling illumination. He exerted the smallest pressure he could and the ceiling gleamed dimly, so dimly that the lower half of the living room remained in semidusk.

He saw enough, however. The main door was closed and the living room lay lifeless and quiet.

He turned the knob back into the off position and moved back to bed.

It was all he needed. The pieces fit. The pattern was complete.

Jessie pleaded with him. "Lije, what's wrong?"

"Nothing's wrong, Jessie. Everything's all right. He's not here."

"The robot? Do you mean he's gone? For good?"

"No, no. He'll be back. And before he does, answer my question."

"What question?"

"What are you afraid of?"

Jessie said nothing.

Baley grew more insistent. "You said you were scared to death."

"Of him."

"No, we went through that. You weren't afraid of him and, besides, you know quite well a robot cannot hurt a human being."

Her words came slowly. "I thought if everyone knew he was a robot there might be a riot. We'd be killed."

"Why kill us?"

"You know what riots are like."

"They don't even know where the robot is, do they?"

"They might find out."

"And that's what you're afraid of, a riot?"

"Well——"

"Sh!" He pressed Jessie down to the pillow.

Then he put his lips to her ear. "He's come back. Now listen and don't say a word. Everything's fine. He'll be gone in the morning and he won't be back. There'll be no riot, nothing."

He was almost contented as he said that, almost completely contented. He felt he could sleep.

He thought again: No riot, nothing. And no declassification.

And just before he actually fell asleep, he thought: Not even a murder investigation. Not even that. The whole thing's solved. . . .

He slept.

7

Excursion Into Spacetown

POLICE COMMISSIONER Julius Enderby polished his glasses with exquisite care and placed them upon the bridge of his nose.

Baley thought: It's a good trick. Keeps you busy while you're thinking what to say, and it doesn't cost money the way lighting up a pipe does.

And because the thought had entered his mind, he drew out his pipe and dipped into his pinched store of rough-cut. One of the few luxury crops still grown on Earth was tobacco, and its end was visibly approaching. Prices had gone up, never down, in Baley's lifetime; quotas down, never up.

Enderby, having adjusted his glasses, felt for the switch at one end of his desk and flicked his door into one-way transparency for a moment. "Where is he now, by the way?"

"He told me he wanted to be shown through the Department, and I let Jack Tobin do the honors." Baley lit his pipe and tightened its baffle carefully. The Commissioner, like most non-indulgers, was petty about tobacco smoke.

"I hope you didn't tell him Daneel was a robot."

"Of course I didn't."

The Commissioner did not relax. One hand remained aimlessly busy with the automatic calendar on his desk.

"How is it?" he asked, without looking at Baley.

"Middling rough."

"I'm sorry, Lije."

Baley said, firmly, "You might have warned me that he looked completely human."

The Commissioner looked surprised. "I didn't?" Then, with sudden petulance, "Damn it, you should have known. I wouldn't have asked you to have him stay at your house if he looked like R. Sammy. Now would I?"

"I know, Commissioner, but I'd never seen a robot like that and you had. I didn't even know such things were possible. I just wish you'd mentioned it, that's all."

"Look, Lije, I'm sorry. I should have told you. You're right. It's just that this job, this whole deal, has me so on edge that half the time I'm just snapping at people for no reason. He, I mean this Daneel thing, is a new-type robot. It's still in the experimental stage."

"So he explained himself."

"Oh. Well, that's it, then."

Baley tensed a little. This was it, now. He said, casually, teeth clenched on pipestem. "R. Daneel has arranged a trip to Spacetown for me."

"To Spacetown!" Enderby looked up with instant indignation.

"Yes. It's the logical next move, Commissioner. I'd like to see the scene of the crime, ask a few questions."

Enderby shook his head decidedly. "I don't think that's a good idea, Lije. We've gone over the ground. I doubt there's anything new to be learned. And they're strange people. Kid gloves! They've got to be handled with kid gloves. You don't have the experience."

He put a plump hand to his forehead and added, with unexpected fervor, "I hate them."

Baley inserted hostility into his voice. "Damn it, the robot came here and I should go there. It's bad enough sharing a front seat with a robot; I hate to take a back seat. Of course, if you don't think I'm capable of running this investigation, Commissioner——"

"It isn't that, Lije. It's not you, it's the Spacers. You don't know what they're like."

Baley deepened his frown. "Well, then, Commissioner, suppose you come along." His right hand rested on his knee, and two of his fingers crossed automatically as he said that.

The Commissioner's eyes widened. "No, Lije. I won't go there. Don't ask me to." He seemed visibly to catch hold of his runaway words. More quietly, he said, with an unconvincing smile, "Lots of work here, you know. I'm days behind."

Baley regarded him thoughtfully. "I tell you what, then. Why not get into it by trimension later on. Just for a while, you understand. In case I need help."

"Well, yes. I suppose I can do that." He sounded unenthusiastic.

"Good." Baley looked at the wall clock, nodded, and got up. "I'll be in touch with you."

Baley looked back as he left the office, keeping the door open for part of an additional second. He saw the Commissioner's head begin bending down toward the crook of one elbow as it rested on the desk. The plain-clothes man could almost swear he heard a sob.

Jehoshaphat! he thought, in outright shock.

He paused in the common room and sat on the corner of a nearby desk, ignoring its occupant, who looked up, murmured a casual greeting, and returned to his work.

Baley unclipped the baffle from the bowl of the pipe and blew into it. He inverted the pipe itself over the desk's small ash vacuum and let the powdery white tobacco ash vanish. He looked regretfully at the empty pipe, readjusted the baffle, and put it away. Another pipeful gone forever!

He reconsidered what had just taken place. In one way, Enderby had not surprised him. He had expected resistance to any attempt on his own part to enter Spacetown. He had heard the Commissioner talk often enough about the difficulties of dealing with Spacers, about the dangers of allowing any but experienced negotiators to have anything to do with them, even over trifles.

He had not expected, however, to have the Commissioner give in so easily. He had supposed, at the very least, that Enderby would have insisted on accompanying him. The pressure of other work was meaningless in the face of the importance of this problem.

And that was not what Baley wanted. He wanted exactly what he had gotten. He wanted the Commissioner to be present by trimensional personification so that he could witness the proceedings from a point of safety.

Safety was the key word. Baley would need a witness that could not be put out of the way immediately. He needed that much as the minimum guarantee of his own safety.

The Commissioner had agreed to that at once. Baley remembered the parting sob, or ghost of one, and thought: Jehoshaphat, the man's into this past his depth.

A cheerful, slurring voice sounded just at Baley's shoulder and Baley started.

"What the devil do you want?" he demanded savagely.

The smile on R. Sammy's face remained foolishly fixed. "Jack says to tell you Daneel is ready, Lije."

"All right. Now get out of here."

He frowned at the robot's departing back. There was nothing so irritating as having that clumsy metal contraption forever making free with your front name. He'd complained about that when R. Sammy first arrived and the Commissioner had shrugged his shoulders and said, "You can't have it both ways, Lije. The public insists that City robots be built with a strong friendship circuit. All right, then. He is drawn to you. He calls you by the friendliest name he knows."

Friendship circuit! No robot built, of any type, could possibly hurt a human being. That was the First Law of Robotics:

"A robot may not injure a human being, or, through inaction, allow a human being to come to harm."

No positronic brain was ever built without that injunction driven so deeply into its basic circuits that no conceivable derangement could displace it. There was no need for specialized friendship circuits.

Yet the Commissioner was right. The Earthman's distrust for robots was something quite irrational and friendship circuits had to be incorporated, just as all robots had to be made smiling. On Earth, at any rate.

R. Daneel, now, never smiled.

Sighing, Baley rose to his feet. He thought: Spacetown, next stop— or, maybe, last stop!

The police forces of the City, as well as certain high officials, could still make use of individual squad cars along the corridors of the City and even along the ancient underground motorways that were barred to foot traffic. There were perennial demands on the part of the Liberals that these motorways be converted to children's playgrounds, to new shopping areas, or to expressway or local-way extensions.

The strong pleas of "Civic safety!" remained unvanquished, however. In cases of fires too large to be handled by local devices, in cases of massive breakdowns in power lines or ventilators, most of all in cases of serious riot, there had to be some means whereby the forces of the City could be mobilized at the stricken point in a hurry. No substitute for the motorways existed or could exist.

Baley had traveled along a motorway several times before in his life, but its indecent emptiness always depressed him. It seemed a million miles from the warm, living pulsation of the City. It stretched out like a blind and hollow worm before his eyes as he sat at the controls of the squad car. It opened continuously into new stretches as he moved around this gentle curve or that. Behind him, he knew without looking, another blind and hollow worm continually contracted and closed. The motorway was well lit, but lighting was meaningless in the silence and emptiness.

R. Daneel did nothing to break that silence or fill that emptiness. He looked straight ahead, as unimpressed by the empty motorway as by the bulging expressway.

In one sounding moment, to the tune of a wild whine of the squad car's siren, they popped out of the motorway and curved gradually into the vehicular lane of a City corridor.

The vehicular lanes were still conscientiously marked down each major corridor in reverence for one vestigial portion of the past. There were no vehicles any longer, except for squad cars, fire engines, and maintenance trucks, and pedestrians used the lanes in complete self-assurance. They scattered in indignant hurry before the advance of Baley's squealing car.

Baley, himself, drew a freer breath as noise surged in about him, but it was an interval only. In less than two hundred yards they turned into the subdued corridors that led to Spacetown Entrance.

They were expected. The guards obviously knew R. Daneel by sight and, although themselves human, nodded to him without the least self-consciousness.

One approached Baley and saluted with perfect, if frigid, military courtesy. He was tall and grave, though not the perfect specimen of Spacer physique that R. Daneel was.

He said, "Your identification card, if you please, sir."

It was inspected quickly but thoroughly. Baley noticed that the guard wore flesh-colored gloves and had an all but unnoticeable filter in each nostril.

The guard saluted again and returned the card. He said, "There is a small Men's Personal here which we would be pleased to have you use if you wish to shower."

It was in Baley's mind to deny the necessity, but R. Daneel plucked gently at his sleeve, as the guard stepped back to his place.

R. Daneel said, "It is customary, partner Elijah, for City dwellers to shower before entering Spacetown. I tell you this since I know you have no desire, through lack of information on this matter, to render yourself or ourselves uncomfortable. It is also advisable for you to attend to any matters of personal hygiene you may think advisable. There will be no facilities within Spacetown for that purpose."

"No facilities!" said Baley, strenuously. "But that's impossible."

"I mean, of course," said R. Daneel, "none for use by City dwellers."

Baley's face filled with a clearly hostile astonishment.

R. Daneel said, "I regret the situation, but it is a matter of custom."

Wordlessly, Baley entered the Personal. He felt, rather than saw, R. Daneel entering behind him.

He thought: Checking on me? Making sure I wash the City dust off myself?

For a furious moment, he reveled in the thought of the shock he was preparing for Spacetown. It seemed to him suddenly minor that he might, in effect, be pointing a blaster at his own chest.

The Personal was small, but it was well appointed and antiseptic in its cleanliness. There was a trace of sharpness in the air. Baley sniffed at it, momentarily puzzled.

Then he thought: Ozone! They've got ultraviolet radiation flooding the place.

A little sign blinked on and off several times, then remained steadily lit. It said, "Visitor will please remove all clothing, including shoes, and place it in the receptacle below."

Baley acquiesced. He unhitched his blaster and blaster strap and recircled it about his naked waist. It felt heavy and uncomfortable.

The receptacle closed and his clothing was gone. The lighted sign blanked out. A new sign flashed ahead.

It said: "Visitor will please tend to personal needs, then make use of the shower indicated by arrow."

Baley felt like a machine tool being shaped by long-distance force edges on an assembly line.

His first act upon entering the small shower cubicle was to draw up the moisture-proof flap on his blaster holster and clip it down firmly all about. He knew by long-standing test that he could still draw and use it in less than five seconds.

There was no knob or hook on which to hang his blaster. There was not even a visible shower head. He placed it in a corner away from the cubicle's entrance door.

Another sign flashed: "Visitor will please hold arms directly out from his body and stand in the central circle with feet in the indicated positions."

As he placed his feet in the small depressions allowed for them, the sign blanked out. As it did so, a stinging, foaming spray hit him from ceiling, floor, and four walls. He felt the water welling up even beneath the soles of his feet. For a full minute it lasted, his skin reddening under the combined force of the heat and pressure and his lungs gasping for air in the warm dampness. There followed another minute of cool, low-pressure spray, and then finally a minute of warm air that left him dry and refreshed.

He picked up his blaster and blaster strap and found that they, too, were dry and warm. He strapped them on and stepped out of the cubicle in time to see R. Daneel emerge from a neighboring shower. Of course! R. Daneel was not a City dweller, but he had accumulated City dust.

Quite automatically, Baley looked away. Then, with the thought that, after all, R. Daneel's customs were not City customs, he forced his unwilling eyes back for one moment. His lips quirked in a tiny smile. R. Daneel's resemblance to humanity was not restricted to his face and hands but had been carried out with painstaking accuracy over the entire body.

Baley stepped forward in the direction he had been traveling continuously since entering the Personal. He found his clothes waiting for him, neatly folded. They had a warm, clean odor to them.

A sign said, "Visitor will please resume his clothing and place his hand in the indicated depression."

Baley did so. He felt a definite tingling in the ball of his middle finger as he laid it down upon the clean, milky surface. He lifted his hand hastily and found a little drop of blood oozing out. As he watched, it stopped flowing.

He shook it off and pinched the finger. No more blood was flowing even then.

Obviously, they were analyzing his blood. He felt a definite pang of anxiety. His own yearly routine examination by Department doctors, he felt sure, was not carried on with the thoroughness or, perhaps, with the knowledge of these cold robot-makers from outer space. He was not sure he wanted too probing an inquiry into the state of his health.

The time of waiting seemed long to Baley, but when the light flashed again, it said simply, "Visitor will proceed."

Baley drew a long breath of relief. He walked onward and stepped through an archway. Two metal rods closed in before him and, written in luminous air, were the words: "Visitor is warned to proceed no further."

"What the devil——" called out Baley, forgetting in his anger the fact that he was still in the Personal.

R. Daneel's voice was in his ear. "The sniffers have detected a power source, I imagine. Are you carrying your blaster, Elijah?"

Baley whirled, his face a deep crimson. He tried twice, then managed to croak out, "A police officer has his blaster on him or in easy reach at all times, on duty and off."

It was the first time he had spoken in a Personal, proper, since he was ten years old. That had been in his uncle Boris's presence and had merely been an automatic complaint when he stubbed his toe. Uncle Boris had beaten him well when he reached home and had lectured him strongly on the necessities of public decency.

R. Daneel said, "No visitor may be armed. It is our custom, Elijah. Even your Commissioner leaves his blaster behind on all visits."

Under almost any other circumstances, Baley would have turned on his heel and walked away, away from Spacetown and away from that robot. Now, however, he was almost mad with desire to go through with his exact plan and have his revenge to the brim in that way.

This, he thought, was the unobtrusive medical examination that had replaced the more detailed one of the early days. He could well understand, he could understand to overflowing, the indignation and anger that had led to the Barrier Riots of his youth.

In black anger, Baley unhitched his blaster belt. R. Daneel took it from him and placed it within a recess in the wall. A thin metal plate slithered across it.

"If you will put your thumb in the depression," said R. Daneel, "only your thumb will open it later on."

Baley felt undressed, far more so, in fact, than he had felt in the shower. He stepped across the point at which the rods had lately barred him, and, finally, out of the Personal.

He was back in a corridor again, but there was an element of strangeness about it. Up ahead, the light had an unfamiliar quality to it. He felt a whiff of air against his face and, automatically, he thought a squad car had passed.

R. Daneel must have read his uneasiness in his face. He said, "You are essentially in open air now, Elijah. It is unconditioned."

Baley felt faintly sick. How could the Spacers be so rigidly careful of a human body, merely because it came from the City, and then breathe the dirty air of the open fields? He tightened his nostrils, as though by pulling them together he could the more effectively screen the ingoing air.

R. Daneel said, "I believe you will find that open air is not deleterious to human health."

"All right," said Baley, faintly.

The air currents hit annoyingly against his face. They were gentle enough, but they were erratic. That bothered him.

Worse came. The corridor opened into blueness and as they approached its end, strong white light washed down. Baley had seen sunlight. He had been in a natural Solarium once in the line of duty. But there, protecting glass had enclosed the place and the sun's own image had been refracted into a generalized glow. Here, all was open.

Automatically, he looked up at the sun, then turned away. His dazzled eyes blinked and watered.

A Spacer was approaching. A moment of misgiving struck Baley.

R. Daneel, however, stepped forward to greet the approaching man with a handshake. The Spacer turned to Baley and said, "Won't you come with me, sir? I am Dr. Han Fastolfe."

Things were better inside one of the domes. Baley found himself goggling at the size of the rooms and the way in which space was so carelessly distributed, but was thankful for the feel of the conditioned air.

Fastolfe said, sitting down and crossing his long legs, "I'm assuming that you prefer conditioning to unobstructed wind."

He seemed friendly enough. There were fine wrinkles on his forehead and a certain flabbiness to the skin below his eyes and just under his chin. His hair was thinning, but showed no signs of gray. His large ears stood away from his head, giving him a humorous and homely appearance that comforted Baley.

Early that morning, Baley had looked once again at those pictures of Spacetown that Enderby had taken. R. Daneel had just arranged the Spacetown appointment and Baley was absorbing the notion that he was to meet Spacers in the flesh. Somehow that was considerably different from speaking to them across miles of carrier wave, as he had done on several occasions before.

The Spacers in those pictures had been, generally speaking, like those that were occasionally featured in the book-films: tall, red-headed, grave, coldly handsome. Like R. Daneel Olivaw, for instance.

R. Daneel named the Spacers for Baley and when Baley suddenly pointed and said, in surprise, "That isn't you, is it?" R. Daneel answered, "No, Elijah, that is my designer, Dr. Sarton."

He said it unemotionally.

"You were made in your maker's image?" asked Baley, sardonically, but there was no answer to that and, in truth, Baley scarcely expected one. The Bible, as he knew, circulated only to the most limited extent on the Outer Worlds.

And now Baley looked at Han Fastolfe, a man who deviated very noticeably from the Spacer norm in looks, and the Earthman felt a pronounced gratitude for that fact.

"Won't you accept food?" asked Fastolfe.

He indicated the table that separated himself and R. Daneel from the Earthman. It bore nothing but a bowl of varicolored spheroids. Baley felt vaguely startled. He had taken them for table decorations.

R. Daneel explained. "These are the fruits of natural plant life grown on Aurora. I suggest you try this kind. It is called an apple and is reputed to be pleasant."

Fastolfe smiled. "R. Daneel does not know this by personal experience, of course, but he is quite right."

Baley brought an apple to his mouth. Its surface was red and green. It was cool to the touch and had a faint but pleasant odor. With an effort, he bit into it and the unexpected tartness of the pulpy contents hurt his teeth.

He chewed it gingerly. City dwellers ate natural food, of course, whenever rations allowed it. He himself had eaten natural meat and bread often. But such food had always been processed in some way. It had been cooked or ground, blended or compounded. Fruit, now, properly speaking, should come in the form of sauce or preserve. What he was holding now must have come straight from the dirt of a planet's soil.

He thought: I hope they've washed it at least.

Again he wondered at the spottiness of Spacer notions concerning cleanliness.

Fastolfe said, "Let me introduce myself a bit more specifically. I am in charge of the investigation of the murder of Dr. Sarton at the Spacetown end as Commissioner Enderby is at the City end. If I can help you in any way, I stand ready to do so. We are as eager for a quiet solution of the affair and prevention of future incidents of the sort as any of you City men can be."

"Thank you, Dr. Fastolfe," said Baley. "Your attitude is appreciated."

So much, he thought, for the amenities. He bit into the center of the apple and hard, dark little ovoids popped into his mouth. He spat automatically. They flew out and fell to the ground. One would have struck Fastolfe's leg had not the Spacer moved it hastily.

Baley reddened, started to bend.

Fastolfe said, pleasantly, "It is quite all right, Mr. Baley. Just leave them, please."

Baley straightened again. He put the apple down gingerly. He had the uncomfortable feeling that once he was gone, the lost little objects would be found and picked up by suction; the bowl of fruit would be burnt or discarded far from Spacetown; the very room they were sitting in would be sprayed with viricide.

He covered his embarrassment with brusqueness. He said, "I would like to ask permission to have Commissioner Enderby join our conference by trimensional personification."

Fastolfe's eyebrows raised. "Certainly, if you wish it. Daneel, would you make the connection?"

Baley sat in stiff discomfort until the shiny surface of the large parallelepiped in one corner of the room dissolved away to show Commissioner Julius Enderby and part of his desk. At that moment, the discomfort eased and Baley felt nothing short of love for that familiar figure, and a longing to be safely back in that office with him, or anywhere in the City, for that matter. Even in the least prepossessing portion of the Jersey yeast-vat districts.

Now that he had his witness, Baley saw no reason for delay. He said, "I believe I have penetrated the mystery surrounding the death of Dr. Sarton."

Out of the corner of his eye, he saw Enderby springing to his feet and grabbing wildly (and successfully) at his flying spectacles. By standing, the Commissioner thrust his head out of the limits of the trimensic receiver and was forced to sit down again, red-faced and speechless.

In a much quieter way, Dr. Fastolfe, head inclined to one side, was as startled. Only R. Daneel was unmoved.

"Do you mean," said Fastolfe, "that you know the murderer?"

"No," said Baley, "I mean there was no murder."

"What!" screamed Enderby.

"One moment, Commissioner Enderby," said Fastolfe, raising a hand. His eyes held Baley's and he said, "Do you mean that Dr. Sarton is alive?"

"Yes, sir, and I believe I know where he is."

"Where?"

"Right there," said Baley, and pointed firmly at R. Daneel Olivaw.

8

Debate Over a Robot

AT THE MOMENT, Baley was most conscious of the thud of his own pulse. He seemed to be living in a moment of suspended time. R. Daneel's expression was, as always, empty of emotion. Han Fastolfe wore a look of well-bred astonishment on his face and nothing more.

It was Commissioner Julius Enderby's reaction that most concerned Baley, however. The trimensic receiver out of which his face stared did not allow of perfect reproduction. There was always that tiny flicker and that not-quite-ideal resolution. Through that imperfection and through the further masking of the Commissioner's spectacles, Enderby's eyes were unreadable.

Baley thought: Don't go to pieces on me, Julius. I need you.

He didn't really think that Fastolfe would act in haste or under emotional impulse. He had read somewhere once that Spacers had no religion, but substituted, instead, a cold and phlegmatic intellectualism raised to the heights of a philosophy. He believed that and counted on it. They would make a point of acting slowly and then only on the basis of reason.

If he were alone among them and had said what he had said, he was certain that he would never have returned to the City. Cold reason would have dictated that. The Spacers' plans were worth more to them, many times over, than the life of a City dweller. There would be some excuse made to Julius Enderby. Maybe they would present his corpse to the Commissioner, shake their heads, and speak of an Earthman conspiracy having struck again. The Commissioner would believe them. It was the way he was built. If he hated Spacers, it was a hatred based on fear. He wouldn't dare disbelieve them.

That was why he had to be an actual witness of events, a witness, moreover, safely out of reach of the Spacers' calculated safety measures.

The Commissioner said, chokingly, "Lije, you're all wrong. I saw Dr. Sarton's corpse."

"You saw the charred remnants of something you were told was Dr. Sarton's corpse," retorted Baley, boldly. He thought grimly of the Commissioner's broken glasses. That had been an unexpected favor for the Spacers.

"No, no, Lije. I knew Dr. Sarton well and his head was undamaged. It was he." The Commissioner put his hand to his glasses uneasily, as though he, too, remembered, and added, "I looked at him closely, very closely."

"How about this one, Commissioner?" asked Baley, pointing to R. Daneel again. "Doesn't he resemble Dr. Sarton?"

"Yes, the way a statue would."

"An expressionless attitude can be assumed, Commissioner. Suppose that were a robot you had seen blasted to death. You say you looked closely. Did you look closely enough to see whether the charred surface at the edge of the blast was really decomposed organic tissue or a deliberately introduced layer of carbonization over fused metal."

The Commissioner looked revolted. He said, "You're being ridiculous."

Baley turned to the Spacer. "Are you willing to have the body exhumed for examination, Dr. Fastolfe?"

Dr. Fastolfe smiled. "Ordinarily, I would have no objection, Mr. Baley, but I'm afraid we do not bury our dead. Cremation is a universal custom among us."

"Very convenient," said Baley.

"Tell me, Mr. Baley," said Dr. Fastolfe, "just how did you arrive at this very extraordinary conclusion of yours?"

Baley thought: He isn't giving up. He'll brazen it out, if he can.

He said, "It wasn't difficult. There's more to imitating a robot than just putting on a frozen expression and adopting a stilted style of conversation. The trouble with you men of the Outer Worlds is that you're too used to robots. You've gotten to accept them almost as human beings. You've grown blind to the differences. On Earth, it's different. We're very conscious of what a robot is.

"Now in the first place, R. Daneel is too good a human to be a robot. My first impression of him was that he was a Spacer. It was quite an effort for me to adjust myself to his statement that he was a robot. And of course, the reason for that was that he *was* a Spacer and *wasn't* a robot."

R. Daneel interrupted, without any sign of self-consciousness at being himself so intimately the topic of debate. He said, "As I told you, partner Elijah, I was designed to take a temporary place in a human society. The resemblance to humanity is purposeful."

"Even," asked Baley, "down to the painstaking duplication of those portions of the body which, in the ordinary course of events, would always be covered by clothes? Even to the duplication of organs which, in a robot, would have no conceivable function?"

Enderby said suddenly, "How did you find that out?"

Baley reddened. "I couldn't help noticing in the—in the Personal."

Enderby looked shocked.

Fastolfe said, "Surely you understand that a resemblance must be complete if it is to be useful. For our purposes, half measures are as bad as nothing at all."

Baley asked abruptly, "May I smoke?"

Three pipefuls in one day was a ridiculous extravagance, but he was riding a rolling torrent of recklessness and needed the release of tobacco. After all, he was talking back to Spacers. He was going to force their lies down their own throats.

Fastolfe said, "I'm sorry, but I'd prefer that you didn't."

It was a "preference" that had the force of a command. Baley felt that. He thrust back the pipe, the bowl of which he had already taken into his hand in anticipation of automatic permission.

Of course not, he thought bitterly. Enderby didn't warn me, because he doesn't smoke himself, but it's obvious. It follows. They don't smoke on their hygienic Outer Worlds, or drink, or have any human vices. No wonder they accept robots in their damned—what did R. Daneel call it?—C/Fe society? No wonder R. Daneel can play the robot as well as he does. They're all robots out there to begin with.

He said, "The too complete resemblance is just one point out of a number. There was a near riot in my section as I was taking *him* home." (He had to point. He could not bring himself to say either

R. Daneel or Dr. Sarton.) "It was he that stopped the trouble and he did it by pointing a blaster at the potential rioters."

"Good Lord," said Enderby, energetically, "the report stated that it was you——"

"I know, Commissioner," said Baley. "The report was based on information that I gave. I didn't want to have it on the record that a robot had threatened to blast men and women."

"No, no. Of course not." Enderby was quite obviously horrified. He leaned forward to look at something that was out of the range of the trimensic receiver.

Baley could guess what it was. The Commissioner was checking the power gauge to see if the transmitter were being tapped.

"Is that a point in your argument?" asked Fastolfe.

"It certainly is. The First Law of Robotics states that a robot cannot harm a human being."

"But R. Daneel did no harm."

"True. He even stated afterward that he wouldn't have fired under any circumstances. Still, no robot I ever heard of could have violated the spirit of the First Law to the extent of threatening to blast a man, even if he really had no intention to do so."

"I see. Are you a robotics expert, Mr. Baley?"

"No, sir. But I've had a course in general robotics and in positronic analysis. I'm not completely ignorant."

"That's nice," said Fastolfe, agreeably, "but you see, I *am* a robotics expert, and I assure you that the essence of the robot mind lies in a completely literal interpretation of the universe. It recognizes no spirit in the First Law, only the letter. The simple models you have on Earth may have their First Law so overlaid with additional safeguards that, to be sure, they may well be incapable of threatening a human. An advanced model such as R. Daneel is another matter. If I gather the situation correctly, Daneel's threat was necessary to prevent a riot. It was intended then to prevent harm to human beings. He was obeying the First Law, not defying it."

Baley squirmed inwardly, but maintained a tight external calm. It would go hard, but he would match this Spacer at his own game.

He said, "You may counter each point separately, but they add up just the same. Last evening in our discussion of the so-called murder, this alleged robot claimed that he had been converted into a detective by the installation of a new drive into his positronic circuits. A drive, if you please, for justice."

"I'll vouch for that," said Fastolfe. "It was done to him three days ago under my own supervision."

"A drive for *justice?* Justice, Dr. Fastolfe, is an abstraction. Only a human being can use the term."

"If you define 'justice' in such a way that it is an abstraction, if you say that it is the rendering of each man his due, that it is adhering to the right, or anything of the sort, I grant you your argument, Mr. Baley. A human understanding of abstractions cannot be built into a positronic brain in the present state of our knowledge."

"You admit that, then—as an expert in robotics?"

"Certainly. The question is, what did R. Daneel mean by using the term 'justice'?"

"From the context of our conversation, he meant what you and I and any human being would mean, but what no robot could mean."

"Why don't you ask him, Mr. Baley, to define the term?"

Baley felt a certain loss of confidence. He turned to R. Daneel. "Well?"

"Yes, Elijah?"

"What is your definition of justice?"

"Justice, Elijah, is that which exists when all the laws are enforced."

Fastolfe nodded. "A good definition, Mr. Baley, for a robot. The desire to see all laws enforced has been built into R. Daneel, now. Justice is a very concrete term to him since it is based on law enforcement, which is in turn based upon the existence of specific and definite laws. There is nothing abstract about it. A human being can recognize the fact that, on the basis of an abstract moral code, some laws may be bad ones and their enforcement unjust. What do you say, R. Daneel?"

"An unjust law," said R. Daneel evenly, "is a contradiction in terms."

"To a robot it is, Mr. Baley. So you see, you mustn't confuse your justice and R. Daneel's."

Baley turned to R. Daneel sharply and said, "You left my apartment last night."

R. Daneel replied, "I did. If my leaving disturbed your sleep, I am sorry."

"Where did you go?"

"To the Men's Personal."

For a moment, Baley was staggered. It was the answer he had already decided was the truth, but he had not expected it to be the answer R. Daneel would give. He felt a little more of his certainty oozing away, yet he held firmly on his track. The Commissioner was watching, his lensed eyes flicking from one to the other as they spoke. Baley *couldn't* back down now, no matter what sophistries they used against him. He had to hold to his point.

He said, "On reaching my section, *he* insisted on entering Personal with me. His excuse was a poor one. During the night, he left to visit Personal again as he has just admitted. If he were a man, I'd say he had every reason and right to do so. Obviously. As a robot, however, the trip was meaningless. The conclusion can only be that he is a man."

Fastolfe nodded. He seemed not in the least put out. He said, "This is most interesting. Suppose we ask Daneel why he made his trip to Personal last night."

Commissioner Enderby leaned forward. "Please, Dr. Fastolfe," he muttered, "it is not proper to——"

"You need not be concerned, Commissioner," said Fastolfe, his thin lips curving back in something that looked like a smile but wasn't, "I am certain that Daneel's answer will not offend your sensibilities or those of Mr. Baley. Won't you tell us, Daneel?"

R. Daneel said, "Elijah's wife, Jessie, left the apartment last night on friendly terms with me. It was quite obvious that she had no reason for thinking me to be other than human. She returned to the apartment knowing I was a robot. The obvious conclusion is that the information to that effect exists outside the apartment. It followed that my conversation with Elijah last night had been overheard. In no other way could the secret of my true nature have become common knowledge.

"Elijah told me that the apartments were well insulated. We spoke together in low voices. Ordinary eavesdropping would not do. Still, it was known that Elijah is a policeman. If a conspiracy exists within the City sufficiently well organized to have planned the murder of Dr. Sarton, they may well have been aware that Elijah had been placed in charge of the murder investigation. It would fall within the realm of possibility then, even of probability, that his apartment had been spybeamed.

"I searched the apartment as well as I could after Elijah and Jessie had gone to bed, but could find no transmitter. This complicated matters. A focused duo-beam could do the trick even in the absence of a transmitter, but that requires rather elaborate equipment.

"Analysis of the situation led to the following conclusion. The one place where a City dweller can do almost anything without being disturbed or questioned is in the Personals. He could even set up a duo-beam. The custom of absolute privacy in the Personals is very strong and other men would not even look at him. The Section Personal is quite close to Elijah's apartment, so that the distance factor is not important. A suitcase model could be used. I went to the Personal to investigate."

"And what did you find?" asked Baley quickly.

"Nothing, Elijah. No sign of a duo-beam."

Dr. Fastolfe said, "Well, Mr. Baley, does this sound reasonable to you?"

But Baley's uncertainty was gone, now. He said, "Reasonable as far as it goes, perhaps, but it stops short of perfection by a hell of a way. What *he* doesn't know is that my wife told me where she got the information and *when*. She learned he was a robot shortly after she left the house. Even then, the rumor had been circulating for hours. So the fact that he was a robot could not have leaked out through spying on our last evening's conversation."

"Nevertheless," said Dr. Fastolfe, "his action last night of going to the Personal stands explained, I think."

"But something is brought up that is *not* explained," retorted Baley, heatedly. "When, where, and how was the leak? How did the news get about that there was a Spacer robot in the City? As far as I know, only two of us knew about the deal, Commissioner Enderby and myself, and we told no one.—Commissioner, did anyone else in the Department know?"

"No," said Enderby, anxiously. "Not even the Mayor. Only we, and Dr. Fastolfe."

"And *he*," added Baley, pointing.

"I?" asked R. Daneel.

"Why not?"

"I was with you at all times, Elijah."

"You were *not*," cried Baley, fiercely. "I was in Personal for half an hour or more before we went to my apartment. During that time, we two were completely out of contact with one another. It was then that you got in touch with your group in the City."

"What group?" asked Fastolfe.

And "What group?" echoed Commissioner Enderby almost simultaneously.

Baley rose from his chair and turned to the trimensic receiver. "Commissioner, I want you to listen closely to this. Tell me if it doesn't all fall into a pattern. A murder is reported and by a curious coincidence it happens just as you are entering Spacetown to keep an appointment with the murdered man. You are shown the corpse of something supposed to be human, but the corpse has since been disposed of and is not available for close examination.

"The Spacers insist an Earthman did the killing, even though the only way they can make such an accusation stick is to suppose that a City man had left the City and cut cross country to Spacetown alone and at night. You know damn well how unlikely that is.

"Next they send a supposed robot into the City; in fact, they *insist* on sending him. The first thing the robot does is to threaten a crowd of human beings with a blaster. The second is to set in motion the rumor that there is a Spacer robot in the City. In fact, the rumor is so specific that Jessie told me it was known that he was working with the police. That means that before long it will be known that it was the robot who handled the blaster. Maybe even now the rumor is spreading across the yeast-vat country and down the Long Island hydroponic plants that there's a killer robot on the loose."

"This is impossible. Impossible!" groaned Enderby.

"No, it isn't. It's exactly what's happening, Commissioner. Don't you see it? There's a conspiracy in the City, all right, but it's run from Spacetown. The Spacers *want* to be able to report a murder. They *want* riots. They *want* an assault on Spacetown. The worse things get, the better the incident—and Spacer ships come down and occupy the Cities of Earth."

Fastolfe said, mildly, "We had an excuse in the Barrier Riots of twenty-five years ago."

"You weren't ready then. You are now." Baley's heart was pounding madly.

"This is quite a complicated plot you're attributing to us, Mr. Baley. If we wanted to occupy Earth, we could do so in much simpler fashion."

"Maybe not, Dr. Fastolfe. Your so-called robot told me that public opinion concerning Earth is by no means unified on your Outer Worlds. I think he was telling the truth at that time, anyway. Maybe an outright occupation wouldn't sit well with the people at home. Maybe an incident is an absolute necessity. A good shocking incident."

"Like a murder, eh? Is that it? You'll admit it would have to be a pretended murder. You won't suggest, I hope, that we'd really kill one of ourselves for the sake of an incident."

"You built a robot to look like Dr. Sarton, blasted the robot, and showed the remains to Commissioner Enderby."

"And then," said Dr. Fastolfe, "having used R. Daneel to impersonate Dr. Sarton in the false murder, we have to use Dr. Sarton to impersonate R. Daneel in the false investigation of the false murder."

"Exactly. I am telling you this in the presence of a witness who is not here in the flesh and whom you cannot blast out of existence and who is important enough to be believed by the City government and by Washington itself. We will be prepared for you and we know what your intentions are. If necessary, our government will report directly to your people, expose the situation for exactly what it is. I doubt if this sort of interstellar rape will be tolerated."

Fastolfe shook his head. "Please, Mr. Baley, you are being unreasonable. Really, you have the most astonishing notions. Suppose now, just quietly suppose, that R. Daneel is really R. Daneel. Suppose he is actually a robot. Wouldn't it follow that the corpse Commissioner Enderby saw was really Dr. Sarton? It would be scarcely reasonable to believe that the corpse were still another robot. Commissioner Enderby witnessed R. Daneel under construction and can vouch for the fact that only one existed."

"If it comes to that," said Baley, stubbornly, "the Commissioner is not a robotics expert. You might have had a dozen such robots."

"Stick to the point, Mr. Baley. What if R. Daneel is really R. Daneel? Would not the entire structure of your reasoning fall to the ground? Would you have any further basis for your belief in this completely melodramatic and implausible interstellar plot you have constructed?"

"*If* he is a robot! I say he is human."

"Yet you haven't really investigated the problem, Mr. Baley," said Fastolfe. "To differentiate a robot, even a very humanoid robot, from a human being, it isn't necessary to make elaborately shaky deductions from little things he says and does. For instance, have you tried sticking a pin into R. Daneel?"

"What?" Baley's mouth fell open.

"It's a simple experiment. There are others perhaps not quite so simple. His skin and hair look real, but have you tried looking at them under adequate magnification. Then again, he seems to breathe, particularly when he is using air to talk, but have you noticed that his breathing is irregular, that minutes may go by during which he has no breath at all. You might even have trapped some of his expired air and measured the carbon dioxide content. You might have tried to draw a sample of blood. You might have tried to detect a pulse in his wrist, or a heartbeat under his shirt. Do you see what I mean, Mr. Baley?"

"That's just talk," said Baley, uneasily. "I'm not going to be bluffed. I might have tried any of those things, but do you suppose this alleged robot would have let me bring a hypodermic to him, or a stethoscope or a microscope?"

"Of course. I see your point," said Fastolfe. He looked at R. Daneel and gestured slightly.

R. Daneel touched the cuff of his right shirt sleeve and the diamagnetic seam fell apart the entire length of his arm. A smooth, sinewy, and apparently entirely human limb lay exposed. Its short, bronze hairs, both in quantity and distribution, were exactly what one would expect of a human being.

Baley said, "So?"

R. Daneel pinched the ball of his right middle finger with the thumb and forefinger of his left hand. Exactly what the details of the manipulation that followed were, Baley could not see.

But, just as the fabric of the sleeve had fallen in two when the diamagnetic field of its seam had been interrupted, so now the arm itself fell in two.

There, under a thin layer of fleshlike material, was the dull blue gray of stainless steel rods, cords, and joints.

"Would you care to examine Daneel's workings more closely, Mr. Baley?" asked Dr. Fastolfe politely.

Baley could scarcely hear the remark for the buzzing in his ears and for the sudden jarring of the Commissioner's high-pitched and hysterical laughter.

9

Elucidation by a Spacer

THE MINUTES PASSED and the buzzing grew louder and drowned out the laughter. The dome and all it contained wavered and Baley's time sense wavered, too.

At least, he found himself sitting in an unchanged position but with a definite feeling of lost time. The Commissioner was gone; the trimensic receiver was milky and opaque; and R. Daneel sat at his side, pinching up the skin of Baley's bared upper arm. Baley could see, just beneath the skin, the small thin darkness of a hypo-sliver. It vanished as he watched, soaking and spreading away into the intercellular fluid, from that into the blood stream and the neighboring cells, from that into all the cells of his body.

His grip on reality heightened.

"Do you feel better, partner Elijah?" asked R. Daneel.

Baley did. He pulled at his arm and the robot let him take it away. He rolled down his sleeve and looked about. Dr. Fastolfe sat where he had been, a small smile softening the homeliness of his face.

Baley said, "Did I black out?"

Dr. Fastolfe said, "In a way, yes. You received a sizable shock, I'm afraid."

It came back to Baley quite clearly. He seized R. Daneel's nearer arm quickly, forcing up the sleeve as far as it would go, exposing the wrist. The robot's flesh felt soft to his fingers, but underneath was the hardness of something more than bone.

R. Daneel let his arm rest easily in the plain-clothes man's grip. Baley stared at it, pinching the skin along the median line. Was there a faint seam?

It was logical, of course, that there should be. A robot, covered with synthetic skin, and deliberately made to look human, could not be repaired in the ordinary fashion. A chest plate could not be unriveted for the purpose. A skull could not be hinged up and outward. Instead, the various parts of the mechanical body would have to be put together along a line of micromagnetic fields. An arm, a head, an entire body, must fall in two at the proper touch, then come together again at a contrary touch.

Baley looked up. "Where's the Commissioner?" he mumbled, hot with mortification.

"Pressing business," said Dr. Fastolfe. "I encouraged him to leave, I'm afraid. I assured him we would take care of you."

"You've taken care of me quite nicely already, thank you," said Baley, grimly. "I think our business is done."

He lifted himself erect on tired joints. He felt an old man, very suddenly. Too old to start over again. He needed no deep insight to foresee that future.

The Commissioner would be half frightened and half furious. He would face Baley whitely, taking his glasses off to wipe them every fifteen seconds. His soft voice (Julius Enderby almost never shouted) would explain carefully that the Spacers had been mortally offended.

"You *can't* talk to Spacers that way, Lije. They won't take it." (Baley could hear Enderby's voice very plainly down to the finest shade of intonation.) "I warned you. No saying how much damage you've done. I can see your point, mind you. I see what you were trying to do. If they were Earthmen, it would be different. I'd say yes, chance it. Run the risk. Smoke them out. But *Spacers!* You might have told me, Lije. You might have consulted me. I know them. I know them inside and out."

And what would Baley be able to say? That Enderby was exactly the man he couldn't tell. That the project was one of tremendous risk and Enderby a man of tremendous caution. That it had been Enderby himself who had pointed up the supreme dangers of either outright failure or of the wrong kind of success. That the one way of defeating declassification was to show that guilt lay in Spacetown itself. . . .

Enderby would say, "There'll have to be a report on this, Lije. There'll be all sorts of repercussions. I know the Spacers. They'll demand your removal from the case, and it'll have to be that way. You understand that, Lije, don't you? I'll try to make it easy on you. You can count on that. I'll protect you as far as I can, Lije."

Baley knew that would be exactly true. The Commissioner would protect him, but only as far as he could, not to the point, for instance, of infuriating further an angry Mayor.

He could hear the Mayor, too. "Damn it, Enderby, what *is* all this? Why wasn't I consulted? Who's running the City? Why was an unauthorized robot allowed inside the City? And just what the devil did this Baley . . ."

If it came to a choice between Baley's future in the Department and the Commissioner's own, what possible result could Baley expect? He could find no reasonable way of blaming Enderby.

The least he could expect was demotion, and that was bad enough. The mere act of living in a modern City insured the bare possibility of existence, even for those entirely declassified. How bare that possibility was he knew only too well.

It was the addition of status that brought the little things: a more comfortable seat here, a better cut of meat there, a shorter wait in line at the other place. To the philosophical mind, these items might seem scarcely worth any great trouble to acquire.

Yet no one, however philosophical, could give up those privileges, *once acquired*, without a pang. That was the point.

What a trifling addition to the convenience of the apartment an activated washbasin was when for thirty years previously the trip to Personal had been an automatic and unregarded one. How useless it was even as a device to prove "status" when it was considered the height of ill form to parade "status." Yet were the washbasin to be deactivated, how humiliating and unbearable would each added trip to Personal be! How yearningly attractive the memory of the bedroom shave! How filled with a sense of lost luxury!

It was fashionable for modern political writers to look back with a smug disapproval at the "fiscalism" of Medieval times, when economy was based on money. The competitive struggle for existence, they said, was brutal. No truly complex society could be maintained because of the strains introduced by the eternal "fight-for-the-buck." (Scholars had varying interpretations of the word "buck," but there was no dispute over the meaning as a whole.)

By contrast, modern "civism" was praised highly as efficient and enlightened.

Maybe so. There were historical novels both in the romantic and the sensational tradition, and the Medievalists thought "fiscalism" had bred such things as individualism and initiative.

Baley wouldn't commit himself, but now he wondered sickly if ever a man fought harder for that buck, whatever it was, or felt its loss more deeply, than a City dweller fought to keep from losing his Sunday night option on a chicken drumstick—a real-flesh drumstick from a once-living bird.

Baley thought: Not me so much. There's Jessie and Ben.

Dr. Fastolfe's voice broke in upon his thoughts. "Mr. Baley, do you hear me?"

Baley blinked. "Yes?" How long had he been standing there like a frozen fool?

"Won't you sit down, sir? Having taken care of the matter on your mind, you may now be interested in some films we have taken of the scene of the crime and of the events immediately following."

"No, thank you. I have business in the City."

"Surely the case of Dr. Sarton comes first."

"Not with me. I imagine I'm off the case already." Suddenly, he boiled over. "Damn it, if you could prove R. Daneel was a robot, why didn't you do it at once? Why did you make such a farce of it all?"

"My dear Mr. Baley, I was very interested in your deductions. As for being off the case, I doubt it. Before the Commissioner left, I made a special point of asking that you be retained. I believe he will co-operate."

Baley sat down, not entirely voluntarily. He said, sharply, "Why?"

Dr. Fastolfe crossed his legs and sighed. "Mr. Baley, in general I have met two kinds of City dwellers, rioters and politicians. Your Commissioner is useful to us, but he is a politician. He tells us what we want to hear. He *handles* us, if you know what I mean. Now you came here and boldly accused us of tremendous crimes and tried to prove your case. I enjoyed the process. I found it a hopeful development."

"How hopeful?" asked Baley sardonically.

"Hopeful enough. You are someone I can deal with frankly. Last night, Mr. Baley, R. Daneel reported to me by shielded subether.

Some things about you interested me very much. For instance, there was the point concerning the nature of the book-films in your apartment."

"What about them?"

"A good many dealt with historical and archaeological subjects. It makes it appear that you are interested in human society and that you know a little about its evolution."

"Even policemen can spend their free time on book-films, if they so choose."

"Quite. I'm glad of your choice in viewing matter. It will help me in what I am trying to do. In the first place, I want to explain, or try to, the exclusivism of the men of the Outer Worlds. We live here in Spacetown; we don't enter the City; we mingle with you City dwellers only in a very rigidly limited fashion. We breathe the open air, but when we do, we wear filters. I sit here now with filters in my nostrils, gloves on my hands, and a fixed determination to come no closer to you than I can help. Why do you suppose that is?"

Baley said, "There's no point in guessing." Let *him* talk now.

"If you guessed as some of your people do, you would say that it was because we despised the men of Earth and refused to lose caste by allowing their shadow to fall upon us. That is not so. The true answer is really quite obvious. The medical examination you went through, as well as the cleansing procedures, were not matters of ritual. They were dictated by necessity."

"Disease?"

"Yes, disease. My dear Mr. Baley, the Earthmen who colonized the Outer Worlds found themselves on planets entirely free of Terrestrial bacteria and viruses. They brought in their own, of course, but they also brought with them the latest medical and microbiological techniques. They had a small community of micro-organisms to deal with and no intermediate hosts. There were no mosquitoes to spread malaria, no snails to spread schistosomiasis. Disease agents were wiped out and symbiotic bacteria allowed to grow. Gradually, the Outer Worlds became disease-free. Naturally, as time went on, entrance requirements for immigrant Earthmen were made more and more rigorous, since less and less could the Outer Worlds endure the possible introduction of disease."

"You've never been sick, Dr. Fastolfe?"

"Not with a parasitic disease, Mr. Baley. We are all liable to degenerative diseases such as atherosclerosis, of course, but I have never had what you would call a cold. If I were to contract one, I might die of it. I've built up no resistance to it whatsoever. That's what's wrong with us here in Spacetown. Those of us who come here run a definite risk. Earth is riddled with diseases to which we have no defense, no *natural* defense. You yourself are carrying the germs of almost every known disease. You are not aware of it, since you keep them all under control at almost all times through the antibodies your body has developed over the years. I, myself, lack the antibodies. Do you wonder that I come no closer to you? Believe me, Mr. Baley, I act aloof only in self-defense."

Baley said, "If this is so, why isn't the fact made known on Earth? I mean, that it is not just queasiness on your part, but a defense against an actual physical danger."

The Spacer shook his head. "We are few, Mr. Baley, and are disliked as foreigners anyway. We maintain our own safety on the basis of a rather shaky prestige as a superior class of being. We cannot afford to lose face by admitting that we are *afraid* to approach an Earthman. Not at least until there is a better understanding between Earthmen and Spacers."

"There won't be, on present terms. It's your supposed superiority that we—they hate you for."

"It is a dilemma. Don't think we aren't aware of it."

"Does the Commissioner know of this?"

"We have never explained it to him flatly, as I have just done to you. He may guess it, however. He is quite an intelligent man."

"If he guessed it, he might have told me," Baley said reflectively.

Dr. Fastolfe lifted his eyebrows. "If he had, then you wouldn't have considered the possibility of R. Daneel being a human Spacer. Is that it?"

Baley shrugged slightly, tossing the matter to one side.

But Dr. Fastolfe went on, "That's quite true, you know. Putting the psychological difficulties to one side, the terrible effect of the noise and crowds upon us, the fact remains that for one of us to enter the City is the equivalent of a death sentence. It is why Dr. Sarton initiated his project of humanoid robots. They were substitute men, designed to enter the City instead of us——"

"Yes. R. Daneel explained this to me."

"Do you disapprove?"

"Look," said Baley, "since we're talking to one another so freely, let me ask a question in simple words. Why have you Spacers come to Earth anyway? Why don't you leave us alone?"

Dr. Fastolfe said, with obvious surprise, "Are you *satisfied* with life on Earth?"

"We get along."

"Yes, but for how long will that continue? Your population goes up continuously; the available calories meet the needs only as a result of greater and greater effort. Earth is in a blind alley, man."

"We get along," repeated Baley stubbornly.

"Barely. A City like New York must spend every ounce of effort getting water in and waste out. The nuclear power plants are kept going by uranium supplies that are constantly more difficult to obtain even from the other planets of the system, and the supply needed goes up steadily. The life of the City depends every moment on the arrival of wood pulp for the yeast vats and minerals for the hydroponic plants. Air must be circulated unceasingly. The balance is a very delicate one in a hundred directions, and growing more delicate each year. What would happen to New York if the tremendous flow of input and outgo were to be interrupted for even a single hour?"

"It never has been."

"Which is no security for the future. In primitive times, individual population centers were virtually self-supporting, living on the produce of neighboring farms. Nothing but immediate disaster, a flood or a pestilence or crop failure, could harm them. As the centers grew and technology improved, localized disasters could be overcome by drawing on help from distant centers, but at the cost of making ever larger areas interdependent. In Medieval times, the open cities, even the largest, could subsist on food stores and on emergency supplies of all sorts for a week at least. When New York first became a City, it could have lived on itself for a day. Now it cannot do so for an hour. A disaster that would have been uncomfortable ten thousand years ago, merely serious a thousand years ago, and acute a hundred years ago would now be surely fatal."

Baley moved restlessly in his chair. "I've heard all this before. The Medievalists want an end to Cities. They want us to get back to the soil and to natural agriculture. Well, they're mad; we can't. There are too many of us and you can't go backward in history, only for-

ward. Of course, if emigration to the Outer Worlds were not restricted——"

"You know why it must be restricted."

"Then what is there to do? You're tapping a dead power line."

"What about emigration to new worlds? There are a hundred billion stars in the Galaxy. It is estimated that there are a hundred million planets that are inhabitable or can be made inhabitable."

"That's ridiculous."

"Why?" asked Dr. Fastolfe, with vehemence. "Why is the suggestion ridiculous? Earthmen have colonized planets in the past.
Over thirty of the fifty Outer Worlds, including my native Aurora,
were directly colonized by Earthmen. Is colonization no longer
possible?"

"Well . . ."

"No answer? Let me suggest that if it *is* no longer possible, it is
because of the development of City culture on Earth. Before the
Cities, human life on Earth wasn't so specialized that they couldn't
break loose and start all over on a raw world. They did it thirty
times. But now, Earthmen are all so coddled, so enwombed in their
imprisoning caves of steel, that they are caught forever. You, Mr.
Baley, won't even believe that a City dweller is capable of crossing
country to get to Spacetown. Crossing space to get to a new world
must represent impossibility squared to you. Civism is ruining Earth,
sir."

Baley said angrily, "And if it does? How does it concern you people? It's our problem. We'll solve it. If not, it's our own particular
road to hell."

"Better your own road to hell than another's road to heaven, eh?
I know how you must feel. It is not pleasant to listen to the preach-
ing of a stranger. Yet I wish your people could preach to us, for we,
too, have a problem, one that is quite analogous to yours."

Baley smiled crookedly. "Overpopulation?"

"Analogous, not identical. Ours is underpopulation. How old
would you say I was?"

The Earthman considered for a moment and then deliberately
overestimated. "Sixty, I'd say."

"A hundred and sixty, you should say."

"What!"

"A hundred and sixty-three next birthday, to be exact. There's no trick to that. I'm using the Standard Earth year as the unit. If I'm fortunate, if I take care of myself, most of all, if I catch no disease on Earth, I may double that age. Men on Aurora have been known to live over three hundred and fifty years. And life expectancy is still increasing."

Baley looked to R. Daneel (who throughout the conversation had been listening in stolid silence), as though he were seeking confirmation.

He said, "How is that possible?"

"In an underpopulated society, it is practical to concentrate study on gerontology, to do research on the aging process. In a world such as yours, a lengthened life expectancy would be disastrous. You couldn't afford the resulting rise in population. On Aurora, there is room for tricentenarians. Then, of course, a long life becomes doubly and triply precious.

"If you were to die now, you would lose perhaps forty years of your life, probably less. If I were to die, I would lose a hundred fifty years, probably more. In a culture such as ours, then, individual life is of prime importance. Our birth rate is low and population increase is rigidly controlled. We maintain a definite robot/man ratio designed to maintain the individual in the greatest comfort. Logically, developing children are carefully screened for physical and mental defects before being allowed to mature."

Baley interrupted. "You mean you kill them if they don't——"

"If they don't measure up. Quite painlessly, I assure you. The notion shocks you, just as the Earthman's uncontrolled breeding shocks us."

"We're controlled, Dr. Fastolfe. Each family is allowed so many children."

Dr. Fastolfe smiled tolerantly. "So many of any kind of children; not so many *healthy* children. And even so, there are many illegitimates and your population increases."

"Who's to judge which children should live?"

"That's rather complicated and not to be answered in a sentence. Some day we may talk it out in detail."

"Well, where's your problem? You sound satisfied with your society."

"It is stable. That's the trouble. It is too stable."

Baley said, "Nothing pleases you. Our civilization is at the ragged edge of chaos, according to you, and your own is too stable."

"It is possible to be too stable. No Outer World has colonized a new planet in two and a half centuries. There is no prospect for colonization in the future. Our lives in the Outer Worlds are too long to risk and too comfortable to upset."

"I don't know about that, Dr. Fastolfe. You've come to Earth. You risk disease."

"Yes, I do. There are some of us, Mr. Baley, who feel that the future of the human race is even worth the possible loss of an extended lifetime. Too few of us, I am sorry to say."

"All right. We're coming to the point. How is Spacetown helping matters?"

"In trying to introduce robots here on Earth, we're doing our best to upset the balance of your City economy."

"That's your way of helping?" Baley's lips quivered. "You mean you're creating a growing group of displaced and declassified men on purpose?"

"Not out of cruelty or callousness, believe me. A group of displaced men, as you call them, are what we need to serve as a nucleus for colonization. Your ancient America was discovered by ships fitted out with men from the prisons. Don't you see that the City's womb has failed the displaced man. He has nothing to lose and worlds to gain by leaving Earth."

"But it isn't working."

"No, it isn't," said Dr. Fastolfe, sadly. "There is something wrong. The resentment of the Earthman for the robot blocks things. Yet those very robots can accompany humans, smooth the difficulties of initial adjustment to a raw world, make colonization practical."

"Then what? More Outer Worlds?"

"No. The Outer Worlds were established before Civism had spread over Earth, before the Cities. The new colonies will be built by humans who have the City background plus the beginnings of a C/Fe culture. It will be a synthesis, a crossbreeding. As it stands now, Earth's own structure must go ricketing down in the near future, the Outer Worlds will slowly degenerate and decay in a somewhat further future, but the new colonies will be a new and healthy strain, combining the best of both cultures. By their reaction upon the older worlds, including Earth, we ourselves may gain new life."

"I don't know. It's all misty, Dr. Fastolfe."

"It's a dream, yes. Think about it." Abruptly the Spacer rose to his feet. "I have spent more time with you than I intended. In fact, more time than our health ordinances allow. You will excuse me?"

Baley and R. Daneel left the dome. Sunlight, at a different angle, somewhat yellower, washed down upon them once again. In Baley, there was a vague wonder whether sunlight might not seem different on another world. Less harsh and brazen perhaps. More acceptable.

Another world? The ugly Spacer with the prominent ears had filled his mind with queer imaginings. Did the doctors of Aurora once look at the child Fastolfe and wonder if he ought to be allowed to mature? Wasn't he too ugly? Or did their criteria include physical appearance at all? When did ugliness become a deformity and what deformities . . .

But when the sunlight vanished and they entered the first door that led to the Personal, the mood became harder to maintain.

Baley shook his head with exasperation. It was all ridiculous. Forcing Earthmen to emigrate, to set up a new society! It was nonsense! What were these Spacers *really* after?

He thought about it and came to no conclusion.

Slowly, their squad car rolled down the vehicular lane. Reality was surging all about Baley. His blaster was a warm and comfortable weight against his hip. The noise and vibrant life of the City was just as warm, just as comfortable.

For a moment, as the City closed in, his nose tingled to a slight and fugitive pungence.

He thought wonderingly: The City smells.

He thought of the twenty million human beings crammed into the steel walls of the great cave and for the first time in his life he smelled them with nostrils that had been washed clean by outdoor air.

He thought: Would it be different on another world? Less people and more air—cleaner?

But the afternoon roar of the City was all around them, the smell faded and was gone, and he felt a little ashamed of himself.

He let the drive rod in slowly and tapped a larger share of the beamed power. The squad car accelerated sharply as it slanted down into the empty motorway.

"Daneel," he said.

"Yes, Elijah."

"Why was Dr. Fastolfe telling me all he did?"

"It seems probable to me, Elijah, that he wished to impress you with the importance of the investigation. We are not here just to solve a murder, but to save Spacetown and with it, the future of the human race."

Baley said dryly, "I think he'd have been better off if he'd let me see the scene of the crime and interview the men who first found the body."

"I doubt if you could have added anything, Elijah. We have been quite thorough."

"Have you? You've got nothing. Not a clue. Not a suspect."

"No, you are right. The answer must be in the City. To be accurate, though, we did have one suspect."

"What? You said nothing of this before."

"I did not feel it to be necessary, Elijah. Surely it is obvious to you that one suspect automatically existed."

"Who? In the devil's name, who?"

"The one Earthman who was on the scene. Commissioner Julius Enderby."

10

Afternoon of a Plain-clothes Man

THE SQUAD CAR veered to one side, halted against the impersonal concrete wall of the motorway. With the humming of its motor stopped, the silence was dead and thick.

Baley looked at the robot next to him and said in an incongruously quiet voice, "What?"

Time stretched while Baley waited for an answer. A small and lonesome vibration rose and reached a minor peak, then faded. It was the sound of another squad car, boring its way past them on some unknown errand, perhaps a mile away. Or else it was a fire car hurrying along toward its own appointment with combustion.

A detached portion of Baley's mind wondered if any one man any longer knew all the motorways that twisted about in New York City's bowels. At no time in the day or night could the entire motorway system be completely empty, and yet there must be individual passages that no man had entered in years. With sudden, devastating clarity, he remembered a short story he had viewed as a youngster.

It concerned the motorways of London and began, quietly enough, with a murder. The murderer fled toward a prearranged hideout in the corner of a motorway in whose dust his own shoeprints had been the only disturbance for a century. In that abandoned hole, he could wait in complete safety till the search died.

But he took a wrong turning and in the silence and loneness of those twisting corridors he swore a mad and blaspheming oath that, in spite of the Trinity and all the saints, he would yet reach his haven.

From that time on, no turning was right. He wandered through an unending maze from the Brighton Sector on the Channel to Norwich and from Coventry to Canterbury. He burrowed endlessly beneath the great City of London from end to end of its sprawl across the southeastern corner of Medieval England. His clothes were rags and his shoes ribbons, his strength wore down but never left him. He was tired, tired, but unable to stop. He could only go on and on with only wrong turnings ahead of him.

Sometimes he heard the sound of passing cars, but they were always in the next corridor, and however fast he rushed (for he would gladly have given himself up by then) the corridors he reached were always empty. Sometimes he saw an exit far ahead that would lead to the City's life and breath, but it always glimmered further away as he approached until he would turn—and it would be gone.

Occasionally, Londoners on official business through the underground would see a misty figure limping silently toward them, a semitransparent arm lifted in pleading, a mouth open and moving, but soundless. As it approached, it would waver and vanish.

It was a story that had lost the attributes of ordinary fiction and had entered the realm of folklore. The "Wandering Londoner" had become a familiar phrase to all the world.

In the depths of New York City, Baley remembered the story and stirred uneasily.

R. Daneel spoke and there was a small echo to his voice. He said, "We may be overheard."

"Down here? Not a chance. Now what about the Commissioner?"

"He was on the scene, Elijah. He is a City dweller. He was inevitably a suspect."

"Was! Is he still a suspect?"

"No. His innocence was quickly established. For one thing, there was no blaster in his possession. There could not very well be one. He had entered Spacetown in the usual fashion; that was quite certain; and, as you know, blasters are removed as a matter of course."

"Was the murder weapon found at all, by the way?"

"No, Elijah. Every blaster in Spacetown was checked and none had been fired for weeks. A check of the radiation chambers was quite conclusive."

"Then whoever had committed the murder had either hidden the weapon so well——"

"It could not have been hidden anywhere in Spacetown. We were quite thorough."

Baley said impatiently, "I'm trying to consider all possibilities. It was either hidden or it was carried away by the murderer when he left."

"Exactly."

"And if you admit only the second possibility, then the Commissioner is cleared."

"Yes. As a precaution, of course, he was cerebroanalyzed."

"What?"

"By cerebroanalysis, I mean the interpretation of the electromagnetic fields of the living brain cells."

"Oh," said Baley, unenlightened. "And what does that tell you?"

"It gives us information concerning the temperamental and emotional makeup of an individual. In the case of Commissioner Enderby, it told us that he was incapable of killing Dr. Sarton. Quite incapable."

"No," agreed Baley. "He isn't the type. I could have told you that."

"It is better to have objective information. Naturally, all our people in Spacetown allowed themselves to be cerebroanalyzed as well."

"All incapable, I suppose."

"No question. It is why we know that the murderer must be a City dweller."

"Well, then, all we have to do is pass the whole City under your cute little process."

"It would not be very practical, Elijah. There might be millions temperamentally capable of the deed."

"Millions," grunted Baley, thinking of the crowds of that long ago day who had screamed at the dirty Spacers, and of the threatening and slobbering crowds outside the shoe store the night before.

He thought: Poor Julius. A suspect!

He could hear the Commissioner's voice describing the period after the discovery of the body: "It was brutal, brutal." No wonder he broke his glasses in shock and dismay. No wonder he did not want to return to Spacetown. "I hate them," he had ground out between his teeth.

Poor Julius. The man who could handle Spacers. The man whose greatest value to the City lay in his ability to get along with them. How much did that contribute to his rapid promotions?

No wonder the Commissioner had wanted Baley to take over. Good old loyal, close-mouthed Baley. College chum! He would keep quiet if he found out about that little incident. Baley wondered how cerebroanalysis was carried out. He imagined huge electrodes, busy pantographs skidding inklines across graphed paper, self-adjusting gears clicking into place now and then.

Poor Julius. If his state of mind were as appalled as it almost had a right to be, he might already be seeing himself at the end of his career with a forced letter of resignation in the hands of the Mayor.

The squad car slanted up into the sublevels of City Hall.

It was 14:30 when Baley arrived back at his desk. The Commissioner was out. R. Sammy, grinning, did not know where the Commissioner was.

Baley spent some time thinking. The fact that he was hungry didn't register.

At 15:20 R. Sammy came to his desk and said, "The Commissioner is in now, Lije."

Baley said, "Thanks."

For once he listened to R. Sammy without being annoyed. R. Sammy, after all, was a kind of relation to R. Daneel, and R. Daneel obviously wasn't a person—or thing, rather—to get annoyed with. Baley wondered how it would be on a new planet with men and robots starting even in a City culture. He considered the situation quite dispassionately.

The Commissioner was going through some documents as Baley entered, stopping occasionally to make notations.

He said, "That was a fairly giant-size blooper you pulled out in Spacetown."

It flooded back strongly. The verbal duel with Fastolfe . . .

His long face took on a lugubrious expression of chagrin. "I'll admit I did, Commissioner. I'm sorry."

Enderby looked up. His expression was keen through his glasses. He seemed more himself than at any time these thirty hours. He said, "No real matter. Fastolfe didn't seem to mind, so we'll forget it. Unpredictable, these Spacers. You don't deserve your luck, Lije. Next time you talk it over with me before you make like a one-man subether hero."

Baley nodded. The whole thing rolled off his shoulders. He had tried a grandstand stunt and it hadn't worked. Okay. He was a little surprised that he could be so casual about it, but there it was.

He said, "Look, Commissioner. I want to have a two-man apartment assigned to Daneel and myself. I'm not taking him home tonight."

"What's all this?"

"The news is out that he's a robot. Remember? Maybe nothing will happen, but if there is a riot, I don't want my family in the middle of it."

"Nonsense, Lije. I've had the thing checked. There's no such rumor in the City."

"Jessie got the story somewhere, Commissioner."

"Well, there's no organized rumor. Nothing dangerous. I've been checking this ever since I got off the trimensic at Fastolfe's dome. It was why I left. I had to track it down, naturally, and fast. Anyway, here are the reports. See for yourself. There's Doris Gillid's report. She went through a dozen Women's Personals in different parts of the City. You know Doris. She's a competent girl. Well, nothing showed. Nothing showed anywhere."

"Then how did Jessie get the rumor, Commissioner?"

"It can be explained. R. Daneel made a show of himself in the shoe store. Did he really pull a blaster, Lije, or were you stretching it a little?"

"He really pulled one. Pointed it, too."

Commissioner Enderby shook his head. "All right. Someone recognized him. As a robot, I mean."

"Hold on," said Baley, indignantly. "You can't tell him for a robot."

"Why not?"

"Could you? I couldn't."

"What does that prove? We're no experts. Suppose there was a technician out of the Westchester robot factories in the crowd. A professional. A man who has spent his life building and designing robots. He notices something queer about R. Daneel. Maybe in the way he talks or holds himself. He speculates about it. Maybe he tells his wife. She tells a few friends. Then it dies. It's too improbable. People don't believe it. Only it got to Jessie before it died."

"Maybe," said Baley, doubtfully. "But how about an assignment to a bachelor room for two, anyway?"

The Commissioner shrugged, lifted the intercom. After a while, he said, "Section Q-27 is all they can do. It's not a very good neighborhood."

"It'll do," said Baley.

"Where's R. Daneel now, by the way?"

"He's at our record files. He's trying to collect information on Medievalist agitators."

"Good Lord, there are millions."

"I know, but it keeps him happy."

Baley was nearly at the door, when he turned, half on impulse, and said, "Commissioner, did Dr. Sarton ever talk to you about Spacetown's program? I mean, about introducing the C/Fe culture?"

"The what?"

"Introducing robots."

"Occasionally." The Commissioner's tone was not one of any particular interest.

"Did he ever explain what Spacetown's point was?"

"Oh, improve health, raise the standard of living. The usual talk; it didn't impress me. Oh, I agreed with him. I nodded my head and all that. What could I do? It's just a matter of humoring them and hoping they'll keep within reason in their notions. Maybe some day . . ."

Baley waited but he didn't say what maybe-some-day might bring.

Baley said, "Did he ever mention anything about emigration?"

"Emigration! Never. Letting an Earthman into an Outer World is like finding a diamond asteroid in the rings of Saturn."

"I mean emigration to new worlds."

But the Commissioner answered that one with a simple stare of incredulousness.

Baley chewed that for a moment, then said with sudden bluntness, "What's cerebroanalysis, Commissioner? Ever hear of it?"

The Commissioner's round face didn't pucker; his eyes didn't blink. He said evenly, "No, what's it supposed to be?"

"Nothing. Just picked it up."

He left the office and at his desk continued thinking. Certainly, the Commissioner wasn't *that* good an actor. Well, then . . .

At 16:05 Baley called Jessie and told her he wouldn't be home that night nor probably any night for a while. It took a while after that to disengage her.

"Lije, is there trouble? Are you in danger?"

A policeman is always in a certain amount of danger, he explained lightly. It didn't satisfy her. "Where will you be staying?"

He didn't tell her. "If you're going to be lonely tonight," he said, "stay at your mother's." He broke connections abruptly, which was probably just as well.

At 16:20 he made a call to Washington. It took a certain length of time to reach the man he wanted and an almost equally long time to convince him he ought to make an air trip to New York the next day. By 16:40, he had succeeded.

At 16:55 the Commissioner left, passing him with an uncertain smile. The day shift left en masse. The sparser population that filled the offices in the evening and through the night made its way in and greeted him in varied tones of surprise.

R. Daneel came to his desk with a sheaf of papers.

"And those are?" asked Baley.

"A list of men and women who might belong to a Medievalist organization."

"How many does the list include?"

"Over a million," said R. Daneel. "These are just part of them."

"Do you expect to check them all, Daneel?"

"Obviously that would be impractical, Elijah."

"You see, Daneel, almost all Earthmen are Medievalists in one way or another. The Commissioner, Jessie, myself. Look at the Commissioner's——" (He almost said, "spectacles," then remembered that Earthmen must stick together and that the Commissioner's face must be protected in the figurative as well as the literal sense.) He concluded, lamely, "eye ornaments."

"Yes," said R. Daneel, "I had noticed them, but thought it indelicate, perhaps, to refer to them. I have not seen such ornaments on other City dwellers."

"It is a very old-fashioned sort of thing."

"Does it serve a purpose of any sort?"

Baley said, abruptly, "How did you get your list?"

"It was a machine that did it for me. Apparently, one sets it for a particular type of offense and it does the rest. I let it scan all disorderly conduct cases involving robots over the past twenty-five years.

Another machine scanned all City newspapers over an equal period for the names of those involved in unfavorable statements concerning robots or men of the Outer Worlds. It is amazing what can be done in three hours. The machine even eliminated the names of non-survivors from the lists."

"You are amazed? Surely you've got computers on the Outer Worlds?"

"Of many sorts, certainly. Very advanced ones. Still, none are as massive and complex as the ones here. You must remember, of course, that even the largest Outer World scarcely has the population of one of your Cities and extreme complexity is not necessary."

Baley said, "Have you ever been on Aurora?"

"No," said R. Daneel, "I was assembled here on Earth."

"Then how do you know about Outer World computers?"

"But surely that is obvious, partner Elijah. My data store is drawn from that of the late Dr. Sarton. You may take it for granted that it is rich in factual material concerning the Outer Worlds."

"I see. Can you eat, Daneel?"

"I am nuclear-powered. I had thought you were aware of that."

"I'm perfectly aware of it. I didn't ask if you needed to eat. I asked if you *could* eat. If you could put food in your mouth, chew it, and swallow it. I should think that would be an important item in seeming to be a man."

"I see your point. Yes, I can perform the mechanical operations of chewing and swallowing. My capacity is, of course, quite limited, and I would have to remove the ingested material from what you might call my stomach sooner or later."

"All right. You can regurgitate, or whatever you do, in the quiet of our room tonight. The point is that I'm hungry. I've missed lunch, damn it, and I want you with me when I eat. And you can't sit there and *not* eat without attracting attention. So if you can eat, that's what I want to hear. Let's go!"

Section kitchens were the same all over the City. What's more, Baley had been in Washington, Toronto, Los Angeles, London, and Budapest in the way of business, and they had been the same there, too. Perhaps it had been different in Medieval times when languages had varied and dietaries as well. Nowadays, yeast products were just the same from Shanghai to Tashkent and from Winnipeg to Buenos

Aires; and English might not be the "English" of Shakespeare or Churchill, but it was the final potpourri that was current over all the continents and, with some modification, on the Outer Worlds as well.

But language and dietary aside, there were the deeper similarities. There was always that particular odor, undefinable but completely characteristic of "kitchen." There was the waiting triple line moving slowly in, converging at the door and splitting up again, right, left, center. There was the rumble of humanity, speaking and moving, and the sharper clatter of plastic on plastic. There was the gleam of simulated wood, highly polished, highlights on glass, long tables, the touch of steam in the air.

Baley inched slowly forward as the line moved (with all possible staggering of meal hours, a wait of at least ten minutes was almost unavoidable) and said to R. Daneel in sudden curiosity, "Can you smile?"

R. Daneel, who had been gazing at the interior of the kitchen with cool absorption, said, "I beg your pardon, Elijah."

"I'm just wondering, Daneel. Can you smile?" He spoke in a casual whisper.

R. Daneel smiled. The gesture was sudden and surprising. His lips curled back and the skin about either end folded. Only the mouth smiled, however. The rest of the robot's face was untouched.

Baley shook his head. "Don't bother, R. Daneel. It doesn't do a thing for you."

They were at the entrance. Person after person thrust his metal food tag through the appropriate slot and had it scanned. Click—click—click—

Someone once calculated that a smoothly running kitchen could allow the entrance of two hundred persons a minute, the tags of each one being fully scanned to prevent kitchen-jumping, meal-jumping, and ration-stretching. They had also calculated how long a waiting line was necessary for maximum efficiency and how much time was lost when any one person required special treatment.

It was therefore always a calamity to interrupt that smooth click—click by stepping to the manual window, as Baley and R. Daneel did, in order to thrust a special-permit pass at the official in charge.

Jessie, filled with the knowledge of an assistant dietitian, had explained it once to Baley.

"It upsets things completely," she had said. "It throws off consumption figures and inventory estimates. It means special checks. You have to match slips with all the different Section kitchens to make sure the balance isn't too unbalanced, if you know what I mean. There's a separate balance sheet to be made out each week. Then if anything goes wrong and you're overdrawn, it's always your fault. It's never the fault of the City Government for passing out special tickets to everybody and his kid sister. Oh, no. And when we have to say that free choice is suspended for the meal, don't the people in line make a fuss. It's always the fault of the people behind the counter. . . ."

Baley had the story in the fullest detail and so he quite understood the dry and poisonous look he received from the woman behind the window. She made a few hurried notes. Home Section, occupation, reason for meal displacement ("official business," a very irritating reason indeed, but quite irrefutable). Then she folded the slip with firm motions of her fingers and pushed it into a slot. A computer seized it, devoured the contents, and digested the information.

She turned to R. Daneel.

Baley let her have the worst. He said, "My friend is out-of-City."

The woman looked finally and completely outraged. She said, "Home City, please."

Baley intercepted the ball for Daneel once again. "All records are to be credited to the Police Department. No details necessary. Official business."

The woman brought down a pad of slips with a jerk of her arm and filled in the necessary matter in dark-light code with practiced pressings of the first two fingers of her right hand.

She said, "How long will you be eating here?"

"Till further notice," said Baley.

"Press fingers here," she said, inverting the information blank.

Baley had a short qualm as R. Daneel's even fingers with their glistening nails pressed downward. Surely, they wouldn't have forgotten to supply him with fingerprints.

The woman took the blank away and fed it into the all-consuming machine at her elbow. It belched nothing back and Baley breathed more easily.

She gave them little metal tags that were in the bright red that meant "temporary."

She said, "No free choices. We're short this week. Take table DF."
They made their way toward DF.

R. Daneel said, "I am under the impression that most of your people eat in kitchens such as these regularly."

"Yes. Of course, it's rather gruesome eating in a strange kitchen. There's no one about whom you know. In your own kitchen, it's quite different. You have your own seat which you occupy all the time. You're with your family, your friends. Especially when you're young, mealtimes are the bright spot of the day." Baley smiled in brief reminiscence.

Table DF was apparently among those reserved for transients. Those already seated watched their plates uneasily and did not talk with one another. They looked with sneaking envy at the laughing crowds at the other tables.

There is no one so uncomfortable, thought Baley, as the man eating out-of-Section. Be it ever so humble, the old saying went, there's no place like home-kitchen. Even the food tastes better, no matter how many chemists are ready to swear it to be no different from the food in Johannesburg.

He sat down on a stool and R. Daneel sat down next to him.

"No free choice," said Baley, with a wave of his fingers, "so just close the switch there and wait."

It took two minutes. A disc slid back in the table top and a dish lifted.

"Mashed potatoes, zymoveal sauce, and stewed apricots. Oh, well," said Baley.

A fork and two slices of whole yeast bread appeared in a recess just in front of the low railing that went down the long center of the table.

R. Daneel said in a low voice, "You may help yourself to my serving, if you wish."

For a moment, Baley was scandalized. Then he remembered and mumbled, "That's bad manners. Go on. Eat."

Baley ate industriously but without the relaxation that allows complete enjoyment. Carefully, he flicked an occasional glance at R. Daneel. The robot ate with precise motions of his jaws. Too precise. It didn't look quite natural.

Strange! Now that Baley knew for a fact that R. Daneel was in truth a robot, all sorts of little items showed up clearly. For instance, there was no movement of an Adam's apple when R. Daneel swallowed.

Yet he didn't mind so much. Was he getting used to the creature? Suppose people started afresh on a new world (how that ran through his mind ever since Dr. Fastolfe had put it there); suppose Bentley, for instance, were to leave Earth; could he get so he didn't mind working and living alongside robots? Why not? The Spacers themselves did it.

R. Daneel said, "Elijah, is it bad manners to watch another man while he is eating?"

"If you mean stare directly at him, of course. That's only common sense, isn't it? A man has a right to his privacy. Ordinary conversation is entirely in order, but you don't peer at a man while he's swallowing."

"I see. Why is it then that I count eight people watching us closely, very closely?"

Baley put down his fork. He looked about as though he were searching for the salt-pinch dispenser. "I see nothing out of the ordinary."

But he said it without conviction. The mob of diners was only a vast conglomeration of chaos to him. And when R. Daneel turned his impersonal brown eyes upon him, Baley suspected uncomfortably that those were not eyes he saw, but scanners capable of noting, with photographic accuracy and in split seconds of time, the entire panorama.

"I am quite certain," said R. Daneel, calmly.

"Well, then, what of it? It's crude behavior, but what does it prove?"

"I cannot say, Elijah, but is it coincidence that six of the watchers were in the crowd outside the shoe store last night?"

11

Escape Along The Strips

BALEY'S GRIP tightened convulsively on his fork.

"Are you sure?" he asked automatically, and as he said it, he realized the uselessness of the question. You don't ask a computer if it is sure of the answer it disgorges; not even a computer with arms and legs.

R. Daneel said, "Quite!"

"Are they close to us?"

"Not very. They are scattered."

"All right, then." Baley returned to his meal, his fork moving mechanically. Behind the frown on his long face, his mind worked furiously.

Suppose the incident last night had been organized by a group of anti-robot fanatics, that it had not been the spontaneous trouble it had seemed. Such a group of agitators could easily include men who had studied robots with the intensity born of deep opposition. One of them might have recognized R. Daneel for what he was. (The Commissioner had suggested that, in a way. Damn it, there were surprising depths to that man.)

It worked itself out logically. Granting they had been unable to act in an organized manner on the spur of last evening's moment, they would still have been able to plan for the future. If they could recognize a robot such as R. Daneel, they could certainly realize that Baley himself was a police officer. A police officer in the unusual company of a humanoid robot would very likely be a responsible man in the organization. (With the wisdom of hindsight, Baley followed the line of reasoning with no trouble at all.)

It followed then that observers at City Hall (or perhaps agents within City Hall) would be bound to spot Baley, R. Daneel, or both before too long a time had passed. That they had done so within twenty-four hours was not surprising. They might have done so in less time if so much of Baley's day had not been spent in Spacetown and along the motorway.

R. Daneel had finished his meal. He sat quietly waiting, his perfect hands resting lightly on the end of the table.

"Had we not better do something?" he asked.

"We're safe here in the kitchen," said Baley. "Now leave this to me. Please."

Baley looked about him cautiously and it was as though he saw a kitchen for the first time.

People! Thousands of them. What was the capacity of an average kitchen? He had once seen the figure. Two thousand two hundred, he thought. This one was larger than average.

Suppose the cry, "Robot," were sent out into the air. Suppose it were tossed among the thousands like a . . .

He was at a loss for a comparison, but it didn't matter. It wouldn't happen.

A spontaneous riot could flare anywhere, in the kitchens as easily as in the corridors or in the elevators. More easily, perhaps. There was a lack of inhibition at mealtimes, a sense of horseplay that could degenerate into something more serious at a trifle.

But a planned riot would be different. Here in the kitchen, the planners would themselves be trapped in a large and mob-filled room. Once the dishes went flying and the tables cracking there would be no easy way to escape. Hundreds would certainly die and they themselves might easily be among them.

No, a safe riot would have to be planned in the avenues of the City, in some relatively narrow passageway. Panic and hysteria would travel slowly along the constriction and there would be time for the quick, prepared fadeaway along the side passage or the unobtrusive step onto an escalating localway that would move them to a higher level and disappearance.

Baley felt trapped. There were probably others waiting outside. Baley and R. Daneel were to be followed to a proper point and the fuse would be set off.

R. Daneel said, "Why not arrest them?"

"That would only start the trouble sooner. You know their faces, don't you? You won't forget?"

"I am not capable of forgetting."

"Then we'll nab them another time. For now, we'll break their net. Follow me. Do exactly as I do."

He rose, turned his dish carefully upside down, centering it on the movable disc from below which it had risen. He put his fork back in its recess. R. Daneel, watching, matched his action. The dishes and utensils dropped out of sight.

R. Daneel said, "They are getting up, too."

"All right. It's my feeling they won't get too close. Not here."

The two moved into line now, drifting toward an exit where the click—click—click of the tags sounded ritualistically, each click recording the expenditure of a ration unit.

Baley looked back through the steamy haze and the noise and, with incongruous sharpness, thought of a visit to the City Zoo with Ben six or seven years ago. No, eight, because Ben had just passed his eighth birthday then. (Jehoshaphat! Where did the time go?)

It had been Ben's first visit and he had been excited. After all, he had never actually seen a cat or a dog before. Then, on top of that, there was the bird cage! Even Baley himself, who had seen it a dozen times before, was not immune to its fascination.

There is something about the first sight of living objects hurtling through air that is incomparably startling. It was feeding time in the sparrow cage and an attendant was dumping cracked oats into a long trough (human beings had grown used to yeast substitutes, but animals, more conservative in their way, insisted on real grain).

The sparrows flocked down in what seemed like hundreds. Wing to wing, with an ear-splitting twitter, they lined the trough. . . .

That was it; that was the picture that came to Baley's mind as he looked back at the kitchen he was leaving. Sparrows at the trough. The thought repelled him.

He thought: Jehoshaphat, there must be a better way.

But what better way? What was wrong with this way? It had never bothered him before.

He said abruptly to R. Daneel, "Ready, Daneel?"

"I am ready, Elijah."

They left the kitchen and escape was now clearly and flatly up to Baley.

There is a game that youngsters know called "running the strips." Its rules vary in trivial fashion from City to City, but its essentials are eternal. A boy from San Francisco can join the game in Cairo with no trouble.

Its object is to get from point A to point B via the City's rapid transit system in such a way that the "leader" manages to lose as many of his followers as possible. A leader who arrives at the destination alone is skillful indeed, as is a follower who refuses to be shaken.

The game is usually conducted during the evening rush hour when the increased density of the commuters makes it at once more hazardous and more complicated. The leader sets off, running up and down the accelerating strips. He does his best to do the unexpected, remaining standing on a given strip as long as possible, then leaping off suddenly in either direction. He will run quickly through several strips, then remain waiting once more.

Pity the follower who incautiously careens forward one strip too far. Before he has caught his mistake, unless he is extraordinarily nimble, he has driven past the leader or fallen behind. The clever leader will compound the error by moving quickly in the appropriate direction.

A move designed to increase the complexity of the task tenfold involves boarding the localways or the expressways themselves, and hurtling off the other side. It is bad form to avoid them completely and also bad form to linger on them.

The attraction of the game is not easy for an adult to understand, particularly for an adult who has never himself been a teenage strip-runner. The players are roughly treated by legitimate travelers into whose path they find themselves inevitably flying. They are persecuted bitterly by the police and punished by their parents. They are denounced in the schools and on the subetherics. No year passes without its four or five teen-agers killed at the game, its dozens hurt, its cases of innocent bystanders meeting tragedy of varying degree.

Yet nothing can be done to wipe out the strip-running gangs. The greater the danger, the more the strip-runners have that most valuable of all prizes, honor in the eyes of their fellows. A successful one may well swagger; a well-known leader is cock-of-the-walk.

Elijah Baley, for instance, remembered with satisfaction even now that he had been a strip-runner once. He had led a gang of twenty from the Concourse Sector to the borders of Queens, crossing three expressways. In two tireless and relentless hours, he had shaken off some of the most agile followers of the Bronx, and arrived at the destination point alone. They talked about that run for months.

Baley was in his forties now, of course. He hadn't run the strips for over twenty years, but he remembered some of the tricks. What he had lost in agility, he made up in another respect. He was a policeman. No one but another policeman as experienced as himself could possibly know the City as well, know where almost every metal-bordered alley began and ended.

He walked away from the kitchen briskly, but not too rapidly. Each moment he expected the cry of "Robot, robot" to ring out behind him. That initial set of moments was the riskiest. He counted the steps until he felt the first accelerating strip moving under him.

He stopped for a moment, while R. Daneel moved smoothly up beside him.

"Are they still behind us, Daneel?" asked Baley in a whisper.

"Yes. They're moving closer."

"That won't last," said Baley confidently. He looked at the strips stretching to either side, with their human cargo whipping to his left more and more rapidly as their distance from him increased. He had felt the strips beneath his feet many times a day almost all the days of his life, but he had not bent his knees in anticipation of running them in seven thousand days and more. He felt the old familiar thrill and his breath grew more rapid.

He quite forgot the one time he had caught Ben at the game. He had lectured him interminably and threatened to have him put under police surveillance.

Lightly, quickly, at double the "safe" rate, he went up the strips. He leaned forward sharply against the acceleration. The localway was humming past. For a moment, it looked as though he would mount, but suddenly he was fading backward, backward, dodging through the crowd to left and right as it thickened on the slower strips.

He stopped, and let himself be carried along at a mere fifteen miles an hour.

"How many are with us, Daneel?"

"Only one, Elijah." The robot was at his side, unruffled, unbreathing.

"He must have been a good one in his day, too, but he won't last either."

Full of self-confidence, he felt a half-remembered sensation of his younger days. It consisted partly of the feeling of immersion in a mystic rite to which others did not belong, partly of the purely physical sensation of wind against hair and face, partly of a tenuous sense of danger.

"They call this the side shuffle," he said to R. Daneel in a low voice.

His long stride ate distance, but he moved along a single strip, dodging the legitimate crowd with a minimum of effort. He kept it up, moving always closer to the strip's edge, until the steady movement of his head through the crowd must have been hypnotic in its constant velocity—as it was intended to be.

And then, without a break in his step, he shifted two inches sideways and was on the adjoining strip. He felt an aching in his thigh muscles as he kept his balance.

He whipped through a cluster of commuters and was on the forty-five-mile strip.

"How is it now, Daneel?" he asked.

"He is still with us," was the calm answer.

Baley's lips tightened. There was nothing for it but to use the moving platforms themselves, and that really required co-ordination; more, perhaps, than he still retained.

He looked about quickly. Exactly where were they now? B-22d Street flashed by. He made rapid calculations and was off. Up the remaining strips, smoothly and steadily, a swing onto the localway platform.

The impersonal faces of men and women, calloused with the ennui of way-riding, were jolted into something like indignation as Baley and R. Daneel clambered aboard and squeezed through the railings.

"Hey, now," called a woman shrilly, clutching at her hat.

"Sorry," said Baley, breathlessly.

He forced his way through the standees and with a wriggle was off on the other side. At the last moment, a jostled passenger thumped his back in anger. He went staggering.

Desperately he tried to regain his footing. He lurched across a strip boundary and the sudden change in velocity forced him to his knees and then over on his side.

He had the sudden, panicky vision of men colliding with him and bowling over, of a spreading confusion on the strips, one of the dreaded "man-jams" that would not fail to put dozens in the hospital with broken limbs.

But R. Daneel's arm was under his back. He felt himself lifted with more than a man's strength.

"Thanks," gasped Baley, and there was no time for more.

Off he went and down the decelerating strips in a complicated pattern so designed that his feet met the V-joint strips of an express-way at the exact point of crossover. Without the loss of rhythm, he was accelerating again, then up and over an expressway.

"Is he with us, Daneel?"

"Not one in sight, Elijah."

"Good. But what a strip-runner you would have been, Daneel!— Oops, now, now!"

Off onto another localway in a whirl and down the strips with a clatter to a doorway, large and official in appearance. A guard rose to his feet.

Baley flashed his identification. "Official business."

They were inside.

"Power plant," said Baley, curtly. "This breaks our tracks completely."

He had been in power plants before, including this one. Familiarity did not lessen his feeling of uncomfortable awe. The feeling was heightened by the haunting thought that once his father had been high in the hierarchy of a plant such as this. That is, before . . .

There was the surrounding hum of the tremendous generators hidden in the central well of the plant, the faint sharpness of ozone in the air, the grim and silent threat of the red lines that marked the limits beyond which no one could pass without protective clothing.

Somewhere in the plant (Baley had no idea exactly where) a pound of fissionable material was consumed each day. Every so often, the radioactive fission products, the so-called "hot ash," were forced by air pressure through leaden pipes to distant caverns ten miles out in the ocean and a half mile below the ocean floor. Baley sometimes wondered what would happen when the caverns were filled.

He said to R. Daneel with sudden gruffness, "Stay away from the red lines." Then, he bethought himself and added sheepishly, "But I suppose it doesn't matter to you."

"Is it a question of radioactivity?" asked Daneel.

"Yes."

"Then it does matter to me. Gamma radiation destroys the delicate balance of a positronic brain. It would affect me much sooner than it would affect you."

"You mean it would *kill* you?"

"I would require a new positronic brain. Since no two can be alike, I would be a new individual. The Daneel you now speak to would be, in a manner of speaking, dead."

Baley looked at the other doubtfully. "I never knew that.—Up these ramps."

"The point isn't stressed. Spacetown wishes to convince Earthmen of the usefulness of such as myself, not of our weaknesses."

"Then why tell me?"

R. Daneel turned his eyes full on his human companion. "You are my partner, Elijah. It is well that you know my weaknesses and shortcomings."

Baley cleared his throat and had nothing more to say on the subject.

"Out in this direction," he said a moment later, "and we're a quarter of a mile from our apartment."

It was a grim, lower-class apartment. One small room and two beds. Two fold-in chairs and a closet. A built-in subetheric screen that allowed no manual adjustment, and would be working only at stated hours, but *would* be working then. No washbasin, not even an unactivated one, and no facilities for cooking or even boiling water. A small trash-disposal pipe was in one corner of the room, an ugly, unadorned, unpleasantly functional object.

Baley shrugged. "This is it. I guess we can stand it."

R. Daneel walked to the trash-disposal pipe. His shirt unseamed at a touch, revealing a smooth and, to all appearances, well-muscled chest.

"What are you doing?" asked Baley.

"Getting rid of the food I ingested. If I were to leave it, it would putrefy and I would become an object of distaste."

R. Daneel placed two fingers carefully under one nipple and pushed in a definite pattern of pressure. His chest opened longitudinally. R. Daneel reached in and from a welter of gleaming metal withdrew a thin, translucent sac, partly distended. He opened it while Baley watched with a kind of horror.

R. Daneel hesitated. He said, "The food is perfectly clean. I do not salivate or chew. It was drawn in through the gullet by suction, you know. It is edible."

"That's all right," said Baley, gently. "I'm not hungry. You just get rid of it."

R. Daneel's food sac was of fluorocarbon plastic, Baley decided. At least the food did not cling to it. It came out smoothly and was placed little by little into the pipe. A waste of good food at that, he thought.

He sat down on one bed and removed his shirt. He said, "I suggest an early start tomorrow."

"For a specific reason?"

"The location of this apartment isn't known to our friends yet. Or at least I hope not. If we leave early, we are that much safer. Once in City Hall, we will have to decide whether our partnership is any longer practical."

"You think it is perhaps not?"

Baley shrugged and said dourly, "We can't go through this sort of thing every day."

"But it seems to me——"

R. Daneel was interrupted by the sharp scarlet sliver of the door signal.

Baley rose silently to his feet and unlimbered his blaster. The door signal flashed once more.

He moved silently to the door, put his thumb on the blaster contact while he threw the switch that activated the one-way transparency patch. It wasn't a good view-patch; it was small and had a distorting effect, but it was quite good enough to show Baley's youngster, Ben, outside the door.

Baley acted quickly. He flung the door open, snatched brutally at Ben's wrist as the boy raised his hand to signal a third time, and pulled him in.

The look of fright and bewilderment faded only slowly from Ben's eyes as he leaned breathlessly against the wall toward which he had been hurled. He rubbed his wrist.

"Dad!" he said in grieved tones. "You didn't have to grab me like that."

Baley was staring through the view-patch of the once-again-closed door. As nearly as he could tell, the corridor was empty.

"Did you see anyone out there, Ben?"

"No. Gee, Dad, I just came to see if you were all right."

"Why shouldn't I be all right?"

"I don't know. It was Mom. She was crying and all like that. She said I had to find you. If I didn't go, she said she would go herself, and then she didn't know what would happen. She *made* me go, Dad."

Baley said, "How did you find me? Did your mother know where I was?"

"No, she didn't. I called up your office."

"And they told you?"

Ben looked startled at his father's vehemence. He said, in a low voice, "Sure. Weren't they supposed to?"

Baley and Daneel looked at one another.

Baley rose heavily to his feet. He said, "Where's your mother now, Ben? At the apartment?"

"No, we went to Grandma's for dinner and stayed there. I'm supposed to go back there now. I mean, as long as you're all right, Dad."

"You'll stay here. Daneel, did you notice the exact location of the floor communo?"

The robot said, "Yes. Do you intend leaving the room to use it?"

"I've got to. I've got to get in touch with Jessie."

"Might I suggest that it would be more logical to let Bentley do that. It is a form of risk and he is less valuable."

Baley stared. "Why, you——"

He thought: Jehoshaphat, what am I getting angry about?

He went on more calmly, "You don't understand, Daneel. Among us, it is not customary for a man to send his young son into possible danger, even if it is logical to do so."

"Danger!" squeaked Ben in a sort of horrified pleasure. "What's going on, Dad? Huh, Dad?"

"Nothing, Ben. Now, this isn't any of your business. Understand?

Get ready for bed. I want you in bed when I get back. You hear me?"

"Aw, gosh. You could tell a fellow. I won't say anything."

"In bed!"

"Gosh!"

Baley hitched his jacket back as he stood at the floor communo, so that his blaster butt was ready for snatching. He spoke his personal number into the mouthpiece and waited while a computer fifteen miles away checked it to make sure the call was permissible. It was a very short wait that was involved, since a plain-clothes man had no limit on the number of his business calls. He spoke the code number of his mother-in-law's apartment.

The small screen at the base of the instrument lit up, and her face looked out at him.

He said, in a low voice, "Mother, put on Jessie."

Jessie must have been waiting for him. She was on at once. Baley looked at her face and then darkened the screen deliberately.

"All right, Jessie. Ben's here. Now, what's the matter?" His eyes roved from side to side continuously, watching.

"Are you all right? You aren't in trouble?"

"I'm obviously all right, Jessie. Now stop it."

"Oh, Lije, I've been so worried."

"What about?" he asked tightly.

"You know. Your friend."

"What about him?"

"I told you last night. There'll be trouble."

"Now, that's nonsense. I'm keeping Ben with me for tonight and you go to bed. Good-by, dear."

He broke connections and waited for two breaths before starting back. His face was gray with apprehension and fear.

Ben was standing in the middle of the room when Baley returned. One of his contact lenses was neatly pocketed in a little suction cup. The other was still in his eye.

Ben said, "Gosh, Dad, isn't there any water in the place? Mr. Olivaw says I can't go to the Personal."

"He's right. You can't. Put that thing back in your eye, Ben. It won't hurt you to sleep with them for one night."

"All right." Ben put it back, put away his suction cup and climbed into bed. "Boy, what a mattress!"

Baley said to R. Daneel, "I suppose you won't mind sitting up."

"Of course not. I was interested, by the way, in the queer glass Bentley wears close to his eyes. Do all Earthmen wear them?"

"No. Just some," said Baley, absently. "I don't, for instance."

"For what reason is it worn?"

Baley was too absorbed with his own thoughts to answer. His own uneasy thoughts.

The lights were out.

Baley remained wakeful. He was dimly aware of Ben's breathing as it turned deep and regular and became a bit rough. When he turned his head, he grew somehow conscious of R. Daneel, sitting in a chair with grave immobility, face turned toward the door.

Then he fell asleep, and when he slept, he dreamed.

He dreamed Jessie was falling into the fission chamber of a nuclear power plant, falling and falling. She held out her arms to him, shrieking, but he could only stand frozenly just outside a scarlet line and watch her distorted figure turn as it fell, growing smaller until it was only a dot.

He could only watch her, in the dream, knowing that it was he, himself, who had pushed her.

12

Words From an Expert

ELIJAH BALEY looked up as Commissioner Julius Enderby entered the office. He nodded wearily.

The Commissioner looked at the clock and grunted, "Don't tell me you've been here all night!"

Baley said, "I won't."

The Commissioner said in a low voice, "Any trouble last night?"

Baley shook his head.

The Commissioner said, "I've been thinking that I could be minimizing the possibility of riots. If there's anything to——"

Baley said tightly, "For God's sake, Commissioner, if anything happened, I'd tell you. There was no trouble of any sort."

"All right." The Commissioner moved away, passing beyond the door that marked off the unusual privacy that became his exalted position.

Baley looked after him and thought: *He* must have slept last night.

Baley bent to the routine report he was trying to write as a cover-up for the real activities of the last two days, but the words he had tapped out by finger touch blurred and danced. Slowly, he became aware of an object standing by his desk.

He lifted his head. "What do you want?"

It was R. Sammy. Baley thought: Julius's private flunky. It pays to be a Commissioner.

R. Sammy said through his fatuous grin, "The Commissioner wants to see you, Lije. He says right away."

Baley waved his hand. "He just saw me. Tell him I'll be in later."

R. Sammy said, "He says right away."

"All right. All right. Go away."

The robot backed away, saying, "The Commissioner wants to see you right away, Lije. He says right away."

"Jehoshaphat," said Baley between his teeth. "I'm going. I'm going." He got up from his desk, headed for the office, and R. Sammy was silent.

Baley said as he entered, "Damn it, Commissioner, *don't* send that thing after me, will you?"

But the Commissioner only said, "Sit down, Lije. Sit down."

Baley sat down and stared. Perhaps he had done old Julius an injustice. Perhaps the man hadn't slept after all. He looked fairly beat.

The Commissioner was tapping the paper before him. "There's a record of a call you made to a Dr. Gerrigel at Washington by insulated beam."

"That's right, Commissioner."

"There's no record of the conversation, naturally, since it was insulated. What's it all about?"

"I'm after background information."

"He's a roboticist, isn't he?"

"That's right."

The Commissioner put out a lower lip and suddenly looked like a child about to pout. "But what's the point? What kind of information are you after?"

"I'm not sure, Commissioner. I just have a feeling that in a case like this, information on robots might help." Baley clamped his mouth shut after that. He wasn't going to be specific, and that was that.

"I wouldn't, Lije. I wouldn't. I don't think it's wise."

"What's your objection, Commissioner?"

"The fewer the people who know about all this, the better."

"I'll tell him as little as I can. Naturally."

"I still don't think it's wise."

Baley was feeling just sufficiently wretched to lose patience. He said, "Are you ordering me not to see him?"

"No. No. You do as you see fit. You're heading this investigation. Only . . ."

"Only what?"

The Commissioner shook his head. "Nothing.—Where is *he*? You know who I mean."

Baley did. He said, "Daneel's still at the files."

The Commissioner paused a long moment, then said, "We're not making much progress, you know."

"We're not making any so far. Still, things may change."

"All right, then," said the Commissioner, but he didn't look as though he really thought it were all right.

R. Daneel was at Baley's desk, when the latter returned.

"Well, and what have *you* got?" Baley asked gruffly.

"I have completed my first, rather hasty, search through the files, partner Elijah, and I have located two of the people who tried to track us last night and who, moreover, were at the shoe store during the former incident."

"Let's see."

R. Daneel placed the small, stamp-size cards before Baley. They were mottled with the small dots that served as code. The robot also produced a portable decoder and placed one of the cards into an appropriate slot. The dots possessed electrical conduction properties different from that of the card as a whole. The electric field passing through the card was therefore distorted in a highly specific manner and in response to that specification the three-by-six screen above the decoder was filled with words. Words which, uncoded, would have filled several sheets of standard size report paper. Words, moreover, which could not possibly be interpreted by anyone not in possession of an official police decoder.

Baley read through the material stolidly. The first person was Francis Clousarr, age thirty-three at time of arrest two years before; cause of arrest, inciting to riot; employee at New York Yeast; home address, so-and-so; parentage, so-and-so; hair, eyes, distinguishing marks, educational history, employment history, psychoanalytic profile, physical profile, data here, data there, and finally reference to tri-photo in the rogues' gallery.

"You checked the photograph?" asked Baley.

"Yes, Elijah."

The second person was Gerhard Paul. Baley glanced at the material on that card and said, "This is all no good."

R. Daneel said, "I am sure that cannot be so. If there is an organization of Earthmen who are capable of the crime we are investigating, these are members. Is that not an obvious likelihood? Should they then not be questioned?"

"We'd get nothing out of them."

"They were there, both at the shoe store and in the kitchen. They cannot deny it."

"Just being there's no crime. Besides which, they *can* deny it. They can just say they weren't there. It's as simple as that. How can we prove they're lying?"

"I saw them."

"That's no proof," said Baley, savagely. "No court, if it ever came to that, would believe that you could remember two faces in a blur of a million."

"It is obvious that *I* can."

"Sure. Tell them what you are. As soon as you do that, you're no witness. Your kind have no status in any court of law on Earth."

R. Daneel said, "I take it, then, that you have changed your mind."

"What do you mean?"

"Yesterday, in the kitchen, you said there was no need to arrest them. You said that as long as I remembered their faces, we could arrest them at any time."

"Well, I didn't think it through," said Baley. "I was crazy. It can't be done."

"Not even for psychological reasons? They would not know we had no legal proof of their complicity in conspiracy."

Baley said, tensely, "Look, I am expecting Dr. Gerrigel of Washington in half an hour. Do you mind waiting till he's been here and gone? Do you mind?"

"I will wait," said R. Daneel.

Anthony Gerrigel was a precise and very polite man of middle height, who looked far from being one of the most erudite roboticists on Earth. He was nearly twenty minutes late, it turned out, and quite apologetic about it. Baley, white with an anger born of apprehension, shrugged off the apologies gracelessly. He checked his reservation on Conference Room D, repeated his instructions that they were not to be disturbed on any account for an hour, and led Dr. Gerrigel and R. Daneel down the corridor, up a ramp, and through a door that led to one of the spy-beam-insulated chambers.

Baley checked the walls carefully before sitting down, listening to the soft burr of the pulsometer in his hand, waiting for any fading of the steady sound which would indicate a break, even a small one, in the insulation. He turned it on the ceiling, floor, and, with particular care, on the door. There was no break.

Dr. Gerrigel smiled a little. He looked like a man who never smiled more than a little. He was dressed with a neatness that could only be described as fussy. His iron-gray hair was smoothed carefully back and his face looked pink and freshly washed. He sat with a posture of prim stiffness as though repeated maternal advice in his younger years concerning the desirability of good posture had rigidified his spine forever.

He said to Baley, "You make this all seem very formidable."

"It's quite important, Doctor. I need information about robots that only you can give me, perhaps. Anything we say here, of course, is top secret and the City will expect you to forget it all when you leave." Baley looked at his watch.

The little smile on the roboticist's face winked away. He said, "Let me explain why I am late." The matter obviously weighed upon him. "I decided not to go by air. I get airsick."

"That's too bad," said Baley. He put away the pulsometer, after checking its standard settings to make last-minute certain that there was nothing wrong with *it*, and sat down.

"Or at least not exactly airsick, but nervous. A mild agoraphobia. It's nothing particularly abnormal, but there it is. So I took the expressways."

Baley felt a sudden sharp interest. "Agoraphobia?"

"I make it sound worse than it is," the roboticist said at once. "It's just the feeling you get in a plane. Have you ever been in one, Mr. Baley?"

"Several times."

"Then you must know what I mean. It's that feeling of being surrounded by nothing; of being separated from—from empty air by a mere inch of metal. It's very uncomfortable."

"So you took the expressway?"

"Yes."

"All the way from Washington to New York?"

"Oh, I've done it before. Since they built the Baltimore-Philadelphia tunnel, it's quite simple."

So it was. Baley had never made the trip himself, but he was perfectly aware that it was possible. Washington, Baltimore, Philadelphia, and New York had grown, in the last two centuries, to the point where all nearly touched. The Four-City Area was almost the official name for the entire stretch of coast, and there were a considerable number of people who favored administrational consolidation and the formation of a single super-City. Baley disagreed with that, himself. New York City by itself was almost too large to be handled by a centralized government. A larger City, with over fifty million population, would break down under its own weight.

"The trouble was," Dr. Gerrigel was saying, "that I missed a connection in Chester Sector, Philadelphia, and lost time. That, and a little difficulty in getting a transient room assignment, ended by making me late."

"Don't worry about that, Doctor. What you say, though, is interesting. In view of your dislike for planes, what would you say to going outside City limits on foot, Dr. Gerrigel?"

"For what reason?" He looked startled and more than a little apprehensive.

"It's just a rhetorical question. I'm not suggesting that you really should. I want to know how the notion strikes you, that's all."

"It strikes me very unpleasantly."

"Suppose you had to leave the City at night and walk cross country for half a mile or more."

"I—I don't think I could be persuaded to."

"No matter how important the necessity?"

"If it were to save my life or the lives of my family, I might try. . . ." He looked embarrassed. "May I ask the point of these questions, Mr. Baley?"

"I'll tell you. A serious crime has been committed, a particularly disturbing murder. I'm not at liberty to give you the details. There is a theory, however, that the murderer, in order to commit the crime, did just what we were discussing; he crossed open country at night and alone. I was just wondering what kind of man could do that."

Dr. Gerrigel shuddered. "No one I know. Certainly not I. Of

course, among millions I suppose you could find a few hardy individuals."

"But you wouldn't say it was a very likely thing for a human being to do?"

"No. Certainly not likely."

"In fact, if there's any other explanation for the crime, any other *conceivable* explanation, it should be considered."

Dr. Gerrigel looked more uncomfortable than ever as he sat bolt upright with his well-kept hands precisely folded in his lap. "Do you have an alternate explanation in mind?"

"Yes. It occurs to me that a robot, for instance, would have no difficulty at all in crossing open country."

Dr. Gerrigel stood up. "Oh, my dear sir!"

"What's wrong?"

"You mean a robot may have committed the crime?"

"Why not?"

"Murder? Of a human being?"

"Yes. Please sit down, Doctor."

The roboticist did as he was told. He said, "Mr. Baley, there are two acts involved: walking cross country, and murder. A human being could commit the latter easily, but would find difficulty in doing the former. A robot could do the former easily, but the latter act would be completely impossible. If you're going to replace an unlikely theory by an impossible one——"

"Impossible is a hell of a strong word, Doctor."

"You've heard of the First Law of Robotics, Mr. Baley?"

"Sure. I can even quote it: A robot may not injure a human being, or, through inaction, allow a human being to come to harm." Baley suddenly pointed a finger at the roboticist and went on, "Why can't a robot be built without the First Law? What's so sacred about it?"

Dr. Gerrigel looked startled, then tittered, "Oh, Mr. Baley."

"Well, what's the answer?"

"Surely, Mr. Baley, if you even know a little about robotics, you must know the gigantic task involved, both mathematically and electronically, in building a positronic brain."

"I have an idea," said Baley. He remembered well his visit to a robot factory once in the way of business. He had seen their library of book-films, long ones, each of which contained the mathematical analysis of a single type of positronic brain. It took more than an hour for the average such film to be viewed at standard scanning speed, condensed though its symbolisms were. And no two brains were alike, even when prepared according to the most rigid specifications. That, Baley understood, was a consequence of Heisenberg's Uncertainty Principle. This meant that each film had to be supplemented by appendices involving possible variations.

Oh, it was a job, all right. Baley wouldn't deny that.

Dr. Gerrigel said, "Well, then, you must understand that a design for a new type of positronic brain, even one where only minor innovations are involved, is not the matter of a night's work. It usually involves the entire research staff of a moderately sized factory and takes anywhere up to a year of time. Even this large expenditure of work would not be nearly enough if it were not that the basic theory of such circuits has already been standardized and may be used as a foundation for further elaboration. The standard basic theory involves the Three Laws of Robotics: the First Law, which you've quoted; the Second Law, which states, 'A robot must obey the orders given it by human beings except where such orders would conflict with the First Law,' and the Third Law, which states, 'A robot must protect its own existence as long as such protection does not conflict with the First or Second Law.' Do you understand?"

R. Daneel, who, to all appearances, had been following the conversation with close attention, broke in. "If you will excuse me, Elijah, I would like to see if I follow Dr. Gerrigel. What you imply, sir, is that any attempt to build a robot, the working of whose positronic brain is not oriented about the Three Laws, would require first the setting up of a new basic theory and that this, in turn, would take many years."

The roboticist looked very gratified. "That is exactly what I mean, Mr. . . ."

Baley waited a moment, then carefully introduced R. Daneel: "This is Daneel Olivaw, Dr. Gerrigel."

"Good day, Mr. Olivaw." Dr. Gerrigel extended his hand and shook Daneel's. He went on, "It is my estimation that it would take fifty years to develop the basic theory of a non-Asenion positronic brain—that is, one in which the basic assumptions of the Three Laws are disallowed—and bring it to the point where robots similar to modern models could be constructed."

"And this has never been done?" asked Baley. "I mean, Doctor, that we've been building robots for several thousand years. In all that time, hasn't anybody or any group had fifty years to spare?"

"Certainly," said the roboticist, "but it is not the sort of work that anyone would care to do."

"I find that hard to believe. Human curiosity will undertake anything."

"It hasn't undertaken the non-Asenion robot. The human race, Mr. Baley, has a strong Frankenstein complex."

"A what?"

"That's a popular name derived from a Medieval novel describing a robot that turned on its creator. I never read the novel myself. But that's beside the point. What I wish to say is that robots without the First Law are simply not built."

"And no theory for it even exists?"

"Not to my knowledge, and my knowledge," he smiled self-consciously, "is rather extensive."

"And a robot with a First Law built in could not kill a man?"

"Never. Unless such killing were completely accidental or unless it were necessary to save the lives of two or more men. In either case, the positronic potential built up would ruin the brain past recovery."

"All right," said Baley. "All this represents the situation on Earth. Right?"

"Yes. Certainly."

"What about the Outer Worlds?"

Some of Dr. Gerrigel's self-assurance seemed to ooze away. "Oh dear, Mr. Baley, I couldn't say of my own knowledge, but I'm sure that if non-Asenion positronic brains were ever designed or if the mathematical theory were worked out, we'd hear of it."

"Would we? Well, let me follow up another thought in my mind, Dr. Gerrigel. I hope you don't mind."

"No. Not at all." He looked helplessly first at Baley, then at R. Daneel. "After all, if it is as important as you say, I'm glad to do all I can."

"Thank you, Doctor. My question is, why humanoid robots? I mean that I've been taking them for granted all my life, but now it occurs to me that I don't know the reason for their existence. Why should a robot have a head and four limbs? Why should he look more or less like a man?"

"You mean, why shouldn't he be built functionally, like any other machine?"

"Right," said Baley. "Why not?"

Dr. Gerrigel smiled a little. "Really, Mr. Baley, you are born too late. The early literature of robotics is riddled with a discussion of that very matter and the polemics involved were something frightful. If you would like a very good reference to the disputations among the functionalists and anti-functionalists, I can recommend Hanford's 'History of Robotics.' Mathematics is kept to a minimum. I think you'd find it very interesting."

"I'll look it up," said Baley, patiently. "Meanwhile, could you give me an idea?"

"The decision was made on the basis of economics. Look here, Mr. Baley, if you were supervising a farm, would you care to buy a tractor with a positronic brain, a reaper, a harrow, a milker, an automobile, and so on, each with a positronic brain; or would you rather have ordinary unbrained machinery with a single positronic robot to run them all. I warn you that the second alternative represents only a fiftieth or a hundredth the expense."

"But why the human form?"

"Because the human form is the most successful generalized form in all nature. We are not a specialized animal, Mr. Baley, except for our nervous systems and a few odd items. If you want a design capable of doing a great many widely various things, all fairly well, you could do no better than to imitate the human form. Besides that, our entire technology is based on the human form. An automobile, for instance, has its controls so made as to be grasped and manipulated most easily by human hands and feet of a certain size and shape, attached to the body by limbs of a certain length and joints of a certain type. Even such simple objects as chairs and tables or knives and forks are designed to meet the requirements of human measurements and manner of working. It is easier to have robots imitate the human shape than to redesign radically the very philosophy of our tools."

"I see. That makes sense. Now isn't it true, Doctor, that the roboticists of the Outer World manufacture robots that are much more humanoid than our own?"

"I believe that is true."

"Could they manufacture a robot so humanoid that it would pass for human under ordinary conditions?"

Dr. Gerrigel lifted his eyebrows and considered that. "I think they could, Mr. Baley. It would be terribly expensive. I doubt that the return could be profitable."

"Do you suppose," went on Baley, relentlessly, "that they could make a robot that would fool *you* into thinking it was human?"

The roboticist tittered. "Oh, my dear Mr. Baley. I doubt that. Really. There's more to a robot than just his appear——"

Dr. Gerrigel froze in the middle of the word. Slowly, he turned to R. Daneel, and his pink face went very pale.

"Oh, dear me," he whispered. "Oh, dear me."

He reached out one hand and touched R. Daneel's cheek gingerly. R. Daneel did not move away but gazed at the roboticist calmly.

"Dear me," said Dr. Gerrigel, with what was almost a sob in his voice, "you *are* a robot."

"It took you a long time to realize that," said Baley, dryly.

"I wasn't expecting it. I never saw one like this. Outer World manufacture?"

"Yes," said Baley.

"It's obvious now. The way he holds himself. The manner of his speaking. It is not a perfect imitation, Mr. Baley."

"It's pretty good though, isn't it?"

"Oh, it's marvelous. I doubt that anyone could recognize the imposture at sight. I am very grateful to you for having me brought face to face with him. May I examine him?" The roboticist was on his feet, eager.

Baley put out a hand. "Please, Doctor. In a moment. First, the matter of the murder, you know."

"Is that real, then?" Dr. Gerrigel was bitterly disappointed and showed it. "I thought perhaps that was just a device to keep my mind engaged and to see how long I could be fooled by——"

"It is not a device, Dr. Gerrigel. Tell me, now, in constructing a robot as humanoid as this one, with the deliberate purpose of having it pass as human, is it not necessary to make its brain possess properties as close to that of the human brain as possible?"

"Certainly."

"Very well. Could not such a humanoid brain lack the First Law? Perhaps it is left out accidentally. You say the theory is unknown. The very fact that it is unknown means that the constructors might set up a brain without the First Law. They would not know what to avoid."

Dr. Gerrigel was shaking his head vigorously. "No. No. Impossible."

"Are you sure? We can test the Second Law, of course.—Daneel, let me have your blaster."

Baley's eyes never left the robot. His own hand, well to one side, gripped his own blaster tightly.

R. Daneel said calmly, "Here it is, Elijah," and held it out, butt first.

Baley said, "A plain-clothes man must never abandon his blaster, but a robot has no choice but to obey a human."

"Except, Mr. Baley," said Dr. Gerrigel, "when obedience involves breaking the First Law."

"Do you know, Doctor, that Daneel drew his blaster on an unarmed group of men and women and threatened to shoot?"

"But I did not shoot," said R. Daneel.

"Granted, but the threat was unusual in itself, wasn't it, Doctor?"

Dr. Gerrigel bit his lip. "I'd need to know the exact circumstances to judge. It sounds unusual."

"Consider this, then. R. Daneel was on the scene at the time of the murder, and if you omit the possibility of an Earthman having moved across open country, carrying a weapon with him, Daneel and Daneel alone of all the persons on the scene could have hidden the weapon."

"Hidden the weapon?" asked Dr. Gerrigel.

"Let me explain. The blaster that did the killing was not found. The scene of the murder was searched minutely and it was not found. Yet it could not have vanished like smoke. There is only one place it could have been, only one place they would not have thought to look."

"Where, Elijah?" asked R. Daneel.

Baley brought his blaster into view, held its barrel firmly in the robot's direction.

"In your food sac," he said. "In your food sac, Daneel!"

Shift to the Machine

"THAT IS not so," said R. Daneel, quietly.

"Yes? We'll let the Doctor decide. Dr. Gerrigel?"

"Mr. Baley?" The roboticist, whose glance had been alternating wildly between the plain-clothes man and the robot as they spoke, let it come to rest upon the human being.

"I've asked you here for an authoritative analysis of this robot. I can arrange to have you use the laboratories of the City Bureau of Standards. If you need any piece of equipment they don't have, I'll get it for you. What I want is a quick and definite answer and hang the expense and trouble."

Baley rose. His words had emerged calmly enough, but he felt a rising hysteria behind them. At the moment, he felt that if he could only seize Dr. Gerrigel by the throat and choke the necessary statements out of him, he would forgo all science.

He said, "Well, Dr. Gerrigel?"

Dr. Gerrigel tittered nervously and said, "My dear Mr. Baley, I won't need a laboratory."

"Why not?" asked Baley apprehensively. He stood there, muscles tense, feeling himself twitch.

"It's not difficult to test the First Law. I've never had to, you understand, but it's simple enough."

Baley pulled air in through his mouth and let it out slowly. He said, "Would you explain what you mean? Are you saying that you can test him here?"

"Yes, of course. Look, Mr. Baley, I'll give you an analogy. If I were a Doctor of Medicine and had to test a patient's blood sugar,

I'd need a chemical laboratory. If I needed to measure his basal metabolic rate, or test his cortical function, or check his genes to pinpoint a congenital malfunction, I'd need elaborate equipment. On the other hand, I could check whether he were blind by merely passing my hand before his eyes and I could test whether he were dead by merely feeling for his pulse.

"What I'm getting at is that the more important and fundamental the property being tested, the simpler the needed equipment. It's the same in a robot. The First Law is fundamental. It affects everything. If it were absent, the robot could not react properly in two dozen obvious ways."

As he spoke, he took out a flat, black object which expanded into a small book-viewer. He inserted a well-worn spool into the receptacle. He then took out a stop watch and a series of white, plastic slivers that fitted together to form something that looked like a slide rule with three independent movable scales. The notations upon it struck no chord of familiarity to Baley.

Dr. Gerrigel tapped his book-viewer and smiled a little, as though the prospect of a bit of field work cheered him.

He said, "It's my *Handbook of Robotics*. I never go anywhere without it. It's part of my clothes." He giggled self-consciously.

He put the eyepiece of the viewer to his eyes and his finger dealt delicately with the controls. The viewer whirred and stopped, whirred and stopped.

"Built-in index," the roboticist said, proudly, his voice a little muffled because of the way in which the viewer covered his mouth. "I constructed it myself. It saves a great deal of time. But then, that's not the point now, is it? Let's see. Umm, won't you move your chair near me, Daneel."

R. Daneel did so. During the roboticist's preparations, he had watched closely and unemotionally.

Baley shifted his blaster.

What followed confused and disappointed him. Dr. Gerrigel proceeded to ask questions and perform actions that seemed without meaning, punctuated by references to his triple slide rule and occasionally to the viewer.

At one time, he asked, "If I have two cousins, five years apart in age, and the younger is a girl, what sex is the older?"

Daneel answered (inevitably, Baley thought), "It is impossible to say on the information given."

To which Dr. Gerrigel's only response, aside from a glance at his stop watch, was to extend his right hand as far as he could sideways and to say, "Would you touch the tip of my middle finger with the tip of the third finger of your left hand?"

Daneel did that promptly and easily.

In fifteen minutes, not more, Dr. Gerrigel was finished. He used his slide rule for a last silent calculation, then disassembled it with a series of snaps. He put away his stop watch, withdrew the *Handbook* from the viewer, and collapsed the latter.

"Is that all?" said Baley, frowning.

"That's all."

"But it's ridiculous. You've asked nothing that pertains to the First Law."

"Oh, my dear Mr. Baley, when a doctor hits your knee with a little rubber mallet and it jerks, don't you accept the fact that it gives information concerning the presence or absence of some degenerative nerve disease? When he looks closely at your eyes and considers the reaction of your iris to light, are you surprised that he can tell you something concerning your possible addiction to the use of certain alkaloids?"

Baley said, "Well, then? What's your decision?"

"Daneel is fully equipped with the First Law!" The roboticist jerked his head in a sharp affirmative.

"You can't be right," said Baley huskily.

Baley would not have thought that Dr. Gerrigel could stiffen into a rigidity that was greater than his usual position. He did so, however, visibly. The man's eyes grew narrow and hard.

"Are you teaching me my job?"

"I don't mean you're incompetent," said Baley. He put out a large, pleading hand. "But couldn't you be mistaken? You've said yourself nobody knows anything about the theory of non-Asenion robots. A blind man could read by using Braille or a sound-scriber. Suppose you didn't know that Braille or sound-scribing existed. Couldn't you, in all honesty, say that a man had eyes because he knew the contents of a certain book-film, and be mistaken?"

"Yes," the roboticist grew genial again, "I see your point. But still a blind man could not read by use of his eyes and it is that which I was testing, if I may continue the analogy. Take my word for it, regardless of what a non-Asenion robot could or could not do, it is certain that R. Daneel is equipped with First Law."

"Couldn't he have falsified his answers?" Baley was floundering, and knew it.

"Of course not. That is the difference between a robot and a man. A human brain, or any mammalian brain, cannot be completely analyzed by any mathematical discipline now known. No response can therefore be counted upon as a certainty. The robot brain is completely analyzable, or it could not be constructed. We know exactly what the responses to given stimuli must be. No robot can truly falsify answers. The thing you call falsification just doesn't exist in the robot's mental horizon."

"Then let's get down to cases. R. Daneel did point a blaster at a crowd of human beings. I saw that. I was there. Granted that he didn't shoot, wouldn't the First Law still have forced him into a kind of neurosis? It didn't, you know. He was perfectly normal afterward."

The roboticist put a hesitant hand to his chin. "That *is* anomalous."

"Not at all," said R. Daneel, suddenly. "Partner Elijah, would you look at the blaster that you took from me?"

Baley looked down upon the blaster he held cradled in his left hand.

"Break open the charge chamber," urged R. Daneel. "Inspect it."

Baley weighed his chances, then slowly put his own blaster on the table beside him. With a quick movement, he opened the robot's blaster.

"It's empty," he said, blankly.

"There is no charge in it," agreed R. Daneel. "If you will look closer, you will see that there has never been a charge in it. The blaster has no ignition bud and cannot be used."

Baley said, "You held an uncharged blaster on the crowd?"

"I had to have a blaster or fail in my role as plain-clothes man," said R. Daneel. "Yet to carry a charged and usable blaster might have made it possible for me to hurt a human being by accident, a thing which is, of course, unthinkable. I would have explained this at the time, but you were angry and would not listen."

Baley stared bleakly at the useless blaster in his hand and said in a low voice, "I think that's all, Dr. Gerrigel. Thank you for helping out."

Baley sent out for lunch, but when it came (yeast-nut cake and a rather extravagant slice of fried chicken on cracker) he could only stare at it.

Round and round went the currents of his mind. The lines on his long face were etched in deep gloom.

He was living in an unreal world, a cruel, topsy-turvy world.

How had it happened? The immediate past stretched behind him like a misty improbable dream dating back to the moment he had stepped into Julius Enderby's office and found himself suddenly immersed in a nightmare of murder and robotics.

Jehoshaphat! It had begun only fifty hours before.

Persistently, he had sought the solution in Spacetown. Twice he had accused R. Daneel, once as a human being in disguise, and once as an admitted and actual robot, each time as a murderer. Twice the accusation had been bent back and broken.

He was being driven back. Against his will he was forced to turn his thoughts into the City, and since last night he dared not. Certain questions battered at his conscious mind, but he would not listen; he felt he could not. If he heard them, he couldn't help but answer them and, oh God, he didn't want to face the answers.

"Lije! Lije!" A hand shook Baley's shoulder roughly.

Baley stirred and said, "What's up, Phil?"

Philip Norris, Plain-clothes man C-5, sat down, put his hands on his knees, and leaned forward, peering at Baley's face. "What happened to you? Been living on knockout drops lately? You were sitting there with your eyes open and, near as I could make out, you were dead."

He rubbed his thinning, pale blond hair, and his close-set eyes appraised Baley's cooling lunch greedily. "Chicken!" he said. "It's getting so you can't get it without a doctor's prescription."

"Take some," said Baley, listlessly.

Decorum won out and Norris said, "Oh, well, I'm going out to eat in a minute. You keep it.—Say, what's doing with the Commish?"

"What?"

Norris attempted a casual attitude, but his hands were restless. He said, "Go on. You know what I mean. You've been living with him ever since he got back. What's up? A promotion in the works?"

Baley frowned and felt reality return somewhat at the touch of office politics. Norris had approximately his own seniority and he was bound to watch most assiduously for any sign of official preference in Baley's direction.

Baley said, "No promotion. Believe me. It's nothing. Nothing. And if it's the Commissioner you're wanting, I wish I could give him to you. Jehoshaphat! Take him!"

Norris said, "Don't get me wrong. I don't care if you get promoted. I just mean that if you've got any pull with the Commish, how about using it for the kid?"

"What kid?"

There was no need of any answer to that. Vincent Barrett, the youngster who had been moved out of his job to make room for R. Sammy, was shuffling up from an unnoticed corner of the room. A skull cap turned restlessly in his hands and the skin over his high cheekbones moved as he tried to smile.

"Hello, Mr. Baley."

"Oh, hello, Vince. How're you doing?"

"Not so good, Mr. Baley."

He was looking about hungrily. Baley thought: He looks lost, half dead—declassified.

Then, savagely, his lips almost moving with the force of his emotion, he thought: But what does he want from me?

He said, "I'm sorry, kid." What else was there to say?

"I keep thinking—maybe something has turned up."

Norris moved in close and spoke into Baley's ear. "Someone's got to stop this sort of thing. They're going to move out Chen-low now."

"What?"

"Haven't you heard?"

"No, I haven't. Damn it, he's a C-3. He's got ten years behind him."

"I grant that. But a machine with legs can do his work. Who's next?"

Young Vince Barrett was oblivious to the whispers. He said out of the depths of his own thinking, "Mr. Baley?"

"Yes, Vince?"

"You know what they say? They say Lyrane Millane, the sub-etherics dancer, is really a robot."

"That's silly."

"Is it? They say they can make robots look just like humans; with a special plastic skin, sort of."

Baley thought guiltily of R. Daneel and found no words. He shook his head.

The boy said, "Do you suppose anyone will mind if I just walk around. It makes me feel better to see the old place."

"Go ahead, kid."

The youngster wandered off. Baley and Norris watched him go. Norris said, "It looks as though the Medievalists are right."

"You mean back to the soil? Is that it, Phil?"

"No. I mean about the robots. Back to the soil. Huh! Old Earth has an unlimited future. We don't need robots, that's all."

Baley muttered, "Eight billion people and the uranium running out! What's unlimited about it?"

"What if the uranium does run out. We'll import it. Or we'll discover other nuclear processes. There's no way you can stop mankind, Lije. You've got to be optimistic about it and have faith in the old human brain. Our greatest resource is ingenuity and we'll never run out of that, Lije."

He was fairly started now. He went on, "For one thing, we can use sunpower and that's good for billions of years. We can build space stations inside Mercury's orbit to act as energy accumulators. We'll transmit energy to Earth by direct beam."

This project was not new to Baley. The speculative fringe of science had been playing with the notion for a hundred and fifty years at least. What was holding it up was the impossibility so far of projecting a beam tight enough to reach fifty million miles without dispersal to uselessness. Baley said as much.

Norris said, "When it's necessary, it'll be done. Why worry?"

Baley had the picture of an Earth of unlimited energy. Population could continue to increase. The yeast farms could expand, hydroponic culture intensify. Energy was the only thing indispensable. The raw minerals could be brought in from the uninhabited rocks of the System. If ever water became a bottleneck, more could be brought in from the moons of Jupiter. Hell, the oceans could be frozen and dragged out into Space where they could circle Earth as moonlets of ice. There they would be, always available for use, while the ocean bottoms would represent more land for exploitation, more room to live. Even carbon and oxygen could be maintained and increased on Earth through utilization of the methane atmosphere of Titan and the frozen oxygen of Umbriel.

Earth's population could reach a trillion or two. Why not? There was a time when the current population of eight billion would have been viewed as impossible. There was a time when a population of a single billion would have been unthinkable. There had always been prophets of Malthusian doom in every generation since Medieval times and they had always been proven wrong.

But what would Fastolfe say? A world of a trillion? Surely! But they would be dependent on imported air and water and upon an energy supply from complicated storehouses fifty million miles away. How incredibly unstable that would be. Earth would be, and remain, a feather's weight away from complete catastrophe at the slightest failure of any part of the System-wide mechanism.

Baley said, "I think it would be easier to ship off some of the surplus population, myself." It was more an answer to the picture he had himself conjured up than to anything Norris had said.

"Who'd have us?" said Norris with a bitter lightness.

"Any uninhabited planet."

Norris rose, patted Baley on the shoulder. "Lije, you eat your chicken, and recover. You *must* be living on knockout pills." He left, chuckling.

Baley watched him leave with a humorless twist to his mouth. Norris would spread the news and it would be weeks before the humor boys of the office (every office has them) would lay off. But at least it got him off the subject of young Vince, of robots, of declassification.

He sighed as he put a fork into the now cold and somewhat stringy chicken.

Baley finished the last of the yeast-nut and it was only then that R. Daneel left his own desk (assigned him that morning) and approached.

Baley eyed him uncomfortably. "Well?"

R. Daneel said, "The Commissioner is not in his office and it is not known when he'll be back. I've told R. Sammy we will use it and that he is to allow no one but the Commissioner to enter."

"What are we going to use it for?"

"Greater privacy. Surely you agree that we must plan our next move. After all, you do not intend to abandon the investigation, do you?"

That was precisely what Baley most longed to do, but obviously, he could not say so. He rose and led the way to Enderby's office.

Once in the office, Baley said, "All right, Daneel. What is it?"

The robot said, "Partner Elijah, since last night, you are not yourself. There is a definite alteration in your mental aura."

A horrible thought sprang full-grown into Baley's mind. He cried, "Are you telepathic?"

It was not a possibility he would have considered at a less disturbed moment.

"No. Of course not," said R. Daneel.

Baley's panic ebbed. He said, "Then what the devil do you mean by talking about my mental aura?"

"It is merely an expression I use to describe a sensation that you do not share with me."

"What sensation?"

"It is difficult to explain, Elijah. You will recall that I was originally designed to study human psychology for our people back in Spacetown."

"Yes, I know. You were adjusted to detective work by the simple installation of a justice-desire circuit." Baley did not try to keep the sarcasm out of his voice.

"Exactly, Elijah. But my original design remains essentially unaltered. I was constructed for the purpose of cerebroanalysis."

"For analyzing brain waves?"

"Why, yes. It can be done by field-measurements without the necessity of direct electrode contact, if the proper receiver exists. My mind is such a receiver. Is that principle not applied on Earth?"

Baley didn't know. He ignored the question and said, cautiously, "If you measure the brain waves, what do you get out of it?"

"Not thoughts, Elijah. I get a glimpse of emotion and most of all, I can analyze temperament, the underlying drives and attitudes of a man. For instance, it was I who was able to ascertain that Commissioner Enderby was incapable of killing a man under the circumstances prevailing at the time of the murder."

"And they eliminated him as a suspect on your say-so."

"Yes. It was safe enough to do so. I am a very delicate machine in that respect."

Again a thought struck Baley. "Wait! Commissioner Enderby didn't know he was being cerebroanalyzed, did he?"

"There was no necessity of hurting his feelings."

"I mean you just stood there and looked at him. No machinery. No electrodes. No needles and graphs."

"Certainly not. I am a self-contained unit."

Baley bit his lower lip in anger and chagrin. It had been the one remaining inconsistency, the one loophole through which a forlorn stab might yet be made in an attempt to pin the crime on Spacetown.

R. Daneel had stated that the Commissioner had been cerebroanalyzed and one hour later the Commissioner himself had, with apparent candor, denied any knowledge of the term. Certainly no man could have undergone the shattering experience of electroencephalographic measurements by electrode and graph under the suspicion of murder without an unmistakable impression of what cerebroanalysis must be.

But now that discrepancy had evaporated. The Commissioner had been cerebroanalyzed and had never known it. R. Daneel told the truth; so had the Commissioner.

"Well," said Baley, sharply, "what does cerebroanalysis tell you about me?"

"You are disturbed."

"That's a great discovery, isn't it? Of course, I'm disturbed."

"Specifically, though, your disturbance is due to a clash between motivations within you. On the one hand your devotion to the principles of your profession urges you to look deeply into this conspiracy of Earthmen who lay siege to us last night. Another motivation, equally strong, forces you in the opposite direction. This much is clearly written in the electric field of your cerebral cells."

"My cerebral cells, *nuts*," said Baley, feverishly. "Look, I'll tell you why there's no point in investigating your so-called conspiracy. It has nothing to do with the murder. I thought it might have. I'll admit that. Yesterday in the kitchen, I thought we were in danger. But what happened? They followed us out, were quickly lost on the strips, and that was that. That was not the action of well-organized and desperate men.

"My own son found out where we were staying easily enough. He called the Department. He didn't even have to identify himself. Our precious conspirators could have done the same if they had really wanted to hurt us."

"Didn't they?"

"Obviously not. If they had wanted riots, they could have started one at the shoe counter, and yet they backed out tamely enough before one man and a blaster. One *robot,* and a blaster which they must have known you would be unable to fire once they recognized what you were. They're Medievalists. They're harmless crackpots. You wouldn't know that, but I should have. And I would have, if it weren't for the fact that this whole business has me thinking in—in foolish melodramatic terms.

"I tell you I know the type of people that become Medievalists. They're soft, dreamy people who find life too hard for them here and get lost in an ideal world of the past that never really existed. If you could cerebroanalyze a movement as you do an individual, you would find they are no more capable of murder than Julius Enderby himself."

R. Daneel said slowly, "I cannot accept your statements at face value."

"What do you mean?"

"Your conversion to this view is too sudden. There are certain discrepancies, too. You arranged the appointment with Dr. Gerrigel hours before the evening meal. You did not know of my food sac then and could not have suspected me as the murderer. Why *did* you call him, then?"

"I suspected you even then."

"And last night you spoke as you slept."

Baley's eyes widened. "What did I say?"

"Merely the one word 'Jessie' several times repeated. I believe you were referring to your wife."

Baley let his tight muscles loosen. He said, shakily, "I had a nightmare. Do you know what that is?"

"I do not know by personal experience, of course. The dictionary definition has it that it is a bad dream."

"And do you know what a dream is?"

"Again, the dictionary definition only. It is an illusion of reality experienced during the temporary suspension of conscious thought which you call sleep."

"All right. I'll buy that. An illusion. Sometimes the illusions can seem damned real. Well, I dreamed my wife was in danger. It's the sort of dream people often have. I called her name. That happens under such circumstances, too. You can take my word for it."

"I am only too glad to do so. But it brings up a thought. How did Jessie find out I was a robot?"

Baley's forehead went moist again. "We're not going into that again, are we? The rumor——"

"I am sorry to interrupt, partner Elijah, but there is no rumor. If there were, the City would be alive with unrest today. I have checked reports coming into the Department and this is not so. There simply is no rumor. Therefore, how did your wife find out?"

"Jehoshaphat! What are you trying to say? Do you think my wife is one of the members of—of . . ."

"Yes, Elijah."

Baley gripped his hands together tightly. "Well, she isn't, and we won't discuss that point any further."

"This is not like you, Elijah. In the course of duty, you accused me of murder twice."

"And is this your way of getting even?"

"I am not sure I understand what you mean by the phrase. Certainly, I approve your readiness to suspect me. You had your reasons. They were wrong, but they might easily have been right. Equally strong evidence points to your wife."

"As a murderess? Why, damn you, Jessie wouldn't hurt her worst enemy. She couldn't set foot outside the City. She couldn't . . . Why, if you were flesh and blood I'd——"

"I merely say that she is a member of the conspiracy. I say that she should be questioned."

"Not on your life. Not on whatever it is you call your life. Now, listen to me. The Medievalists aren't after our blood. It's not the way they do things. But they are trying to get you out of the City. That much is obvious. And they're trying to do it by a kind of psychological attack. They're trying to make life unpleasant for you and for me, since I'm with you. They could easily have found out Jessie was my wife, and it was an obvious move for them to let the news leak to her. She's like any other human being. She doesn't *like* robots. She wouldn't want me to associate with one, especially if she thought it involved danger, and surely they would imply that. I tell you it worked. She begged all night to have me abandon the case or to get you out of the City somehow."

"Presumably," said R. Daneel, "you have a very strong urge to protect your wife against questioning. It seems obvious to me that you are constructing this line of argument without really believing it."

"What the hell do you think you are?" ground out Baley. "You're not a detective. You're a cerebroanalysis machine like the electro-encephalographs we have in this building. You've got arms, legs, a head, and can talk, but you're not one inch more than that machine. Putting a lousy circuit into you doesn't make you a detective, so what do you know? You keep your mouth shut, and let me do the figuring out."

The robot said quietly, "I think it would be better if you lowered your voice, Elijah. Granted that I am not a detective in the sense that you are, I would still like to bring one small item to your attention."

"I'm not interested in listening."

"Please do. If I am wrong, you will tell me so, and it will do no harm. It is only this. Last night you left our room to call Jessie by corridor phone. I suggested that your son go in your place. You told me it was not the custom among Earthmen for a father to send his son into danger. Is it then the custom for a mother to do so?"

"No, of cour——" began Baley, and stopped.

"You see my point," said R. Daneel. "Ordinarily, if Jessie feared for your safety and wished to warn you, she would risk her own life, *not* send her son. The fact that she did send Bentley could only mean that she felt that he would be safe while she herself would not. If the conspiracy consisted of people unknown to Jessie, that would not be the case, or at least she would have no reason to think it to be the case. On the other hand, if she were a member of the conspiracy, she would know, she would *know*, Elijah, that she would be watched for and recognized, whereas Bentley might get through unnoticed."

"Wait now," said Baley, sick at heart, "that's feather-fine reasoning, but——"

There was no need to wait. The signal on the Commissioner's desk was flickering madly. R. Daneel waited for Baley to answer, but the latter could only stare at it helplessly. The robot closed contact.

"What is it?"

R. Sammy's slurring voice said, "There is a lady here who wishes to see Lije. I told her he was busy, but she will not go away. She says her name is Jessie."

"Let her in," said R. Daneel calmly, and his brown eyes rose unemotionally to meet the panicky glare of Baley's.

14

Power of a Name

BALEY REMAINED standing in a tetany of shock, as Jessie ran to him, seizing his shoulders, huddling close.

His pale lips formed the word, "Bentley?"

She looked at him and shook her head, her brown hair flying with the force of her motion. "He's all right."

"Well, then . . ."

Jessie said through a sudden torrent of sobs, in a low voice that could scarcely be made out, "I can't go on, Lije. I can't. I can't sleep or eat. I've got to tell you."

"Don't say anything," Baley said in anguish. "For God's sake, Jessie, not now."

"I must. I've done a terrible thing. Such a terrible thing. Oh, Lije . . ." She lapsed into incoherence.

Baley said, hopelessly, "We're not alone, Jessie."

She looked up and stared at R. Daneel with no signs of recognition. The tears in which her eyes were swimming might easily be refracting the robot into a featureless blur.

R. Daneel said in a low murmur, "Good afternoon, Jessie."

She gasped. "Is it the—the robot?"

She dashed the back of her hand across her eyes and stepped out of Baley's encircling right arm. She breathed deeply and, for a moment, a tremulous smile wavered on her lips. "It *is* you, isn't it?"

"Yes, Jessie."

"You don't mind being called a robot?"

"No, Jessie. It is what I am."

"And I don't mind being called a fool and an idiot and a—a subversive agent, because it's what *I* am."

"Jessie!" groaned Baley.

"It's no use, Lije," she said. "He might as well know if he's your partner. I can't live with it any more. I've had such a time since yesterday. I don't care if I go to jail. I don't care if they send me down to the lowest levels and make me live on raw yeast and water. I don't care if . . . You won't let them, will you, Lije? Don't let them do anything to me. I'm fuh—frightened."

Baley patted her shoulder and let her cry.

He said to R. Daneel, "She isn't well. We can't keep her here. What time is it?"

R. Daneel said without any visible signs of consulting a timepiece, "Fourteen-forty-five."

"The Commissioner could be back any minute. Look, commandeer a squad car and we can talk about this in the motorway."

Jessie's head jerked upright. "The motorway? Oh, no, Lije."

He said, in as soothing a tone as he could manage, "Now, Jessie, don't be superstitious. You can't go on the expressway the way you are. Be a good girl and calm down or we won't even be able to go through the common room. I'll get you some water."

She wiped her face with a damp handkerchief and said drearily, "Oh, look at my makeup."

"Don't worry about your makeup," said Baley. "Daneel, what about the squad car?"

"It's waiting for us now, partner Elijah."

"Come on, Jessie."

"Wait. Wait just a minute, Lije. I've got to do something to my face."

"It doesn't matter now."

But she twisted away. "Please. I can't go through the common room like this. I won't take a second."

The man and the robot waited, the man with little jerky clenchings of his fists, the robot impassively.

Jessie rummaged through her purse for the necessary equipment. (If there were one thing, Baley had once said solemnly, that had resisted mechanical improvement since Medieval times, it was a woman's purse. Even the substitution of magnetic clotures for metal clasps had not proven successful.) Jessie pulled out a small mirror and the silver-chased cosmetokit that Baley had bought her on the occasion of three birthdays before.

The cosmetokit had several orifices and she used each in turn. All but the last spray were invisible. She used them with that fineness of touch and delicacy of control that seems to be the birthright of women even at times of the greatest stress.

The base went on first in a smooth even layer that removed all shininess and roughness from the skin and left it with the faintly golden glow which long experience had taught Jessie was just the shade most suited to the natural coloring of her hair and eyes. Then the touch of tan along the forehead and chin, a gentle brush of rouge on either cheek, tracing back to the angle of the jaw; and a delicate drift of blue on the upper eyelids and along the earlobes. Finally there was the application of the smooth carmine to the lips. That involved the one visible spray, a faintly pink mist that glistened liquidly in air, but dried and deepened richly on contact with the lips.

"There," said Jessie, with several swift pats at her hair and a look of deep dissatisfaction. "I suppose that will do."

The process had taken more than the promised second, but less than fifteen seconds. Nevertheless, it had seemed interminable to Baley.

"Come," he said.

She barely had time to return the cosmetokit to the purse before he had pushed her through the door.

The eerie silence of the motorway lay thick on either side.

Baley said, "All right, Jessie."

The impassivity that had covered Jessie's face since they first left the Commissioner's office showed signs of cracking. She looked at her husband and at Daneel with a helpless silence.

Baley said, "Get it over with, Jessie. Please. Have you committed a crime? An actual crime?"

"A crime?" She shook her head uncertainly.

"Now hold on to yourself. No hysterics. Just say yes or no, Jessie. Have you—" he hesitated a trifle, "killed anyone?"

The look on Jessie's face was promptly transmuted to indignation. "Why, Lije Baley!"

"Yes or no, Jessie."

"No, of course not."

The hard knot in Baley's stomach softened perceptibly. "Have you stolen anything? Falsified ration data? Assaulted anyone? Destroyed property? Speak up, Jessie."

"I haven't done anything—anything specific. I didn't mean anything like that." She looked over her shoulder. "Lije, do we have to stay down here?"

"Right here until this is over. Now, start at the beginning. What did you come to tell us?" Over Jessie's bowed head, Baley's eyes met R. Daneel's.

Jessie spoke in a soft voice that gained in strength and articulateness as she went on.

"It's these people, these Medievalists; *you* know, Lije. They're always around, always talking. Even in the old days when I was an assistant dietitian, it was like that. Remember Elizabeth Thornbowe? She was a Medievalist. She was always talking about how all our troubles came from the City and how things were better before the Cities started.

"I used to ask her how she was so sure that was so, especially after you and I met, Lije (remember the talks we used to have), and then she would quote from those small book-reels that are always floating around. You know, like *Shame of the Cities* that the fellow wrote. I don't remember his name."

Baley said, absently, "Ogrinsky."

"Yes, only most of them were lots worse. Then, when I married you, she was really sarcastic. She said, 'I suppose you're going to be a real City woman now that you've married a policeman.' After that, she didn't talk to me much and then I quit the job and that was that. Lots of things she used to say were just to shock me, I think, or to make herself look mysterious and glamorous. She was an old maid, you know; never got married till the day she died. Lots of those Medievalists don't fit in, one way or another. Remember, you once said, Lije, that people sometimes mistake their own shortcomings for those of society and want to fix the Cities because they don't know how to fix themselves."

Baley remembered, and his words now sounded flip and superficial in his own ears. He said, gently, "Keep to the point, Jessie."

She went on, "Anyway, Lizzy was always talking about how there'd come a day and people had to get together. She said it was all the fault of the Spacers because they wanted to keep Earth weak and decadent. That was one of her favorite words, 'decadent.' She'd look at the menus I'd prepare for the next week and sniff and say, 'Decadent, decadent.' Jane Myers used to imitate her in the cook room and we'd die laughing. She said, Elizabeth did, that someday we were going to break up the Cities and go back to the soil and have an accounting with the Spacers who were trying to tie us forever to the Cities by forcing robots on us. Only she never called them robots. She used to say 'soulless monster-machines,' if you'll excuse the expression, Daneel."

The robot said, "I am not aware of the significance of the adjective you used, Jessie, but in any case, the expression is excused. Please go on."

Baley stirred restlessly. It was that way with Jessie. No emergency, no crisis could make her tell a story in any way but her own circuitous one.

She said, "Elizabeth always tried to talk as though there were lots of people in it with her. She would say, 'At the last meeting,' and then stop and look at me sort of half proud and half scared as though she wanted me to ask about it so she could look important, and yet scared I might get her in trouble. Of course, I never asked her. I wouldn't give her the satisfaction.

"Anyway, after I married you, Lije, it was all over, until . . ."

She stopped.

"Go on, Jessie," said Baley.

"You remember, Lije, that argument we had? About Jezebel, I mean?"

"What about it?" It took a second or two for Baley to remember that it was Jessie's own name, and not a reference to another woman.

He turned to R. Daneel in an automatically defensive explanation. "Jessie's full name is Jezebel. She is not fond of it and doesn't use it."

R. Daneel nodded gravely and Baley thought: Jehoshaphat, why waste worry on *him*?

"It bothered me a lot, Lije," Jessie said. "It really did. I guess it was silly, but I kept thinking and thinking about what you said. I mean about your saying that Jezebel was only a conservative who fought for the ways of her ancestors against the strange ways the newcomers had brought. After all, *I* was Jezebel and I always . . ."

She groped for a word and Baley supplied it. "Identified yourself?"

"Yes." But she shook her head almost immediately and looked away. "Not really, of course. Not literally. The way I thought she was, you know. I wasn't like that."

"I know that, Jessie. Don't be foolish."

"But still I thought of her a lot and, somehow, I got to thinking, it's just the same now as it was then. I mean, we Earth people had our old ways and here were the Spacers coming in with a lot of new ways and trying to encourage the new ways we had stumbled into ourselves and maybe the Medievalists were right. Maybe we *should* go back to our old, good ways. So I went back and found Elizabeth."

"Yes. Go on."

"She said she didn't know what I was talking about and besides I was a cop's wife. I said that had nothing to do with it and finally she said, well, she'd speak to somebody, and then about a month later she came to me and said it was all right and I joined and I've been at meetings ever since."

Baley looked at her sadly. "And you never told me?"

Jessie's voice trembled. "I'm sorry, Lije."

"Well, that won't help. Being sorry, I mean. I want to know about the meetings. In the first place, where were they held?"

A sense of detachment was creeping over him, a numbing of emotions. What he had tried not to believe was so, was openly so, was unmistakably so. In a sense, it was a relief to have the uncertainty over.

She said, "Down here."

"Down here? You mean on this spot? What *do* you mean?"

"Here in the motorway. That's why I didn't want to come down here. It was a wonderful place to meet, though. We'd get together——"

"How many?"

"I'm not sure. About sixty or seventy. It was just a sort of local branch. There'd be folding chairs and some refreshments and someone would make a speech, mostly about how wonderful life was in the old days and how someday we'd do away with the monsters, the robots, that is, and the Spacers, too. The speeches were sort of dull really, because they were all the same. We just endured them. Mostly, it was the fun of getting together and feeling important.

We would pledge ourselves to oaths and there'd be secret ways we could greet each other on the outside."

"Weren't you ever interrupted? No squad cars or fire engines passed?"

"No. Never."

R. Daneel interrupted, "Is that unusual, Elijah?"

"Maybe not," Baley answered thoughtfully. "There are some side-passages that are practically never used. It's quite a trick, knowing which they are, though. Is that all you did at the meetings, Jessie? Make speeches and play at conspiracy?"

"It's about all. And sing songs, sometimes. And of course, refreshments. Not much. Sandwiches, usually, and juice."

"In that case," he said, almost brutally, "what's bothering you now?"

Jessie winced. "You're angry."

"Please," said Baley, with iron patience, "answer my question. If it were all as harmless as that, why have you been in such a panic for the last day and a half?"

"I thought they would hurt you, Lije. For heaven's sake, why do you act as though you don't understand? I've explained it to you."

"No, you haven't. Not yet. You've told me about a harmless little secret kaffee-klatsch you belonged to. Did they ever hold open demonstrations? Did they ever destroy robots? Start riots? Kill people?"

"*Never!* Lije, I wouldn't do any of those things. I wouldn't stay a member if they tried it."

"Well, then, why do you say you've done a terrible thing? Why do you expect to be sent to jail?"

"Well . . . Well, they used to talk about someday when they'd put pressure on the government. We were supposed to get organized and then afterward there would be huge strikes and work stoppages. We could force the government to ban all robots and make the Spacers go back where they came from. I thought it was just talk and then, this thing started; about you and Daneel, I mean. Then they said, 'Now we'll see action,' and 'We're going to make an example of them and put a stop to the robot invasion right now.' Right there in Personal they said it, not knowing it was you they were talking about. But I knew. Right away."

Her voice broke.

Baley softened. "Come on, Jessie. It was all nothing. It was just talk. You can see for yourself that nothing has happened."

"I was so—so suh—scared. And I thought: *I'm* part of it. If there were going to be killing and destruction, *you* might be killed and Bentley and somehow it would be all muh—my fault for taking part in it, and I ought to be sent to jail."

Baley let her sob herself out. He put his arm about her shoulder and stared tight-lipped at R. Daneel, who gazed calmly back.

He said, "Now, I want you to think, Jessie. Who was the head of your group?"

She was quieter now, patting the corners of her eyes with a handkerchief. "A man called Joseph Klemin was the leader, but he wasn't really anybody. He wasn't more than five feet four inches tall and I think he was terribly henpecked at home. I don't think there's any harm in him. You aren't going to arrest him, are you, Lije? On my say-so?" She looked guiltily troubled.

"I'm not arresting anyone just yet. How did Klemin get *his* instructions?"

"I don't know."

"Did any strangers come to meeting? You know what I mean: big shots from Central Headquarters?"

"Sometimes people would come to make speeches. That wasn't very often, maybe twice a year or so."

"Can you name them?"

"No. They were always just introduced as 'one of us' or 'a friend from Jackson Heights' or wherever."

"I see. Daneel!"

"Yes, Elijah," said R. Daneel.

"Describe the men you think you've tabbed. We'll see if Jessie can recognize them."

R. Daneel went through the list with clinical exactness. Jessie listened with an expression of dismay as the categories of physical measurements lengthened and shook her head with increasing firmness.

"It's no use. It's no use," she cried. "How can I remember? I can't remember how any of them looked. I can't——"

She stopped, and seemed to consider. Then she said, "Did you say one of them was a yeast farmer?"

"Francis Clousarr," said R. Daneel, "is an employee at New York Yeast."

"Well, you know, once a man was making a speech and I happened to be sitting in the first row and I kept getting a whiff, just a whiff, really, of raw yeast smell. You know what I mean. The only reason that I remember is that I had an upset stomach that day and the smell kept making me sick. I had to stand up and move to the back and of course I couldn't explain what was wrong. It was so embarrassing. Maybe that's the man you're speaking of. After all, when you work with yeast all the time, the odor gets to stick to your clothes." She wrinkled her nose.

"You don't remember what he looked like?" said Baley.

"No," she replied, with decision.

"All right, then. Look, Jessie, I'm going to take you to your mother's. Bentley will stay with you, and none of you will leave the Section. Ben can stay away from school and I'll arrange to have meals sent in and the corridors around the apartment watched by the police."

"What about you?" quavered Jessie.

"I'll be in no danger."

"But how long?"

"I don't know. Maybe just a day or two." The words sounded hollow even to himself.

They were back in the motorway, Baley and R. Daneel, alone now. Baley's expression was dark with thought.

"It would seem to me," he said, "that we are faced with an organization built up on two levels. First, a ground level with no specific program, designed only to supply mass support for an eventual coup. Secondly, a much smaller elite dedicated to a well-planned program of action. It is this elite we must find. The comic-opera groups that Jessie spoke of can be ignored."

"All this," said R. Daneel, "follows, perhaps, if we can take Jessie's story at face value."

"I think," Baley said stiffly, "that Jessie's story can be accepted as completely true."

"So it would seem," said R. Daneel. "There is nothing about her cerebro-impulses that would indicate a pathological addiction to lying."

Baley turned an offended look upon the robot. "I should say not. And there will be no necessity to mention her name in our reports. Do you understand that?"

"If you wish it so, partner Elijah," said R. Daneel calmly, "but our report will then be neither complete nor accurate."

Baley said, "Well, maybe so, but no real harm will be done. She has come to us with whatever information she had and to mention her name will only put her in the police records. I do not want that to happen."

"In that case, certainly not, provided we are certain that nothing more remains to be found out."

"Nothing remains as far as she's concerned. My guarantee."

"Could you then explain why the word, Jezebel, the mere sound of a name, should lead her to abandon previous convictions and assume a new set? The motivation seems obscure."

They were traveling slowly through the curving, empty tunnel.

Baley said, "It is hard to explain. Jezebel is a rare name. It belonged once to a woman of very bad reputation. My wife treasured that fact. It gave her a vicarious feeling of wickedness and compensated for a life that was uniformly proper."

"Why should a law-abiding woman wish to feel wicked?"

Baley almost smiled. "Women are women, Daneel. Anyway, I did a very foolish thing. In a moment of irritation, I insisted that the historic Jezebel was not particularly wicked and was, if anything, a good wife. I've regretted that ever since.

"It turned out," he went on, "that I had made Jessie bitterly unhappy. I had spoiled something for her that couldn't be replaced. I suppose what followed was her way of revenge. I imagine she wished to punish me by engaging in activity of which she knew I wouldn't approve. I don't say the wish was a conscious one."

"Can a wish be anything but conscious? Is that not a contradiction in terms?"

Baley stared at R. Daneel and despaired at attempting to explain the unconscious mind. He said, instead, "Besides that, the Bible has a great influence on human thought and emotion."

"What is the Bible?"

For a moment Baley was surprised, and then was surprised at himself for having felt surprised. The Spacers, he knew, lived under a thoroughly mechanistic personal philosophy, and R. Daneel could know only what the Spacers knew; no more.

He said, curtly, "It is the sacred book of about half of Earth's population."

"I do not grasp the meaning here of the adjective."

"I mean that it is highly regarded. Various portions of it, when properly interpreted, contain a code of behavior which many men consider best suited to the ultimate happiness of mankind."

R. Daneel seemed to consider that. "Is this code incorporated into your laws?"

"I'm afraid not. The code doesn't lend itself to legal enforcement. It must be obeyed spontaneously by each individual out of a longing to do so. It is in a sense higher than any law can be."

"Higher than law? Is that not a contradiction in terms?"

Baley smiled wryly. "Shall I quote a portion of the Bible for you? Would you be curious to hear it?"

"Please do."

Baley let the car slow to a halt and for a few moments sat with his eyes closed, remembering. He would have liked to use the sonorous Middle English of the Medieval Bible, but to R. Daneel, Middle English would be gibberish.

He began, speaking almost casually in the words of the Modern Revision, as though he were telling a story of contemporary life, instead of dredging a tale out of Man's dimmest past:

" 'Jesus went to the mount of Olives, and at dawn returned to the temple. All the people came to him, and he sat down and preached to them. And the scribes and Pharisees brought to him a woman caught in adultery, and when they had placed her before him, they said to him, "Master, this woman was caught in adultery, in the very act. Now Moses, in the law, commanded us to stone such offenders. What do you say?"

" 'They said this, hoping to trap him, that they might have grounds for accusations against him. But Jesus stooped down, and with his finger wrote on the ground, as though he had not heard them. But when they continued asking him, he stood up and said to them, "He that is without sin among you, let him first cast a stone at her."

" 'And again he stooped down and wrote on the ground. And those that heard this, being convicted by their own conscience, went away one by one, beginning with the oldest, down to the last: and

Jesus was left alone, with the woman standing before him. When Jesus stood up and saw no one but the woman, he said to her, "Woman, where are your accusers? Has no one condemned you?"

" 'She said, "No one, Lord." '

" 'And Jesus said to her, "Nor do I condemn you. Go, and sin no more." ' "

R. Daneel listened attentively. He said, "What is adultery?"

"That doesn't matter. It was a crime and at the time, the accepted punishment was stoning; that is, stones were thrown at the guilty one until she was killed."

"And the woman was guilty?"

"She was."

"Then why was she not stoned?"

"None of the accusers felt he could after Jesus's statement. The story is meant to show that there is something even higher than the justice which you have been filled with. There is a human impulse known as mercy; a human act known as forgiveness."

"I am not acquainted with those words, partner Elijah."

"I know," muttered Baley. "I know."

He started the squad car with a jerk and let it tear forward savagely. He was pressed back against the cushions of the seat.

"Where are we going?" asked R. Daneel.

"To Yeast-town," said Baley, "to get the truth out of Francis Clousarr, conspirator."

"You have a method for doing this, Elijah?"

"Not I, exactly. But you have, Daneel. A simple one."

They sped onward.

15

Arrest of a Conspirator

BALEY COULD sense the vague aroma of Yeast-town growing stronger, more pervasive. He did not find it as unpleasant as some did; Jessie, for instance. He even liked it, rather. It had pleasant connotations.

Every time he smelled raw yeast, the alchemy of sense perception threw him more than three decades into the past. He was a ten-year-old again, visiting his Uncle Boris, who was a yeast farmer. Uncle Boris always had a little supply of yeast delectables: small cookies, chocolaty things filled with sweet liquid, hard confections in the shape of cats and dogs. Young as he was, he knew that Uncle Boris shouldn't really have had them to give away and he always ate them very quietly, sitting in a corner with his back to the center of the room. He would eat them quickly for fear of being caught.

They tasted all the better for that.

Poor Uncle Boris! He had an accident and died. They never told him exactly how, and he had cried bitterly because he thought Uncle Boris had been arrested for smuggling yeast out of the plant. He expected to be arrested and executed himself. Years later, he poked carefully through police files and found the truth. Uncle Boris had fallen beneath the treads of a transport. It was a disillusioning ending to a romantic myth.

Yet the myth would always arise in his mind, at least momentarily, at the whiff of raw yeast.

Yeast-town was not the official name of any part of New York City. It could be found in no gazetteer and on no official map. What was called Yeast-town in popular speech was, to the Post Office, merely the boroughs of Newark, New Brunswick, and Trenton. It was a broad strip across what was once Medieval New Jersey, dotted with residential areas, particularly in Newark Center and Trenton Center, but given over mostly to the many-layered farms in which a thousand varieties of yeast grew and multiplied.

One fifth of the City's population worked in the yeast farms; another fifth worked in the subsidiary industries. Beginning with the mountains of wood and coarse cellulose that were dragged into the City from the tangled forests of the Alleghenies, through the vats of acid that hydrolyzed it to glucose, the carloads of niter and phosphate rock that were the most important additives, down to the jars of organics supplied by the chemical laboratories—it all came to only one thing, yeast and more yeast.

Without yeast, six of Earth's eight billions would starve in a year.

Baley felt cold at the thought. Three days before the possibility existed as deeply as it did now, but three days before it would never have occurred to him.

They whizzed out of the motorway through an exit on the Newark outskirts. The thinly populated avenues, flanked on either side by the featureless blocks that were the farms, offered little to act as a brake on their speed.

"What time is it, Daneel?" asked Baley.

"Sixteen-oh-five," replied R. Daneel.

"Then he'll be at work, if he's on day shift."

Baley parked the squad car in a delivery recess and froze the controls.

"This is New York Yeast then, Elijah?" asked the robot.

"Part of it," said Baley.

They entered into a corridor flanked by a double row of offices. A receptionist at a bend in the corridor was instantly smiles. "Whom do you wish to see?"

Baley opened his wallet. "Police. Is there a Francis Clousarr working for New York Yeast?"

The girl looked perturbed. "I can check."

She connected her switchboard through a line plainly marked "Personnel," and her lips moved slightly, though no sound could be heard.

Baley was no stranger to the throat phones that translated the small movements of the larynx into words. He said, "Speak up, please. Let me hear you."

Her words became audible, but consisted only of, ". . . he says he's a policeman, sir."

A dark, well-dressed man came out a door. He had a thin mustache and his hairline was beginning to retreat. He smiled whitely, and said, "I'm Prescott of Personnel. What's the trouble, Officer?"

Baley stared at him coldly and Prescott's smile grew strained.

Prescott said, "I just don't want to upset the workers. They're touchy about the police."

Baley said, "Tough, isn't it? Is Clousarr in the building now?"

"Yes, Officer."

"Let's have a rod, then. And if he's gone when we get there, I'll be speaking to you again."

The other's smile was quite dead. He muttered, "I'll get you a rod, Officer."

The guide rod was set for Department CG, Section 2. What that meant in factory terminology, Baley didn't know. He didn't have to. The rod was an inconspicuous thing which could be palmed in the hand. Its tip warmed gently when lined up in the direction for which it was set, cooled quickly when turned away. The warmth increased as the final goal was approached.

To an amateur, the guide rod was almost useless, with its quick little differences of heat content, but few City dwellers were amateurs at this particular game. One of the most popular and perennial of the games of childhood was hide-and-seek through the school-level corridors with the use of toy guide rods. ("Hot or Not, Let Hot-Spot Spot. Hot-Spot Guide Rods Are Keen.")

Baley had found his way through hundreds of massive piles by guide rod, and he could follow the shortest course with one of them in his hand as though it had been mapped out for him.

When he stepped into a large and brilliantly lit room after ten minutes, the guide rod's tip was almost hot.

Baley said to the worker nearest the door, "Francis Clousarr here?"

The worker jerked his head. Baley walked in the indicated direction. The odor of yeast was sharply penetrating, despite the laboring air pumps whose humming made a steady background noise.

A man had risen at the other end of the room, and was taking off an apron. He was of moderate height, his face deeply lined despite his comparative youth, and his hair just beginning to grizzle. He had large, knobby hands which he wiped slowly on a celltex towel.

"I'm Francis Clousarr," he said.

Baley looked briefly at R. Daneel. The robot nodded.

"Okay," said Baley. "Anywhere here we can talk?"

"Maybe," said Clousarr slowly, "but it's just about the end of my shift. How about tomorrow?"

"Lots of hours between now and tomorrow. Let's make it now." Baley opened his wallet and palmed it at the yeast farmer.

But Clousarr's hands did not waver in their somber wiping motions. He said, coolly, "I don't know the system in the Police Department, but around here you get tight eating hours with no leeway. I eat at 17:00 to 17:45, or I don't eat."

"It's all right," said Baley. "I'll arrange to have your supper brought to you."

"Well, well," said Clousarr, joylessly. "Just like an aristocrat, or a C-class copper. What's next? Private bath?"

"You just answer questions, Clousarr," said Baley, "and save your big jokes for your girl friend. Where can we talk?"

"If you want to talk, how about the balance room? Suit yourself about that. Me, I've got nothing to say."

Baley thumbed Clousarr into the balance room. It was square and antiseptically white, air-conditioned independently of the larger room (and more efficiently), and with its walls lined with delicate electronic balances, glassed off and manipulable by field forces only. Baley had used cheaper models in his college days. One make, which he recognized, could weigh a mere billion atoms.

Clousarr said, "I don't expect anyone will be in here for a while."

Baley grunted, then turned to Daneel and said, "Would you step out and have a meal sent up here? And if you don't mind, wait outside for it."

He watched R. Daneel leave, then said to Clousarr, "You're a chemist?"

"I'm a zymologist, if you don't mind."

"What's the difference?"

Clousarr looked lofty. "A chemist is a soup-pusher, a stink-operator. A zymologist is a man who helps keep a few billion people alive. I'm a yeast-culture specialist."

"All right," said Baley.

But Clousarr went on, "This laboratory keeps New York Yeast going. There isn't one day, not one damned hour, that we haven't got cultures of every strain of yeast in the company growing in our kettles. We check and adjust the food factor requirements. We make sure it's breeding true. We twist the genetics, start the new strains and weed them out, sort out their properties and mold them again.

"When New Yorkers started getting strawberries out of season a couple of years back, those weren't strawberries, fella. Those were a special high-sugar yeast culture with true-bred color and just a dash of flavor additive. It was developed right here in this room.

"Twenty years ago *Saccharomyces olei Benedictae* was just a scrub strain with a lousy taste of tallow and good for nothing. It still tastes of tallow, but its fat content has been pushed up from 15 per cent to 87 per cent. If you used the expressway today, just remember that it's greased strictly with *S. O. Benedictae, Strain AG-7*. Developed right here in this room.

"So don't call me a chemist. I'm a zymologist."

Despite himself, Baley retreated before the fierce pride of the other.

He said abruptly, "Where were you last night between the hours of eighteen and twenty?"

Clousarr shrugged. "Walking. I like to take a little walk after dinner."

"You visited friends? Or a subetheric?"

"No. Just walked."

Baley's lips tightened. A visit to the subetherics would have involved a notch in Clousarr's ration plack. A meeting with a friend would have involved naming a man or woman, and a cross check.

"No one saw you, then?"

"Maybe someone did. I don't know. Not that I know of, though."

"What about the night before last?"

"Same thing."

"You have no alibi then for either night?"

"If I had done anything criminal, Officer, I'd have one. What do I need an alibi for?"

Baley didn't answer. He consulted his little book. "You were up before the magistrate once. Inciting to riot."

"All right. One of the R things pushed past me and I tripped him up. Is that inciting to riot?"

"The court thought so. You were convicted and fined."

"That ends it, doesn't it? Or do you want to fine me again?"

"Night before last, there was a near riot at a shoe department in the Bronx. You were seen there."

"By whom?"

Baley said, "It was at mealtime for you here. Did you eat the evening meal night before last?"

Clousarr hesitated, then shook his head. "Upset stomach. Yeast gets you that way sometimes. Even an old-timer."

"Last night, there was a near riot in Williamsburg and you were seen *there*."

"By whom?"

"Do you deny you were present on both occasions?"

"You're not giving me anything to deny. Exactly where did these things happen and who says he saw me?"

Baley stared at the zymologist levelly. "I think you know exactly what I'm talking about. I think you're an important man in an unregistered Medievalist organization."

"I can't stop you from thinking, Officer, but thinking isn't evidence. Maybe you know that." Clousarr was grinning.

"Maybe," said Baley, his long face stony, "I can get a little truth out of you right now."

Baley stepped to the door of the balance room and opened it. He said to R. Daneel, who was waiting stolidly outside, "Has Clousarr's evening meal arrived?"

"It is coming now, Elijah."

"Bring it in, will you, Daneel?"

R. Daneel entered a moment later with a metal compartmented tray.

"Put it down in front of Mr. Clousarr, Daneel," said Baley. He sat down on one of the stools lining the balance wall, legs crossed, one shoe swinging rhythmically. He watched Clousarr edge stiffly away as R. Daneel placed the tray on a stool near the zymologist.

"Mr. Clousarr," said Baley. "I want to introduce you to my partner, Daneel Olivaw."

Daneel put out his hand and said, "How do you do, Francis."

Clousarr said nothing. He made no move to grasp Daneel's extended hand. Daneel maintained his position and Clousarr began to redden.

Baley said softly, "You are being rude, Mr. Clousarr. Are you too proud to shake hands with a policeman?"

Clousarr muttered, "If you don't mind, I'm hungry." He unfolded a pocket fork out of a clasp knife he took from his pocket and sat down, eyes bent on his meal.

Baley said, "Daneel, I think our friend is offended by your cold attitude. You are not angry with him, are you?"

"Not at all, Elijah," said R. Daneel.

"Then show that there are no hard feelings. Put your arm about his shoulder."

"I will be glad to," said R. Daneel, and stepped forward.

Clousarr put down his fork. "What is this? What's going on?"

R. Daneel, unruffled, put out his arm.

Clousarr swung backhanded, wildly, knocking R. Daneel's arm to one side. "Damn it, don't touch me."

He jumped up and away, the tray of food tipping and hitting the floor in a messy clatter.

Baley, hard-eyed, nodded curtly to R. Daneel, who thereupon continued a stolid advance toward the retreating zymologist. Baley stepped in front of the door.

Clousarr yelled, "Keep that thing off me."

"That's no way to speak," said Baley with equanimity. "The man's my partner."

"You mean he's a damned robot," shrieked Clousarr.

"Get away from him, Daneel," said Baley promptly.

R. Daneel stepped back and stood quietly against the door just behind Baley. Clousarr, panting harshly, fists clenched, faced Baley.

Baley said, "All right, smart boy. What makes you think Daneel's a robot?"

"Anyone can tell!"

"We'll leave that to a judge. Meanwhile, I think we want you at headquarters, Clousarr. We'd like to have you explain exactly how you knew Daneel was a robot. And lots more, mister, lots more. Daneel, step outside and get through to the Commissioner. He'll be at his home by now. Tell him to come down to the office. Tell him I have a fellow who can't wait to be questioned."

R. Daneel stepped out.

Baley said, "What makes your wheels go round, Clousarr?"

"I want a lawyer."

"You'll get one. Meanwhile, suppose you tell me what makes you Medievalists tick?"

Clousarr looked away in a determined silence.

Baley said, "Jehoshaphat, man, we know all about you *and* your organization. I'm not bluffing. Just tell me for my own curiosity: What do you Medievalists *want?*"

"Back to the soil," said Clousarr in a stifled voice. "That's simple, isn't it?"

"It's simple to say," said Baley. "But it isn't simple to do. How's the soil going to feed eight billions?"

"Did I say back to the soil overnight? Or in a year? Or in a hundred years? Step by step, mister policeman. It doesn't matter how long it takes, but let's get started out of these caves we live in. Let's get out into the fresh air."

"Have *you* ever been out into the fresh air?"

Clousarr squirmed. "All right, so I'm ruined, too. But the children aren't ruined yet. There are babies being born continuously. Get them out, for God's sake. Let them have space and open air and sun. If we've got to, we'll cut our population little by little, too."

"Backward, in other words, to an impossible past." Baley did not really know why he was arguing, except for the strange fever that was burning in his own veins. "Back to the seed, to the egg, to the womb. Why not move forward? Don't cut Earth's population. Use it for export. Go back to the soil, but go back to the soil of other planets. Colonize!"

Clousarr laughed harshly. "And make more Outer Worlds? More Spacers?"

"We won't. The Outer Worlds were settled by Earthmen who came from a planet that did not have Cities, by Earthmen who were individualists and materialists. Those qualities were carried to an unhealthy extreme. We can now colonize out of a society that has built co-operation, if anything, too far. Now environment and tradition can interact to form a new middle way, distinct from either old Earth or the Outer Worlds. Something newer and better."

He was parroting Dr. Fastolfe, he knew, but it was coming out as though he himself had been thinking of it for years.

Clousarr said, "Nuts! Colonize desert worlds with a world of our own at our fingertips? What fools would try?"

"Many. And they wouldn't be fools. There'd be robots to help."

"No," said Clousarr, fiercely. "Never! No robots!"

"Why not, for the love of Heaven? I don't like them, either, but I'm not going to knife myself for the sake of a prejudice. What are we afraid of in robots? If you want my guess, it's a sense of inferiority. We, all of us, feel inferior to the Spacers and hate it. We've got to feel superior somehow, somewhere, to make up for it, and it kills us that we can't at least feel superior to robots. They seem to be better than us—only they're *not*. That's the damned irony of it."

Baley felt his blood heating as he spoke. "Look at this Daneel I've been with for over two days. He's taller than I am, stronger, handsomer. He looks like a Spacer, in fact. He's got a better memory and knows more facts. He doesn't have to sleep or eat. He's not troubled by sickness or panic or love or guilt.

"But he's a machine. I can do anything I want to him, the way I can to that microbalance right there. If I slam the microbalance, it won't hit me back. Neither will Daneel. I can order him to take a blaster to himself and he'll do it.

"We can't ever build a robot that will be even as good as a human being in anything that counts, let alone better. We can't create a robot with a sense of beauty or a sense of ethics or a sense of religion. There's no way we can raise a positronic brain one inch above the level of perfect materialism.

"We can't, damn it, we can't. Not as long as we don't understand what makes our own brains tick. Not as long as things exist that science can't measure. What *is* beauty, or goodness, or art, or love, or God? We're forever teetering on the brink of the unknowable, and trying to understand what can't be understood. It's what makes us men.

"A robot's brain must be finite or it can't be built. It must be calculated to the final decimal place so that it has an end. Jehoshaphat, what are you afraid of? A robot can look like Daneel, he can look like a god, and be no more human than a lump of wood is. Can't you see that?"

Clousarr had tried to interrupt several times and failed against Baley's furious torrent. Now, when Baley paused in sheer emotional exhaustion, he said weakly, "Copper turned philosopher. What do you know?"

R. Daneel re-entered.

Baley looked at him and frowned, partly with the anger that had not yet left him, partly with new annoyance.

He said, "What kept you?"

R. Daneel said, "I had trouble in reaching Commissioner Enderby, Elijah. It turned out he was still at his office."

Baley looked at his watch. "*Now?* What for?"

"There is a certain confusion at the moment. A corpse has been discovered in the Department."

"*What!* For God's sake, who?"

"The errand boy, R. Sammy."

Baley gagged. He stared at the robot and said in an outraged voice, "I thought you said a corpse."

R. Daneel amended smoothly, "A robot with a completely deactivated brain, if you prefer."

Clousarr laughed suddenly and Baley turned on him, saying huskily, "Nothing out of you! Understand?" Deliberately, he unlimbered his blaster. Clousarr was very silent.

Baley said, "Well, what of it? R. Sammy blew a fuse. So what?"

"Commissioner Enderby was evasive, Elijah, but while he did not say so outright, my impression is that the Commissioner believes R. Sammy to have been deliberately deactivated."

Then, as Baley absorbed that silently, R. Daneel added gravely, "Or, if you prefer the phrase—murdered."

16

Questions Concerning a Motive

BALEY REPLACED his blaster, but kept his hand unobtrusively upon its butt.

He said, "Walk ahead of us, Clousarr, to Seventeenth Street Exit B."

Clousarr said, "I haven't eaten."

"Tough," said Baley, impatiently. "There's your meal on the floor where you dumped it."

"I have a right to eat."

"You'll eat in detention, or you'll miss a meal. You won't starve. Get going."

All three were silent as they threaded the maze of New York Yeast, Clousarr moving stonily in advance, Baley right behind him, and R. Daneel in the rear.

It was after Baley and R. Daneel had checked out at the receptionist's desk, after Clousarr had drawn a leave of absence and requested that a man be sent in to clean up the balance room, after they were out in the open just to one side of the parked squad car, that Clousarr said, "Just a minute."

He hung back, turned toward R. Daneel, and, before Baley could make a move to stop him, stepped forward and swung his open hand full against the robot's cheek.

"What the devil," cried Baley, snatching violently at Clousarr.

Clousarr did not resist the plain-clothes man's grasp. "It's all right. I'll go. I just wanted to see for myself." He was grinning.

R. Daneel, having faded with the slap, but not having escaped it entirely, gazed quietly at Clousarr. There was no reddening of his cheek, no mark of any blow.

He said, "That was a dangerous action, Francis. Had I not moved backward, you might easily have damaged your hand. As it is, I regret that I must have caused you pain."

Clousarr laughed.

Baley said, "Get in, Clousarr. You, too, Daneel. Right in the back seat with him. And make sure he doesn't move. I don't care if it means breaking his arm. That's an order."

"What about the First Law?" mocked Clousarr.

"I think Daneel is strong enough and fast enough to stop you without hurting you, but it might do you good to have an arm or two broken at that."

Baley got behind the wheel and the squad car gathered speed. The empty wind ruffled his hair and Clousarr's, but R. Daneel's remained smoothly in place.

R. Daneel said quietly to Clousarr, "Do you fear robots for the sake of your job, Mr. Clousarr?"

Baley could not turn to see Clousarr's expression, but he was certain it would be a hard and rigid mirror of detestation, that he would be sitting stiffly apart, as far as he might, from R. Daneel.

Clousarr's voice said, "And my kids' jobs. And everyone's kids."

"Surely adjustments are possible," said the robot. "If your children, for instance, were to accept training for emigration——"

Clousarr broke in. "You, too? The policeman talked about emigration. He's got good robot training. Maybe he *is* a robot."

Baley growled, "That's enough, you!"

R. Daneel said, evenly, "A training school for emigrants would involve security, guaranteed classification, an assured career. If you are concerned over your children, that is something to consider."

"I wouldn't take anything from a robot, or a Spacer, or any of your trained hyenas in the Government."

That was all. The silence of the motorway engulfed them and there was only the soft whirr of the squad-car motor and the hiss of its wheels on the pavement.

Back at the Department, Baley signed a detention certificate for Clousarr and left him in appropriate hands. Following that, he and R. Daneel took the motospiral up the levels to Headquarters.

R. Daneel showed no surprise that they had not taken the elevators, nor did Baley expect him to. He was becoming used to the robot's queer mixture of ability and submissiveness and tended to leave him out of his calculations. The elevator was the logical method of leaping the vertical gap between Detention and Headquarters. The long moving stairway that was the motospiral was useful only for short climbs or drops of two or three levels at most. People of all sorts and varieties of administrative occupation stepped on and then off in less than a minute. Only Baley and R. Daneel remained on continuously, moving upward in a slow and stolid measure.

Baley felt that he needed the time. It was only minutes at best, but up in Headquarters he would be thrown violently into another phase of the problem and he wanted a rest. He wanted time to think and orient himself. Slowly as it moved, the motospiral went too quickly to satisfy him.

R. Daneel said, "It seems then we will not be questioning Clousarr just yet."

"He'll keep," said Baley, irritably. "Let's find out what the R. Sammy thing is all about." He added in a mutter, far more to himself than to R. Daneel, "It can't be independent; there must be a connection."

R. Daneel said, "It is a pity. Clousarr's cerebric qualities——"

"What about them?"

"They have changed in a strange way. What was it that took place between the two of you in the balance room while I was not present?"

Baley said, absently, "The only thing I did was to preach at him. I passed along the gospel according to St. Fastolfe."

"I do not understand you, Elijah."

Baley sighed and said, "Look, I tried to explain that Earth might as well make use of robots and get its population surplus onto other planets. I tried to knock some of the Medievalist hogwash out of his head. God knows why. I've never thought of myself as the missionary type. Anyway, that's all that happened."

"I see. Well, that makes some sense. Perhaps that can be fitted in. Tell me, Elijah, what did you tell him about robots?"

"You really want to know? I told him robots were simply machines. That was the gospel according to St. Gerrigel. There are any number of gospels, I think."

"Did you by any chance tell him that one could strike a robot with-out fear of a return blow, much as one could strike any other me-chanical object?"

"Except a punching bag, I suppose. Yes. But what made you guess that?" Baley looked curiously at the robot.

"It fits the cerebric changes," said R. Daneel, "and it explains his blow to my face just after we left the factory. He must have been thinking of what you said, so he simultaneously tested your state-ment, worked off his aggressive feelings, and had the pleasure of seeing me placed in what seemed to him a position of inferiority. In order to be so motivated and allowing for the delta variations in his quintic . . ."

He paused a long moment and said, "Yes, it is quite interesting, and now I believe I can form a self-consistent whole of the data."

Headquarters level was approaching. Baley said, "What time is it?"

He thought, pettishly: Nuts, I could look at my watch and take less time that way.

But he knew why he asked him, nevertheless. The motive was not so different from Clousarr's in punching R. Daneel. To give the robot a trivial order that he must fulfill emphasized his roboticity and, contrariwise, Baley's humanity.

Baley thought: We're all brothers. Under the skin, over it, every-where. Jehoshaphat!

R. Daneel said, "Twenty-ten."

They stepped off the motospiral and for a few seconds Baley had the usual queer sensation that went with the necessary adjustment to non-motion after long minutes of steady movement.

He said, "And I haven't eaten. Damn this job, anyway."

Baley saw and heard Commissioner Enderby through the open door of his office. The common room was empty, as though it had been wiped clean, and Enderby's voice rang through it with unusual hollowness. His round face looked bare and weak without its glasses, which he held in his hand, while he mopped his smooth forehead with a flimsy paper napkin.

His eyes caught Baley just as the latter reached the door and his voice rose into a petulant tenor.

"Good God, Baley, where the devil were you?"

Baley shrugged off the remark and said, "What's doing? Where's the night shift?" and then caught sight of the second person in the office with the Commissioner.

He said, blankly, "Dr. Gerrigel!"

The gray-haired roboticist returned the involuntary greeting by nodding briefly. "I'm glad to see you again, Mr. Baley."

The Commissioner readjusted his glasses and stared at Baley through them. "The entire staff is being questioned downstairs. Signing statements. I was going mad trying to find you. It looked queer, your being away."

"*My* being away!" cried Baley, strenuously.

"Anybody's being away. Someone in the Department did it and there's going to be hell to pay for that. What an unholy mess! What an unholy, *rotten* mess!"

He raised his hands as though in expostulation to heaven and as he did so, his eyes fell on R. Daneel.

Baley thought sardonically: First time you've looked Daneel in the face. Take a good look, Julius!

The Commissioner said in a subdued voice, "*He'll* have to sign a statement. Even *I've* had to do it. I!"

Baley said, "Look, Commissioner, what makes you so sure that R. Sammy didn't blow a gasket all by himself? What makes it deliberate destruction?"

The Commissioner sat down heavily. "Ask him," he said, and pointed to Dr. Gerrigel.

Dr. Gerrigel cleared his throat. "I scarcely know how to go about this, Mr. Baley. I take it from your expression that you are surprised to see me."

"Moderately," admitted Baley.

"Well, I was in no real hurry to return to Washington and my visits to New York are few enough to make me wish to linger. And what's more important, I had a growing feeling that it would be criminal for me to leave the City without having made at least one more effort to be allowed to analyze your fascinating robot, whom, by the way," (he looked very eager) "I see you have with you."

Baley stirred restlessly. "That's quite impossible."

The roboticist looked disappointed. "Now, yes. Perhaps later?"

Baley's long face remained woodenly unresponsive.

Dr. Gerrigel went on. "I called you, but you weren't in and no one knew where you could be located. I asked for the Commissioner and he asked me to come to headquarters and wait for you."

The Commissioner interposed quickly. "I thought it might be important. I knew you wanted to see the man."

Baley nodded. "Thanks."

Dr. Gerrigel said, "Unfortunately my guide rod was somewhat off, or perhaps in my overanxiety I misjudged its temperature. In either case I took a wrong turning and found myself in a small room——"

The Commissioner interrupted again. "One of the photographic supply rooms, Lije."

"Yes," said Dr. Gerrigel. "And in it was the prone figure of what was obviously a robot. It was quite clear to me after a brief examination that he was irreversibly deactivated. Dead, you might say. Nor was it very difficult to determine the cause of the deactivation."

"What was it?" asked Baley.

"In the robot's partly clenched right fist," said Dr. Gerrigel, "was a shiny ovoid about two inches long and half an inch wide with a mica window at one end. The fist was in contact with his skull as though the robot's last act had been to touch his head. The thing he was holding was an alpha-sprayer. You know what they are, I suppose?"

Baley nodded. He needed neither dictionary nor handbook to be told what an alpha-sprayer was. He had handled several in his lab courses in physics: a lead-alloy casing with a narrow pit dug into it longitudinally, at the bottom of which was a fragment of a plutonium salt. The pit was capped with a sliver of mica, which was transparent to alpha particles. In that one direction, hard radiation sprayed out.

An alpha-sprayer had many uses, but killing robots was not one of them, not a legal one, at least.

Baley said, "He held it to his head mica first, I take it."

Dr. Gerrigel said, "Yes, and his positronic brain paths were immediately randomized. Instant death, so to speak."

Baley turned to the pale Commissioner. "No mistake? It really *was* an alpha-sprayer?"

The Commissioner nodded, his plump lips thrust out. "Absolutely. The counters could spot it ten feet away. Photographic film in the storeroom was fogged. Cut and dried."

He seemed to brood about it for a moment or two, then said

abruptly, "Dr. Gerrigel, I'm afraid you'll have to stay in the City a day or two until we can get your evidence down on wire-film. I'll have you escorted to a room. You don't mind being under guard, I hope?"

Dr. Gerrigel said nervously, "Do you think it's necessary?"

"It's safer."

Dr. Gerrigel, seeming quite abstracted, shook hands all around, even with R. Daneel, and left.

The Commissioner heaved a sigh. "It's one of us, Lije. That's what bothers me. No outsider would come into the Department just to knock off a robot. Plenty of them outside where it's safer. And it had to be somebody who could pick up an alpha-sprayer. They're hard to get hold of."

R. Daneel spoke, his cool, even voice cutting through the agitated words of the Commissioner. He said, "But what is the motive for this murder?"

The Commissioner glanced at R. Daneel with obvious distaste, then looked away. "We're human, too. I suppose policemen can't get to like robots any more than anyone else can. He's gone now and maybe it's a relief to somebody. He used to annoy you considerably, Lije, remember?"

"That is scarcely murder motive," said R. Daneel.

"No," agreed Baley, with decision.

"It isn't murder," said the Commissioner. "It's property damage. Let's keep our legal terms straight. It's just that it was done inside the Department. Anywhere else it would be nothing. Nothing. Now it could be a first-class scandal. Lije!"

"Yes?"

"When did you last see R. Sammy?"

Baley said, "R. Daneel spoke to R. Sammy after lunch. I should judge it was about 13:30. He arranged to have us use your office, Commissioner."

"My office? What for?"

"I wanted to talk over the case with R. Daneel in moderate privacy. You weren't in, so your office was an obvious place."

"I see." The Commissioner looked dubious, but let the matter ride. "You didn't see him yourself?"

"No, but I heard his voice perhaps an hour afterward."

"Are you sure it was he?"

"Perfectly."

"That would be about 14:30?"

"Or a little sooner."

The Commissioner bit his pudgy lower lip thoughtfully. "Well, that settles one thing."

"It does?"

"Yes. The boy, Vincent Barrett, was here today. Did you know that?"

"Yes. But, Commissioner, he wouldn't do anything like this."

The Commissioner lifted his eyes to Baley's face. "Why not? R. Sammy took his job away. I can understand how he feels. There would be a tremendous sense of injustice. He would want a certain revenge. Wouldn't you? But the fact is that he left the building at 14:00 and you heard R. Sammy alive at 14:30. Of course, he might have given the alpha-sprayer to R. Sammy before he left with instructions not to use it for an hour, but then where could he have gotten an alpha-sprayer? It doesn't bear thinking of. Let's get back to R. Sammy. When you spoke to him at 14:30, what did he say?"

Baley hesitated a perceptible moment, then said carefully, "I don't remember. We left shortly afterward."

"Where did you go?"

"Yeast-town, eventually. I want to talk about that, by the way."

"Later. Later." The Commissioner rubbed his chin. "Jessie was in today, I noticed. I mean, we were checking on all visitors today and I just happened to see her name."

"She was here," said Baley, coldly.

"What for?"

"Personal family matters."

"She'll have to be questioned as a pure formality."

"I understand police routine, Commissioner. Incidentally, what about the alpha-sprayer itself? Has it been traced?"

"Oh, yes. It came from one of the power plants."

"How do they account for having lost it?"

"They don't. They have no idea. But look, Lije, except for routine statements, this has nothing to do with you. You stick to your case. It's just that . . . Well, you stick to the Spacetown investigation."

Baley said, "May I give my routine statements later, Commissioner? The fact is, I haven't eaten yet."

Commissioner Enderby's glassed eyes turned full on Baley. "By all means get something to eat. But stay inside the Department, will you? Your partner's right, though, Lije"—he seemed to avoid addressing R. Daneel or using his name—"it's the motive we need. The motive."

Baley felt suddenly frozen.

Something outside himself, something completely alien, took up the events of this day and the day before and the day before and juggled them. Once again pieces began to dovetail; a pattern began to form.

He said, "Which power plant did the alpha-sprayer come from, Commissioner?"

"The Williamsburg plant. Why?"

"Nothing. Nothing."

The last word Baley heard the Commissioner mutter as he strode out of the office, with R. Daneel immediately behind him, was, "Motive. Motive."

Baley ate a sparse meal in the small and infrequently used Department lunchroom. He devoured the stuffed tomato on lettuce without being entirely aware of its nature and for a second or so after he had gulped down the last mouthful his fork still slithered aimlessly over the slick cardboard of his plate, searching automatically for something that was no longer there.

He became aware of that and put down his fork with a muffled, "Jehoshaphat!"

"He said, "Daneel!"

R. Daneel had been sitting at another table, as though he wished to leave the obviously preoccupied Baley in peace, or as though he required privacy himself. Baley was past caring which.

Daneel stood up, moved to Baley's table, and sat down again. "Yes, partner Elijah?"

Baley did not look at him. "Daneel, I'll need your co-operation."

"In what way?"

"They will question Jessie and myself. That is certain. Let me answer the questions in my own way. Do you understand?"

"I understand what you say, of course. Nevertheless, if I am asked a direct question, how is it possible for me to say anything but what is so?"

"*If* you are asked a direct question, that's another matter. I ask only that you don't volunteer information. You can do that, can't you?"

"I believe so, Elijah, provided it does not appear that I am hurting a human being by remaining silent."

Baley said, grimly, "You will hurt *me* if you don't. I assure you of that."

"I do not quite understand your point of view, partner Elijah. Surely the matter of R. Sammy cannot concern you."

"No? It all centers about motive, doesn't it? You've questioned the motive. The Commissioner questioned it. I do, for that matter. Why should anyone want to kill R. Sammy? Mind you, it's not just a question of who would want to smash up robots in general. Any Earthman, practically, would want to do that. The question is, who would want to single out R. Sammy. Vincent Barrett might, but the Commissioner said he couldn't get hold of an alpha-sprayer, and he's right. We have to look somewhere else, and it so happens that one other person has a motive. It glares out. It yells. It stinks to top level."

"Who is the person, Elijah?"

And Baley said, softly, "I am, Daneel."

R. Daneel's expressionless face did not change under the impact of the statement. He merely shook his head.

Baley said, "You don't agree. My wife came to the office today. They know that already. The Commissioner is even curious. If I weren't a personal friend, he wouldn't have stopped his questioning so soon. Now they'll find out why. That's certain. She was part of a conspiracy; a foolish and harmless one, but a conspiracy just the same. And a policeman can't afford to have his wife mixed up with anything like that. It would be to my obvious interest to see that the matter was hushed up.

"Well, who knew about it? You and I, of course, and Jessie—*and* R. Sammy. He saw her in a state of panic. When he told her that we had left orders not to be disturbed, she must have lost control. You saw the way she was when she first came in."

R. Daneel said, "It is unlikely that she said anything incriminating to him."

"That may be so. But I'm reconstructing the case the way they will. They'll say she did. There's my motive. I killed him to keep him quiet."

"They will not think so."

"They *will* think so. The murder was arranged deliberately in order to throw suspicion on me. Why use an alpha-sprayer? It's a rather risky way. It's hard to get and it can be traced. I think that those were the very reasons it *was* used. The murderer even ordered R. Sammy to go into the photographic supply room and kill himself there. It seems obvious to me that the reason for that was to have the method of murder unmistakable. Even if everyone was so infantile as not to recognize the alpha-sprayer immediately, someone would be bound to notice fogged photographic film in fairly short order."

"How does that all relate to you, Elijah?"

Baley grinned tightly, his long face completely devoid of humor. "Very neatly. The alpha-sprayer was taken from the Williamsburg power plant. You and I passed through the Williamsburg power plant yesterday. We were seen, and the fact will come out. That gives me opportunity to get the weapon as well as motive for the crime. And it may turn out that we were the last ones to see or hear R. Sammy alive, except for the real murderer, of course."

"I was with you in the power plant and I can testify that you did not have the opportunity to steal an alpha-sprayer."

"Thanks," said Baley sadly, "but you're a robot and your testimony will be invalid."

"The Commissioner is your friend. He will listen."

"The Commissioner has a job to keep, and he already is a bit uneasy about me. There's only one chance of saving myself from this very nasty situation."

"Yes?"

"I ask myself, *why* am I being framed? Obviously to get rid of me. But why? Again obviously, because I am dangerous to someone. I am doing my best to be dangerous to whoever killed Dr. Sarton in Spacetown. That might mean the Medievalists, of course, or at least, the inner group among them. It would be this inner group that would know I had passed through the power plant; at least one of them might have followed me along the strips that far, even though you thought we had lost them.

"So the chances are that if I find the murderer of Dr. Sarton, I find the man or men who are trying to get me out of the way. If I think it through, if I crack the case, if I can only crack it, I'll be safe. And Jessie. I couldn't stand to have her . . . But I don't have much time." His fist clenched and unclenched spasmodically. "I don't have much time."

Baley looked at R. Daneel's chiseled face with a sudden burning hope. Whatever the creature was, he was strong and faithful, animated by no selfishness. What more could you ask of any friend? Baley needed a friend and he was in no mood to cavil at the fact that a gear replaced a blood vessel in this particular one.

But R. Daneel was shaking his head.

The robot said, "I am sorry, Elijah"—there was no trace of sorrow on his face, of course—"but I anticipated none of this. Perhaps my action was to your harm. I am sorry if the general good requires that."

"What general good?" stammered Baley.

"I have been in communication with Dr. Fastolfe."

"Jehoshaphat! When?"

"While you were eating."

Baley's lips tightened.

"Well?" he managed to say. "What happened?"

"You will have to clear yourself of suspicion of the murder of R. Sammy through some means other than the investigation of the murder of my designer, Dr. Sarton. Our people at Spacetown, as a result of my information, have decided to bring that investigation to an end, as of today, and to begin plans for leaving Spacetown and Earth."

17

Conclusion of a Project

BALEY LOOKED at his watch with something approaching detachment. It was 21:45. In two and a quarter hours it would be midnight. He had been awake since before six and had been under tension now for two and a half days. A vague sense of unreality pervaded everything.

He kept his voice painfully steady as he reached for his pipe and for the little bag that held his precious crumbs of tobacco. He said, "What's it all about, Daneel?"

R. Daneel said, "Do you not understand? Is it not obvious?"

Baley said, patiently, "I do not understand. It is not obvious."

"We are here," said the robot, "and by we, I mean our people at Spacetown, to break the shell surrounding Earth and force its people into new expansion and colonization."

"I know that. Please don't labor the point."

"I must, since it is the essential one. If we were anxious to exact punishment for the murder of Dr. Sarton, it was not that in doing so we expected to bring Dr. Sarton back to life, you understand; it was only that failure to do so would strengthen the position of our home planet politicians who are against the very idea of Spacetown."

"But now," said Baley, with sudden violence, "you say you're getting ready to go home of your own accord. Why? In heaven's name, why? The answer to the Sarton case is close. It *must* be close or they wouldn't be trying so hard to blast me out of the investigation. I have a feeling I have all the facts I need to work out the answer. It must be in here somewhere." He knuckled his temple wildly. "A sentence might bring it out. A word."

He clenched his eyes fiercely shut, as though the quivering opaque jelly of the last sixty hours were indeed on the point of clarifying and becoming transparent. But it did not. It did not.

Baley drew a shuddering breath and felt ashamed. He was making a weak spectacle of himself before a cold and unimpressed machine that could only stare at him silently.

He said harshly, "Well, never mind that. Why are the Spacers breaking off?"

The robot said, "Our project is concluded. We are satisfied that Earth will colonize."

"You've switched to optimism then?" The plain-clothes man drew in his first calming puff of tobacco smoke and felt his grip upon his own emotions grow firmer.

"I have. For a long time now, we of Spacetown have tried to change Earth by changing its economy. We have tried to introduce our own C/Fe culture. Your planetary and various City governments co-operated with us because it was expedient to do so. Still, in twenty-five years, we have failed. The harder we tried, the stronger the opposing party of the Medievalists grew."

"I know all this," said Baley. He thought: No use. He's got to tell this in his own way, like a field recording. He yelled silently at R. Daneel: *Machine!*

R. Daneel went on, "It was Dr. Sarton who first theorized that we must reverse our tactics. We must first find a segment of Earth's population that desired what we desired or could be persuaded to do so. By encouraging and helping them, we could make the movement a native one rather than a foreign one. The difficulty was in finding the native element best suited for our purposes. You, yourself, Elijah, were an interesting experiment."

"I? I? What do you mean?" demanded Baley.

"We were glad your Commissioner recommended you. From your psychic profile we judged you to be a useful specimen. Cerebroanalysis, a process I conducted upon you as soon as I met you, confirmed our judgment. You are a practical man, Elijah. You do not moon romantically over Earth's past, despite your healthy interest in it. Nor do you stubbornly embrace the City culture of Earth's present day. We felt that people such as yourself were the ones that could lead Earthmen to the stars once more. It was one reason Dr. Fastolfe was anxious to see you yesterday morning.

"To be sure, your practical nature was embarrassingly intense. You refused to understand that the fanatical service of an ideal, even a mistaken ideal, could make a man do things quite beyond his ordinary capacity, as, for instance, crossing open country at night to destroy someone he considered an archenemy of his cause. We were not overly surprised, therefore, that you were stubborn enough and daring enough to attempt to prove the murder a fraud. In a way, it proved you were the man we wanted for our experiment."

"For God's sake, what experiment?" Baley brought his fist down on the table.

"The experiment of persuading you that colonization was the answer to Earth's problems."

"Well, I was persuaded. I'll grant you that."

"Yes, under the influence of the appropriate drug."

Baley's teeth loosened their grip on his pipestem. He caught the pipe as it fell. Once again, he was seeing that scene in the Spacetown dome. Himself swimming back to awareness after the shock of learning that R. Daneel was a robot after all; R. Daneel's smooth fingers pinching up the flesh of his arm; a hypo-sliver standing out darkly under his skin and then fading away.

He said, chokingly, "What was in the hypo-sliver?"

"Nothing that need alarm you, Elijah. It was a mild drug intended only to make your mind more receptive."

"And so I believed whatever was told me. Is that it?"

"Not quite. You would not believe anything that was foreign to the basic pattern of your thought. In fact, the results of the experiment were disappointing. Dr. Fastolfe had hoped you would become fanatical and single-minded on the subject. Instead you became rather distantly approving, no more. Your practical nature stood in the way of anything further. It made us realize that our only hope was the romantics after all, and the romantics, unfortunately, were all Medievalists, actual or potential."

Baley felt incongruously proud of himself, glad of his stubbornness, and happy that he had disappointed them. Let them experiment with someone else.

He grinned savagely. "And so now you've given up and are going home?"

"Why, that is not it. I said a few moments ago that we were satisfied Earth would colonize. It was you that gave us the answer."

"*I* gave it to you? How?"

"You spoke to Francis Clousarr of the advantages of colonization. You spoke rather fervently, I judge. At least our experiment on you had *that* result. And Clousarr's cerebroanalytic properties changed. Very subtly, to be sure, but they changed."

"You mean I convinced him that I was right? I don't believe that."

"No, conviction does not come that easily. But the cerebroanalytic changes demonstrated conclusively that the Medievalist mind is *open* to that sort of conviction. I experimented further myself. When leaving Yeast-town, guessing what might have happened between you two from his cerebric changes, I made the proposition of a school for emigrants as a way of insuring his children's future. He rejected that, but again his aura changed, and it seemed to me quite obvious that it was the proper method of attack."

R. Daneel paused, then spoke on.

"The thing called Medievalism shows a craving for pioneering. To be sure, the direction in which that craving turns itself is toward Earth itself, which is near and which has the precedent of a great past. But the vision of worlds beyond is a similar something and the romantic can turn to it easily, just as Clousarr felt the attraction as a result of one lecture from you.

"So you see, we of Spacetown had already succeeded without knowing it. We ourselves, rather than anything we tried to introduce, were the unsettling factor. We crystallized the romantic impulses on Earth into Medievalism and induced an organization in them. After all, it is the Medievalist who wishes to break the cake of custom, not the City officials who have most to gain from preserving the *status quo*. If we leave Spacetown now, if we do not irritate the Medievalist by our continued presence until he has committed himself to Earth, and only Earth, past redemption, if we leave behind a few obscure individuals or robots such as myself who, together with sympathetic Earthmen such as yourself, can establish the training schools for emigrants that I spoke of, the Medievalist will eventually turn away from Earth. He will need robots and will either get them from us or build his own. He will develop a C/Fe culture to suit himself."

It was a long speech for R. Daneel. He must have realized that himself, for, after another pause, he said, "I tell you all this to explain why it is necessary to do something that may hurt you."

Baley thought bitterly: A robot must not hurt a human being, unless he can think of a way to prove it is for the human being's ultimate good after all.

Baley said, "Just a minute. Let me introduce a practical note. You'll go back to your worlds and say that an Earthman killed a Spacer and is unpunished. The Outer Worlds will demand an indemnity from Earth, and I warn you, Earth is no longer in a mood to endure such treatment. There will be trouble."

"I am sure that will not happen, Elijah. The elements on our planets that would be most interested in pressing for an indemnity would be also most interested in forcing an end to Spacetown. We can easily offer the latter as an inducement to abandon the former. It is what we plan to do, anyway. Earth will be left in peace."

And Baley broke out, his voice hoarse with sudden despair, "And where does that leave me? The Commissioner will drop the Sarton investigation at once if Spacetown is willing, but the R. Sammy thing will have to continue, since it points to corruption inside the Department. He'll be in any minute with a ream of evidence against me. I know that. It's been arranged. I'll be declassified, Daneel. There's Jessie to consider. She'll be smeared as a criminal. There's Bentley——"

R. Daneel said, "You must not think, Elijah, that I do not understand the position in which you find yourself. In the service of humanity's good, the minor wrongs must be tolerated. Dr. Sarton has a surviving wife, two children, parents, a sister, many friends. All must grieve at his death and be saddened at the thought that his murderer has not been found and punished."

"Then why not stay and find him?"

"It is no longer necessary."

Baley said, bitterly, "Why not admit that the entire investigation was an excuse to study us under field conditions? You never gave a damn who killed Dr. Sarton."

"We would have liked to know," said R. Daneel, coolly, "but we were never under any delusions as to which was more important, an individual or humanity. To continue the investigation now would involve interfering with a situation which we now find satisfactory. We could not foretell what damage we might do."

"You mean the murderer might turn out to be a prominent Medievalist and right now the Spacers don't want to do anything to antagonize their new friends."

"It is not as I would say it, but there is truth in your words."

"Where's your justice circuit, Daneel? Is this justice?"

"There are degrees of justice, Elijah. When the lesser is incompatible with the greater, the lesser must give way."

It was as though Baley's mind were circling the impregnable logic of R. Daneel's positronic brain, searching for a loophole, a weakness.

He said, "Have you no personal curiosity, Daneel? You've called yourself a detective. Do you know what that implies? Do you understand that an investigation is more than a job of work? It is a challenge. Your mind is pitted against that of the criminal. It is a clash of intellect. Can you abandon the battle and admit defeat?"

"If no worthy end is served by a continuation, certainly."

"Would you feel no loss? No wonder? Would there be no little speck of dissatisfaction? Frustrated curiosity?"

Baley's hopes, not strong in the first place, weakened as he spoke. The word "curiosity," second time repeated, brought back his own remarks to Francis Clousarr four hours before. He had known well enough then the qualities that marked off a man from a machine. Curiosity *had* to be one of them. A six-week-old kitten was curious, but how could there be a curious machine, be it ever so humanoid?

R. Daneel echoed those thoughts by saying, "What do you mean by curiosity?"

Baley put the best face on it. "Curiosity is the name we give to a desire to extend one's knowledge."

"Such a desire exists within me, when the extension of knowledge is necessary for the performance of an assigned task."

"Yes," said Baley, sarcastically, "as when you ask questions about Bentley's contact lenses in order to learn more of Earth's peculiar customs."

"Precisely," said R. Daneel, with no sign of any awareness of sarcasm. "Aimless extension of knowledge, however, which is what I think you really mean by the term curiosity, is merely inefficiency. I am designed to avoid inefficiency."

It was in that way that the "sentence" he had been waiting for came to Elijah Baley, and the opaque jelly shuddered and settled and changed into luminous transparency.

While R. Daneel spoke, Baley's mouth opened and stayed so.

It could not all have burst full-grown into his mind. Things did not work so. Somewhere, deep inside his unconscious, he had built a case, built it carefully and in detail, but had been brought up short by a single inconsistency. One inconsistency that could be neither jumped over, burrowed under, nor shunted aside. While that inconsistency existed, the case remained buried below his thoughts, beyond the reach of his conscious probing.

But the sentence had come; the inconsistency had vanished; the case was his.

The glare of mental light appeared to have stimulated Baley mightily. At least he suddenly knew what R. Daneel's weakness must be, the weakness of any thinking machine. He thought feverishly, hopefully: The thing *must* be literal-minded.

He said, "Then Project Spacetown is concluded as of today and with it the Sarton investigation. Is that it?"

"That is the decision of our people at Spacetown," agreed R. Daneel, calmly.

"But today is not yet over." Baley looked at his watch. It was 22:30. "There is an hour and a half until midnight."

R. Daneel said nothing. He seemed to consider.

Baley spoke rapidly. "Until midnight, the project continues then. You are my partner and the investigation continues." He was becoming almost telegraphic in his haste. "Let us go on as before. Let me work. It will do your people no harm. It will do them great good. My word upon it. If, in your judgment, I am doing harm, stop me. It is only an hour and a half I ask."

R. Daneel said, "What you say is correct. Today is not over. I had not thought of that, partner Elijah."

Baley was "partner Elijah" again.

He grinned, and said, "Didn't Dr. Fastolfe mention a film of the scene of the murder when I was in Spacetown?"

"He did," said R. Daneel.

Baley said, "Can you get a copy of the film?"

"Yes, partner Elijah."

"I mean now! Instantly!"

"In ten minutes, if I can use the Department transmitter."

The process took less time than that. Baley stared at the small aluminum block he held in his trembling hands. Within it the subtle forces transmitted from Spacetown had strongly fixed a certain atomic pattern.

And at that moment, Commissioner Julius Enderby stood in the doorway. He saw Baley and a certain anxiety passed from his round face, leaving behind it a look of growing thunder.

He said, uncertainly, "Look here, Lije, you're taking a devil of a time, eating."

"I was bone-tired, Commissioner. Sorry if I've delayed you."

"I wouldn't mind, but . . . You'd better come to my office."

Baley's eyes flicked toward R. Daneel, but met no answering look. Together they moved out of the lunchroom.

Julius Enderby tramped the floor before his desk, up and down, up and down. Baley watched him, himself far from composed. Occasionally, he glanced at his watch.

22:45.

The Commissioner moved his glasses up onto his forehead and rubbed his eyes with thumb and forefinger. He left red splotches in the flesh around them, then restored the glasses to their place, blinking at Baley from behind them.

"Lije," he said suddenly, "when were you last in the Williamsburg power plant?"

Baley said, "Yesterday, after I left the office. I should judge at about eighteen or shortly thereafter."

The Commissioner shook his head. "Why didn't you say so?"

"I was going to. I haven't given an official statement yet."

"What were you doing there?"

"Just passing through on my way to our temporary sleeping quarters."

The Commissioner stopped short, standing before Baley, and said, "That's no good, Lije. No one just passes through a power plant to get somewhere else."

Baley shrugged. There was no point in going through the story of the pursuing Medievalists, of the dash along the strips. Not now.

He said, "If you're trying to hint that I had an opportunity to get the alpha-sprayer that knocked out R. Sammy, I'll remind you that

Daneel was with me and will testify that I went right through the plant without stopping and that I had no alpha-sprayer on me when I left."

Slowly, the Commissioner sat down. He did not look in R. Daneel's direction or offer to speak to him. He put his pudgy white hands on the desk before him and regarded them with a look of acute misery on his face.

He said, "Lije, I don't know what to say or what to think. And it's no use having your—your partner as alibi. He can't give evidence."

"I still deny that I took an alpha-sprayer."

The Commissioner's fingers intertwined and writhed. He said, "Lije, why did Jessie come to see you here this afternoon?"

"You asked me that before, Commissioner. Same answer. Family matters."

"I've got information from Francis Clousarr, Lije."

"What kind of information?"

"He claims that a Jezebel Baley is a member of a Medievalist society dedicated to the overthrow of the government by force."

"Are you sure he has the right person? There are many Baleys."

"There aren't many Jezebel Baleys."

"He used her name, did he?"

"He said Jezebel. I heard him, Lije. I'm not giving you a second-hand report."

"All right. Jessie was a member of a harmless lunatic-fringe organization. She never did anything but attend meetings and feel devilish about it."

"It won't look that way to a board of review, Lije."

"You mean I'm going to be suspended and held on suspicion of destroying government property in the form of R. Sammy?"

"I hope not, Lije, but it looks awfully bad. Everyone knows you didn't like R. Sammy. Your wife was seen talking to him this afternoon. She was in tears and some of her words were heard. They were harmless in themselves, but two and two can be added up, Lije. You might feel it was dangerous to leave him in a position to talk. *And* you had an opportunity to obtain the weapon."

Baley interrupted. "If I were wiping out all evidence against Jessie, would I bring in Francis Clousarr? He seems to know a lot more about her than R. Sammy could have. Another thing. I passed through the power plant eighteen hours before R. Sammy spoke to Jessie. Did I know that long in advance that I would have to destroy him and pick up an alpha-sprayer out of clairvoyance?"

The Commissioner said, "Those are good points. I'll do my best. I'm sorry about this, Lije."

"Yes? Do you really believe I didn't do it, Commissioner?"

Enderby said slowly, "I don't know what to think, Lije. I'll be frank with you."

"Then I'll tell you what to think. Commissioner, this is all a careful and elaborate frame."

The Commissioner stiffened. "Now, wait, Lije. Don't strike out blindly. You won't get any sympathy with that line of defense. It's been used by too many bad eggs."

"I'm not after sympathy. I'm just telling the truth. I'm being taken out of circulation to prevent me from learning the facts about the Sarton murder. Unfortunately for my framing pal, it's too late for that."

"*What!*"

Baley looked at his watch. It was 23:00.

He said, "I know who is framing me, and I know how Dr. Sarton was killed and by whom, and I have one hour to tell you about it, catch the man, and end the investigation."

18

End of an Investigation

COMMISSIONER ENDERBY's eyes narrowed and he glared at Baley. "What are you going to do? You tried something like this in Fastolfe's dome yesterday morning. Not again. Please."

Baley nodded. "I know. I was wrong the first time."

He thought, fiercely: Also the second time. But not now, not *this* time, not . . .

The thought faded out, spluttering like a micropile under a positronic damper.

He said, "Judge for yourself, Commissioner. Grant that the evidence against me has been planted. Go that far with me and see where it takes you. Ask yourself who could have planted that evidence. Obviously only someone who'd known I was in the Williamsburg plant yesterday evening."

"All right. Who would that be?"

Baley said, "I was followed out of the kitchen by a Medievalist group. I lost them, or I thought I did, but obviously at least one of them saw me pass through the plant. My only purpose in doing so, you understand, was to help me lose them."

The Commissioner considered. "Clousarr? Was he with them?"

Baley nodded.

Enderby said, "All right, we'll question him. If he's got anything in him, we'll have it out of him. What more can I do, Lije?"

"Wait, now. Don't quit on me. Do you see my point?"

"Well, let's see if I do?" The Commissioner clasped his hands. "Clousarr saw you go into the Williamsburg power plant, or else someone in his group did and passed the information along to him.

He decided to utilize that fact to get you into trouble and off the investigation. Is that what you're saying?"

"It's close to it."

"Good." The Commissioner seemed to warm to the task. "He knew your wife was a member of his organization, naturally, and so he knew you wouldn't face a really close probe into your private life. He thought you would resign rather than fight circumstantial evidence. By the way, Lije, what about a resignation? I mean, if things looked really bad. We could keep things quiet——"

"Not in a million years, Commissioner."

Enderby shrugged. "Well, where was I? Oh, yes, so he got an alpha-sprayer, presumably through a confederate in the plant, and had another confederate arrange the destruction of R. Sammy." His fingers drummed lightly on the desk. "No good, Lije."

"Why not?"

"Too farfetched. Too many confederates. And he has a cast-iron alibi for the night and morning of the Spacetown murder, by the way. We checked that almost right away, though I was the only one who knew the reason for checking that particular time."

Baley said, "I never said it was Clousarr, Commissioner. *You* did. It could be anyone in the Medievalist organization. Clousarr is just the owner of a face that Daneel happened to recognize. I don't even think he's particularly important in the organization. Though there is one queer thing about him."

"What?" asked Enderby, suspiciously.

"He did know Jessie was a member. Does he know every member in the organization, do you suppose?"

"I don't know. He knew about Jessie, anyway. Maybe she was important because she was the wife of a policeman. Maybe he remembered her for that reason."

"You say he came right out and said that Jezebel Baley was a member. Just like that? Jezebel Baley?"

Enderby nodded. "I keep telling you I heard him."

"That's the funny thing, Commissioner. Jessie hasn't used her full first name since before Bentley was born. Not once. I know that for certain. She joined the Medievalists after she dropped her full name. I know that for sure, too. How would Clousarr come to know her as Jezebel, then?"

The Commissioner flushed and said, hastily, "Oh well, if it comes to that, he probably said Jessie. I just filled it in automatically and gave her full name. In fact, I'm sure of that. He said Jessie."

"Until now you were quite sure he said Jezebel. I asked several times."

The Commissioner's voice rose. "You're not saying I'm a liar, are you?"

"I'm just wondering if Clousarr, perhaps, said nothing at all. I'm wondering if you made that up. You've known Jessie for twenty years, and *you* knew her name was Jezebel."

"You're off your head, man."

"Am I? Where were you after lunch today? You were out of your office for two hours at least."

"Are you questioning *me*?"

"I'll answer for you, too. You were in the Williamsburg power plant."

The Commissioner rose from his seat. His forehead glistened and there were dry, white flecks at the corners of his lips. "What the hell are you trying to say?"

"Weren't you?"

"Baley, you're suspended. Hand me your credentials."

"Not yet. Hear me out."

"I don't intend to. You're guilty. You're guilty as the devil, and what gets me is your cheap attempt to make me, *me*, look as though I were conspiring against you." He lost his voice momentarily in a squeak of indignation. He managed to gasp out, "In fact, you're under arrest."

"No," said Baley, tightly, "not yet. Commissioner, I've got a blaster on you. It's pointed straight and it's cocked. Don't fool with me, please, because I'm desperate and I *will* have my say. Afterward, you can do what you please."

With widening eyes, Julius Enderby stared at the wicked muzzle in Baley's hands.

He stammered, "Twenty years for this, Baley, in the deepest prison level in the City."

R. Daneel moved suddenly. His hand clamped down on Baley's wrist. He said, quietly, "I cannot permit this, partner Elijah. You must do no harm to the Commissioner."

For the first time since R. Daneel had entered the City, the Commissioner spoke directly to him. "Hold him, you. First Law!"

Baley said quickly, "I have no intention of hurting him, Daneel, if you will keep him from arresting me. You said you would help me clear this up. I have forty-five minutes."

R. Daneel, without releasing Baley's wrist, said, "Commissioner, I believe Elijah should be allowed to speak. I am in communication with Dr. Fastolfe at this moment——"

"How? How?" demanded the Commissioner, wildly.

"I possess a self-contained subetheric unit," said R. Daneel. The Commissioner stared.

"I am in communication with Dr. Fastolfe," the robot went on inexorably, "and it would make a bad impression, Commissioner, if you were to refuse to listen to Elijah. Damaging inferences might be drawn."

The Commissioner fell back in his chair, quite speechless.

Baley said, "I say you were in the Williamsburg power plant today, Commissioner, and you got the alpha-sprayer and gave it to R. Sammy. You deliberately chose the Williamsburg power plant in order to incriminate me. You even seized Dr. Gerrigel's reappearance to invite him down to the Department and give him a deliberately maladjusted guide rod to lead him to the photographic supply room and allow him to find R. Sammy's remains. You counted on him to make a correct diagnosis."

Baley put away his blaster. "If you want to have me arrested now, go ahead, but Spacetown won't take that for an answer."

"Motive," spluttered Enderby breathlessly. His glasses were fogged and he removed them, looking once again curiously vague and helpless in their absence. "What motive could I have for this?"

"You got me into trouble, didn't you? It will put a spoke in the Sarton investigation, won't it? And all that aside, R. Sammy knew too much."

"About *what*, in Heaven's name?"

"About the way in which a Spacer was murdered five and a half days ago. You see, Commissioner, *you* murdered Dr. Sarton of Spacetown."

It was R. Daneel who spoke. Enderby could only clutch feverishly at his hair and shake his head.

The robot said, "Partner Elijah, I am afraid that this theory is quite untenable. As you know, it is impossible for Commissioner Enderby to have murdered Dr. Sarton."

"Listen, then. Listen to me. Enderby begged *me* to take the case, not any of the men who overranked me. He did that for several reasons. In the first place, we were college friends and he thought he could count on its never occurring to me that an old buddy and respected superior could be a criminal. He counted on my well-known loyalty, you see. Secondly, he knew Jessie was a member of an underground organization and expected to be able to maneuver me out of the investigation or blackmail me into silence if I got too close to the truth. And he wasn't really worried about that. At the very beginning he did his best to arouse my distrust of you, Daneel, and make certain that the two of us worked at cross-purposes. He knew about my father's declassification. He could guess how I would react. You see, it is an advantage for the murderer to be in charge of the murder investigation."

The Commissioner found his voice. He said, weakly, "How could I know about Jessie?" He turned to the robot. "You! If you're transmitting this to Spacetown, tell them it's a lie! It's all a lie!"

Baley broke in, raising his voice for a moment and then lowering it into a queer sort of tense calm. "Certainly you would know about Jessie. You're a Medievalist, and part of the organization. Your old-fashioned spectacles! Your windows! It's obvious your temperament is turned that way. But there's better evidence than that.

"How did Jessie find out Daneel was a robot? It puzzled me at the time. Of course we know now that she found out through her Medievalist organization, but that just shoves the problem one step backward. How did *they* know? You, Commissioner, dismissed it with a theory that Daneel was recognized as a robot during the incident at the shoe counter. I didn't quite believe that. I couldn't. I took him for human when I first saw him, and there's nothing wrong with my eyes.

"Yesterday, I asked Dr. Gerrigel to come in from Washington. Later I decided I needed him for several reasons, but, at the time I first called him, my only purpose was to see if he would recognize Daneel for what he was with no prompting on my part.

"Commissioner, he didn't! I introduced him to Daneel, he shook hands with him, we all talked together, and it was only after the subject got around to humanoid robots that he suddenly caught on. Now, that was Dr. Gerrigel, Earth's greatest expert on robots. Do you mean to say a few Medievalist rioters could do better than he under conditions of confusion and tension, and be so certain about it that they would throw their entire organization into activity based on the feeling that Daneel was a robot?

"It's obvious now that the Medievalists must have known Daneel to be a robot to begin with. The incident at the shoe counter was deliberately designed to show Daneel and, through him, Spacetown, the extent of antirobot feeling in the City. It was meant to confuse the issue, to turn suspicion away from individuals and toward the population as a whole.

"Now, if they knew the truth about Daneel to begin with, who told them? I didn't. I once thought it was Daneel himself, but that's out. The only other Earthman who knew about it was you, Commissioner."

Enderby said, with surprising energy, "There could be spies in the Department, too. The Medievalists could have us riddled with them. Your wife was one, and if you don't find it impossible that I should be one, why not others in the Department?"

The corners of Baley's lips pulled back a savage trifle. "Let's not bring up mysterious spies until we see where the straightforward solution leads us. I say you're the obvious informer and the real one.

"It's interesting now that I look back on it, Commissioner, to see how your spirits rose and fell accordingly as I seemed to be far from a solution or possibly close to it. You were nervous to begin with. When I wanted to visit Spacetown yesterday morning and wouldn't tell you the reason, you were practically in a state of collapse. Did you think I had you pinned, Commissioner? That it was a trap to get you into their hands? You hated them, you told me. You were virtually in tears. For a time, I thought that to be caused by the memory of humiliation in Spacetown when you yourself were a suspect, but then Daneel told me that your sensibilities had been carefully regarded. You had never known you were a suspect. Your panic was due to fear, not humiliation.

"Then when I came out with my completely wrong solution, while you listened over trimensional circuit, and you saw how far, how immensely far, from the truth I was, you were confident again. You even argued with me, defended the Spacers. After that, you were quite master of yourself for a while, quite confident. It surprised me at the time that you so easily forgave my false accusations against the Spacers when earlier you had so lectured me on their sensitivity. You enjoyed my mistake.

"Then I put in my call for Dr. Gerrigel and you wanted to know why and I wouldn't tell you. That plunged you into the abyss again because you feared——"

R. Daneel suddenly raised his hand. "Partner Elijah!"

Baley looked at his watch. 23:42! He said, "What is it?"

R. Daneel said, "He might have been disturbed at thinking you would find out his Medievalist connections, if we grant their existence. There is nothing, though, to connect him with the murder. He cannot have had anything to do with that."

Baley said, "You're quite wrong, Daneel. He didn't know what I wanted Dr. Gerrigel for, but it was quite safe to assume that it was in connection with information about robots. This frightened the Commissioner, because a robot had an intimate connection with his greater crime. Isn't that so, Commissioner?"

Enderby shook his head. "When this is over——" he began, but choked into inarticulacy.

"How was the murder committed?" demanded Baley with a suppressed fury. "C/Fe, damn it! C/Fe! I use your own term, Daneel. You're so full of the benefits of a C/Fe culture, yet you don't see where an Earthman might have used it for at least a temporary advantage. Let me sketch it in for you.

"There is no difficulty in the notion of a robot crossing open country. Even at night. Even alone. The Commissioner put a blaster into R. Sammy's hand, told him where to go and when. He himself entered Spacetown through the Personal and was relieved of his own blaster. He received the other from R. Sammy's hands, killed Dr. Sarton, returned the blaster to R. Sammy, who took it back across the fields to New York City. And today he destroyed R. Sammy, whose knowledge had become dangerous.

"That explains everything. The presence of the Commissioner, the absence of a weapon. And it makes it unnecessary to suppose any human New Yorker had crawled a mile under the open sky at night."

But at the end of Baley's recitation, R. Daneel said, "I am sorry, partner Elijah, though happy for the Commissioner, that your story explains nothing. I have told you that the cerebroanalytic properties of the Commissioner are such that it is impossible for him to have committed deliberate murder. I don't know what English word would be applied to the psychological fact: cowardice, conscience, or compassion. I know the dictionary meanings of all these, but I cannot judge. At any rate, the Commissioner did not murder."

"Thank you," muttered Enderby. His voice gained strength and confidence. "I don't know what your motives are, Baley, or why you should try to ruin me this way, but I'll get to the bottom——"

"Wait," said Baley. "I'm not through. I've got this."

He slammed the aluminum cube on Enderby's desk, and tried to feel the confidence he hoped he was radiating. For half an hour now, he had been hiding from himself one little fact: that he did *not* know what the picture showed. He was gambling, but it was all that was left to do.

Enderby shrank away from the small object. "What is it?"

"It isn't a bomb," said Baley, sardonically. "Just an ordinary microprojector."

"Well? What will that prove?"

"Suppose we see." His fingernail probed at one of the slits in the cube, and a corner of the Commissioner's office blanked out, then lit up in an alien scene in three dimensions.

It reached from floor to ceiling and extended out past the walls of the room. It was awash with a gray light of a sort the City's utilities never provided.

Baley thought, with a pang of mingled distaste and perverse attraction: It must be the dawn they talk about.

The pictured scene was of Dr. Sarton's dome. Dr. Sarton's dead body, a horrible, broken remnant, filled its center.

Enderby's eyes bulged as he stared.

Baley said, "I know the Commissioner isn't a killer. I don't need you to tell me that, Daneel. If I could have gotten around that one fact earlier, I would have had the solution earlier. Actually, I didn't see a way out of it until an hour ago when I carelessly said to you that you had once been curious about Bentley's contact lenses.— That was it, Commissioner. It occurred to me then that your nearsightedness and your glasses were the key. They don't have nearsightedness on the Outer Worlds, I suppose, or they might have reached the true solution of the murder almost at once. Commissioner, when did you break your glasses?"

The Commissioner said, "What do you mean?"

Baley said, "When I first saw you about this case, you told me you had broken your glasses in Spacetown. I assumed that you broke them in your agitation on hearing the news of the murder, but *you* never said so, and I had no reason for making that assumption. Actually, if you were entering Spacetown with crime on your mind, you were already sufficiently agitated to drop and break your glasses *before* the murder. Isn't that so, and didn't that, in fact, happen?"

R. Daneel said, "I do not see the point, partner Elijah."

Baley thought: I'm partner Elijah for ten minutes more. Fast! Talk fast! And think fast!

He was manipulating Sarton's dome image as he spoke. Clumsily, he expanded it, his fingernails unsure in the tension that was overwhelming him. Slowly, in jerks, the corpse widened, broadened, heightened, came closer. Baley could almost smell the stench of its scorched flesh. Its head, shoulders, and one upper arm lolled crazily, connected to hips and legs by a blackened remnant of spine from which charred rib stumps jutted.

Baley cast a side glance at the Commissioner. Enderby had closed his eyes. He looked sick. Baley felt sick, too, but he *had* to look. Slowly he circled the trimensional image by means of the transmitter controls, rotating it, bringing the ground about the corpse to view in successive quadrants. His fingernail slipped and the imaged floor tilted suddenly and expanded till floor and corpse alike were a hazy mass, beyond the resolving power of the transmitter. He brought the expansion down, let the corpse slide away.

He was still talking. He had to. He couldn't stop till he found what he was looking for. And if he didn't, all his talk might be useless. Worse than useless. His heart was throbbing, and so was his head.

He said, "The Commissioner can't commit deliberate murder. True! *Deliberate.* But any man can kill by accident. The Commissioner didn't enter Spacetown to kill Dr. Sarton. He came in to kill you, Daneel, *you!* Is there anything in his cerebroanalysis that says he is incapable of wrecking a machine? *That's* not murder, merely sabotage.

"He is a Medievalist, an earnest one. He worked with Dr. Sarton and knew the purpose for which you were designed, Daneel. He feared that purpose might be achieved, that Earthmen would eventually be weaned away from Earth. So he decided to destroy you,

Daneel. You were the only one of your type manufactured as yet and he had good reason to think that by demonstrating the extent and determination of Medievalism on Earth, he would discourage the Spacers. He knew how strong popular opinion was on the Outer Worlds to end the Spacetown project altogether. Dr. Sarton must have discussed that with him. This, he thought, would be the last nudge in the proper direction.

"I don't say even the thought of killing you, Daneel, was a pleasant one. He would have had R. Sammy do it, I imagine, if you didn't look so human that a primitive robot such as Sammy could not have told the difference, or understood it. First Law would stop him. Or the Commissioner would have had another human do it if he, himself, were not the only one who had ready access to Spacetown at all times.

"Let me reconstruct what the Commissioner's plan might have been. I'm guessing, I admit, but I think I'm close. He made the appointment with Dr. Sarton, but deliberately came early, at dawn, in fact. Dr. Sarton would be sleeping, I imagine, but you, Daneel, would be awake. I assume, by the way, you were living with Dr. Sarton, Daneel."

The robot nodded. "You are quite right, partner Elijah."

Baley said, "Then let me go on. You would come to the dome door, Daneel, receive a blaster charge in the chest or head, and be done with. The Commissioner would leave quickly, through the deserted streets of Spacetown's dawn, and back to where R. Sammy waited. He would give him back the blaster, then slowly walk again to Dr. Sarton's dome. If necessary, he would 'discover' the body himself, though he would prefer to have someone else do that. If questioned concerning his early arrival, he could say, I suppose, that he had come to tell Dr. Sarton of rumors of a Medievalist attack on Spacetown, urge him to take secret precautions to avoid open trouble between Spacers and Earthmen. The dead robot would lend point to his words.

"If they asked about the long interval between your entering Spacetown, Commissioner, and your arrival at Dr. Sarton's dome, you could say—let's see—that you saw someone lurking through the streets and heading for open country. You pursued for a while. That would also encourage them along a false path. As for R. Sammy, no one would notice him. A robot among the truck farms outside the City is just another robot.

"How close am I, Commissioner?"

Enderby writhed, "I didn't——"

"No," said Baley, "you didn't kill Daneel. He's here, and in all the time he's been in the City, you haven't been able to look him in the face or address him by name. Look at him now, Commissioner."

Enderby couldn't. He covered his face with shaking hands.

Baley's shaking hands almost dropped his transmitter. He had found it.

The image was now centered upon the main door to Dr. Sarton's dome. The door was open; it had been slid into its wall receptacle along its shining metal runner grooves. Down within them. There! There!

The sparkle was unmistakable.

"I'll tell you what happened," said Baley. "You were at the dome when you dropped your glasses. You must have been nervous and I've seen you when you're nervous. You take them off; you wipe them. You did that then. But your hands were shaking and you dropped them; maybe you stepped on them. Anyway, they were broken, and just then, the door opened and a figure that looked like Daneel faced you.

"You blasted him, scrabbled up the remains of your glasses, and ran. *They* found the body, not you, and when they came to find you, you discovered that it was not Daneel, but the early-rising Dr. Sarton, that you had killed. Dr. Sarton had designed Daneel in his own image, to his great misfortune, and without your glasses in that moment of tension, you could not tell them apart.

"And if you want the tangible proof, it's there!" The image of Sarton's dome quivered and Baley put the transmitter carefully upon the desk, his hand tightly upon it.

Commissioner Enderby's face was distorted with terror and Baley's with tension. R. Daneel seemed indifferent.

Baley's finger was pointing. "That glitter in the grooves of the door. What was it, Daneel?"

"Two small slivers of glass," said the robot, coolly. "It meant nothing to us."

"It will now. They're portions of concave lenses. Measure their optical properties and compare them with those of the glasses Enderby is wearing now. *Don't smash them, Commissioner!*"

He lunged at the Commissioner and wrenched the spectacles from the other's hand. He held them out to R. Daneel, panting, "That's proof enough, I think, that he was at the dome earlier than he was thought to be."

R. Daneel said, "I am quite convinced. I can see now that I was thrown completely off the scent by the Commissioner's cerebroanalysis. I congratulate you, partner Elijah."

Baley's watch said 24:00. A new day was beginning.

Slowly, the Commissioner's head went down on his arms. His words were muffled wails. "It was a mistake. A mistake. I never meant to kill him." Without warning, he slipped from the chair and lay crumpled on the floor.

R. Daneel sprang to him, saying, "You have hurt him, Elijah. That is too bad."

"He isn't dead, is he?"

"No. But unconscious."

"He'll come to. It was too much for him, I suppose. I had to do it, Daneel, I had to. I had no evidence that would stand up in court, only inferences. I had to badger him and badger him and let it out little by little, hoping he would break down. He did, Daneel. You heard him confess, didn't you?"

"Yes."

"Now, then, I promised this would be to the benefit of Spacetown's project, so—— Wait, he's coming to."

The Commissioner groaned. His eyes fluttered and opened. He stared speechlessly at the two.

Baley said, "Commissioner, do you hear me?"

The Commissioner nodded listlessly.

"All right, then. Now, the Spacers have more on their minds than your prosecution. If you co-operate with them——"

"What? What?" There was a dawning flicker of hope in the Commissioner's eyes.

"You must be a big wheel in New York's Medievalist organization, maybe even in the planetary setup. Maneuver them in the direction of the colonization of space. You can see the propaganda line, can't you? We can go back to the soil all right—but on other planets."

"I don't understand," mumbled the Commissioner.

"It's what the Spacers are after. And God help me, it's what I'm after now, too, since a small conversation I had with Dr. Fastolfe. It's what they want more than anything. They risk death continually by coming to Earth and staying here for that purpose. If Dr. Sarton's murder will make it possible for you to swing Medievalism into line for the resumption of Galactic colonization, they'll probably consider it a worth-while sacrifice. Do you understand now?"

R. Daneel said, "Elijah is quite correct. Help us, Commissioner, and we will forget the past. I am speaking for Dr. Fastolfe and our people generally in this. Of course, if you should agree to help and later betray us, we would always have the fact of your guilt to hold over your head. I hope you understand that, too. It pains me to have to mention that."

"I won't be prosecuted?" asked the Commissioner.

"Not if you help us."

Tears filled his eyes. "I'll do it. It was an accident. Explain that. An accident. I did what I thought right."

Baley said, "If you help us, you *will* be doing right. The colonization of space is the only possible salvation of Earth. You'll realize that if you think about it without prejudice. If you find you cannot, have a short talk with Dr. Fastolfe. And now, you can begin helping by quashing the R. Sammy business. Call it an accident or something. End it!"

Baley got to his feet. "And remember, I'm not the only one who knows the truth, Commissioner. Getting rid of me will ruin you. All Spacetown knows. You see that, don't you?"

R. Daneel said, "It is unnecessary to say more, Elijah. He is sincere and he will help. So much is obvious from his cerebroanalysis."

"All right. Then I'll go home. I want to see Jessie and Bentley and take up a natural existence again. And I want to sleep.— Daneel, will you stay on Earth after the Spacers go?"

R. Daneel said, "I have not been informed. Why do you ask?"

Baley bit his lip, then said, "I didn't think I would ever say anything like this to anyone like you, Daneel, but I trust you. I even— admire you. I'm too old ever to leave Earth myself, but when schools for emigrants are finally established, there's Bentley. If someday, perhaps, Bentley and you, together . . ."

"Perhaps." R. Daneel's face was emotionless.

The robot turned to Julius Enderby, who was watching them with a flaccid face into which a certain vitality was only now beginning to return.

The robot said, "I have been trying, friend Julius, to understand some remarks Elijah made to me earlier. Perhaps I am beginning to, for it suddenly seems to me that the destruction of what should not be, that is, the destruction of what you people call evil, is less just and desirable than the conversion of this evil into what you call good."

He hesitated, then, almost as though he were surprised at his own words, he said, "Go, and sin no more!"

Baley, suddenly smiling, took R. Daneel's elbow, and they walked out the door, arm in arm.

The Naked Sun

To Noreen and Nick Falasca, for inviting me,
To Tony Boucher, for introducing me, and
To One Hundred Unusual Hours.

Contents

1

A Question Is Asked

STUBBORNLY Elijah Baley fought panic.

For two weeks it had been building up. Longer than that, even. It had been building up ever since they had called him to Washington and there calmly told him he was being reassigned.

The call to Washington had been disturbing enough in itself. It came without details, a mere summons; and that made it worse. It included travel slips directing round trip by plane and that made it still worse.

Partly it was the sense of urgency introduced by any order for plane travel. Partly it was the thought of the plane; simply that. Still, that was just the beginning of uneasiness and, as yet, easy to suppress.

After all, Lije Baley had been in a plane four times before. Once he had even crossed the continent. So, while plane travel is never pleasant, it would, at least, not be a complete step into the unknown.

And then, the trip from New York to Washington would take only an hour. The take-off would be from New York Runway Number 2, which, like all official Runways, was decently enclosed, with a lock opening to the unprotected atmosphere only after air speed had been achieved. The arrival would be at Washington Runway Number 5, which was similarly protected.

Furthermore, as Baley well knew, there would be no windows on the plane. There would be good lighting, decent food, all necessary conveniences. The radio-controlled flight would be smooth; there would scarcely be any sensation of motion once the plane was airborne.

He explained all this to himself, and to Jessie, his wife, who had never been air-borne and who approached such matters with terror.

She said, "But I don't *like* you to take a plane, Lije. It isn't natural. Why can't you take the Expressways?"

"Because that would take ten hours"—Baley's long face was set in dour lines—"and because I'm a member of the City Police Force and have to follow the orders of my superiors. At least, I do if I want to keep my C-6 rating."

There was no arguing with that.

Baley took the plane and kept his eyes firmly on the news-strip that unreeled smoothly and continuously from the eye-level dispenser. The City was proud of that service: news, features, humorous articles, educational bits, occasional fiction. Someday the strips would be converted to film, it was said, since enclosing the eyes with a viewer would be an even more efficient way of distracting the passenger from his surroundings.

Baley kept his eyes on the unreeling strip, not only for the sake of distraction, but also because etiquette required it. There were five other passengers on the plane (he could not help noticing that much) and each one of them had his private right to whatever degree of fear and anxiety his nature and upbringing made him feel.

Baley would certainly resent the intrusion of anyone else on his own uneasiness. He wanted no strange eyes on the whiteness of his knuckles where his hands gripped the armrest, or the dampish stain they would leave when he took them away.

He told himself: I'm enclosed. This plane is just a little City.

But he didn't fool himself. There was an inch of steel at his left; he could feel it with his elbow. Past that, nothing——

Well, air! But that was nothing, really.

A thousand miles of it in one direction. A thousand in another. One mile of it, maybe two, straight down.

He almost wished he could see straight down, glimpse the top of the buried Cities he was passing over; New York, Philadelphia, Baltimore, Washington. He imagined the rolling, low-slung cluster-complexes of domes he had never seen but knew to be there. And under them, for a mile underground and dozens of miles in every direction, would be the Cities.

The endless, hiving corridors of the Cities, he thought, alive with people; apartments, community kitchens, factories, Expressways; all comfortable and warm with the evidence of man.

And he himself was isolated in the cold and featureless air in a small bullet of metal, moving through emptiness.

His hands trembled, and he forced his eyes to focus on the strip of paper and read a bit.

It was a short story dealing with Galactic exploration and it was quite obvious that the hero was an Earthman.

Baley muttered in exasperation, then held his breath momentarily in dismay at his boorishness in making a sound.

It was completely ridiculous, though. It was pandering to child-ishness, this pretense that Earthmen could invade space. Galactic exploration! The Galaxy was closed to Earthmen. It was pre-empted by the Spacers, whose ancestors had been Earthmen centuries before. Those ancestors had reached the Outer Worlds first, found themselves comfortable, and their descendants had lowered the bars to immigration. They had penned in Earth and their Earthman cousins. And Earth's City civilization completed the task, imprisoning Earthmen within the Cities by a wall of fear of open spaces that barred them from the robot-run farming and mining areas of their own planet; from even that.

Baley thought bitterly: Jehoshaphat! If we don't like it, let's do something about it. Let's not just waste time with fairy tales.

But there was nothing to do about it, and he knew it.

Then the plane landed. He and his fellow-passengers emerged and scattered away from one another, never looking.

Baley glanced at his watch and decided there was time for fresh-ening before taking the Expressway to the Justice Department. He was glad there was. The sound and clamor of life, the huge vaulted chamber of the airport with City corridors leading off on numerous levels, everything else he saw and heard, gave him the feeling of being safely and warmly enclosed in the bowels and womb of the City. It washed away anxiety and only a shower was necessary to complete the job.

He needed a transient's permit to make use of one of the com-munity bathrooms, but presentation of his travel orders eliminated any difficulties. There was only the routine stamping, with private-stall privileges (the date carefully marked to prevent abuse) and a slim strip of directions for getting to the assigned spot.

Baley was thankful for the feel of the strips beneath his feet. It was with something amounting to luxury that he felt himself accelerate as he moved from strip to moving strip inward toward the speeding Expressway. He swung himself aboard lightly, taking the seat to which his rating entitled him.

It wasn't a rush hour; seats were available. The bathroom, when he reached it, was not unduly crowded either. The stall assigned to him was in decent order with a launderette that worked well.

With his water ration consumed to good purpose and his clothing freshened he felt ready to tackle the Justice Department. Ironically enough, he even felt cheerful.

Undersecretary Albert Minnim was a small, compact man, ruddy of skin, and graying, with the angles of his body smoothed down and softened. He exuded an air of cleanliness and smelled faintly of tonic. It all spoke of the good things of life that came with the liberal rations obtained by those high in Administration.

Baley felt sallow and rawboned in comparison. He was conscious of his own large hands, deep-set eyes, a general sense of cragginess.

Minnim said cordially, "Sit down, Baley. Do you smoke?"

"Only a pipe, sir," said Baley.

He drew it out as he spoke, and Minnim thrust back a cigar he had half drawn.

Baley was instantly regretful. A cigar was better than nothing and he would have appreciated the gift. Even with the increased tobacco ration that went along with his recent promotion from C-5 to C-6 he wasn't exactly swimming in pipe fixings.

"Please light up, if you care to," said Minnim, and waited with a kind of paternal patience while Baley measured out a careful quantity of tobacco and affixed the pipe baffle.

Baley said, his eyes on his pipe, "I have not been told the reason for my being called to Washington, sir."

"I know that," said Minnim. He smiled. "I can fix that right now. You are being reassigned temporarily."

"Outside New York City?"

"Quite a distance."

Baley raised his eyebrows and looked thoughtful. "How temporarily, sir?"

"I'm not sure."

Baley was aware of the advantages and disadvantages of reassignment. As a transient in a City of which he was not a resident, he would probably live on a scale better than his official rating entitled him to. On the other hand, it would be very unlikely that Jessie and their son, Bentley, would be allowed to travel with him. They would be taken care of, to be sure, there in New York, but Baley was a domesticated creature and he did not enjoy the thought of separation.

Then, too, a reassignment meant a specific job of work, which was good, and a responsibility greater than that ordinarily expected of the individual detective, which could be uncomfortable. Baley had, not too many months earlier, survived the responsibility of the investigation of the murder of a Spacer just outside New York. He was not overjoyed at the prospect of another such detail, or anything approaching it.

He said, "Would you tell me where I'm going? The nature of the reassignment? What it's all about?"

He was trying to weigh the Undersecretary's "Quite a distance" and make little bets with himself as to his new base of operations. The "Quite a distance" had sounded emphatic and Baley thought: Calcutta? Sydney?

Then he noticed that Minnim was taking out a cigar after all and was lighting it carefully.

Baley thought: Jehoshaphat! He's having trouble telling me. He doesn't want to say.

Minnim withdrew his cigar from between his lips. He watched the smoke and said, "The Department of Justice is assigning you to temporary duty on Solaria."

For a moment Baley's mind groped for an illusive identification: Solaria, Asia; Solaria, Australia . . . ?

Then he rose from his seat and said tightly, "You mean, one of the Outer Worlds?"

Minnim didn't meet Baley's eyes. "That is right!"

Baley said, "But that's impossible. They wouldn't allow an Earthman on an Outer World."

"Circumstances do alter cases, Plainclothesman Baley. There has been a murder on Solaria."

Baley's lips quirked into a sort of reflex smile. "That's a little out of our jurisdiction, isn't it?"

"They've requested help."

"From us? From Earth?" Baley was torn between confusion and disbelief. For an Outer World to take any attitude other than contempt toward the despised mother planet or, at best, a patronizing social benevolence was unthinkable. To come for help?

"From Earth?" he repeated.

"Unusual," admitted Minnim, "but there it is. They want a Terrestrial detective assigned to the case. It's been handled through diplomatic channels on the highest levels."

Baley sat down again. "Why me? I'm not a young man. I'm forty-three. I've got a wife and child. I couldn't leave Earth."

"That's not our choice, Plainclothesman. You were specifically asked for."

"I?"

"Plainclothesman Elijah Baley, C-6, of the New York City Police Force. They knew what they wanted. Surely you see why."

Baley said stubbornly, "I'm not qualified."

"They think you are. The way you handled the Spacer murder has apparently reached them."

"They must have got it all mixed up. It must have seemed better than it was."

Minnim shrugged. "In any case, they've asked for you and we have agreed to send you. You are reassigned. The papers have all been taken care of and you must go. During your absence, your wife and child will be taken care of at a C-7 level since that will be your temporary rating during your discharge of this assignment." He paused significantly. "Satisfactory completion of the assignment may make the rating permanent."

It was happening too quickly for Baley. None of this could be so. He *couldn't* leave Earth. Didn't they see that?

He heard himself ask in a level voice that sounded unnatural in his own ears. "What kind of a murder? What are the circumstances? Why can't they handle it themselves?"

Minnim rearranged small objects on his desk with carefully kept fingers. He shook his head. "I don't know anything about the murder. I don't know the circumstances."

"Then who does, sir? You don't expect me to go there cold, do you?" And again a despairing inner voice: But I *can't* leave Earth.

"Nobody knows anything about it. Nobody on Earth. The Solarians didn't tell us. That will be your job; to find out what is so important about the murder that they must have an Earthman to solve it. Or, rather, that will be *part* of your job."

Baley was desperate enough to say, "What if I refuse?" He knew the answer, of course. He knew exactly what declassification would mean to himself and, more than that, to his family.

Minnim said nothing about declassification. He said softly, "You can't refuse, Plainclothesman. You have a job to do."

"For Solaria? The hell with them."

"For *us*, Baley. For us." Minnim paused. Then he went on, "You know the position of Earth with respect to the Spacers. I don't have to go into that."

Baley knew the situation and so did every man on Earth. The fifty Outer Worlds, with a far smaller population, in combination, than that of Earth alone, nevertheless maintained a military potential perhaps a hundred times greater. With their underpopulated worlds resting on a positronic robot economy, their energy production per human was thousands of times that of Earth. And it was the amount of energy a single human could produce that dictated military potential, standard of living, happiness, and all besides.

Minnim said, "One of the factors that conspires to keep us in that position is ignorance. Just that. Ignorance. The Spacers know all about us. They send missions enough to Earth, heaven knows. We know nothing about them except what they tell us. No man on Earth has ever as much as set foot on an Outer World. *You* will, though."

Baley began, "I can't . . ."

But Minnim repeated, "You *will*. Your position will be unique. You will be on Solaria on their invitation, doing a job to which they will assign you. When you return, you will have information useful to Earth."

Baley watched the Undersecretary through somber eyes. "You mean I'm to spy for Earth."

"No question of spying. You need do nothing they don't ask you to do. Just keep your eyes and mind open. Observe! There will be specialists on Earth when you return to analyze and interpret your observations."

Baley said, "I take it there's a crisis, sir."

"Why do you say that?"

"Sending an Earthman to an Outer World is risky. The Spacers hate us. With the best will in the world and even though I'm there on invitation, I could cause an interstellar incident. The Terrestrial Government could easily avoid sending me if they chose. They could say I was ill. The Spacers are pathologically afraid of disease. They wouldn't want me for any reason if they thought I were ill."

"Do you suggest," said Minnim, "we try that trick?"

"No. If the government had no other motive for sending me, they would think of that or something better without my help. So it follows that it is the question of spying that is the real essential. And if that is so, there must be more to it than just a see-what-you-can-see to justify the risk."

Baley half expected an explosion and would have half welcomed one as a relief of pressure, but Minnim only smiled frostily and said, "You can see past the non-essentials, it seems. But then, I expected no less."

The Undersecretary leaned across his desk toward Baley. "Here is certain information which you will discuss with no one, not even with other government officials. Our sociologists have been coming to certain conclusions concerning the present Galactic situation. Fifty Outer Worlds, underpopulated, roboticized, powerful, with people that are healthy and long-lived. We ourselves, crowded, technologically underdeveloped, short-lived, under their domination. It is unstable."

"Everything is in the long run."

"This is unstable in the short run. A hundred years is the most we're allowed. The situation will last our time, to be sure, but we have children. Eventually we will become too great a danger to the Outer Worlds to be allowed to survive. There are eight billions on Earth who hate the Spacers."

Baley said, "The Spacers exclude us from the Galaxy, handle our trade to their own profit, dictate to our government, and treat us with contempt. What do they expect? Gratitude?"

"True, and yet the pattern is fixed. Revolt, suppression, revolt, suppression—and within a century Earth will be virtually wiped out as a populated world. So the sociologists say."

Baley stirred uneasily. One didn't question sociologists and their computers. "But what do you expect me to accomplish if all this is so?"

"Bring us information. The big flaw in sociological forecast is our lack of data concerning the Spacers. We've had to make assumptions on the basis of the few Spacers they sent out here. We've had to rely on what they choose to tell us of themselves, so it follows we know their strengths and only their strengths. Damn it, they have their robots and their low numbers and their long lives. But do they have weaknesses? Is there some factor or factors which, if we but knew, would alter the sociologic inevitability of destruction; something that could guide our actions and better the chance of Earth's survival."

"Hadn't you better send a sociologist, sir?"

Minnim shook his head. "If we could send whom we pleased, we would have sent someone out ten years ago, when these conclusions were first being arrived at. This is our first excuse to send someone and they ask for a detective and that suits us. A detective is a sociologist, too; a rule-of-thumb, practicing sociologist, or he wouldn't be a good detective. Your record proves you a good one."

"Thank you, sir," said Baley mechanically. "And if I get into trouble?"

Minnim shrugged. "That's the risk of a policeman's job." He dismissed the point with a wave of his hand and added, "In any case, you must go. Your time of departure is set. The ship that will take you is waiting."

Baley stiffened. "Waiting? When do I leave?"

"In two days."

"I've got to get back to New York then. My wife——"

"*We* will see your wife. She can't know the nature of your job, you know. She will be told not to expect to hear from you."

"But this is inhuman. I must see her. I may never see her again."

Minnim said, "What I say now may sound even more inhuman, but isn't it true that there is never a day you set about your duties on which you cannot tell yourself she may never see you again? Plainclothesman Baley, we must all do our duty."

Baley's pipe had been out for fifteen minutes. He had never noticed it.

No one had more to tell him. No one knew anything about the murder. Official after official simply hurried him on to the moment when he stood at the base of a spaceship, all unbelieving still.

It was like a gigantic cannon aimed at the heavens, and Baley shivered spasmodically in the raw, open air. The night closed in (for which Baley was thankful) like dark black walls melting into a black ceiling overhead. It was cloudy, and though he had been to Planetaria, a bright star, stabbing through a rift in the cloud, startled him when it caught his eyes.

A little spark, far, far away. He stared curiously, almost unafraid of it. It looked quite close, quite insignificant, and yet around things like that circled planets of which the inhabitants were lords of the Galaxy. The sun was a thing like that, he thought, except much closer, shining now on the other side of the Earth.

He thought of the Earth suddenly as a ball of stone with a film of moisture and gas, exposed to emptiness on every side, with its Cities barely dug into the outer rim, clinging precariously between rock and air. His skin crawled!

The ship was a Spacer vessel, of course. Interstellar trade was entirely in Spacer hands. He was alone now, just outside the rim of the City. He had been bathed and scraped and sterilized until he was considered safe, by Spacer standards, to board the ship. Even so, they sent only a robot out to meet him, bearing as he did a hundred varieties of disease germs from the sweltering City to which he himself was resistant but to which the eugenically hothoused Spacers were not.

The robot bulked dimly in the night, its eyes a dull red glow. "Plainclothesman Elijah Baley?"

"That's right," said Baley crisply, the hair on the nape of his neck stirring a bit. He was enough of an Earthman to get angry goose flesh at the sight of a robot doing a man's job. There had been R. Daneel Olivaw, who had partnered with him in the Spacer murder affair, but that had been different. Daneel had been——

"You will follow me, please," said the robot, and a white light flooded a path toward the ship.

Baley followed. Up the ladder and into the ship he went, along corridors, and into a room.

The robot said, "This will be your room, Plainclothesman Baley. It is requested that you remain in it for the duration of the trip."

Baley thought: Sure, seal me off. Keep me safe. Insulated.

The corridors along which he had traveled had been empty. Robots were probably disinfecting them now. The robot facing him would probably step through a germicidal bath when it left.

The robot said, "There is a water supply and plumbing. Food will be supplied. You will have viewing matter. The ports are controlled from this panel. They are closed now but if you wish to view space——"

Baley said with some agitation, "That's all right, boy. Leave the ports closed."

He used the "boy" address that Earthmen always used for robots, but the robot showed no adverse response. It couldn't, of course. Its responses were limited and controlled by the Laws of Robotics.

The robot bent its large metal body in the travesty of a respectful bow and left.

Baley was alone in his room and could take stock. It was better than the plane, at least. He could see the plane from end to end. He could see its limits. The spaceship was large. It had corridors, levels, rooms. It was a small City in itself. Baley could almost breathe freely.

Then lights flashed and a robot's metallic voice sounded over the communo and gave him specific instructions for guarding himself against take-off acceleration.

There was the push backward against webbing and a yielding hydraulic system, a distant rumble of force-jets heated to fury by the proton micro-pile. There was the hiss of tearing atmosphere, growing thinner and high-pitched and fading into nothingness after an hour.

They were in space.

It was as though all sensation had numbed, as though nothing were real. He told himself that each second found him thousands of miles farther from the Cities, from Jessie, but it didn't register.

On the second day (the third?—there was no way of telling time except by the intervals of eating and sleeping) there was a queer momentary sensation of being turned inside out. It lasted an instant and Baley knew it was a Jump, that oddly incomprehensible, almost mystical, momentary transition through hyperspace that transferred a ship and all it contained from one point in space to another, light-years away. Another lapse of time and another Jump, still another lapse, still another Jump.

Baley told himself now that he was light-years away, tens of light-years, hundreds, thousands.

He didn't know how many. No one on Earth as much as knew

Solaria's location in space. He would bet on that. They were ignorant, every one of them.

He felt terribly alone.

There was the feel of deceleration and the robot entered. Its somber, ruddy eyes took in the details of Baley's harness. Efficiently it tightened a wing nut; quickly it surveyed the details of the hydraulic system.

It said, "We will be landing in three hours. You will remain, if you please, in this room. A man will come to escort you out and to take you to your place of residence."

"Wait," said Baley tensely. Strapped in as he was, he felt helpless. "When we land, what time of day will it be?"

The robot said at once, "By Galactic Standard Time, it will be——"

"Local time, boy. Local time! Jehoshaphat!"

The robot continued smoothly, "The day on Solaria is twenty-eight point thirty-five Standard hours in length. The Solarian hour is divided into ten decads, each of which is divided into a hundred centads. We are scheduled to arrive at an airport at which the day will be at the twentieth centad of the fifth decad."

Baley hated that robot. He hated it for its obtuseness in not understanding; for the way it was making him ask the question directly and exposing his own weakness.

He had to. He said flatly, "Will it be daytime?"

And after all that the robot answered, "Yes, sir," and left.

It would be day! He would have to step out onto the unprotected surface of a planet in daytime.

He was not quite sure how it would be. He had seen glimpses of planetary surfaces from certain points within the City; he had even been out upon it for moments. Always, though, he had been surrounded by walls or within reach of one. There was always safety at hand.

Where would there be safety now? Not even the false walls of darkness.

And because he would not display weakness before the Spacers—he'd be damned if he would—he stiffened his body against the webbing that held him safe against the forces of deceleration, closed his eyes, and stubbornly fought panic.

2

A Friend Is Encountered

BALEY WAS losing his fight. Reason alone was not enough.

Baley told himself over and over: Men live in the open all their lives. The Spacers do so now. Our ancestors on Earth did it in the past. There is no real harm in wall-lessness. It is only my mind that tells me differently, and it is wrong.

But all that did not help. Something above and beyond reason cried out for walls and would have none of space.

As time passed, he thought he would not succeed. He would be cowering at the end, trembling and pitiful. The Spacer they would send for him (with filters in his nose to keep out germs, and gloves on his hands to prevent contact) would not even honestly despise him. The Spacer would feel only disgust.

Baley held on grimly.

When the ship stopped and the deceleration harness automatically uncoupled, while the hydraulic system retracted into the wall, Baley remained in his seat. He was afraid, and determined not to show it.

He looked away at the first quiet sound of the door of his room opening. There was the eye-corner flash of a tall, bronze-haired figure entering; a Spacer, one of those proud descendants of Earth who had disowned their heritage.

The Spacer spoke. "Partner Elijah!"

Baley's head turned toward the speaker with a jerk. His eyes rounded and he rose almost without volition.

He stared at the face; at the broad, high cheekbones, the absolute calm of the facial lines, the symmetry of the body, most of all at that level look out of nerveless blue eyes.

"D-daneel."

The Spacer said, "It is pleasant that you remember me, Partner Elijah."

"Remember you!" Baley felt relief wash over him. This being was a bit of Earth, a friend, a comfort, a savior. He had an almost unbearable desire to rush to the Spacer and embrace him, to hug him wildly, and laugh and pound his back and do all the foolish things old friends did when meeting once again after a separation.

But he didn't. He couldn't. He could only step forward, and hold out his hand and say, "I'm not likely to forget you, Daneel."

"That is pleasant," said Daneel, nodding gravely. "As you are well aware, it is quite impossible for me, while in working order, to forget you. It is well that I see you again."

Daneel took Baley's hand and pressed it with firm coolness, his fingers closing to a comfortable but not painful pressure and then releasing it.

Baley hoped earnestly that the creature's unreadable eyes could not penetrate Baley's mind and see that wild moment, just past and not yet entirely subsided, when all of Baley had concentrated into a feeling of an intense friendship that was almost love.

After all, one could not love as a friend this Daneel Olivaw, who was not a man at all, but only a robot.

The robot that looked so like a man said, "I have asked that a robot-driven ground-transport vessel be connected to this ship by air-tube——"

Baley frowned. "An air-tube?"

"Yes. It is a common technique, frequently used in space, in order that personnel and matériel be transferred from one vessel to another without the necessity of special equipment against vacuum. It would seem then that you are not acquainted with the technique."

"No," said Baley, "but I get the picture."

"It is, of course, rather complicated to arrange such a device between spaceship and ground vehicle, but I have requested that it be done. Fortunately, the mission on which you and I are engaged is one of high priority. Difficulties are smoothed out quickly."

"Are you assigned to the murder case too?"

"Have you not been informed of that? I regret not having told you at once." There was, of course, no sign of regret on the robot's perfect face. "It was Dr. Han Fastolfe, whom you met on Earth during our previous partnership and whom I hope you remember, who first suggested you as an appropriate investigator in this case. He made it a condition that I be assigned to work with you once more."

Baley managed a smile. Dr. Fastolfe was a native of Aurora and Aurora was the strongest of the Outer Worlds. Apparently the advice of an Auroran bore weight.

Baley said, "A team that works shouldn't be broken up, eh?" (The first exhilaration of Daneel's appearance was fading and the compression about Baley's chest was returning.)

"I do not know if that precise thought was in his mind, Partner Elijah. From the nature of his orders to me, I should think that he was interested in having assigned to work with you one who would have experience with your world and would know of your consequent peculiarities."

"Peculiarities!" Baley frowned and felt offended. It was not a term he liked in connection with himself.

"So that I could arrange the air-tube, for example. I am well aware of your aversion to open spaces as a result of your upbringing in the Cities of Earth."

Perhaps it was the effect of being called "peculiar," the feeling that he had to counterattack or lose caste to a machine, that drove Baley to change the subject sharply. Perhaps it was just that life-long training prevented him from leaving any logical contradiction undisturbed.

He said, "There was a robot in charge of my welfare on board this ship; a robot" (a touch of malice intruded itself here) "that looks like a robot. Do you know it?"

"I spoke to it before coming on board."

"What's its designation? How do I make contact with it?"

"It is RX-2475. It is customary on Solaria to use only serial numbers for robots." Daneel's calm eyes swept the control panel near the door. "This contact will signal it."

Baley looked at the control panel himself and, since the contact to which Daneel pointed was labeled RX, its identification seemed quite unmysterious.

Baley put his finger over it and in less than a minute, the robot, the one that looked like a robot, entered.

Baley said, "You are RX-2475."

"Yes, sir."

"You told me earlier that someone would arrive to escort me off the ship. Did you mean him?" Baley pointed at Daneel.

The eyes of the two robots met. RX-2475 said, "His papers identify him as the one who was to meet you."

"Were you told in advance anything about him other than his papers? Was he described to you?"

"No, sir. I was given his name, however."

"Who gave you the information?"

"The captain of the ship, sir."

"Who is a Solarian?"

"Yes, sir."

Baley licked his lips. The next question would be decisive.

He said, "What were you told would be the name of the one you were expecting?"

RX-2475 said, "Daneel Olivaw, sir."

"Good boy! You may leave now."

There was the robotic bow and then the sharp about-face. RX-2475 left.

Baley turned to his partner and said thoughtfully, "You are not telling me all the truth, Daneel."

"In what way, Partner Elijah?" asked Daneel.

"While I was talking to you earlier, I recalled an odd point. RX-2475, when it told me I would have an escort said a *man* would come for me. I remember that quite well."

Daneel listened quietly and said nothing.

Baley went on. "I thought the robot might have made a mistake. I thought also that perhaps a man had indeed been assigned to meet me and had later been replaced by you, RX-2475 not being informed of the change. But you heard me check that. Your papers were described to it and it was given your name. But it was not quite given your name at that, was it, Daneel?"

"Indeed, it was not given my entire name," agreed Daneel.

"Your name is not Daneel Olivaw, but R. Daneel Olivaw, isn't it? Or, in full, Robot Daneel Olivaw."

"You are quite correct, Partner Elijah."

"From which it all follows that RX-2475 was never informed that you are a robot. It was allowed to think of you as a man. With your manlike appearance, such a masquerade is possible."

"I have no quarrel with your reasoning."

"Then let's proceed." Baley was feeling the germs of a kind of savage delight. He was on the trace of something. It couldn't be anything much, but this was the kind of tracking he could do well. It was something he could do well enough to be called half across space to do. He said, "Now why should anyone want to deceive a miserable robot? It doesn't matter to it whether you are man or robot. It follows orders in either case. A reasonable conclusion then is that the Solarian captain who informed the robot and the Solarian officials who informed the Captain did not themselves know you were a robot. As I say, that is one reasonable conclusion, but perhaps not the only one. Is this one true?"

"I believe it is."

"All right, then. Good guess. Now why? Dr. Han Fastolfe, in recommending you as my partner allows the Solarians to think you are a human. Isn't that a dangerous thing? The Solarians, if they find out, may be quite angry. Why was it done?"

The humanoid robot said, "It was explained to me thus, Partner Elijah. Your association with a human of the Outer Worlds would raise your status in the eyes of the Solarians. Your association with a robot would lower it. Since I was familiar with your ways and could work with you easily, it was thought reasonable to allow the Solarians to accept me as a man without actually deceiving them by a positive statement to that effect."

Baley did not believe it. It seemed like the kind of careful consideration for an Earthman's feelings that did not come naturally to a Spacer, not even to as enlightened a one as Fastolfe.

He considered an alternative and said, "Are the Solarians well known among the Outer Worlds for the production of robots?"

"I am glad," said Daneel, "that you have been briefed concerning the inner economy of Solaria."

"Not a word," said Baley. "I can guess the spelling of the word Solaria and there my knowledge stops."

"Then I do not see, Partner Elijah, what it was that impelled you to ask that question, but it is a most pertinent one. You have hit the mark. My mind-store of information includes the fact that, of the fifty Outer Worlds, Solaria is by far the best known for the variety and excellence of robot models it turns out. It exports specialized models to all the other Outer Worlds."

Baley nodded in grim satisfaction. Naturally Daneel did not follow an intuitive mental leap that used human weakness as a starting point. Nor did Baley feel impelled to explain the reasoning. *If* Solaria turned out to be a world expert in robotics, Dr. Han Fastolfe and his associates might have purely personal and very human motives for demonstrating their own prize robot. It would have nothing at all to do with an Earthman's safety or feelings.

They would be asserting their own superiority by allowing the expert Solarians to be fooled into accepting a robot of Auroran handiwork as a fellow-man.

Baley felt much better. Strange that all the thought, all the intellectual powers he could muster, could not succeed in lifting him out of panic; and yet a sop to his own vainglory succeeded at once.

The recognition of the vainglory of the Spacers helped too.

He thought: Jehoshaphat, we're all human; even the Spacers.

Aloud he said, almost flippantly, "How long do we have to wait for the ground-car? I'm ready."

The air-tube gave signs of not being well adapted to its present use. Man and humanoid stepped out of the spaceship erect, moving along flexible mesh that bent and swayed under their weight. (In space, Baley imagined hazily, men transferring weightlessly from ship to ship might easily skim along the length of the tube, impelled by an initial Jump.)

Toward the other end the tube narrowed clumsily, its meshing bunching as though some giant hand had constricted it. Daneel, carrying the flashlight, got down on all fours and so did Baley. They traveled the last twenty feet in that fashion, moving at last into what was obviously a ground-car.

Daneel closed the door through which they had entered, sliding it shut carefully. There was a heavy, clicking noise that might have been the detachment of the air-tube.

Baley looked about curiously. There was nothing too exotic about the ground-car. There were two seats in tandem, each of which could hold three. There were doors at each end of each seat. The glossy sections that might ordinarily have been windows were black and opaque, as a result, undoubtedly, of appropriate polarization. Baley was acquainted with that.

The interior of the car was lit by two round spots of yellow illumination in the ceiling and, in short, the only thing Baley felt to be strange was the transmitter set into the partition immediately before the front seat and, of course, the added fact that there were no visible controls.

Baley said, "I suppose the driver is on the other side of this partition."

Daneel said, "Exactly so, Partner Elijah. And we can give our orders in this fashion." He leaned forward slightly and flicked a toggle switch that set a spot of red light to flickering. He said quietly, "You may start now. We are ready."

There was a muted whir that faded almost at once, a very slight, very transitory pressing against the back of the seat, and then nothing.

Baley said in surprise, "Are we moving?"

Daneel said, "We are. The car does not move on wheels but glides along a diamagnetic force-field. Except for acceleration and deceleration, you will feel nothing."

"What about curves?"

"The car will bank automatically to compensate. Its level is maintained when traveling up- or downhill."

"The controls must be complicated," said Baley dryly.

"Quite automatic. The driver of the vehicle is a robot."

"Umm." Baley had about all he wanted on the ground-car. He said, "How long will this take?"

"About an hour. Air travel would have been speedier, but I was concerned to keep you enclosed and the aircraft models available on Solaria do not lend themselves to complete enclosure as does a ground-car such as that in which we are now riding."

Baley felt annoyed at the other's "concern." He felt like a baby in the charge of its nurse. He felt almost as annoyed, oddly enough, at Daneel's sentences. It seemed to him that such needlessly formal sentence structure might easily betray the robotic nature of the creature.

For a moment Baley stared curiously at R. Daneel Olivaw. The robot, looking straight ahead, was motionless and unself-conscious under the other's gaze.

Daneel's skin texture was perfect, the individual hairs on head and body had been lovingly and intricately manufactured and placed. The muscle movement under the skin was most realistic. No pains, however extravagant, had been spared. Yet Baley knew, from personal knowledge, that limbs and chest could be split open along invisible seams so that repairs might be made. He knew there was metal and silicone under that realistic skin. He knew a positronic brain, most advanced but only positronic, nestled in the hollow of the skull. He knew that Daneel's "thoughts" were only short-lived positronic currents flowing along paths rigidly designed and foreordained by the manufacturer.

But what were the signs that would give that away to the expert eye that had no foreknowledge? The trifling unnaturalness of Daneel's manner of speech? The unemotional gravity that rested so steadily upon him? The very perfection of his humanity?

But he was wasting time. Baley said, "Let's get on with it, Daneel. I suppose that before arriving here, you were briefed on matters Solarian?"

"I was, Partner Elijah."

"Good. That's more than they did for me. How large is the world?"

"Its diameter is 9500 miles. It is the outermost of three planets and the only inhabited one. In climate and atmosphere it resembles Earth; its percentage of fertile land is higher; its useful mineral content lower, but of course less exploited. The world is self-supporting and can, with the aid of its robot exports, maintain a high standard of living."

Baley said, "What's the population?"

"Twenty thousand people, Partner Elijah."

Baley accepted that for a moment, then he said mildly, "You mean twenty million, don't you?" His scant knowledge of the Outer Worlds was enough to tell him that, although the worlds were underpopulated by Earthly standards, the individual populations *were* in the millions.

"Twenty thousand people, Partner Elijah," said the robot again.

"You mean the planet has just been settled?"

"Not at all. It has been independent for nearly two centuries, and it was settled for a century or more before that. The population is deliberately maintained at twenty thousand, that being considered optimum by the Solarians themselves."

"How much of the planet do they occupy?"

"All the fertile portions."

"Which is, in square miles?"

"Thirty million square miles, including marginal areas."

"For twenty thousand people?"

"There are also some two hundred million working positronic robots, Partner Elijah."

"Jehoshaphat! That's—that's ten thousand robots per human."

"It is by far the highest such ratio among the Outer Worlds, Partner Elijah. The next highest, on Aurora, is only fifty to one."

"What can they use so many robots for? What do they want with all that food?"

"Food is a relatively minor item. The mines are more important, and power production more important still."

Baley thought of all those robots and felt a trifle dizzy. Two hundred million robots! So many among so few humans. The robots must litter the landscape. An observer from without might think Solaria a world of robots altogether and fail to notice the thin human leaven.

He felt a sudden need to see. He remembered the conversation with Minnim and the sociologic prediction of Earth's danger. It seemed far off, a bit unreal, but he remembered. His personal dangers and difficulties since leaving Earth dimmed the memory of Minnim's voice stating enormities with cool and precise enunciation, but never blotted it out altogether.

Baley had lived too long with duty to allow even the overwhelming fact of open space to stop him in its performance. Data collected from a Spacer's words, or from those of a Spacer robot for that matter, was the sort of thing that was already available to Earth's sociologists. What was needed was direct observation and it was his job, however unpleasant, to collect it.

He inspected the upper portion of the ground-car. "Is this thing a convertible, Daneel?"

"I beg your pardon, Partner Elijah, but I do not follow your meaning."

"Can the car's top be pushed back? Can it be made open to the—the sky?" (He had almost said "dome" out of habit.)

"Yes, it can."

"Then have that done, Daneel. I would like to take a look."

The robot responded gravely, "I am sorry, but I cannot allow that."

Baley felt astonished. He said, "Look, R. Daneel" (he stressed the R.). "Let's rephrase that. I order you to lower the top."

The creature was a robot, manlike or not. It *had* to follow orders.

But Daneel did not move. He said, "I must explain that it is my first concern to spare you harm. It has been clear to me on the basis both of my instructions and of my own personal experience that you would suffer harm at finding yourself in large, empty spaces. I cannot, therefore, allow you to expose yourself to that."

Baley could feel his face darkening with an influx of blood and at the same time could feel the complete uselessness of anger. The creature *was* a robot, and Baley knew the First Law of Robotics well.

It went: *A robot may not injure a human being, or, through inaction, allow a human being to come to harm.*

Everything else in a robot's positronic brain—that of any robot on any world in the Galaxy—had to bow to that prime consideration. Of course a robot had to follow orders, but with one major, all-important qualification. Following orders was only the Second Law of Robotics.

It went: *A robot must obey the orders given it by human beings except where such orders would conflict with the First Law.*

Baley forced himself to speak quietly and reasonably. "I think I can endure it for a short time, Daneel."

"That is not my feeling, Partner Elijah."

"Let me be the judge, Daneel."

"If that is an order, Partner Elijah, I cannot follow it."

Baley let himself lounge back against the softly upholstered seat. The robot would, of course, be quite beyond the reach of force. Daneel's strength, if exerted fully, would be a hundred times that of flesh and blood. He would be perfectly capable of restraining Baley without ever hurting him.

Baley was armed. He could point a blaster at Daneel, but, except for perhaps a momentary sensation of mastery, that action would only succeed in greater frustration. A threat of destruction was useless against a robot. Self-preservation was only the Third Law.

It went: *A robot must protect its own existence, as long as such protection does not conflict with the First or Second Laws.*

It would not trouble Daneel to be destroyed if the alternative were breaking the First Law. And Baley did not wish to destroy Daneel. Definitely not.

Yet he did want to see out the car. It was becoming an obsession with him. He couldn't allow this nurse-infant relationship to build up.

For a moment he thought of pointing the blaster at his own temple. Open the car top or I'll kill myself. Oppose one application of the First Law by a greater and more immediate one.

Baley knew he couldn't do it. Too undignified. He disliked the picture conjured up by the thought.

He said wearily, "Would you ask the driver how close in miles we are to destination?"

"Certainly, Partner Elijah."

Daneel bent forward and pushed the toggle switch. But as he did so, Baley leaned forward too, crying out, "Driver! Lower the top of the car!"

And it was the human hand that moved quickly to the toggle switch and closed it again. The human hand held its place firmly thereafter.

Panting a bit, Baley stared at Daneel.

For a second Daneel was motionless, as though his positronic paths were momentarily out of stability in their effort to adjust to the new situation. But that passed quickly and then the robot's hand was moving.

Baley had anticipated that. Daneel would remove the human hand from the switch (gently, not hurting it), reactivate the transmitter, and countermand the order.

Baley said, "You won't get my hand away without hurting me. I warn you. You will probably have to break my finger."

That was not so. Baley knew that. But Daneel's movements stopped. Harm against harm. The positronic brain had to weigh probabilities and translate them into opposing potentials. It meant just a bit more hesitation.

Baley said, "It's too late."

His race was won. The top was sliding back and pouring into the car, now open, was the harsh white light of Solaria's sun.

Baley wanted to shut his eyes in initial terror, but fought the sensation. He faced the enormous wash of blue and green, incredible quantities of it. He could feel the undisciplined rush of air against his face, but could make out no details of anything. A moving something flashed past. It might have been a robot or an animal or an unliving something caught in a puff of air. He couldn't tell. The car went past it too quickly.

Blue, green, air, noise, motion—and over it all, beating down, furiously, relentlessly, frighteningly, was the white light that came from a ball in the sky.

For one fleeting split moment he bent his head back and stared directly at Solaria's sun. He stared at it, unprotected by the diffusing glass of the Cities' uppermost-Level sun-porches. He stared at the naked sun.

And at the very moment he felt Daneel's hands clamping down upon his shoulders. His mind crowded with thought during that unreal, whirling moment. He had to see! He had to see all he could. And Daneel must be there with him to keep him from seeing.

But surely a robot would not dare use violence on a man. That thought was dominant. Daneel could not prevent him forcibly, and yet Baley felt the robot's hands forcing him down.

Baley lifted his arms to force those fleshless hands away and lost all sensation.

3

A Victim Is Named

BALEY WAS back in the safety of enclosure. Daneel's face wavered before his eyes, and it was splotched with dark spots that turned to red when he blinked.

Baley said, "What happened?"

"I regret," said Daneel, "that you have suffered harm despite my presence. The direct rays of the sun are damaging to the human eye, but I believe that the damage from the short exposure you suffered will not be permanent. When you looked up, I was forced to pull you down and you lost consciousness."

Baley grimaced. That left the question open as to whether he had fainted out of overexcitement (or fright?) or had been knocked unconscious. He felt his jaw and head and found no pain. He forbore asking the question direct. In a way he didn't want to know.

He said, "It wasn't so bad."

"From your reactions, Partner Elijah, I should judge you had found it unpleasant."

"Not at all," said Baley stubbornly. The splotches before his eyes were fading and they weren't tearing so. "I'm only sorry I saw so little. We were moving too fast. Did we pass a robot?"

"We passed a number of them. We are traveling across the Kinbald estate, which is given over to fruit orchards."

"I'll have to try again," said Baley.

"You must not, in my presence," said Daneel. "Meanwhile, I have done as you requested."

"As I requested?"

"You will remember, Partner Elijah, that before you ordered the driver to lower the top of the car, you had ordered me to ask the driver how close in miles we were to destination. We are ten miles away now and shall be there in some six minutes."

Baley felt the impulse to ask Daneel if he were angry at having been outwitted if only to see that perfect face become imperfect, but he repressed it. Of course Daneel would simply answer no, without rancor or annoyance. He would sit there as calm and as grave as ever, unperturbed and imperturbable.

Baley said quietly, "Just the same, Daneel, I'll have to get used to it, you know."

The robot regarded his human partner. "To what is it that you refer?"

"Jehoshaphat! To the—the outdoors. It's all this planet is made of."

"There will be no necessity for facing the outdoors," said Daneel. Then, as though that disposed of the subject, he said, "We are slowing down, Partner Elijah. I believe we have arrived. It will be necessary to wait now for the connection of another air-tube leading to the dwelling that will serve as our base of operations."

"An air-tube is unnecessary, Daneel. If I am to be working outdoors, there is no point in delaying the indoctrination."

"There will be no reason for you to work outdoors, Partner Elijah."

The robot started to say more, but Baley waved him quiet with a peremptory motion of the hand.

At the moment he was not in the mood for Daneel's careful consolations, for soothings, for assurances that all would be well and that he would be taken care of.

What he really wanted was an inner knowledge that he could take care of himself and fulfill his assignment. The sight and feel of the open had been hard to take. It might be that when the time came he would lack the hardihood to dare face it again, at the cost of his self-respect and, conceivably, of Earth's safety. All over a small matter of emptiness.

His face grew grim even at the glancing touch of that thought. He would face air, sun, and empty space yet!

Elijah Baley felt like an inhabitant of one of the smaller Cities, say Helsinki, visiting New York and counting the Levels in awe. He had thought of a "dwelling" as something like an apartment unit, but this was nothing like it at all. He passed from room to room endlessly. Panoramic windows were shrouded closely, allowing no hint of disturbing day to enter. Lights came to life noiselessly from hidden sources as they stepped into a room and died again as quietly when they left.

"So many rooms," said Baley with wonder. "So many. It's like a very tiny City, Daneel."

"It would seem so, Partner Elijah," said Daneel with equanimity.

It seemed strange to the Earthman. Why was it necessary to crowd so many Spacers together with him in close quarters? He said, "How many will be living here with me?"

Daneel said, "There will be myself, of course, and a number of robots."

Baley thought: He ought to have said, a number of *other* robots.

Again he found it obvious that Daneel had the intention of playing the man thoroughly even for no other audience than Baley, who knew the truth so well.

And then that thought popped into nothing under the force of a second, more urgent one. He cried, *"Robots?* How many *humans?"*

"None, Partner Elijah."

They had just stepped into a room, crowded from floor to ceiling with book films. Three fixed viewers with large twenty-four-inch viewing panels set vertically were in three corners of the room. The fourth contained an animation screen.

Baley looked about in annoyance. He said, "Did they kick everyone out just to leave me rattling around alone in this mausoleum?"

"It is meant only for you. A dwelling such as this for one person is customary on Solaria."

"Everyone lives like this?"

"Everyone."

"What do they need all the rooms for?"

"It is customary to devote a single room to a single purpose. This is the library. There is also a music room, a gymnasium, a kitchen, a bakery, a dining room, a machine shop, various robot-repair and testing rooms, two bedrooms——"

"Stop! How do you know all this?"

"It is part of the information pattern," said Daneel smoothly, "made available to me before I left Aurora."

"Jehoshaphat! Who takes care of all of this?" He swung his arm in a wide arc.

"There are a number of household robots. They have been assigned to you and will see to it that you are comfortable."

"But I don't need all this," said Baley. He had the urge to sit down and refuse to budge. He wanted to see no more rooms.

"We can remain in one room if you so desire, Partner Elijah. That was visualized as a possibility from the start. Nevertheless, Solarian customs being what they are, it was considered wiser to allow this house to be built——"

"*Built!*" Baley stared. "You mean this was built for me? All this? Specially?"

"A thoroughly roboticized economy——"

"Yes, I see what you're going to say. What will they do with the house when all this is over?"

"I believe they will tear it down."

Baley's lips clamped together. Of course! Tear it down! Build a tremendous structure for the special use of one Earthman and then tear down everything he touched. Sterilize the soil the house stood on! Fumigate the air he breathed! The Spacers might seem strong, but they, too, had their foolish fears.

Daneel seemed to read his thoughts, or to interpret his expression at any rate. He said, "It may appear to you, Partner Elijah, that it is to escape contagion that they will destroy the house. If such are your thoughts, I suggest that you refrain from making yourself uncomfortable over the matter. The fear of disease on the part of Spacers is by no means so extreme. It is just that the effort involved in building the house is, to them, very little. Nor does the waste involved in tearing it down once more seem great to them.

"And by law, Partner Elijah, this place cannot be allowed to remain standing. It is on the estate of Hannis Gruer and there can only be one legal dwelling place on any estate, that of the owner. This house was built by special dispensation, for a specific purpose. It is meant to house us for a specific length of time, till our mission is completed."

"And who is Hannis Gruer?" asked Baley.

"The head of Solarian security. We are to see him on arrival."

"Are we? Jehoshaphat, Daneel, when do I begin to learn anything at all about anything? I'm working in a vacuum and I don't like it. I might as well go back to Earth. I might as well——"

He felt himself working up into resentment and cut himself short.

Daneel never wavered. He merely waited his chance to speak. He said, "I regret the fact that you are annoyed. My general knowledge of Solaria does seem to be greater than yours. My knowledge of the murder case itself is as limited as is your own. It is Agent Gruer who will tell us what we must know. The Solarian Government has arranged this."

"Well, then, let's get to this Gruer. How long a trip will it be?" Baley winced at the thought of more travel and the familiar constriction in his chest was making itself felt again.

Daneel said, "No travel is necessary, Partner Elijah. Agent Gruer will be waiting for us in the conversation room."

"A room for conversation, too?" Baley murmured wryly. Then, in a louder voice, "Waiting for us now?"

"I believe so."

"Then let's get to him, Daneel!"

Hannis Gruer was bald, and that without qualification. There was not even a fringe of hair at the sides of his skull. It was completely naked.

Baley swallowed and tried, out of politeness, to keep his eyes off that skull, but couldn't. On Earth there was the continuous acceptance of Spacers at the Spacers' own evaluation. The Spacers were the unquestioned lords of the Galaxy; they were tall, bronze of skin and hair, handsome, large, cool, aristocratic.

In short, they were all R. Daneel Olivaw was, but with the fact of humanity in addition.

And the Spacers who were sent to Earth often did look like that; perhaps were deliberately chosen for that reason.

But here was a Spacer who might have been an Earthman for all his appearance. He was bald. And his nose was misshapen, too. Not much, to be sure, but on a Spacer even a slight asymmetry was noteworthy.

Baley said, "Good afternoon, sir. I am sorry if we kept you waiting."

No harm in politeness. He would have to work with these people.

He had the momentary urge to step across the expanse of room (how ridiculously large) and offer his hand in greeting. It was an urge easy to fight off. A Spacer certainly would not welcome such a greeting: a hand covered with Earthly germs?

Gruer sat gravely, as far away from Baley as he could get, his hands resting within long sleeves, and probably there were filters in his nostrils, although Baley couldn't see them.

It even seemed to him that Gruer cast a disapproving look at Daneel as though to say: You're a queer Spacer, standing that close to an Earthman.

That would mean Gruer simply did not know the truth. Then Baley noticed suddenly that Daneel was standing at some distance, at that; farther than he usually did.

Of course! Too close, and Gruer might find the proximity unbelievable. Daneel was intent on being accepted as human.

Gruer spoke in a pleasant, friendly voice, but his eyes tended to remain furtively on Daneel; looking away, then drifting back. He said, "I haven't been waiting long. Welcome to Solaria, gentlemen. Are you comfortable?"

"Yes, sir. Quite," said Baley. He wondered if etiquette would require that Daneel as the "Spacer" should speak for the two, but rejected that possibility resentfully. Jehoshaphat! It was he, himself, who had been requested for the investigation and Daneel had been added afterward. Under the circumstances Baley felt he would not play the secondary to a genuine Spacer; it was out of the question when a robot was involved, even such a robot as Daneel.

But Daneel made no attempt to take precedence over Baley, nor did Gruer seem surprised or displeased at that. Instead, he turned his attention at once to Baley to the exclusion of Daneel.

Gruer said, "You have been told nothing, Plainclothesman Baley, about the crime for which your services have been solicited. I imagine you are quite curious about that." He shook his arms so that the sleeves fell backward and clasped his hands loosely in his lap. "Won't you gentlemen sit down?"

They did so and Baley said, "We *are* curious." He noted that Gruer's hands were not protected by gloves.

Gruer went on. "That was on purpose, Plainclothesman. We wanted you to arrive here prepared to tackle the problem with a fresh mind. We wanted no preconceived notions. You will have available to you shortly a full report of the details of the crime and of the investigations we have been able to conduct. I am afraid, Plainclothesman, that you will find our investigations ridiculously incomplete from the standpoint of your own experience. We have no police force on Solaria."

"None at all?" asked Baley.

Gruer smiled and shrugged. "No crime, you see. Our population is tiny and widely scattered. There is no occasion for crime; therefore no occasion for police."

"I see. But for all that, you *do* have crime now."

"True, but the first crime of violence in two centuries of history."

"Unfortunate, then, that you must begin with murder."

"Unfortunate, yes. More unfortunately still, the victim was a man we could scarcely afford to lose. A most inappropriate victim. And the circumstances of the murder were particularly brutal."

Baley said, "I suppose the murderer is completely unknown." (Why else would the crime be worth the importation of an Earthly detective?)

Gruer looked particularly uneasy. He glanced sideways at Daneel, who sat motionless, an absorptive, quiet mechanism. Baley knew that Daneel would, at any time in the future, be able to reproduce any conversation he heard, of whatever length. He was a recording machine that walked and talked like a man.

Did Gruer know that? His look at Daneel had certainly something of the furtive about it.

Gruer said, "No, I cannot say the murderer is completely unknown. In fact, there is only one person that can possibly have done the deed."

"Are you sure you don't mean only one person who is *likely* to have done the deed?" Baley distrusted overstatement and had no liking for the armchair deducer who discovered certainty rather than probability in the workings of logic.

But Gruer shook his bald head. "No. Only one possible person. Anyone else is impossible. Completely impossible."

"Completely?"

"I assure you."

"Then you have no problem."

"On the contrary. We do have a problem. That one person couldn't have done it either."

Baley said calmly, "Then no one did it."

"Yet the deed was done. Rikaine Delmarre is dead."

That's something, thought Baley. Jehoshaphat, I've got *something*. I've got the victim's name.

He brought out his notebook and solemnly made note of it, partly out of a wry desire to indicate that he had scraped up, at last, a nubbin of fact, and partly to avoid making it too obvious that he sat by the side of a recording machine who needed no notes.

He said, "How is the victim's name spelled?"

Gruer spelled it.

"His profession, sir?"

"Fetologist."

Baley spelled that as it sounded and let it go. He said, "Now who would be able to give me a personal account of the circumstances surrounding the murder? As firsthand as possible."

Gruer's smile was grim and his eyes shifted to Daneel again, and then away. "His wife, Plainclothesman."

"His wife . . . ?"

"Yes. Her name is Gladia." Gruer pronounced it in three syllables, accenting the second.

"Any children?" Baley's eyes were fixed on his notebook. When no answer came, he looked up. "Any children?"

But Gruer's mouth had pursed up as though he had tasted something sour. He looked sick. Finally he said, "I would scarcely know."

Baley said, "What?"

Gruer added hastily, "In any case, I think you had better postpone actual operations till tomorrow. I know you've had a hard trip, Mr. Baley, and that you are tired and probably hungry."

Baley, about to deny it, realized suddenly that the thought of food had an uncommon attraction for him at the moment. He said, "Will you join us at our meal?" He didn't think Gruer would, being a Spacer. (Yet he had been brought to the point of saying "Mr. Baley" rather than "Plainclothesman Baley," which was something.)

As expected, Gruer said, "A business engagement makes that impossible. I will have to leave. I am sorry."

Baley rose. The polite thing would be to accompany Gruer to the door. In the first place, however, he wasn't at all anxious to approach the door and the unprotected open. And in the second he wasn't sure where the door was.

He remained standing in uncertainty.

Gruer smiled and nodded. He said, "I will see you again. Your robots will know the combination if you wish to talk to me."

And he was gone.

Baley exclaimed sharply.

Gruer and the chair he was sitting on were simply not there. The wall behind Gruer, the floor under his feet changed with explosive suddenness.

Daneel said calmly, "He was not there in the flesh at any time. It was a trimensional image. It seemed to me you would know. You have such things on Earth."

"Not like this," muttered Baley.

A trimensional image on Earth was encased in a cubic force-field that glittered against the background. The image itself had a tiny flicker. On Earth there was no mistaking image for reality. Here . . .

No wonder Gruer had worn no gloves. He needed no nose filters, for that matter.

Daneel said, "Would you care to eat now, Partner Elijah?"

Dinner was an unexpected ordeal. Robots appeared. One set the table. One brought in the food.

"How many are there in the house, Daneel?" Baley asked.

"About fifty, Partner Elijah."

"Will they stay here while we eat?" (One had backed into a corner, his glossy, glowing-eyed face turned toward Baley.)

"It is the usual practice," said Daneel, "for one to do so in case its service is called upon. If you do not wish that, you have only to order it to leave."

Baley shrugged. "Let it stay!"

Under normal conditions Baley might have found the food delicious. Now he ate mechanically. He noted abstractedly that Daneel ate also, with a kind of unimpassioned efficiency. Later on, of course, he would empty the fluorocarbon sac within him into which the "eaten" food was now being stored. Meanwhile Daneel maintained his masquerade.

"Is it night outside?" asked Baley.

"It is," replied Daneel.

Baley stared somberly at the bed. It was too large. The whole bedroom was too large. There were no blankets to burrow under, only sheets. They would make a poor enclosure.

Everything was difficult! He had already gone through the unnerving experience of showering in a stall that actually adjoined the bedroom. It was the height of luxury in a way, yet, on the other hand, it seemed an unsanitary arrangement.

He said abruptly, "How is the light put out?" The headboard of the bed gleamed with a soft light. Perhaps that was to facilitate book viewing before sleeping, but Baley was in no mood for that.

"It will be taken care of once you're in bed, if you compose yourself for sleep."

"The robots watch, do they?"

"It is their job."

"Jehoshaphat! What do these Solarians do for *themselves?*" Baley muttered. "I wonder now why a robot didn't scrub my back in the shower."

With no trace of humor Daneel said, "One would have, had you required it. As for the Solarians, they do what they choose. No robot performs his duty if ordered not to, except, of course, where the performance is necessary to the well-being of the human."

"Well, good night, Daneel."

"I will be in another bedroom, Partner Elijah. If, at any time during the night, you need anything——"

"I know. The robots will come."

"There is a contact patch on the side table. You have only to touch it. I will come too."

Sleep eluded Baley. He kept picturing the house he was in, balanced precariously at the outer skin of the world, with emptiness waiting just outside like a monster.

On Earth his apartment—his snug, comfortable, crowded apartment—sat nestled beneath many others. There were dozens of Levels and thousands of people between himself and the rim of Earth.

Even on Earth, he tried to tell himself, there were people on the topmost Level. They would be immediately adjacent to the outside. Sure! But that's what made those apartments low-rent.

Then he thought of Jessie, a thousand light-years away.

He wanted terribly to get out of bed right now, dress, and walk to her. His thoughts grew mistier. If there were only a tunnel, a nice, safe tunnel burrowing its way through safe, solid rock and metal from Solaria to Earth, he would walk and walk and walk. . . .

He would walk back to Earth, back to Jessie, back to comfort and security. . . .

Security.

Baley's eyes opened. His arms grew rigid and he rose up on his elbow, scarcely aware that he was doing so.

Security! This man, Hannis Gruer, was head of Solarian security. So Daneel had said. What did "security" mean? If it meant the same as it meant on Earth, and surely it must, this man Gruer was responsible for the protection of Solaria against invasion from without and subversion from within.

Why was he interested in a murder case? Was it because there were no police on Solaria and the Department of Security would come the closest to knowing what to do about a murder?

Gruer had seemed at ease with Baley, yet there had been those furtive glances, again and again, in the direction of Daneel.

Did Gruer suspect the motives of Daneel? Baley, himself, had been ordered to keep his eyes open and Daneel might very likely have received similar instructions.

It would be natural for Gruer to suspect that espionage was possible. His job made it necessary for him to suspect that in any case where it was conceivable. And he would not fear Baley overmuch, an Earthman, representative of the least formidable world in the Galaxy.

But Daneel was a native of Aurora, the oldest and largest and strongest of the Outer Worlds. That would be different.

Gruer, as Baley now remembered, had not addressed one word to Daneel.

For that matter, why should Daneel pretend so thoroughly to be a man? The earlier explanation that Baley had posed for himself, that it was a vainglorious game on the part of Daneel's Auroran designers, seemed trivial. It seemed obvious now that the masquerade was something more serious.

A man could be expected to receive diplomatic immunity; a certain courtesy and gentleness of treatment. A robot could not. But then why did not Aurora send a real man in the first place. Why gamble so desperately on a fake? The answer suggested itself instantly to Baley. A real man of Aurora, a real Spacer, would not care to associate too closely or for too long a time with an Earthman.

But if all this were true, why should Solaria find a single murder so important that it must allow an Earthman and an Auroran to come to their planet?

Baley felt trapped.

He was trapped on Solaria by the necessities of his assignment. He was trapped by Earth's danger, trapped in an environment he could scarcely endure, trapped by a responsibility he could not shirk. And, to add to all this, he was trapped somehow in the midst of a Spacer conflict the nature of which he did not understand.

4

A Woman Is Viewed

HE SLEPT at last. He did not remember when he actually made the transition to sleep. There was just a period when his thoughts grew more erratic and then the headboard of his bed was shining and the ceiling was alight with a cool, daytime glow. He looked at his watch.

Hours had passed. The robots who ran the house had decided it was time for him to wake up and had acted accordingly.

He wondered if Daneel were awake and at once realized the illogic of the thought. Daneel could not sleep. Baley wondered if he had counterfeited sleep as part of the role he was playing. Had he undressed and put on nightclothes?

As though on cue Daneel entered. "Good morning, Partner Elijah."

The robot was completely dressed and his face was in perfect repose. He said, "Did you sleep well?"

"Yes," said Baley dryly, "did you?"

He got out of bed and tramped into the bathroom for a shave and for the remainder of the morning ritual. He shouted, "If a robot comes in to shave me, send him out again. They get on my nerves. Even if I don't see them, they get on my nerves."

He stared at his own face as he shaved, marveling a bit that it looked so like the mirrored face he saw on Earth. If only the image were another Earthman with whom he could consult instead of only the light-mimicry of himself. If he could go over what he had already learned, small as it was . . .

"Too small! Get more," he muttered to the mirror.

He came out, mopping his face, and pulled trousers over fresh shorts. (Robots supplied everything, damn them.)

He said, "Would you answer a few questions, Daneel?"

"As you know, Partner Elijah, I answer all questions to the best of my knowledge."

Or to the letter of your instructions, thought Baley. He said, "Why are there only twenty thousand people on Solaria?"

"That is a mere fact," said Daneel. "A datum. A figure that is the result of a counting process."

"Yes, but you're evading the matter. The planet can support millions; why, then, only twenty thousand? You said the Solarians consider twenty thousand optimum. Why?"

"It is their way of life."

"You mean they practice birth control?"

"Yes."

"And leave the planet empty?" Baley wasn't sure why he was pounding away at this one point, but the planet's population was one of the few hard facts he had learned about it and there was little else he could ask about.

Daneel said, "The planet is not empty. It is parceled out into estates, each of which is supervised by a Solarian."

"You mean each lives on his estate. Twenty thousand estates, each with a Solarian."

"Fewer estates than those, Partner Elijah. Wives share the estate."

"No Cities?" Baley felt cold.

"None at all, Partner Elijah. They live completely apart and never see one another except under the most extraordinary circumstances."

"Hermits?"

"In a way, yes. In a way, no."

"What does that mean?"

"Agent Gruer visited you yesterday by trimensional image. Solarians visit one another freely that way and in no other way."

Baley stared at Daneel. He said, "Does that include us? Are we expected to live that way?"

"It is the custom of the world."

"Then how do I investigate this case? If I want to see someone——"

"From this house, Partner Elijah, you can obtain a trimensional view of anyone on the planet. There will be no problem. In fact, it will save you the annoyance of leaving this house. It was why I said when we arrived that there would be no occasion for you to feel it necessary to grow accustomed to facing the outdoors. And that is well. Any other arrangement would be most distasteful to you."

"I'll judge what's distasteful to me," said Baley. "First thing today, Daneel, I get in touch with the Gladia woman, the wife of the murdered man. If the trimensional business is unsatisfactory, I will go out to her place, personally. It's a matter for my decision."

"We shall see what is best and most feasible, Partner Elijah," said Daneel noncommittally. "I shall arrange for breakfast." He turned to leave.

Baley stared at the broad robotic back and was almost amused. Daneel Olivaw acted the master. If his instructions had been to keep Baley from learning any more than was absolutely necessary, a trump card had been left in Baley's hand.

The other was only R. Daneel Olivaw, after all. All that was necessary was to tell Gruer, or any Solarian, that Daneel was a robot and not a man.

And yet, on the other hand, Daneel's pseudo humanity could be of great use, too. A trump card need not be played at once. Sometimes it was more useful in the hand.

Wait and see, he thought, and followed Daneel out to breakfast.

Baley said, "Now how does one go about establishing trimensional contact?"

"It is done for us, Partner Elijah," said Daneel, and his finger sought out one of the contact patches that summoned robots.

A robot entered at once.

Where do they come from, Baley wondered. As one wandered aimlessly about the uninhabited maze that constituted the mansion, not one robot was ever visible. Did they scramble out of the way as humans approached? Did they send messages to one another and clear the path?

Yet whenever a call went out, one appeared without delay.

Baley stared at the robotic newcomer. It was sleek, but not glossy. Its surface had a muted, grayish finish, with a checkerboard pattern on the right shoulder as the only bit of color. Squares in white and yellow (silver and gold, really, from the metallic luster) were placed in what seemed an aimless pattern.

Daneel said, "Take us to the conversation room."

The robot bowed and turned, but said nothing.

Baley said, "Wait, boy. What's your name?"

The robot faced Baley. It spoke in clear tones and without hesitation. "I have no name, master. My serial number"—and a metal finger lifted and rested on the shoulder patch—"is ACX-2745."

Daneel and Baley followed into a large room, which Baley recognized as having held Gruer and his chair the day before.

Another robot was waiting for them with the eternal, patient nonboredom of the machine. The first bowed and left.

Baley compared shoulder patches of the two as the first bowed and started out. The pattern of silver and gold was different. The checkerboard was made up of a six-by-six square. The number of possible arrangements would be 2^{36} then, or seventy billion. More than enough.

Baley said, "Apparently, there is one robot for everything. One to show us here. One to run the viewer."

Daneel said, "There is much robotic specialization in Solaria, Partner Elijah."

"With so many of them, I can understand why." Baley looked at the second robot. Except for the shoulder patch, and, presumably, for the invisible positronic patterns within its spongy platinum-iridium brain it was the duplicate of the first. He said, "And your serial number?"

"ACC-1129, master."

"I'll just call you boy. Now I want to speak to a Mrs. Gladia Delmarre, wife of the late Rikaine Delmarre—— Daneel, is there an address, some way of pin-pointing her location?"

Daneel said gently, "I do not believe any further information is necessary. If I may question the robot——"

"Let me do that," Baley said. "All right, boy, do you know how the lady is to be reached?"

"Yes, master. I have knowledge of the connection pattern of all masters." This was said without pride. It was a mere fact, as though it were saying: I am made of metal, master.

Daneel interposed, "That is not surprising, Partner Elijah. There are less than ten thousand connections that need be fed into the memory circuits, and that is a small number."

Baley nodded. "Is there more than one Gladia Delmarre, by any chance? There might be that chance of confusion."

"Master?" After the question the robot remained blankly silent.

"I believe," said Daneel, "that this robot does not understand your question. It is my belief that duplicate names do not occur on Solaria. Names are registered at birth and no name may be adopted unless it is unoccupied at the time."

"All right," said Baley, "we learn something every minute. Now see here, boy, you tell me how to work whatever it is I am supposed to work; give me the connection pattern, or whatever you call it, and then step out."

There was a perceptible pause before the robot answered. It said, "Do you wish to make contact yourself, sir?"

"That's right."

Daneel touched Baley's sleeve gently. "One moment, Partner Elijah."

"Now what is it?"

"It is my belief that the robot could make the necessary contact with greater ease. It is his specialization."

Baley said grimly, "I'm sure he can do it better than I can. Doing it myself, I may make a mess of it." He stared levelly at the impassive Daneel. "Just the same, I prefer to make contact myself. Do I give the orders or don't I?"

Daneel said, "You give the orders, Partner Elijah, and your orders, where First Law permits, will be obeyed. However, with your permission, I would like to give you what pertinent information I have concerning the Solarian robots. Far more than on any other world, the robots on Solaria are specialized. Although Solarian robots are physically capable of many things, they are heavily equipped mentally for one particular type of job. To perform functions outside their specialty requires the high potentials produced by direct application of one of the Three Laws. Again, for them *not* to perform the duty for which they *are* equipped also requires the direct application of the Three Laws."

"Well, then, a direct order from me brings the Second Law into play, doesn't it?"

"True. Yet the potential set up by it is 'unpleasant' to the robot. Ordinarily, the matter would not come up, since almost never does a Solarian interfere with the day-to-day workings of a robot. For one thing, he would not care to do a robot's work; for another, he would feel no need to."

"Are you trying to tell me, Daneel, that it hurts the robot to have me do its work?"

"As you know, Partner Elijah, pain in the human sense is not applicable to robotic reactions."

Baley shrugged. "Then?"

"Nevertheless," went on Daneel, "the experience which the robot undergoes is as upsetting to it as pain is to a human, as nearly as I can judge."

"And yet," said Baley, "I'm not a Solarian. I'm an Earthman. I don't like robots doing what I want to do."

"Consider, too," said Daneel, "that to cause distress to a robot might be considered on the part of our hosts to be an act of impoliteness since in a society such as this there must be a number of more or less rigid beliefs concerning how it is proper to treat a robot and how it is not. To offend our hosts would scarcely make our task easier."

"All right," said Baley. "Let the robot do its job."

He settled back. The incident had not been without its uses. It was an educational example of how remorseless a robotic society could be. Once brought into existence, robots were not so easily removed, and a human who wished to dispense with them even temporarily found he could not.

His eyes half closed, he watched the robot approach the wall. Let the sociologists on Earth consider what had just occurred and draw their conclusions. He was beginning to have certain notions of his own.

Half a wall slid aside and the control panel that was revealed would have done justice to a City Section power station.

Baley longed for his pipe. He had been briefed that smoking on non-smoking Solaria would be a terrible breach of decorum, so he had not even been allowed to take his fixings. He sighed. There were moments when the feel of pipestem between teeth and a warm bowl in his hand would have been infinitely comforting.

The robot was working quickly, adjusting variable resistances a trifle here and there and intensifying field-forces in proper pattern by quick finger pressures.

Daneel said, "It is necessary first to signal the individual one desires to view. A robot will, of course, receive the message. If the individual being signaled is available and wishes to receive the view, full contact is established."

"Are all those controls necessary?" asked Baley. "The robot's hardly touching most of the panel."

"My information on the matter is not complete, Partner Elijah. There is, however, the necessity of arranging, upon occasion, for multiple viewings and for mobile viewings. The latter, particularly, call for complicated and continuing adjustment."

The robot said, "Masters, contact is made and approved. When you are ready, it will be completed."

"Ready," growled Baley, and as though the word were a signal, the far half of the room was alive with light.

Daneel said at once, "I neglected to have the robot specify that all visible openings to the outside be draped. I regret that and we must arrange——"

"Never mind," said Baley, wincing. "I'll manage. Don't interfere."

It was a bathroom he was staring at, or he judged it to be so from its fixtures. One end of it was, he guessed, a kind of beautician's establishment and his imagination pictured a robot (or robots?) working with unerring swiftness on the details of a woman's coiffure and on the externals that made up the picture she presented to the world.

Some gadgets and fittings he simply gave up on. There was no way of judging their purpose in the absence of experience. The walls were inlaid with an intricate pattern that all but fooled the eye into believing some natural object was being represented before fading away into an abstraction. The result was soothing and almost hypnotic in the way it monopolized attention.

What might have been the shower stall, a large one, was shielded off by nothing that seemed material, but rather by a trick of lighting that set up a wall of flickering opacity. No human was in sight.

Baley's glance fell to the floor. Where did his room end and the other begin? It was easy to tell. There was a line where the quality of the light changed and that must be it.

He stepped toward the line and after a moment's hesitation pushed his hand beyond it.

He felt nothing, any more than he would have had he shoved the hand into one of Earth's crude trimensionals. There, at least, he would have seen his own hand still; faintly, perhaps, and overlaid by the image, but he would have seen it. Here it was lost completely. To his vision, his arm ended sharply at the wrist.

What if he stepped across the line altogether? Probably his own vision would become inoperative. He would be in a world of complete blackness. The thought of such efficient enclosure was almost pleasant.

A voice interrupted him. He looked up and stepped backward with an almost clumsy haste.

Gladia Delmarre was speaking. At least Baley assumed it was she. The upper portion of the flickering light across the shower stall had faded and a head was clearly visible.

It smiled at Baley. "I said hello, and I'm sorry to keep you waiting. I'll be dry soon."

Hers was a triangular face, rather broad at the cheekbones (which grew prominent when she smiled) and narrowing with a gentle curve past full lips to a small chin. Her head was not high above the ground. Baley judged her to be about five feet two in height. (This was not typical. At least not to Baley's way of thinking. Spacer women were supposed to lean toward the tall and stately.) Nor was her hair the Spacer bronze. It was light brown, tinging toward yellow, and worn moderately long. At the moment it was fluffed out in what Baley imagined must be a stream of warm air. The whole picture was quite pleasing.

Baley said in confusion, "If you want us to break contact and wait till you're through——"

"Oh no. I'm almost done, and we can talk meanwhile. Hannis Gruer told me you would be viewing. You're from Earth, I understand." Her eyes rested full on him, seemed to drink him in.

Baley nodded and sat down. "My companion is from Aurora."

She smiled and kept her glance fixed on Baley as though *he* remained the curiosity nevertheless, and of course, Baley thought, so he was.

She lifted her arms above her head, running her fingers through the hair and spreading it out as though to hasten drying. Her arms were slim and graceful. Very attractive, Baley thought.

Then he thought uneasily: Jessie wouldn't like this.

Daneel's voice broke in. "Would it be possible, Mrs. Delmarre, to have the window we see polarized or draped. My partner is disturbed by the sight of daylight. On Earth, as you may have heard——"

The young woman (Baley judged her to be twenty-five but had the doleful thought that the apparent ages of Spacers could be most deceptive) put her hands to her cheeks and said, "Oh my, yes. I know all about that. How ridiculously silly of me. Forgive me, please, but it won't take a moment. I'll have a robot in here——"

She stepped out of the drying cabinet, her hand extended toward the contact-patch, still talking. "I'm always thinking I ought to have more than one contact-patch in this room. A house is just no good if it doesn't have a patch within reach no matter where you stand—say not more than five feet away. It just—— Why, what's the matter?"

She stared in shock at Baley, who, having jumped out of his chair and upset it behind him, had reddened to his hairline and hastily turned away.

Daneel said calmly, "It would be better, Mrs. Delmarre, if, after you have made contact with the robot, you would return to the stall or, failing that, proceed to put on some articles of clothing."

Gladia looked down at her nudity in surprise and said, "Well, of course."

5

A Crime Is Discussed

"IT WAS only viewing, you see," said Gladia contritely. She was wrapped in something that left her arms and shoulders free. One leg showed to mid-thigh, but Baley, entirely recovered and feeling an utter fool, ignored it stoically.

He said, "It was the surprise, Mrs. Delmarre——"

"Oh, please. You can call me Gladia, unless—unless that's against your customs."

"Gladia, then. It's all right. I just want to assure you there was nothing repulsive about it, you understand. Just the surprise." Bad enough for him to have acted the fool, he thought, without having the poor girl think he found her unpleasant. As a matter of fact, it had been rather—rather . . .

Well, he didn't have the phrase, but he knew quite certainly that there was no way he would ever be able to talk of this to Jessie.

"I know I offended you," Gladia said, "but I didn't mean to. I just wasn't thinking. Of course I realize one must be careful about the customs of other planets, but the customs are so queer sometimes; at least, not queer," she hastened to add, "I don't mean queer. I mean strange, you know, and it's so easy to forget. As I forgot about keeping the windows darkened."

"Quite all right," muttered Baley. She was in another room now with all the windows draped and the light had the subtly different and more comfortable texture of artificiality.

"But about the other thing," she went on earnestly, "it's just *viewing,* you see. After all, you didn't mind talking to me when I was in the drier and I wasn't wearing anything then, either."

"Well," said Baley, wishing she would run down as far as that subject was concerned, "hearing you is one thing, and seeing you is another."

"But that's exactly it. Seeing isn't involved." She reddened a trifle and looked down. "I hope you don't think I'd ever do anything like that, I mean, just step out of the drier, if anyone were *seeing* me. It was just *viewing*."

"Same thing, isn't it?" said Baley.

"Not at all the same thing. You're viewing me right now. You can't touch me, can you, or smell me, or anything like that. You could if you were seeing me. Right now, I'm two hundred miles away from you at *least*. So how can it be the same thing?"

Baley grew interested. "But I see you with my eyes."

"No, you don't see me. You see my image. You're viewing me."

"And that makes a difference?"

"All the difference there is."

"I see." In a way he did. The distinction was not one he could make easily, but it had a kind of logic to it.

She said, bending her head a little to one side, "Do you *really* see?"

"Yes."

"Does that mean you wouldn't mind if I took off my wrapper?" She was smiling.

He thought: She's teasing and I ought to take her up on it.

But aloud he said, "No, it would take my mind off my job. We'll discuss it another time."

"Do you mind my being in the wrapper, rather than something more formal? Seriously."

"I don't mind."

"May I call you by your first name?"

"If you have the occasion."

"What is your first name?"

"Elijah."

"All right." She snuggled into a chair that looked hard and almost ceramic in texture, but it slowly gave as she sat until it embraced her gently.

Baley said, "To business, now."

She said, "To business."

Baley found it all extraordinarily difficult. There was no way even to make a beginning. On Earth he would ask name, rating, City and Sector of dwelling, a million different routine questions. He might even know the answers to begin with, yet it would be a device to ease into the serious phase. It would serve to introduce him to the person, make his judgment of the tactics to pursue something other than a mere guess.

But here? How could he be certain of anything? The very verb "to see" meant different things to himself and to the woman. How many other words would be different? How often would they be at cross-purposes without his being aware of it?

He said, "How long were you married, Gladia?"

"Ten years, Elijah."

"How old are you?"

"Thirty-three."

Baley felt obscurely pleased. She might easily have been a hundred thirty-three.

He said, "Were you happily married?"

Gladia looked uneasy. "How do you mean that?"

"Well——" For a moment Baley was at a loss. How do you define a happy marriage. For that matter, what would a Solarian consider a happy marriage? He said, "Well, you saw one another often?"

"What? I should hope not. We're not animals, you know."

Baley winced. "You did live in the same mansion? I thought——"

"Of course, we did. We were married. But I had my quarters and he had his. He had a very important career which took much of his time and I have my own work. We viewed each other whenever necessary."

"He *saw* you, didn't he?"

"It's not a thing one talks about but he *did* see me."

"Do you have any children?"

Gladia jumped to her feet in obvious agitation. "That's too much. Of all the indecent——"

"Now wait. *Wait!*" Baley brought his fist down on the arm of his chair. "Don't be difficult. This is a murder investigation. Do you understand? Murder. And it was your husband who was murdered. Do you want to see the murderer found and punished or don't you?"

"Then *ask* about the murder, not about—about——"

"I have to ask all sorts of things. For one thing I want to know whether you're sorry your husband is dead." He added with calculated brutality, "You don't seem to be."

She stared at him haughtily. "I'm sorry when anyone dies, especially when he's young and useful."

"Doesn't the fact that he was your husband make it just a little more than that?"

"He was assigned to me and, well, we *did* see each other when scheduled and—and"—she hurried the next words—"and, if you must know, we don't have children because none have been assigned us yet. I don't see what all that has to do with being sorry over someone being dead."

Maybe it had nothing to do with it, Baley thought. It depended on the social facts of life and with those he was not acquainted.

He changed the subject. "I'm told you have personal knowledge of the circumstances of the murder."

For a moment she seemed to grow taut. "I—discovered the body. Is that the way I should say it?"

"Then you didn't witness the actual murder?"

"Oh no," she said faintly.

"Well, suppose you tell me what happened. Take your time and use your own words." He sat back and composed himself to listen.

She began, "It was on three-two of the fifth——"

"When was that in Standard Time?" asked Baley quickly.

"I'm not sure. I really don't know. You can check, I suppose."

Her voice seemed shaky and her eyes had grown large. They were a little too gray to be called blue, he noted.

She said, "He came to my quarters. It was our assigned day for seeing and I knew he'd come."

"He always came on the assigned day?"

"Oh yes. He was a very conscientious man, a good Solarian. He never skipped an assigned day and always came at the same time. Of course, he didn't stay long. We have not been assigned ch——"

She couldn't finish the word, but Baley nodded.

"Anyway," she said, "he always came at the same time, you know, so that everything would be comfortable. We spoke a few minutes; seeing *is* an ordeal, but he always spoke quite normally to me. It was his way. Then he left to attend to some project he was involved with; I'm not sure what. He had a special laboratory in my quarters to which he could retire on seeing days. He had a much bigger one in his quarters, of course."

Baley wondered what he did in those laboratories. Fetology, perhaps, whatever that was.

He said, "Did he seem unnatural in any way? Worried?"

"No. No. He was never worried." She came to the edge of a small laugh and buried it at the last moment. "He always had perfect control, like your friend there." For a brief moment her small hand reached out and indicated Daneel, who did not stir.

"I see. Well, go on."

Gladia didn't. Instead she whispered, "Do you mind if I have myself a drink?"

"Please do."

Gladia's hand slipped along the arm of her chair momentarily. In less than a minute, a robot moved in silently and a warm drink (Baley could see the steam) was in her hand. She sipped slowly, then set the drink down.

She said, "That's better. May I ask a personal question?"

Baley said, "You may always ask."

"Well, I've read a lot about Earth. I've always been interested, you know. It's such a *queer* world." She gasped and added immediately, "I didn't mean that."

Baley frowned a little. "Any world is queer to people who don't live on it."

"I mean it's different. You know. Anyway, I want to ask a rude question. At least, I hope it doesn't seem rude to an Earthman. I wouldn't ask it of a Solarian, of course. Not for anything."

"Ask what, Gladia?"

"About you and your friend—Mr. Olivaw, is it?"

"Yes."

"You two aren't viewing, are you?"

"How do you mean?"

"I mean each other. You're seeing. You're there, both of you."

Baley said, "We're physically together. Yes."

"You could touch him, if you wanted to."

"That's right."

She looked from one to the other and said, "Oh."

It might have meant anything. Disgust? Revulsion?

Baley toyed with the idea of standing up, walking to Daneel and placing his hand flat on Daneel's face. It might be interesting to watch her reaction.

He said, "You were about to go on with the events of that day when your husband came to see you." He was morally certain that her digression, however interesting it might have been intrinsically to her, was primarily motivated by a desire to avoid just that.

She returned to her drink for a moment. Then: "There isn't much to tell. I saw he would be engaged, and I knew he would be, anyway, because he was always at some sort of constructive work, so I went back to my own work. Then, perhaps fifteen minutes later, I heard a shout."

There was a pause and Baley prodded her. "What kind of a shout?"

She said, "Rikaine's. My husband's. Just a shout. No words. A kind of fright. No! Surprise, shock. Something like that. I'd never heard him shout before."

She lifted her hands to her ears as though to shut out even the memory of the sound and her wrapper slipped slowly down to her waist. She took no notice and Baley stared firmly at his notebook.

He said, "What did you do?"

"I ran. I ran. I didn't know where he was——"

"I thought you said he had gone to the laboratory he maintained in your quarters."

"He did, E-Elijah, but I didn't know where that was. Not for sure, anyway. I never went there. It was his. I had a general idea of its direction. I knew it was somewhere in the west, but I was so upset, I didn't even think to summon any robot. One of them would have guided me easily, but of course none came without being summoned. When I did get there—I found it somehow—he was dead."

She stopped suddenly and, to Baley's acute discomfort, she bent her head and wept. She made no attempt to obscure her face. Her eyes simply closed and tears slowly trickled down her cheeks. It was quite soundless. Her shoulders barely trembled.

Then her eyes opened and looked at him through swimming tears. "I never saw a dead man before. He was all bloody and his head was—just—all—— I managed to get a robot and he called others and I suppose they took care of me and of Rikaine. I don't remember. I don't——"

Baley said, "What do you mean, they took care of Rikaine?"

"They took him away and cleaned up." There was a small wedge of indignation in her voice, the lady of the house careful of its condition. "Things were a mess."

"And what happened to the body?"

She shook her head. "I don't know. Burned, I suppose. Like any dead body."

"You didn't call the police?"

She looked at him blankly and Baley thought: No police!

He said, "You told somebody, I suppose. People found out about the matter."

She said, "The robots called a doctor. And I had to call Rikaine's place of work. The robots there had to know he wouldn't be back."

"The doctor was for you, I suppose."

She nodded. For the first time, she seemed to notice her wrapper draped about her hips. She pulled it up into position, murmuring forlornly, "I'm sorry. I'm sorry."

Baley felt uncomfortable, watching her as she sat there helpless, shivering, her face contorted with the absolute terror that had come over her with the memory.

She had never seen a dead body before. She had never seen blood and a crushed skull. And if the husband-wife relationship on Solaria was something thin and shallow, it was still a dead human being with whom she had been confronted.

Baley scarcely knew what to say or do next. He had the impulse to apologize, and yet, as a policeman, he was doing only his duty.

But there were no police on this world. Would she understand that this was his duty?

Slowly, and as gently as he could, he said, "Gladia, did you hear anything at all? Anything besides your husband's shout."

She looked up, her face as pretty as ever, despite its obvious distress—perhaps because of it. She said, "Nothing."

"No running footsteps? No other voice?"

She shook her head. "I didn't hear anything."

"When you found your husband, he was completely alone? You two were the only ones present?"

"Yes."

"No signs of anyone else having been there?"

"None that I could see. I don't see how anyone could have been there, anyway."

"Why do you say that?"

For a moment she looked shocked. Then she said dispiritedly, "You're from Earth. I keep forgetting. Well, it's just that nobody could have been there. My husband never saw anybody except me; not since he was a boy. He certainly wasn't the sort to see anybody. Not Rikaine. He was very strict; very custom-abiding."

"It might not have been his choice. What if someone had just come to see him without an invitation, without your husband knowing anything about it? He couldn't have helped seeing the intruder regardless of how custom-abiding he was."

She said, "Maybe, but he would have called robots at once and had the man taken away. He would have! Besides no one would try to see my husband without being invited to. I couldn't conceive of such a thing. And Rikaine certainly would never invite anyone to see him. It's ridiculous to think so."

Baley said softly, "Your husband was killed by being struck on the head, wasn't he? You'll admit that."

"I suppose so. He was—all——"

"I'm not asking for the details at the moment. Was there any sign of some mechanical contrivance in the room that would have enabled someone to crush his skull by remote control."

"Of course not. At least, I didn't see any."

"If anything like that had been there, I imagine you would have seen it. It follows then that a hand held something capable of crushing a man's skull and that hand swung it. Some person had to be within four feet of your husband to do that. So someone did see him."

"No one would," she said earnestly. "A Solarian just wouldn't see anyone."

"A Solarian who would commit murder wouldn't stick at a bit of seeing, would he?"

(To himself that statement sounded dubious. On Earth he had known the case of a perfectly conscienceless murderer who had been caught only because he could not bring himself to violate the custom of absolute silence in the community bathroom.)

Gladia shook her head. "You don't understand about seeing. Earthmen just see anybody they want to all the time, so you don't understand it. . . ."

Curiosity seemed to be struggling within her. Her eyes lightened a bit. "Seeing does seem perfectly normal to you, doesn't it?"

"I've always taken it for granted," said Baley.

"It doesn't trouble you?"

"Why should it?"

"Well, the films don't say, and I've always wanted to know—— Is it all right if I ask a question?"

"Go ahead," said Baley stolidly.

"Do you have a wife assigned to you?"

"I'm married. I don't know about the assignment part."

"And I know you see your wife any time you want to and she sees you and neither of you thinks anything of it."

Baley nodded.

"Well, when you see her, suppose you just want to——" She lifted her hands elbow-high, pausing as though searching for the proper phrase. She tried again, "Can you just—any time . . ." She let it dangle.

Baley didn't try to help.

She said, "Well, never mind. I don't know why I should bother you with that sort of thing now anyway. Are you through with me?" She looked as though she might cry again.

Baley said, "One more try, Gladia. Forget that no one would see your husband. Suppose someone *did*. Who might it have been?"

"It's just useless to guess. It couldn't be anyone."

"It has to be someone. Agent Gruer says there is reason to suspect some one person. So you see there must be someone."

A small, joyless smile flickered over the girl's face. "I know who he thinks did it."

"All right. Who?"

She put a small hand on her breast. "I."

6

A Theory Is Refuted

"I SHOULD have said, Partner Elijah," said Daneel, speaking suddenly, "that that is an obvious conclusion."

Baley cast a surprised look at his robot partner. "Why obvious?" he asked.

"The lady herself," said Daneel, "states that she was the only person who did or who would see her husband. The social situation on Solaria is such that even she cannot plausibly present anything else as the truth. Certainly Agent Gruer would find it reasonable, even obligatory, to believe that a Solarian husband would be seen only by his wife. Since only one person could be in seeing range, only one person could strike the blow and only one person could be the murderer. Or murderess, rather. Agent Gruer, you will remember, said that only one person could have done it. Anyone else he considered impossible. Well?"

"He also said," said Baley, "that that one person couldn't have done it, either."

"By which he probably meant that there was no weapon found at the scene of the crime. Presumably Mrs. Delmarre could explain that anomaly."

He gestured with cool robotic politeness toward where Gladia sat, still in viewing focus, her eyes cast down, her small mouth compressed.

Jehoshaphat, thought Baley, we're forgetting the lady.

Perhaps it was annoyance that had caused him to forget. It was Daneel who annoyed him, he thought, with his unemotional approach to problems. Or perhaps it was himself, with his emotional approach. He did not stop to analyze the matter.

He said, "That will be all for now, Gladia. However one goes about it, break contact. Good-by."

She said softly, "Sometimes one says, 'Done viewing,' but I like 'Good-by' better. You seem disturbed, Elijah. I'm sorry, because I'm used to having people think I did it, so you don't need to feel disturbed."

Daneel said, "*Did* you do it, Gladia?"

"No," she said angrily.

"Good-by, then."

With the anger not yet washed out of her face she was gone. For a moment, though, Baley could still feel the impact of those quite extraordinary gray eyes.

She might say she was used to having people think her a murderess, but that was very obviously a lie. Her anger spoke more truly than her words. Baley wondered of how many other lies she was capable.

And now Baley found himself alone with Daneel. He said, "All right, Daneel, I'm not altogether a fool."

"I have never thought you were, Partner Elijah."

"Then tell me what made you say there was no murder weapon found at the site of the crime? There was nothing in the evidence so far, nothing in anything I've heard that would lead us to that conclusion."

"You are correct. I have additional information not yet available to you."

"I was sure of that. What kind?"

"Agent Gruer said he would send a copy of the report of their own investigation. I have that copy. It arrived this morning."

"Why haven't you shown it to me?"

"I felt that it would perhaps be more fruitful for you to conduct your investigation, at least in the initial stages, according to your own ideas, without being prejudiced by the conclusions of other people who, self-admittedly, have reached no satisfactory conclusion. It was because I, myself, felt my logical processes might be influenced by those conclusions that I contributed nothing to the discussion."

Logical processes! Unbidden, there leaped into Baley's mind the fragment of a conversation he had once had with a roboticist. A robot, the man had said, is logical but not reasonable.

He said, "You entered the discussion at the end."

"So I did, Partner Elijah, but only because by that time I had independent evidence bearing out Agent Gruer's suspicions."

"What kind of independent evidence?"

"That which could be deduced from Mrs. Delmarre's own behavior."

"Let's be specific, Daneel."

"Consider that if the lady were guilty and were attempting to prove herself innocent, it would be useful to her to have the detective in the case believe her innocent."

"Well?"

"If she could warp his judgment by playing upon a weakness of his, she might do so, might she not?"

"Strictly hypothetical."

"Not at all," was the calm reply. "You will have noticed, I think, that she concentrated her attention entirely on you."

"I was doing the talking," said Baley.

"Her attention was on you from the start; even before she could guess that you would be doing the talking. In fact, one might have thought she would, logically, have expected that I, as an Auroran, would take the lead in the investigation. Yet she concentrated on you."

"And what do you deduce from this?"

"That it was upon you, Partner Elijah, that she pinned her hopes. You were the Earthman."

"What of that?"

"She had studied Earth. She implied that more than once. She knew what I was talking about when I asked her to blank out the outer daylight at the very start of the interview. She did not act surprised or uncomprehending, as she would most certainly have done had she not had actual knowledge of conditions on Earth."

"Well?"

"Since she has studied Earth, it is quite reasonable to suppose that she discovered one weakness Earthmen possess. She must know of the nudity tabu, and of how such a display must impress an Earthman."

"She—she explained about viewing——"

"So she did. Yet did it seem entirely convincing to you? Twice she allowed herself to be seen in what you would consider a state of improper clothing——"

"Your conclusion," said Baley, "is that she was trying to seduce me. Is that it?"

"Seduce you away from your professional impersonality. So it would seem to me. And though I cannot share human reactions to stimuli, I would judge, from what has been imprinted on my instruction circuits, that the lady meets any reasonable standard of physical attractiveness. From your behavior, moreover, it seems to me that you were aware of that and that you approved her appearance. I would even judge that Mrs. Delmarre acted rightly in thinking her mode of behavior would predispose you in her favor."

"Look," said Baley uncomfortably, "regardless of what effect she might have had on me, I am still an officer of the law in full possession of my sense of professional ethics. Get that straight. Now let's see the report."

Baley read through the report in silence. He finished, turned back, and read it through a second time.

"This brings in a new item," he said. "The robot."

Daneel Olivaw nodded.

Baley said thoughtfully, "She didn't mention it."

Daneel said, "You asked the wrong question. You asked if he was alone when she found the body. You asked if anyone else had been present at the death scene. A robot isn't 'anybody else.'"

Baley nodded. If he himself were a suspect and were asked who else had been at the scene of a crime, he would scarcely have replied: "No one but this table."

He said, "I suppose I should have asked if any robots were present?" (Damn it, what questions does one ask anyway on a strange world?) He said, "How legal is robotic evidence, Daneel?"

"What do you mean?"

"Can a robot bear witness on Solaria? Can it give evidence?"

"Why should you doubt it?"

"A robot isn't human, Daneel. On Earth, it cannot be a legal witness."

"And yet a footprint can, Partner Elijah, although that is much less a human than a robot is. The position of your planet in this respect is illogical. On Solaria, robotic evidence, when competent, is admissible."

Baley did not argue the point. He rested his chin on the knuckles of one hand and went over this matter of the robot in his mind.

In the extremity of terror Gladia Delmarre, standing over her husband's body, had summoned robots. By the time they came she was unconscious.

The robots reported having found her there together with the dead body. And something else was present as well; a robot. That robot had not been summoned; it was already there. It was not one of the regular staff. No other robot had seen it before or knew its function or assignment.

Nor could anything be discovered from the robot in question. It was not in working order. When found, its motions were disorganized and so, apparently, was the functioning of its positronic brain. It could give none of the proper responses, either verbal or mechanical, and after exhaustive investigation by a robotics expert it was declared a total loss.

Its only activity that had any trace of organization was its constant repetition of "You're going to kill me—you're going to kill me— you're going to kill me . . ."

No weapon that could possibly have been used to crush the dead man's skull was located.

Baley said suddenly, "I'm going to eat, Daneel, and then we see Agent Gruer again—or view him, anyway."

Hannis Gruer was still eating when contact was established. He ate slowly, choosing each mouthful carefully from a variety of dishes, peering at each anxiously as though searching for some hidden combination he would find most satisfactory.

Baley thought: He may be a couple of centuries old. Eating may be getting dull for him.

Gruer said, "I greet you, gentlemen. You received our report, I believe." His bald head glistened, as he leaned across the table to reach a titbit.

"Yes. We have spent an interesting session with Mrs. Delmarre also," said Baley.

"Good, good," said Gruer. "And to what conclusion, if any, did you come?"

Baley said, "That she is innocent, sir."

Gruer looked up sharply. "Really?"

Baley nodded.

Gruer said, "And yet she was the only one who could see him, the only one who could possibly be within reach. . . ."

Baley said, "That's been made clear to me, and no matter how firm social customs are on Solaria, the point is not conclusive. May I explain?"

Gruer had returned to his dinner. "Of course."

"Murder rests on three legs," said Baley, "each equally important. They are motive, means, and opportunity. For a good case against any suspect, each of the three must be satisfied. Now I grant you that Mrs. Delmarre had the opportunity. As for the motive, I've heard of none."

Gruer shrugged. "We know of none." For a moment his eyes drifted to the silent Daneel.

"All right. The suspect has no known motive, but perhaps she's a pathological killer. We can let the matter ride for a while, and continue. She is in his laboratory with him and there's some reason why she wants to kill him. She waves some club or other heavy object threateningly. It takes him a while to realize that his wife really intends to hurt him. He shouts in dismay, 'You're going to kill me,' and so she does. He turns to run as the blow descends and it crushes the back of his head. Did a doctor examine the body, by the way?"

"Yes and no. The robots called a doctor to attend Mrs. Delmarre and, as a matter of course, he looked at the dead body, too."

"That wasn't mentioned in the report."

"It was scarcely pertinent. The man was dead. In fact, by the time the doctor could view the body, it had been stripped, washed, and prepared for cremation in the usual manner."

"In other words, the robots had destroyed evidence," said Baley, annoyed. Then: "Did you say he *viewed* the body? He didn't *see* it?"

"Great Space," said Gruer, "what a morbid notion. He viewed it, of course, from all necessary angles and at close focus, I'm sure. Doctors can't avoid seeing patients under some conditions, but I can't conceive of any reason why they should have to see corpses. Medicine is a dirty job, but even doctors draw the line somewhere."

"Well, the point is this. Did the doctor report anything about the nature of the wound that killed Dr. Delmarre?"

"I see what you're driving at. You think that perhaps the wound was too severe to have been caused by a woman."

"A woman is weaker than a man, sir. And Mrs. Delmarre is a small woman."

"But quite athletic, Plainclothesman. Given a weapon of the proper type, gravity and leverage would do most of the work. Even not allowing for that, a woman in frenzy can do surprising things."

Baley shrugged. "You speak of a weapon. Where is it?"

Gruer shifted position. He held out his hand toward an empty glass and a robot entered the viewing field and filled it with a colorless fluid that might have been water.

Gruer held the filled glass momentarily, then put it down as though he had changed his mind about drinking. He said, "As is stated in the report, we have not been able to locate it."

"I know the report says that. I want to make absolutely certain of a few things. The weapon was searched for?"

"Thoroughly."

"By yourself?"

"By robots, but under my own viewing supervision at all times. We could locate nothing that might have been the weapon."

"That weakens the case against Mrs. Delmarre, doesn't it?"

"It does," said Gruer calmly. "It is one of several things about the case we don't understand. It is one reason why we have not acted against Mrs. Delmarre. It is one reason why I told you that the guilty party could not have committed the crime, either. Perhaps I should say that she apparently could not have committed the crime."

"Apparently?"

"She must have disposed of the weapon someway. So far, we have lacked the ingenuity to find it."

Baley said dourly, "Have you considered all possibilities?"

"I think so."

"I wonder. Let's see. A weapon has been used to crush a man's skull and it is not found at the scene of the crime. The only alternative is that it has been carried away. It could not have been carried away by Rikaine Delmarre. He was dead. Could it have been carried away by Gladia Delmarre?"

"It must have been," said Gruer.

"How? When the robots arrived, she was on the floor unconscious. Or she may have been feigning unconsciousness, but anyway she was there. How long a time between the murder and the arrival of the first robot?"

"That depends upon the exact time of the murder, which we don't know," said Gruer uneasily.

"I read the report, sir. One robot reported hearing a disturbance and a cry it identified as Dr. Delmarre's. It was apparently the closest to the scene. The summoning signal flashed five minutes afterward. It would take the robot less than a minute to appear on the scene." (Baley remembered his own experiences with the rapid-fire appearance of robots when summoned.) "In five minutes, even ten, how far could Mrs. Delmarre have carried a weapon and returned in time to assume unconsciousness?"

"She might have destroyed it in a disposer unit."

"The disposer unit was investigated, according to the report, and the residual gamma-ray activity was quite low. Nothing sizable had been destroyed in it for twenty-four hours."

"I know that," said Gruer. "I simply present it as an example of what might have been done."

"True," said Baley, "but there may be a very simple explanation. I suppose the robots belonging to the Delmarre household have been checked and all were accounted for."

"Oh yes."

"And all in reasonable working order?"

"Yes."

"Could any of those have carried away the weapon, perhaps without being aware of what it was?"

"Not one of them had removed anything from the scene of the crime. Or touched anything, for that matter."

"That's not so. They certainly removed the body and prepared it for cremation."

"Well, yes, of course, but that scarcely counts. You would expect them to do that."

"Jehoshaphat!" muttered Baley. He had to struggle to keep calm. He said, "Now suppose someone else had been on the scene."

"Impossible," said Gruer. "How could someone invade Dr. Delmarre's personal presence?"

"Suppose!" cried Baley. "Now there was never any thought in the robots' minds that an intruder might have been present. I don't suppose any of them made an immediate search of the grounds about the house. It wasn't mentioned in the report."

"There was no search till we looked for the weapon, but that was a considerable time afterward."

"Nor any search for signs of a ground-car or an air vehicle on the grounds?"

"No."

"Then if someone had nerved himself to invade Dr. Delmarre's personal presence, as you put it, he could have killed him and then walked away leisurely. No one would have stopped him or even seen him. Afterward, he could rely on everyone being sure no one could have been there."

"And no one could," said Gruer positively.

Baley said, "One more thing. Just one more. There was a robot involved. A robot was at the scene."

Daneel interposed for the first time. "The robot was not at the scene. Had it been there, the crime would not have been committed."

Baley turned his head sharply. And Gruer, who had lifted his glass a second time as though about to drink, put it down again to stare at Daneel.

"Is that not so?" asked Daneel.

"Quite so," said Gruer. "A robot would have stopped one person from harming another. First Law."

"All right," said Baley. "Granted. But it must have been close. It was on the scene when the other robots arrived. Say it was in the next room. The murderer is advancing on Delmarre and Delmarre cries out, 'You're going to kill me.' The robots of the household did not hear those words; at most they heard a cry, so, unsummoned, they did not come. But this particular robot heard the words and First Law made it come unsummoned. It was too late. Probably, it actually saw the murder committed."

"It must have seen the last stages of the murder," agreed Gruer. "That is what disordered it. Witnessing harm to a human without having prevented it is a violation of the First Law and, depending upon circumstances, more or less damage to the positronic brain is induced. In this case, it was a great deal of damage."

Gruer stared at his fingertips as he turned the glass of liquid to and fro, to and fro.

Baley said, "Then the robot was a witness. Was it questioned?"

"What use? He was disordered. It could only say 'You're going to kill me.' I agree with your reconstruction that far. They were probably Delmarre's last words burned into the robot's consciousness when everything else was destroyed."

"But I'm told Solaria specializes in robots. Was there no way in which the robot could be repaired? No way in which its circuits could be patched?"

"None," said Gruer sharply.

"And where is the robot, now?"

"Scrapped," said Gruer.

Baley raised his eyebrows. "This is a rather peculiar case. No motive, no means, no witnesses, no evidence. Where there was some evidence to begin with, it was destroyed. You have only one suspect and everyone seems convinced of her guilt; at least, everyone is certain no one else can be guilty. That's your opinion, too, obviously. The question then is: Why was I sent for?"

Gruer frowned. "You seem upset, Mr. Baley." He turned abruptly to Daneel. "Mr. Olivaw."

"Yes, Agent Gruer."

"Won't you please go through the dwelling and make sure all windows are closed and blanked out? Plainclothesman Baley may be feeling the effects of open space."

The statement astonished Baley. It was his impulse to deny Gruer's assumption and order Daneel to keep his place when, on the brink, he caught something of panic in Gruer's voice, something of glittering appeal in his eyes.

He sat back and let Daneel leave the room.

It was as though a mask had dropped from Gruer's face, leaving it naked and afraid. Gruer said, "That was easier than I had thought. I'd planned so many ways of getting you alone. I never thought the Auroran would leave at a simple request, and yet I could think of nothing else to do."

Baley said, "Well, I'm alone now."

Gruer said, "I couldn't speak freely in his presence. He's an Auroran and he is here because he was forced on us as the price of having you." The Solarian leaned forward. "There's something more to this than murder. I am not concerned only with the matter of who did it. There are parties on Solaria, secret organizations. . . ."

Baley stared. "Surely, I can't help you there."

"Of course you can. Now understand this: Dr. Delmarre was a Traditionalist. He believed in the old ways, the good ways. But there are new forces among us, forces for change, and Delmarre has been silenced."

"By Mrs. Delmarre?"

"Hers must have been the hand. That doesn't matter. There is an organization behind her and that is the important matter."

"Are you sure? Do you have evidence?"

"Vague evidence, only. I can't help that. Rikaine Delmarre was on the track of something. He assured me *his* evidence was good, and I believe him. I knew him well enough to know him as neither fool nor child. Unfortunately, he told me very little. Naturally, he wanted to complete his investigation before laying the matter completely open to the authorities. He must have gotten close to completion, too, or they wouldn't have dared the risk of having him openly slaughtered by violence. One thing Delmarre told me, though. The whole human race is in danger."

Baley felt himself shaken. For a moment it was as though he were listening to Minnim again, but on an even larger scale. Was *everyone* going to turn to him with cosmic dangers?

"Why do you think I can help?" he asked.

"Because you're an Earthman," said Gruer. "Do you understand? We on Solaria have no experience with these things. In a way, we don't understand people. There are too few of us here."

He looked uneasy. "I don't like to say this, Mr. Baley. My colleagues laugh at me and some grow angry, but it is a definite feeling I have. It seems to me that you Earthmen *must* understand people far better than we do, just by living among such crowds of them. And a detective more than anyone. Isn't that so?"

Baley half nodded and held his tongue.

Gruer said, "In a way, this murder was fortunate. I have not dared speak to the others about Delmarre's investigation, since I wasn't sure who might be involved in the conspiracy, and Delmarre himself was not ready to give any details till his investigation was complete. And even if Delmarre had completed his work, how would we deal with the matter afterward? How does one deal with hostile human beings? I don't know. From the beginning, I felt we needed an Earthman. When I heard of your work in connection with the murder in Spacetown on Earth, I knew we needed you. I got in touch with Aurora, with whose men you had worked most closely, and through them approached the Earth government. Yet my own colleagues could not be persuaded into agreeing to this. Then came the murder and that was enough of a shock to give me the agreement I needed. At the moment, they would have agreed to anything."

Gruer hesitated, then added, "It's not easy to ask an Earthman to help, but I must do so. Remember, whatever it is, the human race is in danger. Earth, too."

Earth was doubly in danger, then. There was no mistaking the desperate sincerity in Gruer's voice.

But then, if the murder were so fortunate a pretext for allowing Gruer to do what he so desperately wanted to do all the time, was it entirely fortune? It opened new avenues of thought that were not reflected in Baley's face, eyes, or voice.

Baley said, "I have been sent here, sir, to help. I will do so to the best of my ability."

Gruer finally lifted his long-delayed drink and looked over the rim of the glass at Baley. "Good," he said. "Not a word to the Auroran, please. Whatever this is about, Aurora may be involved. Certainly they took an unusually intense interest in the case. For instance, they insisted on including Mr. Olivaw as your partner. Aurora is powerful; we had to agree. They say they include Mr. Olivaw only because he worked with you before, but it may well be that they wish a reliable man of their own on the scene, eh?"

He sipped slowly, his eyes on Baley.

Baley passed the knuckles of one hand against his long cheek, rubbing it thoughtfully. "Now if that——"

He didn't finish, but leaped from his chair and almost hurled himself toward the other, before remembering it was only an image he was facing.

For Gruer, staring wildly at his drink, clutched his throat, whispering hoarsely, "Burning . . . burning . . ."

The glass fell from his hand, its contents spilling. And Gruer dropped with it, his face distorted with pain.

7

A Doctor Is Prodded

DANEEL STOOD in the doorway. "What happened, Partner Eli——"

But no explanation was needed. Daneel's voice changed to a loud ringing shout. "Robots of Hannis Gruer! Your master is hurt! Robots!"

At once a metal figure strode into the dining room and after it, in a minute or two, a dozen more entered. Three carried Gruer gently away. The others busily engaged in straightening the disarray and picking up the tableware strewn on the floor.

Daneel called out suddenly, "You there, robots, never mind the crockery. Organize a search. Search the house for any human being. Alert any robots on the grounds outside. Have them go over every acre of the estate. If you find a master, hold him. Do not hurt him" (unnecessary advice) "but do not let him leave, either. If you find no master present, let me know. I will remain at this viewer combination."

Then, as robots scattered, Elijah muttered to Daneel, "That's a beginning. It was poison, of course."

"Yes. That much is obvious, Partner Elijah." Daneel sat down queerly, as though there were a weakness in his knees. Baley had never seen him give way so, not for an instant, to any action that resembled anything so human as a weakness in the knees.

Daneel said, "It is not well with my mechanism to see a human being come to harm."

"There was nothing you could do."

"That I understand and yet it is as though there were certain cloggings in my thought paths. In human terms what I feel might be the equivalent to shock."

"If that's so, get over it." Baley felt neither patience nor sympathy for a queasy robot. "We've got to consider the little matter of responsibility. There is no poison without a poisoner."

"It might have been food-poisoning."

"Accidental food-poisoning? On a world this neatly run? Never. Besides, the poison was in a liquid and the symptoms were sudden and complete. It was a poisoned dose and a large one. Look, Daneel, I'll go into the next room to think this out a bit. You get Mrs. Delmarre. Make sure she's at home and check the distance between her estate and Gruer's."

"Is it that you think she——"

Baley held up a hand. "Just find out, will you?"

He strode out of the room, seeking solitude. Surely there could not be two independent attempts at murder so close together in time on a world like Solaria. And if a connection existed, the easiest assumption to make was that Gruer's story of a conspiracy was true.

Baley felt a familiar excitement growing within him. He had come to this world with Earth's predicament in his mind, and his own. The murder itself had been a faraway thing, but now the chase was really on. The muscles in his jaw knotted.

After all, the murderer or murderers (or murderess) had struck in his presence and he was stung by that. Was he held in so little account? It was professional pride that was hurt and Baley knew it and welcomed the fact. At least it gave him a firm reason to see this thing through as a murder case, simply, even without reference to Earth's dangers.

Daneel had located him now and was striding toward him. "I have done as you asked me to, Partner Elijah. I have viewed Mrs. Delmarre. She is at her home, which is somewhat over a thousand miles from the estate of Agent Gruer."

Baley said, "I'll see her myself later. View her, I mean." He stared thoughtfully at Daneel. "Do you think she has any connection with this crime?"

"Apparently not a direct connection, Partner Elijah."

"Does that imply there might be an indirect connection?"

"She might have persuaded someone else to do it."

"Someone else?" Baley asked quickly. "Who?"

"That, Partner Elijah, I cannot say."

"If someone were acting for her, that someone would have to be at the scene of the crime."

"Yes," said Daneel, "someone must have been there to place the poison in the liquid."

"Isn't it possible that the poisoned liquid might have been prepared earlier in the day? Perhaps much earlier?"

Daneel said quietly, "I had thought of that, Partner Elijah, which is why I used the word 'apparently' when I stated that Mrs. Delmarre had no direct connection with the crime. It is within the realm of possibility for her to have been on the scene earlier in the day. It would be well to check her movements."

"We will do that. We will check whether she was physically present at any time."

Baley's lips twitched. He had guessed that in some ways robotic logic must fall short and he was convinced of it now. As the roboticist had said: Logical but not reasonable.

He said, "Let's get back into the viewing room and get Gruer's estate back in view."

The room sparkled with freshness and order. There was no sign at all that less than an hour before a man had collapsed in agony.

Three robots stood, backs against the wall, in the usual robotic attitude of respectful submission.

Baley said, "What news concerning your master?"

The middle robot said, "The doctor is attending him, master."

"Viewing or seeing?"

"Viewing, master."

"What does the doctor say? Will your master live?"

"It is not yet certain, master."

Baley said, "Has the house been searched?"

"Thoroughly, master."

"Was there any sign of another master beside your own?"

"No, master."

"Were there any signs of such presence in the near past?"

"Not at all, master."

"Are the grounds being searched?"

"Yes, master."

"Any results so far?"

"No, master."

Baley nodded and said, "I wish to speak to the robot that served at the table this night."

"It is being held for inspection, master. Its reactions are erratic."

"Can it speak?"

"Yes, master."

"Then get it here without delay."

There *was* delay and Baley began again. "I said——"

Daneel interrupted smoothly. "There is interradio communication among these Solarian types. The robot you desire is being summoned. If it is slow in coming, it is part of the disturbance that has overtaken it as the result of what has occurred."

Baley nodded. He might have guessed at interradio. In a world so thoroughly given over to robots some sort of intimate communication among them would be necessary if the system were not to break down. It explained how a dozen robots could follow when one robot had been summoned, but only when needed and not otherwise.

A robot entered. It limped, one leg dragging. Baley wondered why and then shrugged. Even among the primitive robots on Earth reactions to injury of the positronic paths were never obvious to the layman. A disrupted circuit might strike a leg's functioning, as here, and the fact would be most significant to a roboticist and completely meaningless to anyone else.

Baley said cautiously, "Do you remember a colorless liquid on your master's table, some of which you poured into a goblet for him?"

The robot said, "Yeth, mathter."

A defect in oral articulation, too!

Baley said, "What was the nature of the liquid?"

"It wath water, mathter."

"Just water? Nothing else?"

"Jutht water, mathter."

"Where did you get it?"

"From the rethervoir tap, mathter."

"Had it been standing in the kitchen before you brought it in?"

"The mathter preferred it not too cold, mathter. It wath a thtanding order that it be poured an hour before mealth."

How convenient, thought Baley, for anyone who knew that fact.

He said, "Have one of the robots connect me with the doctor viewing your master as soon as he is available. And while that is being done, I want another one to explain how the reservoir tap works. I want to know about the water supply here."

The doctor was available with little delay. He was the oldest Spacer Baley had ever seen, which meant, Baley thought, that he might be over three hundred years old. The veins stood out on his hands and his close-cropped hair was pure white. He had a habit of tapping his ridged front teeth with a fingernail, making a little clicking noise that Baley found annoying. His name was Altim Thool.

The doctor said, "Fortunately, he threw up a good deal of the dose. Still, he may not survive. It is a tragic event." He sighed heavily.

"What was the poison, Doctor?" asked Baley.

"I'm afraid I don't know." (Click-click-click.)

Baley said, "What? Then how are you treating him?"

"Direct stimulation of the neuromuscular system to prevent paralysis, but except for that I am letting nature take its course." His face, with its faintly yellow skin, like well-worn leather of superior quality, wore a pleading expression. "We have very little experience with this sort of thing. I don't recall another case in over two centuries of practice."

Baley stared at the other with contempt. "You know there are such things as poisons, don't you?"

"Oh yes." (Click-click.) "Common knowledge."

"You have book-film references where you can gain some knowledge."

"It would take days. There are numerous mineral poisons. We make use of insecticides in our society, and it is not impossible to obtain bacterial toxins. Even with descriptions in the films it would take a long time to gather the equipment and develop the techniques to test for them."

"If no one on Solaria knows," said Baley grimly, "I'd suggest you get in touch with one of the other worlds and find out. Meanwhile, you had better test the reservoir tap in Gruer's mansion for poison. Get there in person, if you have to, and do it."

Baley was prodding a venerable Spacer roughly, ordering him about like a robot and was quite unconscious of the incongruity of it. Nor did the Spacer make any protest.

Dr. Thool said doubtfully, "How could the reservoir tap be poisoned? I'm sure it couldn't be."

"Probably not," agreed Baley, "but test it anyway to make sure."

The reservoir tap was a dim possibility indeed. The robot's explanation had shown it to be a typical piece of Solarian self-care. Water might enter it from whatever source and be tailored to suit. Microorganisms were removed and non-living organic matter eliminated. The proper amount of aeration was introduced, as were various ions in just those trace amounts best suited to the body's needs. It was very unlikely that any poison could survive one or another of the control devices.

Still, if the safety of the reservoir were directly established, then the time element would be clear. There would be the matter of the hour before the meal, when the pitcher of water (exposed to *air*, thought Baley sourly) was allowed to warm slowly, thanks to Gruer's idiosyncrasy.

But Dr. Thool, frowning, was saying, "But how would I test the reservoir tap?"

"Jehoshaphat! Take an animal with you. Inject some of the water you take out of the tap into its veins, or have it drink some. Use your head, man. And do the same for what's left in the pitcher, and if that's poisoned, as it must be, run some of the tests the reference films describe. Find some simple ones. Do *something*."

"Wait, wait. What pitcher?"

"The pitcher in which the water was standing. The pitcher from which the robot poured the poisoned drink."

"Well, dear me—I presume it has been cleaned up. The household retinue would surely not leave it standing about."

Baley groaned. Of course not. It was *impossible* to retain evidence with eager robots forever destroying it in the name of household duty. He should have *ordered* it preserved, but of course, this society was not his own and he never reacted properly to it.

Jehoshaphat!

Word eventually came through that the Gruer estate was clear; no sign of any unauthorized human present anywhere.

Daneel said, "That rather intensifies the puzzle, Partner Elijah, since it seems to leave no one in the role of poisoner."

Baley, absorbed in thought, scarcely heard. He said, "What? . . . Not at all. Not at all. It clarifies the matter." He did not explain, knowing quite well that Daneel would be incapable of understanding or believing what Baley was certain was the truth.

Nor did Daneel ask for an explanation. Such an invasion of a human's thoughts would have been most unrobotic.

Baley prowled back and forth restlessly, dreading the approach of the sleep period, when his fears of the open would rise and his longing for Earth increase. He felt an almost feverish desire to keep things happening.

He said to Daneel, "I might as well see Mrs. Delmarre again. Have the robot make contact."

They walked to the viewing room and Baley watched a robot work with deft metal fingers. He watched through a haze of obscuring thought that vanished in startled astonishment when a table, elaborately spread for dinner, suddenly filled half the room.

Gladia's voice said, "Hello." A moment later she stepped into view and sat down. "Don't look surprised, Elijah. It's just dinnertime. And I'm very carefully dressed. See?"

She was. The dominant color of her dress was a light blue and it shimmered down the length of her limbs to wrists and ankles. A yellow ruff clung about her neck and shoulders, a little lighter than her hair, which was now held in disciplined waves.

Baley said, "I did not mean to interrupt your meal."

"I haven't begun yet. Why don't you join me?"

He eyed her suspiciously. "Join you?"

She laughed. "You Earthmen are so funny. I don't mean join me in personal presence. How could you do that? I mean, go to your own dining room and then you and the other one can dine with me."

"But if I leave——"

"Your viewing technician can maintain contact."

Daneel nodded gravely at that, and with some uncertainty Baley turned and walked toward the door. Gladia, together with her table, its setting, and its ornaments moved with him.

Gladia smiled encouragingly. "See? Your viewing technician is keeping us in contact."

Baley and Daneel traveled up a moving ramp that Baley did not recall having traversed before. Apparently there were numerous possible routes between any two rooms in this impossible mansion and he knew only few of them. Daneel, of course, knew them all.

And, moving through walls, sometimes a bit below floor level, sometimes a bit above, there was always Gladia and her dinner table.

Baley stopped and muttered, "This takes getting used to."

Gladia said at once, "Does it make you dizzy?"

"A little."

"Then I tell you what. Why don't you have your technicians freeze me right here. Then when you're in your dining room and all set, he can join us up."

Daneel said, "I will order that done, Partner Elijah."

Their own dinner table was set when they arrived, the plates steaming with a dark brown soup in which diced meat was bobbing, and in the center a large roast fowl was ready for the carving. Daneel spoke briefly to the serving robot and, with smooth efficiency, the two places that had been set were drawn to the same end of the table.

As though that were a signal, the opposite wall seemed to move outward, the table seemed to lengthen and Gladia was seated at the opposite end. Room joined to room and table to table so neatly that but for the varying pattern in wall and floor covering and the differing designs in tableware it would have been easy to believe they were all dining together in actual fact.

"There," said Gladia with satisfaction. "Isn't this comfortable?"

"Quite," said Baley. He tasted his soup gingerly, found it delicious, and helped himself more generously. "You know about Agent Gruer?"

Trouble shadowed her face at once and she put her spoon down. "Isn't it terrible? Poor Hannis."

"You use his first name. Do you know him?"

"I know almost all the important people on Solaria. Most Solarians do know one another. Naturally."

Naturally, indeed, thought Baley. How many of them were there, after all?

Baley said, "Then perhaps you know Dr. Altim Thool. He's taking care of Gruer."

Gladia laughed gently. Her serving robot sliced meat for her and added small, browned potatoes and slivers of carrots. "Of course I know him. He treated me."

"Treated you when?"

"Right after the—the trouble. About my husband, I mean."

Baley said in astonishment, "Is he the only doctor on the planet?"

"Oh no." For a moment her lips moved as though she were counting to herself. "There are at least ten. And there's one youngster I know of who's studying medicine. But Dr. Thool is one of the best. He has the most experience. Poor Dr. Thool."

"Why poor?"

"Well, you know what I mean. It's such a nasty job, being a doctor. Sometimes you just have to see people when you're a doctor and even touch them. But Dr. Thool seems so resigned to it and he'll always do some seeing when he feels he must. He's always treated me since I was a child and was always so friendly and kind and I honestly feel I almost wouldn't mind if he did have to see me. For instance, he saw me this last time."

"After your husband's death, you mean?"

"Yes. You can imagine how he felt when he saw my husband's dead body and me lying there."

"I was told he viewed the body," said Baley.

"The body, yes. But after he made sure I was alive and in no real danger, he ordered the robots to put a pillow under my head and give me an injection of something or other, and then get out. He came over by jet. Really! By jet. It took less than half an hour and he took care of me and made sure all was well. I was so woozy when I came to that I was sure I was only viewing him, you know, and it wasn't till he touched me that I knew we were seeing, and I screamed. Poor Dr. Thool. He was awfully embarrassed, but I knew he meant well."

Baley nodded. "I suppose there's not much use for doctors on Solaria?"

"I should hope *not*."

"I know there are no germ diseases to speak of. What about metabolic disorders? Atherosclerosis? Diabetes? Things like that?"

"It happens and it's pretty awful when it does. Doctors can make life more livable for such people in a physical way, but that's the least of it."

"Oh?"

"Of course. It means the gene analysis was imperfect. You don't suppose we allow defects like diabetes to develop on purpose. Anyone who develops such things has to undergo very detailed re-analysis. The mate assignment has to be retracted, which is terribly embarrassing for the mate. And it means no—no"—her voice sank to a whisper—"children."

Baley said in a normal voice, "No children?"

Gladia flushed. "It's a terrible thing to say. Such a word! Ch-children!"

"It comes easy after a while," said Baley dryly.

"Yes, but if I get into the habit, I'll say it in front of another Solarian someday and I'll just sink into the ground. . . . Anyway, if the two of them have had children (see, I've said it again) already, the children have to be found and examined—that was one of Rikaine's jobs, by the way—and well, it's just a mess."

So much for Thool, thought Baley. The doctor's incompetence was a natural consequence of the society, and held nothing sinister. Nothing *necessarily* sinister. Cross him off, he thought, but lightly.

He watched Gladia as she ate. She was neat and precisely delicate in her movements and her appetite seemed normal. (His own fowl was delightful. In one respect, anyway—food—he could easily be spoiled by these Outer Worlds.)

He said, "What is your opinion of the poisoning, Gladia?"

She looked up. "I'm trying not to think of it. There are so many horrors lately. Maybe it wasn't poisoning."

"It was."

"But there wasn't anyone around?"

"How do you know?"

"There couldn't have been. He has no wife, these days, since he's all through with his quota of ch—you know what. So there was no one to put the poison in anything, so how could he be poisoned?"

"But he was poisoned. That's a fact and must be accepted."

Her eyes clouded over. "Do you suppose," she said, "he did it himself?"

"I doubt it. Why should he? And so publicly?"

"Then it couldn't be done, Elijah. It just couldn't."

Baley said, "On the contrary, Gladia. It could be done very easily. And I'm sure I know exactly how."

8

A Spacer Is Defied

GLADIA SEEMED to be holding her breath for a moment. It came out through puckered lips in what was almost a whistle. She said, "I'm sure I don't see how. Do you know *who* did it?"

Baley nodded. "The same one who killed your husband."

"Are you sure?"

"Aren't you? Your husband's murder was the first in the history of Solaria. A month later there is another murder. Could that be a coincidence? Two separate murderers striking within a month of each other on a crime-free world? Consider, too, that the second victim was investigating the first crime and therefore represented a violent danger to the original murderer."

"Well!" Gladia applied herself to her dessert and said between mouthfuls, "If you put it that way, I'm innocent."

"How so, Gladia?"

"Why, Elijah. I've never been near the Gruer estate, never in my whole life. So I certainly couldn't have poisoned Agent Gruer. And if I haven't—why, neither did I kill my husband."

Then, as Baley maintained a stern silence, her spirit seemed to fade and the corners of her small mouth drooped. "Don't you think so, Elijah?"

"I can't be sure," said Baley. "I've told you I know the method used to poison Gruer. It's an ingenious one and anyone on Solaria could have used it, whether they were on the Gruer estate or not; whether they were ever on the Gruer estate or not."

Gladia clenched her hands into fists. "Are you saying I did it?"

"I'm not saying that."

"You're implying it." Her lips were thin with fury and her high cheekbones were splotchy. "Is that all your interest in viewing me? To ask me sly questions? To trap me?"

"Now wait——"

"You seemed so sympathetic. So understanding. You—you Earthman!"

Her contralto had become a tortured rasp with the last word.

Daneel's perfect face leaned toward Gladia and he said, "If you will pardon me, Mrs. Delmarre, you are holding a knife rather tightly and may cut yourself. Please be careful."

Gladia stared wildly at the short, blunt, and undoubtedly quite harmless knife she held in her hand. With a spasmodic movement she raised it high.

Baley said, "You couldn't reach me, Gladia."

She gasped. "Who'd want to reach you? Ugh!" She shuddered in exaggerated disgust and called out, "Break contact at once!"

The last must have been to a robot out of the line of sight, and Gladia and her end of the room were gone and the original wall sprang back.

Daneel said, "Am I correct in believing you now consider this woman guilty?"

"No," said Baley flatly. "Whoever did this needed a great deal more of certain characteristics than this poor girl has."

"She has a temper."

"What of that? Most people do. Remember, too, that she has been under a considerable strain for a considerable time. If I had been under a similar strain and someone had turned on me as she imagined I had turned on her, I might have done a great deal more than wave a foolish little knife."

Daneel said, "I have not been able to deduce the technique of poisoning at a distance, as you say you have."

Baley found it pleasant to be able to say, "I know you haven't. You lack the capacity to decipher this particular puzzle."

He said it with finality and Daneel accepted the statement as calmly and as gravely as ever.

Baley said, "I have two jobs for you, Daneel."

"And what are they, Partner Elijah?"

"First, get in touch with this Dr. Thool and find out Mrs. Delmarre's condition at the time of the murder of her husband. How long she required treatment and so on."

"Do you want to determine something in particular?"

"No. I'm just trying to accumulate data. It isn't easy on this world. Secondly, find out who will be taking Gruer's place as head of security and arrange a viewing session for me first thing in the morning. As for me," he said without pleasure in his mind, and with none in his voice, "I'm going to bed and eventually, I hope, I'll sleep." Then, almost petulantly, "Do you suppose I could get a decent book-film in this place?"

Daneel said, "I would suggest that you summon the robot in charge of the library."

Baley felt only irritation at having to deal with the robot. He would much rather have browsed at will.

"No," he said, "not a classic; just an ordinary piece of fiction dealing with everyday life on contemporary Solaria. About half a dozen of them."

The robot submitted (it would have to) but even as it manipulated the proper controls that plucked the requisite book-films out of their niches and transferred them first to an exit slot and then to Baley's hand, it rattled on in respectful tones about all the other categories in the library.

The master might like an adventure romance of the days of exploration, it suggested, or an excellent view of chemistry, perhaps, with animated atom models, or a fantasy, or a Galactography. The list was endless.

Baley waited grimly for his half dozen, said, "These will do," reached with his own hands (his *own* hands) for a scanner and walked away.

When the robot followed and said, "Will you require help with the adjustment, master?" Baley turned and snapped, "No. Stay where you are."

The robot bowed and stayed.

Lying in bed, with the headboard aglow, Baley almost regretted his decision. The scanner was like no model he had ever used and he began with no idea at all as to the method for threading the film. But he worked at it obstinately, and, eventually, by taking it apart and working it out bit by bit, he managed something.

At least he could view the film and, if the focus left a bit to be desired, it was small payment for a moment's independence from the robots.

In the next hour and a half he had skipped and switched through four of the six films and was disappointed.

He had had a theory. There was no better way, he had thought, to get an insight into Solarian ways of life and thought than to read their novels. He needed that insight if he were to conduct the investigation sensibly.

But now he had to abandon his theories. He had viewed novels and had succeeded only in learning of people with ridiculous problems who behaved foolishly and reacted mysteriously. Why should a woman abandon her job on discovering her child had entered the same profession and refuse to explain her reasons until unbearable and ridiculous complications had resulted? Why should a doctor and an artist be humiliated at being assigned to one another and what was so noble about the doctor's insistence on entering robotic research?

He threaded the fifth novel into the scanner and adjusted it to his eyes. He was bone-weary.

So weary, in fact, that he never afterward recalled anything of the fifth novel (which he believed to be a suspense story) except for the opening in which a new estate owner entered his mansion and looked through the past account films presented him by a respectful robot.

Presumably he fell asleep then with the scanner on his head and all lights blazing. Presumably a robot, entering respectfully, had gently removed the scanner and put out the lights.

In any case, he slept and dreamed of Jessie. All was as it had been. He had never left Earth. They were ready to travel to the community kitchen and then to see a subetheric show with friends. They would travel over the Expressways and see people and neither of them had a care in the world. He was happy.

And Jessie was beautiful. She had lost weight somehow. Why should she be so slim? And so beautiful?

And one other thing was wrong. Somehow the sun shone down on them. He looked up and there was only the vaulted base of the upper Levels visible, yet the sun shone down, blazing brightly on everything, and no one was afraid.

Baley woke up, disturbed. He let the robots serve breakfast and did not speak to Daneel. He said nothing, asked nothing, downed excellent coffee without tasting it.

Why had he dreamed of the visible-invisible sun? He could understand dreaming of Earth and of Jessie, but what had the sun to do with it? And why should the thought of it bother him, anyway?

"Partner Elijah," said Daneel gently.

"What?"

"Corwin Attlebish will be in viewing contact with you in half an hour. I have arranged that."

"Who the hell is Corwin Whatchamacullum?" asked Baley sharply, and refilled his coffee cup.

"He was Agent Gruer's chief aide, Partner Elijah, and is now Acting Head of Security."

"Then get him now."

"The appointment, as I explained, is for half an hour from now."

"I don't care when it's for. Get him now. That's an order."

"I will make the attempt, Partner Elijah. He may not, however, agree to receive the call."

"Let's take the chance, and get on with it, Daneel."

The Acting Head of Security accepted the call and, for the first time on Solaria, Baley saw a Spacer who looked like the usual Earthly conception of one. Attlebish was tall, lean, and bronze. His eyes were a light brown, his chin large and hard.

He looked faintly like Daneel. But whereas Daneel was idealized, almost godlike, Corwin Attlebish had lines of humanity in his face.

Attlebish was shaving. The small abrasive pencil gave out its spray of fine particles that swept over cheek and chin, biting off the hair neatly and then disintegrating into impalpable dust.

Baley recognized the instrument through hearsay but had never seen one used before.

"You the Earthman?" asked Attlebish slurringly through barely cracked lips, as the abrasive dust passed under his nose.

Baley said, "I'm Elijah Baley, Plainclothesman C-7. I'm from Earth."

"You're early." Attlebish snapped his shaver shut and tossed it somewhere outside Baley's range of vision. "What's on your mind, Earthman?"

Baley would not have enjoyed the other's tone of voice at the best of times. He burned now. He said, "How is Agent Gruer?"

Attlebish said, "He's still alive. He may stay alive."

Baley nodded. "Your poisoners here on Solaria don't know dosages. Lack of experience. They gave Gruer too much and he threw it up. Half the dose would have killed him."

"Poisoners? There is no evidence for poison."

Baley stared. "Jehoshaphat! What else do you think it is?"

"A number of things. Much can go wrong with a person." He rubbed his face, looking for roughness with his fingertips. "You would scarcely know the metabolic problems that arise past the age of two fifty."

"If that's the case, have you obtained competent medical advice?"

"Dr. Thool's report——"

That did it. The anger that had been boiling inside Baley since waking burst through. He cried at the top of his voice, "I don't care about Dr. Thool. I said competent medical advice. Your doctors don't know anything, any more than your detectives would, if you had any. You had to get a detective from Earth. Get a doctor as well."

The Solarian looked at him coolly. "Are you telling me what to do?"

"Yes, and without charge. Be my guest. Gruer *was* poisoned. I witnessed the process. He drank, retched, and yelled that his throat was burning. What do you call it when you consider that he was investigating——" Baley came to a sudden halt.

"Investigating what?" Attlebish was unmoved.

Baley was uncomfortably aware of Daneel at his usual position some ten feet away. Gruer had not wanted Daneel, as an Auroran, to know of the investigation. He said lamely, "There were political implications."

Attlebish crossed his arms and looked distant, bored, and faintly hostile. "We have no politics on Solaria in the sense we hear of it on other worlds. Hannis Gruer has been a good citizen, but he is imaginative. It was he who, having heard some story about you, urged that we import you. He even agreed to accept an Auroran companion for you as a condition. I did not think it necessary. There is no mystery. Rikaine Delmarre was killed by his wife and we shall find out how and why. Even if we do not, she will be genetically analyzed and the proper measures taken. As for Gruer, your fantasy concerning poisoning is of no importance."

Baley said incredulously, "You seem to imply that I'm not needed here."

"I believe not. If you wish to return to Earth, you may do so. I may even say we urge you to."

Baley was amazed at his own reaction. He cried, "No, sir. I don't budge."

"We hired you, Plainclothesman. We can discharge you. You will return to your home planet."

"*No!* You listen to me. I'd advise you to. You're a big-time Spacer and I'm an Earthman, but with all respect, with deepest and most humble apologies, you're scared."

"Withdraw that statement!" Attlebish drew himself to his six-foot-plus, and stared down at the Earthman haughtily.

"You're scared as hell. You think you'll be next if you pursue this thing. You're giving in so they'll let you alone; so they'll leave you your miserable life." Baley had no notion who the "they" might be or if there were any "they" at all. He was striking out blindly at an arrogant Spacer and enjoying the thud his phrases made as they hit against the other's self-control.

"You will leave," said Attlebish, pointing his finger in cold anger, "within the hour. There'll be no diplomatic considerations about this, I assure you."

"Save your threats, Spacer. Earth is nothing to you, I admit, but I'm not the only one here. May I introduce my partner, Daneel Olivaw. He's from Aurora. He doesn't talk much. He's not here to talk. I handle that department. But he listens awfully well. He doesn't miss a word.

"Let me put it straight, Attlebish"—Baley used the unadorned name with relish—"whatever monkeyshines are going on here on Solaria, Aurora and forty-odd other Outer Worlds are interested. If you kick us off, the next deputation to visit Solaria will consist of warships. I'm from Earth and I know how the system works. Hurt feelings mean warships by return trip."

Attlebish transferred his regard to Daneel and seemed to be considering. His voice was gentler. "There is nothing going on here that need concern anyone outside the planet."

"Gruer thought otherwise and my partner heard him." This was no time to cavil at a lie.

Daneel turned to look at Baley, at the Earthman's last statement, but Baley paid no attention. He drove on: "I intend to pursue this investigation. Ordinarily, there's nothing I wouldn't do to get back to Earth. Even just dreaming about it gets me so restless I can't sit. If I owned this robot-infested palace I'm living in now, I'd give it with the robots thrown in and you and all your lousy world to boot for a ticket home.

"But I won't be ordered off by you. Not while there's a case to which I've been assigned that's still open. Try getting rid of me against my will and you'll be looking down the throats of space-based artillery.

"What's more, from now on, this murder investigation is going to be run *my* way. I'm in charge. I see the people I want to see. I *see* them. I don't view them. I'm used to seeing and that's the way it's going to be. I'll want the official approval of your office for all of that."

"This is impossible, unbearable——"

"Daneel, you tell him."

The humanoid's voice said dispassionately, "As my partner has informed you, Agent Attlebish, we have been sent here to conduct a murder investigation. It is essential that we do so. We, of course, do not wish to disturb any of your customs and perhaps actual seeing will be unnecessary, although it would be helpful if you were to give approval for such seeing as becomes necessary as Plainclothesman Baley has requested. As to leaving the planet against our will, we feel that would be inadvisable, although we regret any feeling on your part or on the part of any Solarian that our remaining would be unpleasant."

Baley listened to the stilted sentence structure with a dour stretching of his lips that was not a smile. To one who knew Daneel as a robot, it was all an attempt to do a job without giving offense to any human, not to Baley and not to Attlebish. To one who thought Daneel was an Auroran, a native of the oldest and most powerful militarily of the Outer Worlds, it sounded like a series of subtly courteous threats.

Attlebish put the tips of his fingers to his forehead. "I'll think about it."

"Not too long," said Baley, "because I have some visiting to do within the hour, and not by viewer. Done viewing!"

He signaled the robot to break contact, then he stared with surprise and pleasure at the place where Attlebish had been. None of this had been planned. It had all been impulse born of his dream and of Attlebish's unnecessary arrogance. But now that it had happened, he was glad. It was what he had wanted, really—to take control.

He thought: Anyway, that was telling the dirty Spacer!

He wished the entire population of Earth could have been here to watch. The man *looked* such a Spacer, and that made it all the better, of course. All the better.

Only, why this feeling of vehemence in the matter of seeing? Baley scarcely understood that. He knew what he planned to do, and seeing (not viewing) was part of it. All right. Yet there had been the tight lift to his spirit when he spoke of seeing, as though he were ready to break down the walls of this mansion even though it served no purpose.

Why?

There was something impelling him beside the case, something that had nothing to do even with the question of Earth's safety. But what?

Oddly, he remembered his dream again; the sun shining down through all the opaque layers of the gigantic underground Cities of Earth.

Daneel said with thoughtfulness (as far as his voice could carry a recognizable emotion), "I wonder, Partner Elijah, if this is entirely safe."

"Bluffing this character? It worked. And it wasn't really a bluff. I think it *is* important to Aurora to find out what's going on on Solaria, and that Aurora knows it. Thank you, by the way, for not catching me out in a misstatement."

"It was the natural decision. To have borne you out did Agent Attlebish a certain rather subtle harm. To have given you the lie would have done you a greater and more direct harm."

"Potentials countered and the higher one won out, eh, Daneel?"

"So it was, Partner Elijah. I understand that this process, in a less definable way, goes on within the human mind. I repeat, however, that this new proposal of yours is not safe."

"Which new proposal is this?"

"I do not approve your notion of seeing people. By that I mean seeing as opposed to viewing."

"I understand you. I'm not asking for your approval."

"I have my instructions, Partner Elijah. What it was that Agent Hannis Gruer told you during my absence last night I cannot know. That he did say something is obvious from the change in your attitude toward this problem. However, in the light of my instructions, I can guess. He must have warned you of the possibility of danger to other planets arising from the situation on Solaria."

Slowly Baley reached for his pipe. He did that occasionally and always there was the feeling of irritation when he found nothing and remembered he could not smoke. He said, "There are only twenty thousand Solarians. What danger can they represent?"

"My masters on Aurora have for some time been uneasy about Solaria. I have not been told all the information at their disposal——"

"And what little you have been told you have been told not to repeat to me. Is that it?" demanded Baley.

Daneel said, "There is a great deal to find out before this matter can be discussed freely."

"Well, what are the Solarians doing? New weapons? Paid subversion? A campaign of individual assassination? What can twenty thousand people do against hundreds of millions of Spacers?"

Daneel remained silent.

Baley said, "I intend to find out, you know."

"But not the way you have now proposed, Partner Elijah. I have been instructed most carefully to guard your safety."

"You would have to anyway. First Law!"

"Over and above that, as well. In conflict between your safety and that of another I must guard yours."

"Of course. I understand that. If anything happens to me, there is no further way in which you can remain on Solaria without complications that Aurora is not yet ready to face. As long as I'm alive, I'm here at Solaria's original request and so we can throw our weight around, if necessary, and make them keep us. If I'm dead, the whole situation is changed. Your orders are, then, to keep Baley alive. Am I right, Daneel?"

Daneel said, "I cannot presume to interpret the reasoning behind my orders."

Baley said, "All right, don't worry. The open space won't kill me, if I do find it necessary to see anyone. I'll survive. I may even get used to it."

"It is not the matter of open space alone, Partner Elijah," said Daneel. "It is this matter of seeing Solarians. I do not approve of it."

"You mean the Spacers won't like it. Too bad if they don't. Let them wear nose filters and gloves. Let them spray the air. And if it offends their nice morals to see me in the flesh, let them wince and blush. But I intend to see them. I consider it necessary to do so and I *will* do so."

"But I cannot allow you to."

"*You* can't allow *me?*"

"Surely you see why, Partner Elijah."

"I do not."

"Consider, then, that Agent Gruer, the key Solarian figure in the investigation of this murder, has been poisoned. Does it not follow that if I permit you to proceed in your plan for exposing yourself indiscriminately in actual person, the next victim will necessarily be you yourself. How then can I possibly permit you to leave the safety of this mansion?"

"How will you stop me, Daneel?"

"By force, if necessary, Partner Elijah," said Daneel calmly. "Even if I must hurt you. If I do not do so, you will surely die."

9

A Robot Is Stymied

BALEY SAID, "So the higher potential wins out again, Daneel. You will hurt me to keep me alive."

"I do not believe hurting you will be necessary, Partner Elijah. You know that I am superior to you in strength and you will not attempt a useless resistance. If it should become necessary, however, I will be compelled to hurt you."

"I could blast you down where you stand," said Baley. "Right now! There is nothing in *my* potentials to prevent me."

"I had thought you might take this attitude at some time in our present relationship, Partner Elijah. Most particularly, the thought occurred to me during our trip to this mansion, when you grew momentarily violent in the ground-car .The destruction of myself is unimportant in comparison with your safety, but such destruction would cause you distress eventually and disturb the plans of my masters. It was one of my first cares, therefore, during your first sleeping period, to deprive your blaster of its charge."

Baley's lips tightened. He was left without a charged blaster! His hand dropped instantly to his holster. He drew his weapon and stared at the charge reading. It hugged zero.

For a moment he balanced the lump of useless metal as though to hurl it directly into Daneel's face. What good? The robot would dodge efficiently.

Baley put the blaster back. It could be recharged in good time.

Slowly, thoughtfully, he said, "I'm not fooled by you, Daneel."

"In what way, Partner Elijah."

"You are too much the master. I am too completely stopped by you. Are you a robot?"

"You have doubted me before," said Daneel.

"On Earth last year, I doubted whether R. Daneel Olivaw was truly a robot. It turned out he was. I believe he still is. My question, however is this: Are you R. Daneel Olivaw?"

"I am."

"Yes? Daneel was designed to imitate a Spacer closely. Why could not a Spacer be made up to imitate Daneel closely?"

"For what reason?"

"To carry on an investigation here with greater initiative and capacity than ever a robot could. And yet by assuming Daneel's role, you could keep me safely under control by giving me a false consciousness of mastery. After all, you are working through me and I must be kept pliable."

"All this is not so, Partner Elijah."

"Then why do all the Solarians we meet assume you to be human? They are robotic experts. Are they so easily fooled? It occurs to me that I cannot be one right against many wrong. It is far more likely that I am one wrong against many right."

"Not at all, Partner Elijah."

"Prove it," said Baley, moving slowly toward an end table and lifting a scrap-disposal unit. "You can do that easily enough, if you *are* a robot. Show the metal beneath your skin."

Daneel said, "I assure you——"

"Show the metal," said Baley crisply. "That is an order! Or don't you feel compelled to obey orders?"

Daneel unbuttoned his shirt. The smooth, bronze skin of his chest was sparsely covered with light hair. Daneel's fingers exerted a firm pressure just under the right nipple, and flesh and skin split bloodlessly the length of the chest, with the gleam of metal showing beneath.

And as that happened, Baley's fingers, resting on the end table, moved half an inch to the right and stabbed at a contact patch. Almost at once a robot entered.

"Don't move, Daneel," cried Baley. "That's an order! Freeze!"

Daneel stood motionless, as though life, or the robotic imitation thereof, had departed from him.

Baley shouted to the robot, "Can you get two more of the staff in here without yourself leaving? If so, do it."

The robot said, "Yes, master."

Two more robots entered, answering a radioed call. The three lined up abreast.

"Boys!" said Baley. "Do you see this creature whom you thought a master?"

Six ruddy eyes had turned solemnly on Daneel. They said in unison, "We see him, master."

Baley said, "Do you also see that this so-called master is actually a robot like yourself since it is metal within. It is only designed to look like a man."

"Yes, master."

"You are not required to obey any order it gives you. Do you understand that?"

"Yes, master."

"I, on the other hand," said Baley, "am a true man."

For a moment the robots hesitated. Baley wondered if, having had it shown to them that a thing might seem a man yet be a robot, they would accept *anything* in human appearance as a man, anything at all.

But then one robot said, "You are a man, master," and Baley drew breath again.

He said, "Very well, Daneel. You may relax."

Daneel moved into a more natural position and said calmly, "Your expressed doubt as to my identity, then, was merely a feint designed to exhibit my nature to these others, I take it."

"So it was," said Baley, and looked away. He thought: The thing is a machine, not a man. You can't double-cross a machine.

And yet he couldn't entirely repress a feeling of shame. Even as Daneel stood there, chest open, there seemed something so human about him, something capable of being betrayed.

Baley said, "Close your chest, Daneel, and listen to me. Physically, you are no match for three robots. You see that, don't you?"

"That is clear, Partner Elijah."

"Good! . . . Now you boys," and he turned to the other robots again. "You are to tell no one, human or master, that this creature is a robot. Never at any time, without further instructions from myself and myself alone."

"I thank you," interposed Daneel softly.

"However," Baley went on, "this manlike robot is not to be allowed to interfere with my actions in any way. If it attempts any such interference, you will restrain it by force, taking care not to damage it unless absolutely necessary. Do not allow it to establish contact with humans other than myself, or with robots other than yourselves, either by seeing or by viewing. And do not leave it at any time. Keep it in this room and remain here yourselves. Your other duties are suspended until further notice. Is all this clear?"

"Yes, master," they chorused.

Baley turned to Daneel again. "There is nothing you can do now, so don't try to stop me."

Daneel's arms hung loosely at his side. He said, "I may not, through inaction, allow you to come to harm, Partner Elijah. Yet under the circumstances, nothing but inaction is possible. The logic is unassailable. I shall do nothing. I trust you will remain safe and in good health."

There it was, thought Baley. Logic was logic and robots had nothing else. Logic told Daneel he was completely stymied. Reason might have told him that all factors are rarely predictable, that the opposition might make a mistake.

None of that. A robot is logical only, not reasonable.

Again Baley felt a twinge of shame and could not forbear an attempt at consolation. He said, "Look, Daneel, even if I were walking into danger, *which I'm not*" (he added that hurriedly, with a quick glance at the other robots) "it would only be my job. It is what I'm paid to do. It is as much my job to prevent harm to mankind as a whole as yours is to prevent harm to man as an individual. Do you see?"

"I do not, Partner Elijah."

"Then that is because you're not made to see. Take my word for it that if you were a man, you would see."

Daneel bowed his head in acquiescence and remained standing, motionless, while Baley walked slowly toward the door of the room. The three robots parted to make room for him and kept their photoelectric eyes fixed firmly on Daneel.

Baley was walking to a kind of freedom and his heart beat rapidly in anticipation of the fact, then skipped a beat. Another robot was approaching the door from the other side.

Had something gone wrong?

"What is it, boy?" he snapped.

"A message has been forwarded to you, master, from the office of Acting Head of Security Attlebish."

Baley took the personal capsule handed to him and it opened at once. A finely inscribed strip of paper unrolled. (He wasn't startled. Solaria would have his fingerprints on file and the capsule would be adjusted to open at the touch of his particular convolutions.)

He read the message and his long face mirrored satisfaction. It was his official permission to arrange "seeing" interviews, subject to the wishes of the interviewees, who were nevertheless urged to give "Agents Baley and Olivaw" every possible co-operation.

Attlebish had capitulated, even to the extent of putting the Earthman's name first. It was an excellent omen with which to begin, finally, an investigation conducted as it should be conducted.

Baley was in an air-borne vessel again, as he had been on that trip from New York to Washington. This time, however, there was a difference. The vessel was not closed in. The windows were left transparent.

It was a clear, bright day and from where Baley sat the windows were so many patches of blue. Unrelieved, featureless. He tried not to huddle. He buried his head in his knees only when he could absolutely no longer help it.

The ordeal was of his own choosing. His state of triumph, his unusual sense of freedom at having beaten down first Attlebish and then Daneel, his feeling of having asserted the dignity of Earth against the Spacers, almost demanded it.

He had begun by stepping across open ground to the waiting plane with a kind of lightheaded dizziness that was almost enjoyable, and he had ordered the windows left unblanked in a kind of manic self-confidence.

I have to get used to it, he thought, and stared at the blue until his heart beat rapidly and the lump in his throat swelled beyond endurance.

He had to close his eyes and bury his head under the protective cover of his arms at shortening intervals. Slowly his confidence trickled away and even the touch of the holster of his freshly recharged blaster could not reverse the flow.

He tried to keep his mind on his plan of attack. First, learn the ways of the planet. Sketch in the background against which everything must be placed or fail to make sense.

See a sociologist!

He had asked a robot for the name of the Solarian most eminent as a sociologist. And there was that comfort about robots; they asked no questions.

The robot gave the name and vital statistics, and paused to remark that the sociologist would most probably be at lunch and would, therefore, possibly ask to delay contact.

"Lunch!" said Baley sharply. "Don't be ridiculous. It's not noon by two hours."

The robot said, "I am using local time, master."

Baley stared, then understood. On Earth, with its buried Cities, day and night, waking and sleeping, were man-made periods, adjusted to suit the needs of the community and the planet. On a planet such as this one, exposed nakedly to the sun, day and night were not a matter of choice at all, but were imposed on man willy-nilly.

Baley tried to picture a world as a sphere being lit and unlit as it turned. He found it hard to do and felt scornful of the so-superior Spacers who let such an essential thing as time be dictated to them by the vagaries of planetary movements.

He said, "Contact him anyway."

Robots were there to meet the plane when it landed and Baley, stepping out into the open again, found himself trembling badly.

He muttered to the nearest of the robots, "Let me hold your arm, boy."

The sociologist waited for him down the length of a hall, smiling tightly. "Good afternoon, Mr. Baley."

Baley nodded breathlessly. "Good evening, sir. Would you blank out the windows?"

The sociologist said, "They are blanked out already. I know something of the ways of Earth. Will you follow me?"

Baley managed it without robotic help, following at a considerable distance, across and through a maze of hallways. When he finally sat down in a large and elaborate room, he was glad of the opportunity to rest.

The walls of the room were set with curved, shallow alcoves. Statuary in pink and gold occupied each niche; abstract figures that pleased the eye without yielding instant meaning. A large, boxlike affair with white and dangling cylindrical objects and numerous pedals suggested a musical instrument.

Baley looked at the sociologist standing before him. The Spacer looked precisely as he had when Baley had viewed him earlier that day. He was tall and thin and his hair was pure white. His face was strikingly wedge-shaped, his nose prominent, his eyes deep-set and alive.

His name was Anselmo Quemot.

They stared at one another until Baley felt he could trust his voice to be reasonably normal. And then his first remark had nothing to do with the investigation. In fact it was nothing he had planned.

He said, "May I have a drink?"

"A drink?" The sociologist's voice was a trifle too high-pitched to be entirely pleasant. He said, "You wish water?"

"I'd prefer something alcoholic."

The sociologist's look grew sharply uneasy, as though the obligations of hospitality were something with which he was unacquainted.

And that, thought Baley, was literally so. In a world where viewing was the thing, there would be no sharing of food and drink.

A robot brought him a small cup of smooth enamel. The drink was a light pink in color. Baley sniffed at it cautiously and tasted it even more cautiously. The small sip of liquid evaporated warmly in his mouth and sent a pleasant message along the length of his esophagus. His next sip was more substantial.

Quemot said, "If you wish more——"

"No, thank you, not now. It is good of you, sir, to agree to see me."

Quemot tried a smile and failed rather markedly, "It has been a long time since I've done anything like this. Yes."

He almost squirmed as he spoke.

Baley said, "I imagine you find this rather hard."

"Quite." Quemot turned away sharply and retreated to a chair at the opposite end of the room. He angled the chair so that it faced more away from Baley than toward him and sat down. He clasped his gloved hands and his nostrils seemed to quiver.

Baley finished his drink and felt warmth in his limbs and even the return of something of his confidence.

He said, "Exactly how *does* it feel to have me here, Dr. Quemot?"

The sociologist muttered, "That is an uncommonly personal question."

"I know it is. But I think I explained when I viewed you earlier that I was engaged in a murder investigation and that I would have to ask a great many questions, some of which were bound to be personal."

"I'll help if I can," said Quemot. "I hope the questions will be decent ones." He kept looking away as he spoke. His eyes, when they struck Baley's face, did not linger, but slipped away.

Baley said, "I don't ask about your feelings out of curiosity only. This is essential to the investigation."

"I don't see how."

"I've got to know as much as I can about this world. I must understand how Solarians feel about ordinary matters. Do you see that?"

Quemot did not look at Baley at all now. He said slowly, "Ten years ago, my wife died. Seeing her was never very easy, but, of course, it is something one learns to bear in time and she was not the intrusive sort. I have been assigned no new wife since I am past the age of—of"—he looked at Baley as though requesting him to supply the phrase, and when Baley did not do so, he continued in a lower voice—"siring. Without even a wife, I have grown quite unused to this phenomenon of seeing."

"But how does it feel?" insisted Baley. "Are you in panic?" He thought of himself on the plane.

"No. Not in panic." Quemot angled his head to catch a glimpse of Baley and almost instantly withdrew. "But I will be frank, Mr. Baley. I imagine I can smell you."

Baley automatically leaned back in his chair, painfully self-conscious. "Smell me?"

"Quite imaginary, of course," said Quemot. "I cannot say whether you do have an odor or how strong it is, but even if you had a strong one, my nose filters would keep it from me. Yet, imagination . . ." He shrugged.

"I understand."

"It's worse. You'll forgive me, Mr. Baley, but in the actual presence of a human, I feel strongly as though something slimy were about to touch me. I keep shrinking away. It is most unpleasant."

Baley rubbed his ear thoughtfully and fought to keep down annoyance. After all, it was the other's neurotic reaction to a simple state of affairs.

He said, "If all this is so, I'm surprised you agreed to see me so readily. Surely you anticipated this unpleasantness."

"I did. But you know, I was curious. You're an Earthman."

Baley thought sardonically that that should have been another argument against seeing, but he said only, "What does that matter?"

A kind of jerky enthusiasm entered Quemot's voice. "It's not something I can explain easily. Not even to myself, really. But I've worked on sociology for ten years now. Really worked. I've developed propositions that are quite new and startling, and yet basically true. It is one of these propositions that makes me most extraordinarily interested in Earth and Earthmen. You see, if you were to consider Solaria's society and way of life carefully, it will become obvious to you that the said society and way of life is modeled directly and closely on that of Earth itself."

10

A Culture Is Traced

BALEY COULD not prevent himself from crying out, "What!"

Quemot looked over his shoulder as the moments of silence passed and said finally, "Not Earth's present culture. No."

Baley said, "Oh."

"But in the past, yes. Earth's ancient history. As an Earthman, you know it, of course."

"I've viewed books," said Baley cautiously.

"Ah. Then you understand."

Baley, who did not, said, "Let me explain exactly what I want, Dr. Quemot. I want you to tell me what you can about why Solaria is so different from the other Outer Worlds, why there are so many robots, why you behave as you do. I'm sorry if I seem to be changing the subject."

Baley most definitely wanted to change the subject. Any discussion of a likeness or unlikeness between Solaria's culture and Earth's would prove too absorbing by half. He might spend the day there and come away none the wiser as far as useful information was concerned.

Quemot smiled. "You want to compare Solaria and the other Outer Worlds and not Solaria and Earth."

"I know Earth, sir."

"As you wish." The Solarian coughed slightly. "Do you mind if I turn my chair completely away from you? It would be more—more comfortable."

"As you wish, Dr. Quemot," said Baley stiffly.

"Good." A robot turned the chair at Quemot's low-voiced order,

ans established homes, and Solaria became what I like to call a 'villa planet.' And of the settlers, more and more took to remaining on the planet all year round and carrying on their business on Nexon through proxies. Robot factories were established on Solaria. Farms and mines began to be exploited to the point where exports were possible.

"In short, Mr. Baley, it became obvious that Solaria, in the space of a century or less, would be as crowded as Nexon had been. It seemed ridiculous and wasteful to find such a new world and then lose it through lack of foresight.

"To spare you a great deal of complicated politics, I need say only that Solaria managed to establish its independence and make it stick without war. Our usefulness to other Outer Worlds as a source of specialty robots gained us friends and helped us, of course.

"Once independent, our first care was to make sure that population did not grow beyond reasonable limits. We regulate immigration and births and take care of all needs by increasing and diversifying the robots we use."

Baley said, "Why is it the Solarians object to seeing one another?" He felt annoyed at the manner in which Quemot chose to expound sociology.

Quemot peeped around the corner of his chair and retreated almost at once. "It follows inevitably. We have huge estates. An estate ten thousand square miles in area is not uncommon, although the largest ones contain considerable unproductive areas. My own estate is nine hundred fifty square miles in area but every bit of it is good land.

"In any case, it is the size of an estate, more than anything else, that determines a man's position in society. And one property of a large estate is this: You can wander about in it almost aimlessly with little or no danger of entering a neighbor's territory and thus encountering your neighbor. You see?"

Baley shrugged. "I suppose I do."

"In short, a Solarian takes pride in not meeting his neighbor. At the same time, his estate is so well run by robots and so self-sufficient that there is no reason for him to have to meet his neighbor. The desire not to do so led to the development of ever more perfect viewing equipment, and as the viewing equipment grew better there was less and less need ever to see one's neighbor. It was a reinforcing cycle, a kind of feed-back. Do you see?"

Baley said, "Look here, Dr. Quemot. You don't have to make all this so simple for me. I'm not a sociologist but I've had the usual elementary courses in college. It's only an Earth college, of course," Baley added with a reluctant modesty designed to ward off the same comment, in more insulting terms, from the other, "but I can follow mathematics."

"Mathematics?" said Quemot, his voice squeaking the last syllable.

"Well, not the stuff they use in robotics, which I *wouldn't* follow, but sociological relationships I can handle. For instance, I'm familiar with the Teramin Relationship."

"The what, sir?"

"Maybe you have a different name for it. The differential of inconveniences suffered with privileges granted: dee eye sub jay taken to the nth——"

"What are you talking about?" It was the sharp and peremptory tone of a Spacer that Baley heard and he was silenced in bewilderment.

Surely the relationship between inconveniences suffered and privileges granted was part of the very essentials of learning how to handle people without an explosion. A private stall in the community bathroom for one person, given for cause, would keep x persons waiting patiently for the same lightning to strike them, the value of x varying in known ways with known variations in environment and human temperament, as quantitatively described in the Teramin Relationship.

But then again, in a world where all was privilege and nothing inconvenience, the Teramin Relationship might reduce to triviality. Perhaps he had chosen the wrong example.

He tried again. "Look, sir, it's one thing to get a qualitative fill-in on the growth of this prejudice against seeing, but it isn't helpful for my purposes. I want to know the exact analysis of the prejudice so I can counteract it effectively. I want to persuade people to see me, as you are doing now."

"Mr. Baley," said Quemot, "you can't treat human emotions as though they were built about a positronic brain."

"I'm not saying you can. Robotics is a deductive science and sociology an inductive one. But mathematics can be made to apply in either case."

There was silence for a moment. Then Quemot spoke in a voice that trembled. "You have admitted you are not a sociologist."

"I know. But I was told you *were* one. The best on the planet."

"I am the only one. You might almost say I have invented the science."

"Oh?" Baley hesitated over the next question. It sounded impertinent even to himself. "Have you viewed books on the subject?"

"I've looked at some Auroran books."

"Have you looked at books from Earth?"

"Earth?" Quemot laughed uneasily. "It wouldn't have occurred to me to read any of Earth's scientific productions. No offense intended."

"Well, I'm sorry. I had thought I would be able to get specific data that would make it possible for me to interview others face to face without having to——"

Quemot made a queer, grating, inarticulate sound and the large chair in which he sat scraped backward, then went over with a crash.

A muffled "My apologies" was caught by Baley.

Baley had a momentary glimpse of Quemot running with an ungainly stride, then he was out the room and gone.

Baley's eyebrows lifted. What the devil had he said this time? Jehoshaphat! What wrong button had he pushed?

Tentatively he rose from his seat, and stopped halfway as a robot entered.

"Master," said the robot, "I have been directed to inform you that the master will view you in a few moments."

"*View* me, boy?"

"Yes, master. In the meanwhile, you may desire further refreshment."

Another beaker of the pink liquid was at Baley's elbow and this time a dish of some confectionary, warm and fragrant, was added.

Baley took his seat again, sampled the liquor cautiously and put it down. The confectionary was hard to the touch and warm, but the crust broke easily in the mouth and the inner portion was at once considerably warmer and softer. He could not identify the com-

The Robot Novels

ponents of the taste and wondered if it might not be a product of the native spices or condiments of Solaria.

Then he thought of the restricted, yeast-derived dietary of Earth and wondered if there might be a market for yeast strains designed to imitate the tastes of Outer World products.

But his thoughts broke off sharply as sociologist Quemot appeared out of nowhere and faced him. *Faced* him this time! He sat in a smaller chair in a room in which the walls and floor clashed sharply with those surrounding Baley. And he was smiling now, so that fine wrinkles in his face deepened and, paradoxically, gave him a more youthful appearance by accentuating the life in his eyes.

He said, "A thousand pardons, Mr. Baley. I thought I was enduring personal presence so well, but that was a delusion. I was quite on edge and your phrase pushed me over it, in a manner of speaking."

"What phrase was that, sir?"

"You said something about interviewing people face to——" He shook his head, his tongue dabbing quickly at his lips. "I would rather not say it. I think you know what I mean. The phrase conjured up the most striking picture of the two of us breathing—breathing one another's breath." The Solarian shuddered. "Don't you find that repulsive?"

"I don't know that I've ever thought of it so."

"It seems so filthy a habit. And as you said it and the picture arose in my mind, I realized that after all we *were* in the same room and even though I was not facing you, puffs of air that had been in your lungs must be reaching me and entering mine. With my sensitive frame of mind——"

Baley said, "Molecules all over Solaria's atmosphere have been in thousands of lungs. Jehoshaphat! They've been in the lungs of animals and the gills of fish."

"That *is* true," said Quemot with a rueful rub of his cheek, "and I'd just as soon not think of that, either. However there was a sense of immediacy to the situation with yourself actually there and with both of us inhaling and exhaling. It's amazing the relief I feel in viewing."

"I'm still in the same house, Dr. Quemot."

"That's precisely what is so amazing about the relief. You are in the same house and yet just the use of the trimensionals makes all the difference. At least I know what seeing a stranger feels like now. I won't try it again."

"That sounds as though you were experimenting with seeing."

"In a way," said the Spacer, "I suppose I was. It was a minor motivation. And the results were interesting, even if they were disturbing as well. It was a good test and I may record it."

"Record what?" asked Baley, puzzled.

"My feelings!" Quemot returned puzzled stare for puzzled stare.

Baley sighed. Cross-purposes. Always cross-purposes. "I only asked because somehow I assumed you would have instruments of some sort to measure emotional responses. An electroencephalograph, perhaps." He looked about fruitlessly, "Though I suppose you could have a pocket version of the same that works without direct electrical connection. We don't have anything like that on Earth."

"I trust," said the Solarian stiffly, "that I am able to estimate the nature of my own feelings without an instrument. They were pronounced enough."

"Yes, of course, but for quantitative analysis . . ." began Baley.

Quemot said querulously, "I don't know what you're driving at. Besides I'm trying to tell you something else, my own theory, in fact, something I have viewed in no books, something I am quite proud of——"

Baley said, "Exactly what is that, sir?"

"Why, the manner in which Solaria's culture is based on one existing in Earth's past."

Baley sighed. If he didn't allow the other to get it off his chest, there might be very little co-operation thereafter. He said, "And that is?"

"Sparta!" said Quemot, lifting his head so that for a moment his white hair glistened in the light and seemed almost a halo. "I'm sure you've heard of Sparta!"

Baley felt relieved. He had been mightily interested in Earth's ancient past in his younger days (it was an attractive study to many Earthmen—an Earth supreme because it was an Earth alone; Earthmen the masters because there were no Spacers), but Earth's past was a large one. Quemot might well have referred to some phase with which Baley was unacquainted and that would have been embarrassing.

As it was, he could say cautiously, "Yes. I've viewed films on the subject."

"Good. Good. Now Sparta in its heydey consisted of a relatively small number of Spartiates, the only full citizens, plus a somewhat larger number of second-class individuals, the Perioeci, and a really large number of outright slaves, the Helots. The Helots outnumbered the Spartiates a matter of twenty to one, and the Helots were men with human feelings and human failings.

"In order to make certain that a Helot rebellion could never be successful despite their overwhelming numbers, the Spartans became military specialists. Each lived the life of a military machine, and the society achieved its purpose. There was never a successful Helot revolt.

"Now we human beings on Solaria are equivalent, in a way, to the Spartiates. We have our Helots, but our Helots aren't men but machines. They cannot revolt and need not be feared even though they outnumber us a thousand times as badly as the Spartans' human Helots outnumbered them. So we have the advantage of Spartiate exclusiveness without any need to sacrifice ourselves to rigid mastery. We can, instead, model ourselves on the artistic and cultural way of life of the Athenians, who were contemporaries of the Spartans and who——"

Baley said, "I've viewed films on the Athenians, too."

Quemot grew warmer as he spoke. "Civilizations have always been pyramidal in structure. As one climbs toward the apex of the social edifice, there is increased leisure and increasing opportunity to pursue happiness. As one climbs, one finds also fewer and fewer people to enjoy this more and more. Invariably, there is a preponderance of the dispossessed. And remember this, no matter how well off the bottom layers of the pyramid might be on an absolute scale, they are always dispossessed in comparison with the apex. For instance, even the most poorly off humans on Aurora are better off than Earth's aristocrats, but they are dispossessed with respect to Aurora's aristocrats, and it is with the masters of their own world that they compare themselves.

"So there is always social friction in ordinary human societies. The action of social revolution and the reaction of guarding against such revolution or combating it once it has begun are the causes of a great deal of the human misery with which history is permeated.

"Now here on Solaria, for the first time, the apex of the pyramid stands alone. In the place of the dispossessed are the robots. We have the first new society, the first really new one, the first great social invention since the farmers of Sumeria and Egypt invented cities."

He sat back now, smiling.

Baley nodded. "Have you published this?"

"I may," said Quemot with an affectation of carelessness, "some-day. I haven't yet. This is my third contribution."

"Were the other two as broad as this?"

"They weren't in sociology. I have been a sculptor in my time. The work you see about you"—he indicated the statuary—"is my own. And I have been a composer, too. But I am getting older and Rikaine Delmarre always argued strongly in favor of the applied arts rather than the fine arts and I decided to go into sociology."

Baley said, "That sounds as though Delmarre was a good friend of yours."

"We knew one another. At my time in life, one knows all adult Solarians. But there is no reason not to agree that Rikaine Delmarre and I were well acquainted."

"What sort of a man was Delmarre?" (Strangely enough, the name of the man brought up the picture of Gladia in Baley's mind and he was plagued with a sudden, sharp recall of her as he had last seen her, furious, her face distorted with anger at him.)

Quemot looked a bit thoughtful. "He was a worthy man; devoted to Solaria and to its way of life."

"An idealist, in other words."

"Yes. Definitely. You could see that in the fact that he volunteered for his job as—as fetal engineer. It was an applied art, you see, and I told you his feelings about that."

"Was volunteering unusual?"

"Wouldn't *you* say—— But I forget you're an Earthman. Yes, it is unusual. It's one of those jobs that must be done, yet finds no volun-tary takers. Ordinarily, someone must be assigned to it for a period of so many years and it isn't pleasant to be the one chosen. Delmarre volunteered, and for life. He felt the position was too important to be left to reluctant draftees, and he persuaded me into that opinion, too. Yet I certainly would never have volunteered. I couldn't possibly make the personal sacrifice. And it was more of a sacrifice for him, since he was almost a fanatic in personal hygiene."

"I'm still not certain I understand the nature of his job."

Quemot's old cheeks flushed gently. "Hadn't you better discuss that with his assistant?"

Baley said, "I would certainly have done so by now, sir, if anyone had seen fit to tell me before this moment that he had an assistant."

"I'm sorry about that," said Quemot, "but the existence of the assistant is another measure of his social responsibility. No previous occupant of the post provided for one. Delmarre, however, felt it necessary to find a suitable youngster and conduct the necessary training himself so as to leave a professional heir behind when the time came for him to retire or, well, to die." The old Solarian sighed heavily. "Yet I outlived him and he was so much younger. I used to play chess with him. Many times."

"How did you manage that?"

Quemot's eyebrows lifted. "The usual way."

"You saw one another?"

Quemot looked horrified. "What an idea! Even if I could stomach it, Delmarre would never allow it for an instant. Being fetal engineer didn't blunt his sensibilities. He was a finicky man."

"Then how——"

"With two boards as any two people would play chess." The Solarian shrugged in a sudden gesture of tolerance. "Well, you're an Earthman. My moves registered on his board, and his on mine. It's a simple matter."

Baley said, "Do you know Mrs. Delmarre?"

"We've viewed one another. She's a field colorist, you know, and I've viewed some of her showings. Fine work in a way but more interesting as curiosities than as creations. Still, they're amusing and show a perceptive mind."

"Is she capable of killing her husband, would you say?"

"I haven't given it thought. Women are surprising creatures. But then, there's scarcely room for argument, is there? Only Mrs. Delmarre could have been close enough to Rikaine to kill him. Rikaine would never, under any circumstances, have allowed anyone else seeing privileges for any reason. Extremely finicky. Perhaps finicky is the wrong word. It was just that he lacked any trace of abnormality; anything of the perverse. He was a good Solarian."

"Would you call your granting me seeing privileges perverse?" asked Baley.

Quemot said, "Yes, I think I would. I should say there was a bit of scatophilia involved."

"Could Delmarre have been killed for political reasons?"

"What?"

"I've heard him called a Traditionalist."

"Oh, we all are."

"You mean there is no group of Solarians who are *not* Traditionalists?"

"I dare say there are some," said Quemot slowly, "who think it is dangerous to be too Traditionalist. They are overconscious of our small population, of the way the other worlds outnumber us. They think we are defenseless against possible aggression from the other Outer Worlds. They're quite foolish to think so and there aren't many of them. I don't think they're a force."

"Why do you say they are foolish? Is there anything about Solaria that would affect the balance of power in spite of the great disadvantage of numbers? Some new type of weapon?"

"A weapon, certainly. But not a new one. The people I speak of are more blind than foolish not to realize that such a weapon is in operation continuously and cannot be resisted."

Baley's eyes narrowed. "Are you serious?"

"Certainly."

"Do you know the nature of the weapon?"

"All of us must. *You* do, if you stop to think of it. I see it a trifle easier than most, perhaps, since I am a sociologist. To be sure, it isn't used as a weapon ordinarily is used. It doesn't kill or hurt, but it is irresistible even so. All the more irresistible because no one notices it."

Baley said with annoyance, "And just what is this non-lethal weapon?"

Quemot said, "The positronic robot."

11

A Farm Is Inspected

FOR A MOMENT Baley went cold. The positronic robot was the symbol of Spacer superiority over Earthmen. That was weapon enough.

He kept his voice steady. "It's an economic weapon. Solaria is important to the other Outer Worlds as a source of advanced models and so it will not be harmed by them."

"That's an obvious point," said Quemot indifferently. "That helped us establish our independence. What I have in mind is something else, something more subtle and more cosmic." Quemot's eyes were fixed on his fingers' ends and his mind was obviously fixed on abstractions.

Baley said, "Is this another of your sociological theories?"

Quemot's poorly suppressed look of pride all but forced a short smile out of the Earthman.

The sociologist said, "It is indeed mine. Original, as far as I know, and yet obvious if population data on the Outer Worlds is carefully studied. To begin with, ever since the positronic robot was invented, it has been used more and more intensively everywhere."

"Not on Earth," said Baley.

"Now, now, Plainclothesman. I don't know much of your Earth, but I know enough to know that robots are entering your economy. You people live in large Cities and leave most of your planetary surface unoccupied. Who runs your farms and mines, then?"

"Robots," admitted Baley. "But if it comes to that, Doctor, Earthmen invented the positronic robot in the first place."

"They did? Are you sure?"

"You can check. It's true."

"Interesting. Yet robots made the least headway there." The sociologist said thoughtfully, "Perhaps that is because of Earth's large population. It would take that much longer. Yes . . . Still, you have robots even in your Cities."

"Yes," said Baley.

"More now than, say, fifty years ago."

Baley nodded impatiently. "Yes."

"Then it fits. The difference is only one of time. Robots tend to displace human labor. The robot economy moves in only one direction. More robots and fewer humans. I've studied population data *very* carefully and I've plotted it and made a few extrapolations." He paused in sudden surprise. "Why, that's rather an application of mathematics to sociology, isn't it?"

"It is," said Baley.

"There may be something to it, at that. I will have to give the matter thought. In any case, these are the conclusions I have come to, and I am convinced there is no doubt as to their correctness. The robot-human ratio in any economy that has accepted robot labor tends continuously to increase despite any laws that are passed to prevent it. The increase is slowed, but never stopped. At first the human population increases, but the robot population increases much more quickly. Then, after a certain critical point is reached . . ."

Quemot stopped again, then said, "Now let's see. I wonder if the critical point could be determined exactly; if you could really put a figure to it. There's your mathematics again."

Baley stirred restlessly. "What happens after the critical point is reached, Dr. Quemot?"

"Eh? Oh, the human population begins actually to decline. A planet approaches a true social stability. Aurora will have to. Even your Earth will have to. Earth may take a few more centuries, but it is inevitable."

"What do you mean by social stability?"

"The situation here. In Solaria. A world in which the humans are the leisure class only. So there is no reason to fear the other Outer Worlds. We need only wait a century perhaps and they shall all be Solarias. I suppose that will be the end of human history, in a way; at least, its fulfillment. Finally, finally, all men will have all they can need and want. You know, there is a phrase I once picked up; I don't know where it comes from; something about the pursuit of happiness."

Baley said thoughtfully, "All men are 'endowed by their Creator with certain unalienable rights . . . among these are life, liberty, and the pursuit of happiness.' "

"You've hit it. Where's that from?"

"Some old document," said Baley.

"Do you see how that is changed here on Solaria and eventually in all the Galaxy? The pursuit will be over. The rights mankind will be heir to will be life, liberty, and happiness. Just that. Happiness."

Baley said dryly, "Maybe so, but a man has been killed on your Solaria and another may yet die."

He felt regret almost the moment he spoke, for the expression on Quemot's face was as though he had been struck with an open palm. The old man's head bowed. He said without looking up, "I have answered your questions as well as I could. Is there anything else you wish?"

"I have enough. Thank you, sir. I am sorry to have intruded on your grief at your friend's death."

Quemot looked up slowly. "It will be hard to find another chess partner. He kept our appointments most punctually and he played an extraordinarily even game. He was a good Solarian."

"I understand," said Baley softly. "May I have your permission to use your viewer to make contact with the next person I must see?"

"Of course," said Quemot. "My robots are yours. And now I will leave you. Done viewing."

A robot was at Baley's side within thirty seconds of Quemot's disappearance and Baley wondered once again how these creatures were managed. He had seen Quemot's fingers move toward a contact as he had left and that was all.

Perhaps the signal was quite a generalized one, saying only, "Do your duty!" Perhaps robots listened to all that went on and were always aware of what a human might desire at any given moment, and if the particular robot was not designed for a particular job in either mind or body, the radio web that united all robots went into action and the correct robot was spurred into action.

For a moment Baley had the vision of Solaria as a robotic net with holes that were small and continually growing smaller, with every human being caught neatly in place. He thought of Quemot's picture of worlds turning into Solarias; of nets forming and tightening even on Earth, until——

His thoughts were disrupted as the robot who had entered spoke with the quiet and even respect of the machine.

"I am ready to help you, master."

Baley said, "Do you know how to reach the place where Rikaine Delmarre once worked?"

"Yes, master."

Baley shrugged. He would never teach himself to avoid asking useless questions. The robots knew. Period. It occurred to him that, to handle robots with true efficiency, one must needs be expert, a sort of roboticist. How well did the average Solarian do, he wondered? Probably only so-so.

He said, "Get Delmarre's place and contact his assistant. If the assistant is not there, locate him wherever he is."

"Yes, master."

As the robot turned to go, Baley called after it, "Wait! What time is it at the Delmarre workplace?"

"About 0630, master."

"In the morning?"

"Yes, master."

Again Baley felt annoyance at a world that made itself victim of the coming and going of a sun. It was what came of living on bare planetary surface.

He thought fugitively of Earth, then tore his mind away. While he kept firmly to the matter in hand, he managed well. Slipping into homesickness would ruin him.

He said, "Call the assistant, anyway, boy, and tell him it's government business—and have one of the other boys bring something to eat. A sandwich and a glass of milk will do."

He chewed thoughtfully at the sandwich, which contained a kind of smoked meat, and with half his mind thought that Daneel Olivaw would certainly consider every article of food suspect after what had happened to Gruer. And Daneel might be right, too.

He finished the sandwich without ill effects, however (immediate ill effects, at any rate), and sipped at the milk. He had not learned from Quemot what he had come to learn, but he had learned something. As he sorted it out in his mind, it seemed he had learned a good deal.

Little about the murder, to be sure, but more about the larger matter.

The robot returned. "The assistant will accept contact, master."

"Good. Was there any trouble about it?"

"The assistant was asleep, master."

"Awake now, though?"

"Yes, master."

The assistant was facing him suddenly, sitting up in bed and wearing an expression of sullen resentment.

Baley reared back as though a force-barrier had been raised before him without warning. Once again a piece of vital information had been withheld from him. Once again he had not asked the right questions.

No one had thought to tell him that Rikaine Delmarre's assistant was a woman.

Her hair was a trifle darker than ordinary Spacer bronze and there was a quantity of it, at the moment in disorder. Her face was oval, her nose a trifle bulbous, and her chin large. She scratched slowly at her side just above the waist and Baley hoped the sheet would remain in position. He remembered Gladia's free attitude toward what was permitted while viewing.

Baley felt a sardonic amusement at his own disillusion at that moment. Earthmen assumed, somehow, that all Spacer women were beautiful, and certainly Gladia had reinforced that assumption. This one, though, was plain even by Earthly standards.

It therefore surprised Baley that he found her contralto attractive when she said, "See here, do you know what time it is?"

"I do," said Baley, "but since I will be seeing you, I felt I should warn you."

"*Seeing* me? Skies above——" Her eyes grew wide and she put a hand to her chin. (She wore a ring on one finger, the first item of personal adornment Baley had yet seen on Solaria.) "Wait, you're not my new assistant, are you?"

"No. Nothing like that. I'm here to investigate the death of Rikaine Delmarre."

"Oh? Well, investigate, then."

"What is your name?"

"Klorissa Cantoro."

"And how long have you been working with Dr. Delmarre?"

"Three years."

"I assume you're now at the place of business." (Baley felt uncomfortable at that noncommittal phrase, but he did not know what to call a place where a fetal engineer worked.)

"If you mean, am I at the farm?" said Klorissa discontentedly, "I certainly am. I haven't left it since the old man was done in, and I won't leave it, looks like, till an assistant is assigned me. Can *you* arrange that, by the way?"

"I'm sorry, ma'am. I have no influence with anyone here."

"Thought I'd ask."

Klorissa pulled off the sheet and climbed out of bed without any self-consciousness. She was wearing a one-piece sleeping suit and her hand went to the notch of the seam, where it ended at the neck.

Baley said hurriedly, "Just one moment. If you'll agree to see me, that will end my business with you for now and you may dress in privacy."

"In privacy?" She put out her lower lip and stared at Baley curiously. "You're finicky, aren't you? Like the boss."

"Will you see me? I would like to look over the farm."

"I don't get this business about seeing, but if you want to view the farm I'll tour you. If you'll give me a chance to wash and take care of a few things and wake up a little, I'll enjoy the break in routine."

"I don't want to view anything. I want to *see*."

The woman cocked her head to one side and her keen look had something of professional interest in it. "Are you a pervert or something? When was the last time you underwent a gene analysis?"

"Jehoshaphat!" muttered Baley. "Look, I'm Elijah Baley. I'm from Earth."

"From Earth?" She cried vehemently. "Skies above! Whatever are you doing here? Or is this some kind of complicated joke?"

"I'm not joking. I was called in to investigate Delmarre's death. I'm a plainclothesman, a detective."

"You mean that kind of investigation. But I thought everyone knew his wife did it."

"No, ma'am, there's some question about it in my mind. May I have your permission to see the farm and you. As an Earthman, you understand, I'm not accustomed to viewing. It makes me uncomfortable. I have permission from the Head of Security to see people who might help me. I will show you the document, if you wish."

"Let's see it."

Baley held the official strip up before her imaged eyes.

She shook her head. "Seeing! It's filthy. Still, skies above, what's a little more filth in this filthy job? Look here, though, don't you come close to me. You stay a good distance away. We can shout or send messages by robot, if we have to. You understand?"

"I understand."

Her sleeping suit split open at the seam just as contact broke off and the last word he heard from her was a muttered: "Earthman!"

"That's close enough," said Klorissa.

Baley, who was some twenty-five feet from the woman, said, "It's all right this distance, but I'd like to get indoors quickly."

It had not been so bad this time, somehow. He had scarcely minded the plane trip, but there was no point in overdoing it. He kept himself from yanking at his collar to allow himself to breathe more freely.

Klorissa said sharply, "What's wrong with you? You look kind of beat."

Baley said, "I'm not used to the outdoors."

"That's right! Earthman! You've got to be cooped up or something. Skies above!" Her tongue passed over her lips as though it tasted something unappetizing. "Well, come in, then, but let me move out of the way first. All right. Get in."

Her hair was in two thick braids that wound about her head in a complicated geometrical pattern. Baley wondered how long it took to arrange like that and then remembered that, in all probability, the unerring mechanical fingers of a robot did the job.

The hair set off her oval face and gave it a kind of symmetry that made it pleasant if not pretty. She did not wear any facial make-up, nor, for that matter, were her clothes meant to do more than cover her serviceably. For the most part they were a subdued dark blue except for her gloves, which covered her to mid-arm and were a badly clashing lilac in color. Apparently they were not part of her ordinary costume. Baley noted the thickening of one finger of the gloves owing to the presence of the ring underneath.

They remained at opposite ends of the room, facing one another.

Baley said, "You don't like this, do you, ma'am?"

Klorissa shrugged. "Why should I like it? I'm not an animal. But I can stand it. You get pretty hardened, when you deal with—with" —she paused, and then her chin went up as though she had made up her mind to say what she had to say without mincing—"with children." She pronounced the word with careful precision.

"You sound as though you don't like the job you have."

"It's an important job. It must be done. Still, I don't like it."

"Did Rikaine Delmarre like it?"

"I suppose he didn't, but he never showed it. He was a good Solarian."

"And he was finicky."

Klorissa looked surprised.

Baley said, "You yourself said so. When we were viewing and I said you might dress in private, you said I was finicky like the boss."

"Oh. Well, he *was* finicky. Even viewing he never took any liberties. Always proper."

"Was that unusual?"

"It shouldn't be. Ideally, you're supposed to be proper, but no one ever is. Not when viewing. There's no personal presence involved so why take any pains? You know? I don't take pains when viewing, except with the boss. You had to be formal with him."

"Did you admire Dr. Delmarre?"

"He was a good Solarian."

Baley said, "You've called this place a farm and you've mentioned children. Do you bring up children here?"

"From the age of a month. Every fetus on Solaria comes here."

"Fetus?"

"Yes." She frowned. "We get them a month after conception. Does this embarrass you?"

"No," Baley said shortly. "Can you show me around?"

"I can. But keep your distance."

Baley's long face took on a stony grimness as he looked down the length of the long room from above. There was glass between the room and themselves. On the other side, he was sure, was perfectly controlled heat, perfectly controlled humidity, perfectly controlled asepsis. Those tanks, row on row, each contained its little creature floating in a watery fluid of precise composition, infused with a nutrient mixture of ideal proportions. Life and growth went on.

Little things, some smaller than half his fist, curled on themselves, with bulging skulls and tiny budding limbs and vanishing tails.

Klorissa, from her position twenty feet away, said, "How do you like it, Plainclothesman?"

Baley said, "How many do you have?"

"As of this morning, one hundred and fifty-two. We receive fifteen to twenty each month and we graduate as many to independence."

"Is this the only such institution on the planet?"

"That's right. It's enough to keep the population steady, counting on a life expectancy of three hundred years and a population of twenty thousand. This building is quite new. Dr. Delmarre supervised its construction and made many changes in our procedures. Our fetal death rate now is virtually zero."

Robots threaded their way among the tanks. At each tank they stopped and checked controls in a tireless, meticulous way, looking in at the tiny embryos within.

"Who operates on the mother?" asked Baley. "I mean, to get the little things."

"Doctors," answered Klorissa.

"Dr. Delmarre?"

"Of course not. *Medical* doctors. You don't think Dr. Delmarre would ever stoop to—— Well, never mind."

"Why can't robots be used?"

"Robots in surgery? First Law makes that very difficult, Plainclothesman. A robot might perform an appendectomy to save a human life, if he knew how, but I doubt that he'd be usable after that without major repairs. Cutting human flesh would be quite a traumatic experience for a positronic brain. Human doctors can manage to get hardened to it. Even to the personal presence required."

Baley said, "I notice that robots tend the fetuses, though. Do you and Dr. Delmarre ever interfere?"

"We have to, sometimes, when things go wrong. If a fetus has developmental trouble, for instance. Robots can't be trusted to judge the situation accurately when human life is involved."

Baley nodded. "Too much risk of a misjudgment and a life lost, I suppose."

"Not at all. Too much risk of overvaluing a life and saving one improperly." The woman looked stern. "As fetal engineers, Baley, we see to it that healthy children are born; *healthy* ones. Even the best gene analysis of parents can't assure that all gene permutations and combinations will be favorable, to say nothing of the possibility of mutations. That's our big concern, the unexpected mutation. We've got the rate of those down to less than one in a thousand, but that means that, on the average, once a decade, we have trouble."

She motioned him along the balcony and he followed her.

She said, "I'll show you the infants' nurseries and the youngsters' dormitories. They're much more a problem than the fetuses are. With them, we can rely on robot labor only to a limited extent."

"Why is that?"

"You would know, Baley, if you ever tried to teach a robot the importance of discipline. First Law makes them almost impervious to that fact. And don't think youngsters don't learn that about as soon as they can talk. I've seen a three-year-old holding a dozen robots motionless by yelling, 'You'll hurt me. I'm hurt.' It takes an extremely advanced robot to understand that a child might be deliberately lying."

"Could Delmarre handle the children?"

"Usually."

"How did he do that? Did he get out among them and shake sense into them?"

"Dr. Delmarre? Touch them? Skies above! Of course not! But he could *talk* to them. And he could give a robot specific orders. I've seen him viewing a child for fifteen minutes, and keeping a robot in spanking position all that time, getting it to spank—spank—spank. A few like that and the child would risk fooling with the boss no more. And the boss was skillful enough about it so that usually the robot didn't need more than a routine readjustment afterward."

"How about you? Do you get out among the children?"

"I'm afraid I have to sometimes. I'm not like the boss. Maybe someday I'll be able to handle the long-distance stuff, but right now if I tried, I'd just ruin robots. There's an art to handling robots really well, you know. When I think of it, though. Getting out among the children. Little animals!"

She looked back at him suddenly. "I suppose you wouldn't mind seeing them."

"It wouldn't bother me."

She shrugged and stared at him with amusement. "Earthman!"

She walked on again. "What's all this about, anyway? You'll have to end up with Gladia Delmarre as murderess. You'll *have* to."

"I'm not quite sure of that," said Baley.

"How could you be anything else but sure? Who else could it possibly be?"

"There are possibilities, ma'am."

"Who, for instance?"

"Well, you, for instance!"

And Klorissa's reaction to that quite surprised Baley.

12

A Target Is Missed

SHE LAUGHED.

The laughter grew and fed on itself till she was gasping for breath and her plump face had reddened almost to purple. She leaned against the wall and gasped for breath.

"No, don't come—closer," she begged. "I'm all right."

Baley said gravely, "Is the possibility that humorous?"

She tried to answer and laughed again. Then, in a whisper, she said, "Oh, you *are* an Earthman? How could it ever be me?"

"You knew him well," said Baley. "You knew his habits. You could have planned it."

"And you think I would *see* him? That I would get close enough to bash him over the head with something? You just don't know anything at all about it, Baley."

Baley felt himself redden. "Why couldn't you get close enough to him, ma'am. You've had practice—uh—mingling."

"With the *children.*"

"One thing leads to another. You seem to be able to stand my presence."

"At twenty feet," she said contemptuously.

"I've just visited a man who nearly collapsed because he had to endure my presence for a while."

Klorissa sobered and said, "A difference in degree."

"I suggest that a difference in degree is all that is necessary. The habit of seeing children makes it possible to endure seeing Delmarre just long enough."

"I would like to point out, Mr. Baley," said Klorissa, no longer appearing the least amused, "that it doesn't matter a speck what I can endure. Dr. Delmarre was the finicky one. He was almost as bad as Leebig himself. Almost. Even if I could endure seeing him, he would never endure seeing me. Mrs. Delmarre is the only one he could possibly have allowed within seeing distance."

Baley said, "Who's this Leebig you mentioned?"

Klorissa shrugged. "One of these odd-genius types, if you know what I mean. He's done work with the boss on robots."

Baley checked that off mentally and returned to the matter at hand. He said, "It could also be said you had a motive."

"What motive?"

"His death put you in charge of this establishment, gave you position."

"You call that a motive? Skies above, who could *want* this position? Who on Solaria? This is a motive for keeping him alive. It's a motive for hovering over him and protecting him. You'll have to do better than that, Earthman."

Baley scratched his neck uncertainly with one finger. He saw the justice of that.

Klorissa said, "Did you notice my ring, Mr. Baley?"

For a moment it seemed she was about to strip the glove from her right hand, but she refrained.

"I noticed it," said Baley.

"You don't know its significance, I suppose?"

"I don't." (He would never have done with ignorance, he thought bitterly.)

"Do you mind a small lecture, then?"

"If it will help me make sense of this damned world," blurted out Baley, "by all means."

"Skies above!" Klorissa smiled. "I suppose we seem to you as Earth would seem to us. Imagine. Say, here's an empty chamber. Come in here and we'll sit down—no, the room's not big enough. Tell you what, though. You take a seat in there and I'll stand out here."

She stepped farther down the corridor, giving him space to enter the room, then returned, taking up her stand against the opposite wall at a point from which she could see him.

Baley took his seat with only the slightest quiver of chivalry countering it. He thought rebelliously: Why not? Let the Spacer woman stand.

Klorissa folded her muscular arms across her chest and said, "Gene analysis is the key to our society. We don't analyze for genes directly, of course. Each gene, however, governs one enzyme, and we can analyze for enzymes. Know the enzymes, know the body chemistry. Know the body chemistry, know the human being. You see all that?"

"I understand the theory," said Baley. "I don't know how it's applied."

"That part's done here. Blood samples are taken while the infant is still in the late fetal stage. That gives us our rough first approximation. Ideally, we should catch all mutations at that point and judge whether birth can be risked. In actual fact, we still don't quite know enough to eliminate all possibility of mistake. Someday, maybe. Anyway, we continue testing after birth; biopsies as well as body fluids. In any case, long before adulthood, we know exactly what our little boys and girls are made of."

(Sugar and spice . . . A nonsense phrase went unbidden through Baley's mind.)

"We wear coded rings to indicate our gene constitution," said Klorissa. "It's an old custom, a bit of the primitive left behind from the days when Solarians had not yet been weeded eugenically. Nowadays, we're all healthy."

Baley said, "But you still wear yours. Why?"

"Because I'm exceptional," she said with an unembarrassed, unblunted pride. "Dr. Delmarre spent a long time searching for an assistant. He *needed* someone exceptional. Brains, ingenuity, industry, stability. Most of all, stability. Someone who could learn to mingle with children and not break down."

"He couldn't, could he? Was that a measure of his instability?"

Klorissa said, "In a way, it was, but at least it was a desirable type of instability under most circumstances. You wash your hands, don't you?"

Baley's eyes dropped to his hands. They were as clean as need be. "Yes," he said.

"All right. I suppose it's a measure of instability to feel such revulsion at dirty hands as to be unable to clean an oily mechanism by hand even in an emergency. Still, in the *ordinary* course of living, the revulsion keeps you clean, which is good."

"I see. Go ahead."

"There's nothing more. My genic health is the third-highest ever recorded on Solaria, so I wear my ring. It's a record I enjoy carrying with me."

"I congratulate you."

"You needn't sneer. It may not be my doing. It may be the blind permutation of parental genes, but it's a proud thing to own, anyway. And no one would believe me capable of so seriously psychotic an act as murder. Not with my gene make-up. So don't waste accusations on me."

Baley shrugged and said nothing. The woman seemed to confuse gene make-up and evidence and presumably the rest of Solaria would do the same.

Klorissa said, "Do you want to see the youngsters now?"

"Thank you. Yes."

The corridors seemed to go on forever. The building was obviously a tremendous one. Nothing like the huge banks of apartments in the Cities of Earth, of course, but for a single building clinging to the outside skin of a planet it must be a mountainous structure.

There were hundreds of cribs, with pink babies squalling, or sleeping, or feeding. Then there were playrooms for the crawlers.

"They're not too bad even at this age," said Klorissa grudgingly, "though they take up a tremendous sum of robots. It's practically a robot per baby till walking age."

"Why is that?"

"They sicken if they don't get individual attention."

Baley nodded. "Yes, I suppose the requirement for affection is something that can't be done away with."

Klorissa frowned and said brusquely, "Babies require attention."

Baley said, "I am a little surprised that robots can fulfill the need for affection."

She whirled toward him, the distance between them not sufficing to hide her displeasure. "See here, Baley, if you're trying to shock me by using unpleasant terms, you won't succeed. Skies above, don't be childish."

"Shock you?"

"I can use the word too. Affection! Do you want a short word, a good four-letter word. I can say that, too. Love! Love! Now if it's out of your system, behave yourself."

Baley did not trouble to dispute the matter of obscenity. He said, "Can robots really give the necessary attention, then?"

"Obviously, or this farm would not be the success it is. They fool with the child. They nuzzle it and snuggle it. The child doesn't care that it's only a robot. But then, things grow more difficult between three and ten."

"Oh?"

"During that interval, the children insist on playing with one another. Quite indiscriminately."

"I take it you let them."

"We have to, but we never forget our obligation to teach them the requirements of adulthood. Each has a separate room that can be closed off. Even from the first, they must sleep alone. We insist on that. And then we have an isolation time every day and that increases with the years. By the time a child reaches ten, he is able to restrict himself to viewing for a week at a time. Of course, the viewing arrangements are elaborate. They can view outdoors, under mobile conditions, and can keep it up all day."

Baley said, "I'm surprised you can counter an instinct so thoroughly. You do counter it; I see that. Still, it surprises me."

"What instinct?" demanded Klorissa.

"The instinct of gregariousness. There is one. You say yourself that as children they insist on playing with each other."

Klorissa shrugged. "Do you call that instinct? But then, what if it is? Skies above, a child has an instinctive fear of falling, but adults can be trained to work in high places even where there is constant danger of falling. Haven't you ever seen gymnastic exhibitions on high wires? There are some worlds where people live in tall buildings. And children have instinctive fear of loud noises, too, but are you afraid of them?"

"Not within reason," said Baley.

"I'm willing to bet that Earth people couldn't sleep if things were really quiet. Skies above, there isn't an instinct around that can't give way to a good, persistent education. Not in human beings, where instincts are weak anyway. In fact, if you go about it right, education gets easier with each generation. It's a matter of evolution."

Baley said, "How is that?"

"Don't you see? Each individual repeats his own evolutionary history as he develops. Those fetuses back there have gills and a tail for a time. Can't skip those steps. The youngster has to go through the social-animal stage in the same way. But just as a fetus can get through in one month a stage that evolution took a hundred million years to get through, so our children can hurry through the social-animal stage. Dr. Delmarre was of the opinion that with the generations, we'd get through that stage faster and faster."

"Is that so?"

"In three thousand years, he estimated, at the present rate of progress, we'd have children who'd take to viewing at once. The boss had other notions, too. He was interested in improving robots to the point of making them capable of disciplining children without becoming mentally unstable. Why not? Discipline today for a better life tomorrow is a true expression of First Law if robots could only be made to see it."

"Have such robots been developed yet?"

Klorissa shook her head. "I'm afraid not. Dr. Delmarre and Leebig had been working hard on some experimental models."

"Did Dr. Delmarre have some of the models sent out to his estate? Was he a good enough roboticist to conduct tests himself?"

"Oh yes. He tested robots frequently."

"Do you know that he had a robot with him when he was murdered?"

"I've been told so."

"Do you know what kind of a model it was?"

"You'll have to ask Leebig. As I told you, he's the roboticist who worked with Dr. Delmarre."

"You know nothing about it?"

"Not a thing."

"If you think of anything, let me know."

"I will. And don't think new robot models are all that Dr. Delmarre was interested in. Dr. Delmarre used to say the time would come when unfertilized ova would be stored in banks at liquid-air temperatures and utilized for artificial insemination. In that way, eugenic principles could be truly applied and we could get rid of the last vestige of any need for seeing. I'm not sure that I quite go along with him so far, but he was a man of advanced notions; a very good Solarian."

She added quickly, "Do you want to go outside? The five-through-eight group are encouraged to take part in outdoor play and you could see them in action."

Baley said cautiously, "I'll try that. I may have to come back inside on rather short notice."

"Oh yes, I forgot. Maybe you'd rather not go out at all?"

"No." Baley forced a smile. "I'm trying to grow accustomed to the outdoors."

The wind was hard to bear. It made breathing difficult. It wasn't cold, in a direct physical sense, but the feel of it, the feel of his clothes moving against his body, gave Baley a kind of chill.

His teeth chattered when he tried to talk and he had to force his words out in little bits. It hurt his eyes to look so far at a horizon so hazy green and blue and there was only limited relief when he looked at the pathway immediately before his toes. Above all, he avoided looking up at the empty blue, empty, that is, but for the piled-up white of occasional clouds and the glare of the naked sun.

And yet he could fight off the urge to run, to return to enclosure.

He passed a tree, following Klorissa by some ten paces, and he reached out a cautious hand to touch it. It was rough and hard to the touch. Frondy leaves moved and rustled overhead, but he did not raise his eyes to look at them. A living tree!

Klorissa called out. "How do you feel?"

"All right."

"You can see a group of youngsters from here," she said. "They're involved in some kind of game. The robots organize the games and see to it that the little animals don't kick each other's eyes out. With personal presence you can do just that, you know."

Baley raised his eyes slowly, running his glance along the cement of the pathway out to the grass and down the slope, farther and farther out—very carefully—ready to snap back to his toes if he grew frightened—feeling with his eyes . . .

There were the small figures of boys and girls racing madly about, uncaring that they raced at the very outer rim of a world with nothing but air and space above them. The glitter of an occasional robot moved nimbly among them. The noise of the children was a far-off incoherent squeaking in the air.

"They love it," said Klorissa. "Pushing and pulling and squabbling and falling down and getting up and just generally contacting. Skies above! How do children ever manage to grow up?"

"What are those older children doing?" asked Baley. He pointed at a group of isolated youngsters standing to one side.

"They're viewing. They're not in a state of personal presence. By viewing, they can walk together, talk together, race together, play together. Anything except physical contact."

"Where do children go when they leave here?"

"To estates of their own. The number of deaths is, on the average, equal to the number of graduations."

"To their parents' estates?"

"Skies above, no! It would be an amazing coincidence, wouldn't it, to have a parent die just as a child is of age. No, the children take any one that falls vacant. I don't know that any of them would be particularly happy, anyway, living in a mansion that once belonged to their parents, supposing, of course, they knew who their parents were."

"Don't they?"

She raised her eyebrows. "Why should they?"

"Don't parents visit their children here?"

"What a mind you have. Why should they want to?"

Baley said, "Do you mind if I clear up a point for myself? Is it bad manners to ask a person if they have had children?"

"It's an intimate question, wouldn't you say?"

"In a way."

"I'm hardened. Children are my business. Other people aren't."

Baley said, "Have you any children?"

Klorissa's Adam's apple made a soft but clearly visible motion in her throat as she swallowed. "I deserve that, I suppose. And you deserve an answer. I haven't."

"Are you married?"

"Yes, and I have an estate of my own and I would be there but for the emergency here. I'm just not confident of being able to control all the robots if I'm not here in person."

She turned away unhappily, and then pointed. "Now there's one of them gone tumbling and of course he's crying."

A robot was running with great space-devouring strides.

Klorissa said, "He'll be picked up and cuddled and if there's any real damage, I'll be called in." She added nervously, "I hope I don't have to be."

Baley took a deep breath. He noted three trees forming a small triangle fifty feet to the left. He walked in that direction, the grass soft and loathsome under his shoes, disgusting in its softness (like walking through corrupting flesh, and he nearly retched at the thought).

He was among them, his back against one trunk. It was almost like being surrounded by imperfect walls. The sun was only a wavering series of glitters through the leaves, so disconnected as almost to be robbed of horror.

Klorissa faced him from the path, then slowly shortened the distance by half.

"Mind if I stay here awhile?" asked Baley.

"Go ahead," said Klorissa.

Baley said, "Once the youngsters graduate out of the farm, how do you get them to court one another?"

"Court?"

"Get to know one another," said Baley, vaguely wondering how the thought could be expressed safely, "so they can marry."

"That's not their problem," said Klorissa. "They're matched by gene analysis, usually when they are quite young. That's the sensible way, isn't it?"

"Are they always willing?"

"To be married? They never are! It's a very traumatic process. At first they have to grow accustomed to one another, and a little bit of seeing each day, once the initial queasiness is gone, can do wonders."

"What if they just don't like their partner?"

"What? If the gene analysis indicates a partnership what difference does it——"

"I understand," said Baley hastily. He thought of Earth and sighed.

Klorissa said, "Is there anything else you would like to know?"

Baley wondered if there were anything to be gained from a longer stay. He would not be sorry to be done with Klorissa and fetal engineering so that he might pass on to the next stage.

He had opened his mouth to say as much, when Klorissa called out at some object far off, "You, child, you there! What are you doing?" Then, over her shoulder: "Earthman! Baley! Watch out! Watch *out!*"

Baley scarcely heard her. He responded to the note of urgency in her voice. The nervous effort that held his emotions taut snapped wide and he flamed into panic. All the terror of the open air and the endless vault of heaven broke in upon him.

Baley gibbered. He heard himself mouth meaningless sounds and felt himself fall to his knees and slowly roll over to his side as though he were watching the process from a distance.

Also from a distance he heard the sighing hum piercing the air above him and ending with a sharp thwack.

Baley closed his eyes and his fingers clutched a thin tree root that skimmed the surface of the ground and his nails burrowed into dirt.

He opened his eyes (it must only have been moments after). Klorissa was scolding sharply at a youngster who remained at a distance. A robot, silent, stood closer to Klorissa. Baley had only time to notice the youngster held a stringed object in his hand before his eyes sheered away.

Breathing heavily, Baley struggled to his feet. He stared at the shaft of glistening metal that remained in the trunk of the tree against which he had been standing. He pulled at it and it came out readily. It had not penetrated far. He looked at the point but did not touch it. It was blunted, but it would have sufficed to tear his skin had he not dropped when he did.

It took him two tries to get his legs moving. He took a step toward Klorissa and called, "You. Youngster."

Klorissa turned, her face flushed. She said, "It was an accident. Are you hurt?"

"No! What is this thing?"

"It's an arrow. It is fired by a bow, which makes a taut string do the work."

"Like this," called the youngster impudently, and he shot another arrow into the air, then burst out laughing. He had light hair and a lithe body.

Klorissa said, "You will be disciplined. Now leave!"

"Wait, wait," cried Baley. He rubbed his knee where a rock had caught and bruised him as he had fallen. "I have some questions. What is your name?"

"Bik," he said carelessly.

"Did you shoot that arrow at me, Bik?"

"That's right," said the boy.

"Do you realize you would have hit me if I hadn't been warned in time to duck?"

Bik shrugged. "I was aiming to hit."

Klorissa spoke hurriedly. "You must let me explain. Archery is an encouraged sport. It is competitive without requiring contact. We have contests among the boys using viewing only. Now I'm afraid some of the boys will aim at robots. It amuses them and it doesn't hurt the robots. I'm the only adult human on the estate and when the boy saw you, he must have assumed you were a robot."

Baley listened. His mind was clearing, and the natural dourness of his long face intensified. He said, "Bik, did you think I was a robot?"

"No," said the youngster. "You're an Earthman."

"All right. Go now."

Bik turned and raced off whistling. Baley turned to the robot. "You! How did the youngster know I was an Earthman, or weren't you with him when he shot?"

"I was with him, master. I told him you were an Earthman."

"Did you tell him what an Earthman was?"

"Yes, master."

"What is an Earthman?"

"An inferior sort of human that ought not to be allowed on Solaria because he breeds disease, master."

"And who told you that, boy?"

The robot maintained silence.

Baley said, "Do you know who told you?"

"I do not, master. It is in my memory store."

"So you told the boy I was a disease-breeding inferior and he immediately shot at me. Why didn't you stop him?"

"I would have, master. I would not have allowed harm to come to a human, even an Earthman. He moved too quickly and I was not fast enough."

"Perhaps you thought I was just an Earthman, not completely a human, and hesitated a bit."

"No, master."

It was said with quiet calm, but Baley's lips quirked grimly. The robot might deny it in all faith, but Baley felt that was exactly the factor involved.

Baley said, "What were you doing with the boy?"

"I was carrying his arrows, master."

"May I see them?"

He held out his hand. The robot approached and delivered a dozen of them. Baley put the original arrow, the one that had hit the tree, carefully at his feet, and looked the others over one by one. He handed them back and lifted the original arrow again.

He said, "Why did you give this particular arrow to the boy?"

"No reason, master. He had asked for an arrow some time earlier and this was the one my hand touched first. He looked about for a target, then noticed you and asked who the strange human was. I explained——"

"I know what you explained. This arrow you handed him is the only one with gray vanes at the rear. The others have black vanes."

The robot simply stared.

Baley said, "Did you guide the youngster here?"

"We walked randomly, master."

The Earthman looked through the gap between two trees through which the arrow had hurled itself toward its mark. He said, "Would it happen, by any chance, that this youngster, Bik, was the best archer you have here?"

The robot bent his head. "He is the best, master."

Klorissa gaped. "How did you ever come to guess that?"

"It follows," said Baley dryly. "Now please observe this gray-vaned arrow and the others. The gray-vaned arrow is the only one that seems oily at the point. I'll risk melodrama, ma'am, by saying that your warning saved my life. This arrow that missed me is poisoned."

13

A Roboticist Is Confronted

KLORISSA SAID, "Impossible! Skies above, absolutely impossible!"

"Above or below or any way you wish it. Is there an animal on the farm that's expendable? Get it and scratch it with the arrow and see what happens."

"But why should anyone want to——"

Baley said harshly, "I know why. The question is, who?"

"No one."

Baley felt the dizziness returning and he grew savage. He threw the arrow at her and she eyed the spot where it fell.

"Pick it up," Baley cried, "and if you don't want to test it, destroy it. Leave it there and you'll have an accident if the children get at it."

She picked it up hurriedly, holding it between forefinger and thumb.

Baley ran for the nearest entrance to the building and Klorissa was still holding the arrow, gingerly, when she followed him back indoors.

Baley felt a certain measure of equanimity return with the comfort of enclosure. He said, "Who poisoned the arrow?"

"I can't imagine."

"I suppose it isn't likely the boy did it himself. Would you have any way of telling who his parents were?"

"We could check the records," said Klorissa gloomily.

"Then you do keep records of relationships?"

"We have to for gene analysis."

"Would the youngster know who his parents were?"

"Never," said Klorissa energetically.

"Would he have any way of finding out?"

"He would have to break into the records room. Impossible."

"Suppose an adult visited the estate and wanted to know who his child was——"

Klorissa flushed. "Very unlikely."

"But suppose. Would he be told if he were to ask?"

"I don't know. It isn't exactly illegal for him to know. It certainly isn't customary."

"Would *you* tell him?"

"I'd try not to. I know Dr. Delmarre wouldn't have. He believed knowledge of relationship was for gene analysis only. Before him things may have been looser. . . . Why do you ask all this, anyway?"

"I don't see how the youngster could have a motive on his own account. I thought that through his parents he might have."

"This is all horrible." In her disturbed state of mind Klorissa approached more closely than at any previous time. She even stretched out an arm in his direction. "How can it all be happening? The boss killed; you nearly killed. We have no motives for violence on Solaria. We all have all we can want, so there is no personal ambition. We have no knowledge of relationship, so there is no family ambition. We are all in good genic health."

Her face cleared all at once. "Wait. This arrow can't be poisoned. I shouldn't let you convince me it is."

"Why have you suddenly decided that?"

"The robot with Bik. He would never have allowed poison. It's inconceivable that he could have done anything that might bring harm to a human being. The First Law of Robotics makes sure of that."

Baley said, "Does it? What is the First Law, I wonder?"

Klorissa stared blankly. "What do you mean?"

"Nothing. You have the arrow tested and you will find it poisoned." Baley himself was scarcely interested in the matter. He knew it for poison beyond any internal questionings. He said, "Do you still believe Mrs. Delmarre to have been guilty of her husband's death?"

"She was the only one present."

"I see. And you are the only other human adult present on this estate at a time when I have just been shot at with a poisoned arrow."

She cried energetically, "I had nothing to do with it."

"Perhaps not. And perhaps Mrs. Delmarre is innocent as well. May I use your viewing apparatus?"

"Yes, of course."

Baley knew exactly whom he intended to view and it was *not* Gladia. It came as a surprise to himself then to hear his voice say, "Get Gladia Delmarre."

The robot obeyed without comment, and Baley watched the manipulations with astonishment, wondering why he had given the order.

Was it that the girl had just been the subject of discussion, or was it that he had been a little disturbed over the manner of the end of their last viewing, or was it simply the sight of the husky, almost overpoweringly practical figure of Klorissa that finally enforced the necessity of a glimpse of Gladia as a kind of counterirritant?

He thought defensively: Jehoshaphat! Sometimes a man has to play things by ear.

She was there before him all at once, sitting in a large, upright chair that made her appear smaller and more defenseless than ever. Her hair was drawn back and bound into a loose coil. She wore pendant earrings bearing gems that looked like diamonds. Her dress was a simple affair that clung tightly at the waist.

She said in a low voice, "I'm glad you viewed, Elijah. I've been trying to reach you."

"Good morning, Gladia." (Afternoon? Evening? He didn't know Gladia's time and he couldn't tell from the manner in which she was dressed what time it might be.) "Why have you been trying to reach me?"

"To tell you I was sorry I had lost my temper last time we viewed. Mr. Olivaw didn't know where you were to be reached."

Baley had a momentary vision of Daneel still bound fast by the overseeing robots and almost smiled. He said, "That's all right. In a few hours, I'll be seeing you."

"Of course, if—— *Seeing* me?"

"Personal presence," said Baley gravely.

Her eyes grew wide and her fingers dug into the smooth plastic of the chair arms. "Is there any reason for that?"

"It is necessary."

"I don't think——"

"Would you allow it?"

She looked away. "Is it absolutely necessary?"

"It is. First, though, there is someone else I must see. Your husband was interested in robots. You told me that, and I have heard it from other sources, but he wasn't a roboticist, was he?"

"That wasn't his training, Elijah." She still avoided his eyes.

"But he worked with a roboticist, didn't he?"

"Jothan Leebig," she said at once. "He's a good friend of mine."

"He is?" said Baley energetically.

Gladia looked startled. "Shouldn't I have said that?"

"Why not, if it's the truth?"

"I'm always afraid that I'll say things that will make me seem as though—— You don't know what it's like when everyone is sure you've done something."

"Take it easy. How is it that Leebig is a friend of yours?"

"Oh, I don't know. He's in the next estate, for one thing. Viewing energy is just about nil, so we can just view all the time in free motion with hardly any trouble. We go on walks together all the time; or we did, anyway."

"I didn't know you could go on walks together with anyone."

Gladia flushed. "I said *viewing*. Oh well, I keep forgetting you're an Earthman. Viewing in free motion means we focus on ourselves and we can go anywhere we want to without losing contact. I walk on my estate and he walks on his and we're together." She held her chin high. "It can be pleasant."

Then, suddenly, she giggled. "Poor Jothan."

"Why do you say that?"

"I was thinking of you thinking we walked together without viewing. He'd die if he thought anyone could think that."

"Why?"

"He's terrible that way. He told me that when he was five years old he stopped seeing people. Insisted on viewing only. Some children are like that. Rikaine"—she paused in confusion, then went on —"Rikaine, my husband, once told me, when I talked about Jothan, that more and more children would be like that too. He said it was a kind of social evolution that favored survival of pro-viewing. Do you think that's so?"

"I'm no authority," said Baley.

"Jothan won't even get married. Rikaine was angry with him, told him he was anti-social and that he had genes that were necessary in the common pool, but Jothan just refused to consider it."

"Has he a right to refuse?"

"No-o," said Gladia hesitantly, "but he's a very brilliant roboticist, you know, and roboticists are valuable on Solaria. I suppose they stretched a point. Except I think Rikaine was going to stop working with Jothan. He told me once Jothan was a bad Solarian."

"Did he tell Jothan that?"

"I don't know. He was working with Jothan to the end."

"But he thought Jothan was a bad Solarian for refusing to marry?"

"Rikaine once said that marriage was the hardest thing in life, but that it had to be endured."

"What did you think?"

"About what, Elijah?"

"About marriage. Did you think it was the hardest thing in life?"

Her expression grew slowly blank as though she were painstakingly washing emotion out of it. She said, "I never thought about it."

Baley said, "You said you go on walks with Jothan Leebig all the time, then corrected yourself and put that in the past. You don't go on walks with him any more, then?"

Gladia shook her head. Expression was back in her face. Sadness. "No. We don't seem to. I viewed him once or twice. He always seemed busy and I didn't like to—— You know."

"Was this since the death of your husband?"

"No, even some time before. Several months before."

"Do you suppose Dr. Delmarre ordered him not to pay further attention to you?"

Gladia looked startled. "Why should he? Jothan isn't a robot and neither am I. How can we take orders and why should Rikaine give them?"

Baley did not bother to try to explain. He could have done so only in Earth terms and that would make things no clearer to her. And if it did manage to clarify, the result could only be disgusting to her.

Baley said, "Only a question. I'll view you again, Gladia, when I'm done with Leebig. What time do you have, by the way?" He was sorry at once for asking the question. Robots would answer in Terrestrial equivalents, but Gladia might answer in Solarian units and Baley was weary of displaying ignorance.

But Gladia answered in purely qualitative terms. "Midafternoon," she said.

"Then that's it for Leebig's estate also?"

"Oh yes."

"Good. I'll view you again as soon as I can and we'll make arrangements for seeing."

Again she grew hesitant. "Is it absolutely necessary?"

"It is."

She said in a low voice, "Very well."

There was some delay in contacting Leebig and Baley utilized it in consuming another sandwich, one that was brought to him in its original packaging. But he had grown more cautious. He inspected the seal carefully before breaking it, then looked over the contents painstakingly.

He accepted a plastic container of milk, not quite unfrozen, bit an opening with his own teeth, and drank from it directly. He thought gloomily that there were such things as odorless, tasteless, slow-acting poisons that could be introduced delicately by means of hypodermic needles or high-pressure needle jets, then put the thought aside as being childish.

So far murders and attempted murders had been committed in the most direct possible fashion. There was nothing delicate or subtle about a blow on the head, enough poison in a glass to kill a dozen men, or a poisoned arrow shot openly at the victim.

And then he thought, scarcely less gloomily, that as long as he hopped between time zones in this fashion, he was scarcely likely to have regular meals. Or, if this continued, regular sleep.

The robot approached him. "Dr. Leebig directs you to call sometime tomorrow. He is engaged in important work."

Baley bounced to his feet and roared, "You tell that guy——"

He stopped. There was no use in yelling at a robot. That is, you could yell if you wished, but it would achieve results no sooner than a whisper.

He said in a conversational tone, "You tell Dr. Leebig, or his robot if that is as far as you've reached, that I am investigating the murder of a professional associate of his and a good Solarian. You tell him that I cannot wait on his work. You tell him that if I am not viewing him in five minutes, I will be in a plane and at his estate *seeing* him in less than an hour. You use that word, seeing, so there's no mistake."

He returned to his sandwich.

The five minutes were not quite gone, when Leebig, or at least a Solarian whom Baley presumed to be Leebig, was glaring at him.

Baley glared back. Leebig was a lean man, who held himself rigidly erect. His dark, prominent eyes had a look of intense abstraction about them, compounded now with anger. One of his eyelids drooped slightly.

He said, "Are you the Earthman?"

"Elijah Baley," said Baley, "Plainclothesman C-7, in charge of the investigation into the murder of Dr. Rikaine Delmarre. What is your name?"

"I'm Dr. Jothan Leebig. Why do you presume to annoy me at my work?"

"It's easy," said Baley quietly. "It's my business."

"Then take your business elsewhere."

"I have a few questions to ask first, Doctor. I believe you were a close associate of Dr. Delmarre. Right?"

One of Leebig's hands clenched suddenly into a fist and he strode hastily toward a mantelpiece on which tiny clockwork contraptions went through complicated periodic motions that caught hypnotically at the eye.

The viewer kept focused on Leebig so that his figure did not depart from central projection as he walked. Rather the room behind him seemed to move backward in little rises and dips as he strode.

Leebig said, "If you are the foreigner whom Gruer threatened to bring in——"

"I am."

"Then you are here against my advice. Done viewing."

"Not yet. Don't break contact." Baley raised his voice sharply and a finger as well. He pointed it directly at the roboticist, who shrank visibly away from it, full lips spreading into an expression of disgust.

Baley said, "I wasn't bluffing about seeing you, you know."

"No Earthman vulgarity, please."

"A straightforward statement is what it is intended to be. I will see you, if I can't make you listen any other way. I will grab you by the collar and make you listen."

Leebig stared back. "You are a filthy animal."

"Have it your way, but I will do as I say."

"If you try to invade my estate, I will—I will——"

Baley lifted his eyebrows. "Kill me? Do you often make such threats?"

"I made no threat."

"Then talk now. In the time you have wasted, a good deal might have been accomplished. You were a close associate of Dr. Delmarre. Right?"

The roboticist's head lowered. His shoulders moved slightly to a slow, regular breathing. When he looked up, he was in command of himself. He even managed a brief, sapless smile.

"I was."

"Delmarre was interested in new types of robots, I understand."

"He was."

"What kind?"

"Are you a roboticist?"

"No. Explain it for the layman."

"I doubt that I can."

"Try! For instance, I think he wanted robots capable of disciplining children. What would that involve?"

Leebig raised his eyebrows briefly and said, "To put it very simply, skipping all the subtle details, it means a strengthening of the C-integral governing the Sikorovich tandem route response at the W-65 level."

"Double-talk," said Baley.

"The truth."

"It's double-talk to me. How else can you put it?"

"It means a certain weakening of the First Law."

"Why so? A child is disciplined for its own future good. Isn't that the theory?"

"Ah, the future good!" Leebig's eyes glowed with passion and he seemed to grow less conscious of his listener and correspondingly more talkative. "A simple concept, you think. How many human beings are willing to accept a trifling inconvenience for the sake of a large future good? How long does it take to train a child that what tastes good now means a stomach-ache later, and what tastes bad now will correct the stomach-ache later? Yet you want a robot to be able to understand?

"Pain inflicted by a robot on a child sets up a powerful disruptive potential in the positronic brain. To counteract that by an anti-potential triggered through a realization of future good requires enough paths and bypaths to increase the mass of the positronic brain by 50 per cent, unless other circuits are sacrificed."

Baley said, "Then you haven't succeeded in building such a robot."

"No, nor am I likely to succeed. Nor anyone."

"Was Dr. Delmarre testing an experimental model of such a robot at the time of his death?"

"Not of *such* a robot. We were interested in other more practical things also."

Baley said quietly, "Dr. Leebig, I am going to have to learn a bit more about robotics and I am going to ask you to teach me."

Leebig shook his head violently, and his drooping eyelid dipped further in a ghastly travesty of a wink. "It should be obvious that a course in robotics takes more than a moment. I lack the time."

"Nevertheless, you must teach me. The smell of robots is the one thing that pervades everything on Solaria. If it is time we require, then more than ever I must see you. I am an Earthman and I cannot work or think comfortably while viewing."

It would not have seemed possible to Baley for Leebig to stiffen his stiff carriage further, but he did. He said, "Your phobias as an Earthman don't concern me. Seeing is impossible."

"I think you will change your mind when I tell you what I chiefly want to consult you about."

"It will make no difference. Nothing can."

"No? Then listen to this. It is my belief that throughout the history of the positronic robot, the First Law of Robotics has been deliberately misquoted."

Leebig moved spasmodically. "Misquoted? Fool! Madman! Why?"

"To hide the fact," said Baley with complete composure, "that robots can commit murder."

14

A Motive Is Revealed

LEEBIG'S MOUTH widened slowly. Baley took it for a snarl at first and then, with considerable surprise, decided that it was the most unsuccessful attempt at a smile that he had ever seen.

Leebig said, "Don't say that. Don't ever say that."

"Why not?"

"Because anything, however small, that encourages distrust of robots is harmful. Distrusting robots is a human *disease!*"

It was as though he were lecturing a small child. It was as though he were saying something gently that he wanted to yell. It was as though he were trying to persuade when what he really wanted was to enforce on penalty of death.

Leebig said, "Do you know the history of robotics?"

"A little."

"On Earth, you should. Yes. Do you know robots started with a Frankenstein complex against them? They were suspect. Men distrusted and feared robots. Robotics was almost an undercover science as a result. The Three Laws were first built into robots in an effort to overcome distrust and even so Earth would never allow a robotic society to develop. One of the reasons the first pioneers left Earth to colonize the rest of the Galaxy was so that they might establish societies in which robots would be allowed to free men of poverty and toil. Even *then*, there remained a latent suspicion not far below, ready to pop up at any excuse."

"Have you yourself had to counter distrust of robots?" asked Baley.

"Many times," said Leebig grimly.

"Is that why you and other roboticists are willing to distort the facts just a little in order to avoid suspicion as much as possible?"

"There is no distortion!"

"For instance, aren't the Three Laws misquoted?"

"*No!*"

"I can demonstrate that they are, and unless you convince me otherwise, I will demonstrate it to the whole Galaxy, if I can."

"You're mad. Whatever argument you may think you have is fallacious, I assure you."

"Shall we discuss it?"

"If it does not take too long."

"Face to face? Seeing?"

Leebig's thin face twisted. "*No!*"

"Good-by, Dr. Leebig. Others will listen to me."

"Wait. Great Galaxy, man, wait!"

"Seeing?"

The roboticist's hands wandered upward, hovered about his chin. Slowly a thumb crept into his mouth and remained there. He stared, blankly, at Baley.

Baley thought: Is he regressing to the pre-five-year-old stage so that it will be legitimate for him to see me?

"Seeing?" he said.

But Leebig shook his head slowly. "I can't. I can't," he moaned, the words all but stifled by the blocking thumb. "Do whatever you want."

Baley stared at the other and watched him turn away and face the wall. He watched the Solarian's straight back bend and the Solarian's face hide in shaking hands.

Baley said, "Very well, then, I'll agree to view."

Leebig said, back still turned, "Excuse me a moment. I'll be back."

Baley tended to his own needs during the interval and stared at his fresh-washed face in the bathroom mirror. Was he getting the feel of Solaria and Solarians? He wasn't sure.

He sighed and pushed a contact and a robot appeared. He didn't turn to look at it. He said, "Is there another viewer at the farm, besides the one I'm using?"

"There are three other outlets, master."

"Then tell Klorissa Cantoro—tell your mistress that I will be using this one till further notice and that I am not to be disturbed."

"Yes, master."

Baley returned to his position where the viewer remained focused on the empty patch of room in which Leebig had stood. It was still empty and he settled himself to wait.

It wasn't long. Leebig entered and the room once more jiggled as the man walked. Evidently focus shifted from room center to man center without delay. Baley remembered the complexity of viewing controls and began to feel a kind of appreciation of what was involved.

Leebig was quite master of himself now, apparently. His hair was slicked back and his costume had been changed. His clothes fitted loosely and were of a material that glistened and caught highlights. He sat down in a slim chair that folded out of the wall.

He said soberly, "Now what is this notion of yours concerning First Law?"

"Will we be overheard?"

"No. I've taken care."

Baley nodded. He said, "Let me quote the First Law."

"I scarcely need that."

"I know, but let me quote it, anyway: A robot may not harm a human being or, through inaction, allow a human being to come to harm."

"Well?"

"Now when I first landed on Solaria, I was driven to the estate assigned for my use in a ground-car. The ground-car was a specially enclosed job designed to protect me from exposure to open space. As an Earthman——"

"I know about that," said Leebig impatiently. "What has this to do with the matter?"

"The robots who drove the car did *not* know about it. I asked that the car be opened and was at once obeyed. Second Law. They had to follow orders. I was uncomfortable, of course, and nearly collapsed before the car was enclosed again. Didn't the robots harm me?"

"At your order," snapped Leebig.

"I'll quote the Second Law: A robot must obey the orders given it by human beings except where such orders would conflict with the First Law. So you see, my order should have been ignored."

"This is nonsense. The robot lacked knowledge——"

Baley leaned forward in his chair. "Ah! We have it. Now let's recite the First Law as it should be stated: A robot may do nothing that, *to its knowledge*, will harm a human being; nor, through inaction, *knowingly* allow a human being to come to harm."

"This is all understood."

"I think not by ordinary men. Otherwise, ordinary men would realize robots could commit murder."

Leebig was white. "Mad! Lunacy!"

Baley stared at his finger ends. "A robot may perform an innocent task, I suppose; one that has no damaging effect on a human being?"

"If ordered to do so," said Leebig.

"Yes, of course. If ordered to do so. And a second robot may perform an innocent task, also, I suppose; one that also can have no damaging effect on a human being? If ordered to do so?"

"Yes."

"And what if the two innocent tasks, each completely innocent, completely, amount to murder when added together?"

"What?" Leebig's face puckered into a scowl.

"I want your expert opinion on the matter," said Baley. "I'll set you a hypothetical case. Suppose a man says to a robot, 'Place a small quantity of this liquid into a glass of milk that you will find in such and such a place. The liquid is harmless. I wish only to know its effect on milk. Once I know the effect, the mixture will be poured out. After you have performed this action, forget you have done so.'"

Leebig, still scowling, said nothing.

Baley said, "If I had told the robot to add a mysterious liquid to milk and then offer it to a man, First Law would force it to ask, 'What is the nature of the liquid? Will it harm a man?' And if it were assured the liquid was harmless, First Law might still make the robot hesitate and refuse to offer the milk. Instead, however, it is told the milk will be poured out. First Law is not involved. Won't the robot do as it is told?"

Leebig glared.

Baley said, "Now a second robot has poured out the milk in the first place and is unaware that the milk has been tampered with. In all innocence, it offers the milk to a man and the man dies."

Leebig cried out, "*No!*"

"Why not? Both actions are innocent in themselves. Only together are they murder. Do you deny that that sort of thing can happen?"

"The murderer would be the man who gave the order," cried Leebig.

"If you want to be philosophical, yes. The robots would have been the immediate murderers, though, the instruments of murder."

"No man would give such orders."

"A man would. A man has. It was exactly in this way that the murder attempt on Dr. Gruer must have been carried through. You've heard about that, I suppose."

"On Solaria," muttered Leebig, "one hears about everything."

"Then you know Gruer was poisoned at his dinner table before the eyes of myself and my partner, Mr. Olivaw of Aurora. Can you suggest any other way in which the poison might have reached him? There was no other human on the estate. As a Solarian, you must appreciate that point."

"I'm not a detective. I have no theories."

"I've presented you with one. I want to know if it is a possible one. I want to know if two robots might not perform two separate actions, each one innocent in itself, the two together resulting in murder. You're the expert, Dr. Leebig. *Is it possible?*"

And Leebig, haunted and harried, said, "Yes," in a voice so low that Baley scarcely heard him.

Baley said, "Very well, then. So much for the First Law."

Leebig stared at Baley and his drooping eyelid winked once or twice in a slow tic. His hands, which had been clasped, drew apart, though the fingers maintained their clawed shape as though each hand still entwined a phantom hand of air. Palms turned downward and rested on knees and only then did the fingers relax.

Baley watched it all in abstraction.

Leebig said, "Theoretically, yes. Theoretically! But don't dismiss the First Law that easily, Earthman. Robots would have to be ordered very cleverly in order to circumvent the First Law."

"Granted," said Baley. "I am only an Earthman. I know next to nothing about robots and my phrasing of the orders was only by way of example. A Solarian would be much more subtle and do much better. I'm sure of that."

Leebig might not have been listening. He said loudly, "If a robot can be manipulated into doing harm to a man, it means only that we must extend the powers of the positronic brain. One *might* say we ought to make the human better. That is impossible, so we will make the robot more foolproof.

"We advance continuously. Our robots are more varied, more specialized, more capable, and more unharming than those of a century ago. A century hence, we will have still greater advances. Why have a robot manipulate controls when a positronic brain can be built into the controls itself? That's specialization, but we can generalize, also. Why not a robot with replaceable and interchangeable limbs. Eh? Why not? If we——"

Baley interrupted. "Are you the only roboticist on Solaria?"

"Don't be a fool."

"I only wondered. Dr. Delmarre was the only—uh—fetal engineer, except for an assistant."

"Solaria has over twenty roboticists."

"Are you the best?"

"I am," Leebig said without self-consciousness.

"Delmarre worked with you."

"He did."

Baley said, "I understand that he was planning to break the partnership toward the end."

"No sign of it. What gave you the idea?"

"I understand he disapproved of your bachelorhood."

"He may have. He was a thorough Solarian. However, it did not affect our business relationships."

"To change the subject. In addition to developing new model robots, do you also manufacture and repair existing types?"

Leebig said, "Manufacture and repair are largely robot-conducted. There is a large factory and maintenance shop on my estate."

"Do robots require much in the way of repair, by the way?"

"Very little."

"Does that mean that robot repair is an undeveloped science?"

"Not at all." Leebig said that stiffly.

"What about the robot that was at the scene of Dr. Delmarre's murder?"

Leebig looked away, and his eyebrows drew together as though a painful thought were being barred entrance to his mind. "It was a complete loss."

"Really complete? Could it answer any questions at all?"

"None at all. It was absolutely useless. Its positronic brain was completely short-circuited. Not one pathway was left intact. Consider! It had witnessed a murder it had been unable to halt——"

"Why was it unable to halt the murder, by the way?"

"Who can tell? Dr. Delmarre was experimenting with that robot. I do not know in what mental condition he had left it. He might have ordered it, for instance, to suspend all operations while he checked one particular circuit element. If someone whom neither Dr. Delmarre nor the robot suspected of harm were suddenly to launch a homicidal attack, there might be a perceptible interval before the robot could use First Law potential to overcome Dr. Delmarre's freezing order. The length of the interval would depend on the nature of the attack and the nature of Dr. Delmarre's freezing order. I could invent a dozen other ways of explaining why the robot was unable to prevent the murder. Being unable to do so was a First Law violation, however, and that was sufficient to blast every positronic pathway in the robot's mind."

"But if the robot was physically unable to prevent the murder, was it responsible? Does the First Law ask impossibilities?"

Leebig shrugged. "The First Law, despite your attempts to make little of it, protects humanity with every atom of possible force. It allows no excuses. If the First Law is broken, the robot is ruined."

"That is a universal rule, sir?"

"As universal as robots."

Baley said, "Then I've learned something."

"Then learn something else. Your theory of murder by a series of robotic actions, each innocent in itself, will not help you in the case of Dr. Delmarre's death."

"Why not?"

"The death was not by poisoning, but by bludgeoning. Something had to hold the bludgeon, and that had to be a human arm. No robot could swing a club and smash a skull."

"Suppose," said Baley, "a robot were to push an innocent button which dropped a booby-trap weight on Delmarre's head."

Leebig smiled sourly. "Earthman, I've viewed the scene of the crime. I've heard all the news. The murder was a big thing here on Solaria, you know. So I know there was no sign of any machinery at the scene of the crime, or of any fallen weight."

Baley said, "Or of any blunt instrument, either."

Leebig said scornfully, "You're a detective. Find it."

"Granting that a robot was not responsible for Dr. Delmarre's death, who was, then?"

"Everyone knows who was," shouted Leebig. "His wife! Gladia!"

Baley thought: At least there's a unanimity of opinion.

Aloud he said, "And who was the mastermind behind the robots who poisoned Gruer?"

"I suppose . . ." Leebig trailed off.

"You don't think there are two murderers, do you? If Gladia was responsible for one crime, she must be responsible for the second attempt, also."

"Yes. You must be right." His voice gained assurance. "No doubt of it."

"No doubt?"

"Nobody else could get close enough to Dr. Delmarre to kill him. He allowed personal presence no more than I did, except that he made an exception in favor of his wife, and I make no exceptions. The wiser I." The roboticist laughed harshly.

"I believe you knew her," said Baley abruptly.

"Whom?"

"Her. We are discussing only one 'her.' Gladia!"

"Who told you I knew her any more than I know anyone else?" demanded Leebig. He put his hand to his throat. His fingers moved slightly and opened the neck-seam of his garment for an inch downward, leaving more freedom to breathe.

"Gladia herself did. You two went for walks."

"So? We were neighbors. It is a common thing to do. She seemed a pleasant person."

"You approved of her, then?"

Leebig shrugged. "Talking to her was relaxing."

"What did you talk about?"

"Robotics." There was a flavor of surprise about the word as though there were wonder that the question could be asked.

"And she talked robotics too?"

"She knew nothing about robotics. Ignorant! But she listened. She has some sort of field-force rigmarole she plays with; field coloring, she calls it. I have no patience with that, but I listened."

"All this without personal presence?"

Leebig looked revolted and did not answer.

Baley tried again, "Were you attracted to her?"

"What?"

"Did you find her attractive? Physically?"

Even Leebig's bad eyelid lifted and his lips quivered. "Filthy animal," he muttered.

"Let me put it this way, then. When did you cease finding Gladia pleasant? You used that word yourself, if you remember."

"What do you mean?"

"You said you found her pleasant. Now you believe she murdered her husband. That isn't the mark of a pleasant person."

"I was mistaken about her."

"But you decided you were mistaken before she killed her husband, if she did so. You stopped walking with her some time before the murder. Why?"

Leebig said, "Is that important?"

"Everything is important till proven otherwise."

"Look, if you want information from me as a roboticist, ask it. I won't answer personal questions."

Baley said, "You were closely associated with both the murdered man and the chief suspect. Don't you see that personal questions are unavoidable? Why did you stop walking with Gladia?"

Leebig snapped, "There came a time when I ran out of things to say; when I was too busy; when I found no reason to continue the walks."

"When you no longer found her pleasant, in other words."

"All right. Put it so."

"Why was she no longer pleasant?"

Leebig shouted, "I have no reason."

Baley ignored the other's excitement. "You are still someone who has known Gladia well. What could her motive be?"

"Her motive?"

"No one has suggested any motive for the murder. Surely Gladia wouldn't commit murder without a motive."

"Great Galaxy!" Leebig leaned his head back as though to laugh, but didn't. "No one told you? Well, perhaps no one knew. I knew, though. She told me. She told me frequently."

"Told you what, Dr. Leebig?"

"Why, that she quarreled with her husband. Quarreled bitterly and frequently. She hated him, Earthman. Didn't anyone tell you that? Didn't *she* tell you?"

15

A Portrait Is Colored

BALEY TOOK it between the eyes and tried not to show it.

Presumably, living as they did, Solarians considered one another's private lives to be sacrosanct. Questions concerning marriage and children were in bad taste. He supposed then that chronic quarreling could exist between husband and wife and be a matter into which curiosity was equally forbidden.

But even when murder had been committed? Would no one commit the social crime of asking the suspect if she quarreled with her husband? Or of mentioning the matter if they happened to know of it?

Well, Leebig had.

Baley said, "What did the quarrels concern?"

"You had better ask her, I think."

He better had, thought Baley. He rose stiffly, "Thank you, Dr. Leebig, for your co-operation. I may need your help again later. I hope you will keep yourself available."

"Done viewing," said Leebig, and he and the segment of his room vanished abruptly.

For the first time Baley found himself not minding a plane flight through open space. Not minding it at all. It was almost as though he were in his own element.

He wasn't even thinking of Earth or of Jessie. He had been away from Earth only a matter of weeks, yet it might as well have been years. He had been on Solaria only the better part of three days and yet it seemed forever.

How fast could a man adapt to nightmare?

Or was it Gladia? He would be seeing her soon, not viewing her. Was that what gave him confidence and this odd feeling of mixed apprehension and anticipation?

Would she endure it? he wondered. Or would she slip away after a few moments of seeing, begging off as Quemot had done?

She stood at the other end of a long room when he entered. She might almost have been an impressionistic representation of herself, she was reduced so to essentials.

Her lips were faintly red, her eyebrows lightly penciled, her earlobes faintly blue, and, except for that, her face was untouched. She looked pale, a little frightened, and very young.

Her brown-blond hair was drawn back, and her gray-blue eyes were somehow shy. Her dress was a blue so dark as to be almost black, with a thin white edging curling down each side. She wore long sleeves, white gloves, and flat-heeled shoes. Not an inch of skin showed anywhere but in her face. Even her neck was covered by a kind of unobtrusive ruching.

Baley stopped where he was. "Is this close enough, Gladia?"

She was breathing with shallow quickness. She said, "I had forgotten what to expect really. It's just like viewing, isn't it? I mean, if you don't think of it as seeing."

Baley said, "It's all quite normal to me."

"Yes, on Earth." She closed her eyes. "Sometimes I try to imagine it. Just crowds of people everywhere. You walk down a road and there are others walking with you and still others walking in the other direction. Dozens——"

"Hundreds," said Baley. "Did you ever view scenes on Earth in a book-film? Or view a novel with an Earth setting?"

"We don't have many of those, but I've viewed novels set on the other Outer Worlds where seeing goes on all the time. It's different in a novel. It just seems like a multiview."

"Do people ever kiss in novels?"

She flushed painfully. "I don't read that kind."

"Never?"

"Well—there are always a few dirty films around, you know, and sometimes, just out of curiosity—— It's sickening, really."

"Is it?"

She said with sudden animation, "But Earth is so different. So many people. When you walk, Elijah, I suppose you even t-touch people. I mean, by accident."

Baley half smiled. "You even knock them down by accident." He thought of the crowds on the Expressways, tugging and shoving, bounding up and down the strips, and for a moment, inevitably, he felt the pang of homesickness.

Gladia said, "You don't have to stay way out there."

"Would it be all right if I came closer?"

"I think so. I'll tell you when I'd rather you wouldn't any more."

Stepwise Baley drew closer, while Gladia watched him, wide-eyed.

She said suddenly, "Would you like to see some of my field colorings?"

Baley was six feet away. He stopped and looked at her. She seemed small and fragile. He tried to visualize her, something in her hand (what?), swinging furiously at the skull of her husband. He tried to picture her, mad with rage, homicidal with hate and anger.

He had to admit it could be done. Even a hundred and five pounds of woman could crush a skull if she had the proper weapon and were wild enough. And Baley had known murderesses (on Earth, of course) who, in repose, were bunny rabbits.

He said, "What are field colorings, Gladia?"

"An art form," she said.

Baley remembered Leebig's reference to Gladia's art. He nodded. "I'd like to see some."

"Follow me, then."

Baley maintained a careful six-foot distance between them. At that, it was less than a third the distance Klorissa had demanded.

They entered a room that burst with light. It glowed in every corner and every color.

Gladia looked pleased, proprietary. She looked up at Baley, eyes anticipating.

Baley's response must have been what she expected, though he said nothing. He turned slowly, trying to make out what he saw, for it was light only, no material object at all.

The gobbets of light sat on embracing pedestals. They were living geometry, lines and curves of color, entwined into a coalescing whole yet maintaining distinct identities. No two specimens were even remotely alike.

Baley groped for appropriate words and said, "Is it supposed to mean anything?"

Gladia laughed in her pleasant contralto. "It means whatever you like it to mean. They're just light-forms that might make you feel angry or happy or curious or whatever *I* felt when I constructed one. I could make one for you, a kind of portrait. It might not be very good, though, because I would just be improvising quickly."

"Would you? I would be very interested."

"All right," she said, and half-ran to a light-figure in one corner, passing within inches of him as she did so. She did not seem to notice.

She touched something on the pedestal of the light-figure and the glory above died without a flicker.

Baley gasped and said, "Don't do that."

"It's all right. I was tired of it, anyway. I'll just fade the others temporarily so they don't distract me." She opened a panel along one featureless wall and moved a rheostat. The colors faded to something scarcely visible.

Baley said, "Don't you have a robot to do this? Closing contacts?"

"Shush, now," she said impatiently. "I don't keep robots in here. This is *me*." She looked at him, frowning. "I don't know you well enough. That's the trouble."

She wasn't looking at the pedestal, but her fingers rested lightly on its smooth upper surface. All ten fingers were curved, tense, waiting.

One finger moved, describing a half curve over smoothness. A bar of deep yellow light grew and slanted obliquely across the air above. The finger inched backward a fraction and the light grew slightly less deep in shade.

She looked at it momentarily. "I suppose that's it. A kind of strength without weight."

"Jehoshaphat," said Baley.

"Are you offended?" Her fingers lifted and the yellow slant of light remained solitary and stationary.

"No, not at all. But what is it? How do you do it?"

"That's hard to explain," said Gladia, looking at the pedestal thoughtfully, "considering I don't really understand it myself. It's a kind of optical illusion, I've been told. We set up force-fields at different energy levels. They're extrusions of hyperspace, really, and don't have the properties of ordinary space at all. Depending on the energy level, the human eye sees light of different shades. The shapes and colors are controlled by the warmth of my fingers against appropriate spots on the pedestal. There are all sorts of controls inside each pedestal."

"You mean if I were to put my finger there——" Baley advanced and Gladia made way for him. He put a hesitant forefinger down upon the pedestal and felt a soft throbbing.

"Go ahead. Move your finger, Elijah," said Gladia.

Baley did so and a dirty-gray jag of light lifted upward, skewing the yellow light. Baley withdrew his finger sharply and Gladia laughed and then was instantly contrite.

"I shouldn't laugh," she said. "It's really very hard to do, even for people who've tried a long time." Her own hand moved lightly and too quickly for Baley to follow and the monstrosity he had set up disappeared, leaving the yellow light in isolation again.

"How did you learn to do this?" asked Baley.

"I just kept on trying. It's a new art form, you know, and only one or two really know how——"

"And you're the best," said Baley somberly. "On Solaria everyone is either the only or the best or both."

"You needn't laugh. I've had some of my pedestals on display. I've given shows." Her chin lifted. There was no mistaking her pride.

She continued, "Let me go on with your portrait." Her fingers moved again.

There were few curves in the light-form that grew under her ministrations. It was all sharp angles. And the dominant color was blue.

"That's Earth, somehow," said Gladia, biting her lower lip. "I always think of Earth as blue. All those people and seeing, seeing, seeing. Viewing is more rose. How does it seem to you?"

"Jehoshaphat, I can't picture things as colors."

"Can't you?" she asked abstractedly. "Now you say 'Jehoshaphat' sometimes and that's just a little blob of violet. A little sharp blob because it usually comes out ping, like that." And the little blob was there, glowing just off-center.

"And then," she said, "I can finish it like this." And a flat, luster-less hollow cube of slate gray sprang up to enclose everything. The light within shone through it, but dimmer; imprisoned, somehow.

Baley felt a sadness at it, as though it were something enclosing him, keeping him from something he wanted. He said, "What's that last?"

Gladia said, "Why, the walls about you. That's what's most in you, the way you can't go outside, the way you have to be inside. You *are* inside there. Don't you see?"

Baley saw and somehow he disapproved. He said, "Those walls aren't permanent. I've been out today."

"You have? Did you mind?"

He could not resist a counterdig. "The way you mind seeing me. You don't like it but you can stand it."

She looked at him thoughtfully. "Do you want to come out now? With me? For a walk?"

It was Baley's impulse to say: Jehoshaphat, no.

She said, "I've never walked with anyone, seeing. It's still daytime, and it's pleasant weather."

Baley looked at his abstractionist portrait and said, "If I go, will you take away the gray?"

She smiled and said, "I'll see how you behave."

The structure of light remained as they left the room. It stayed behind, holding Baley's imprisoned soul fast in the gray of the Cities.

Baley shivered slightly. Air moved against him and there was a chill to it.

Gladia said, "Are you cold?"

"It wasn't like this before," muttered Baley.

"It's late in the day now, but it isn't really cold. Would you like a coat? One of the robots could bring one in a minute."

"No. It's all right." They stepped forward along a narrow paved path. He said, "Is this where you used to walk with Dr. Leebig?"

"Oh no. We walked way out among the fields, where you only see an occasional robot working and you can hear the animal sounds. You and I will stay near the house though, just in case."

"In case what?"

"Well, in case you want to go in."

"Or in case you get weary of seeing?"

"It doesn't bother me," she said recklessly.

There was the vague rustle of leaves above and an all-pervading yellowness and greenness. There were sharp, thin cries in the air about, plus a strident humming, and shadows, too.

He was especially aware of the shadows. One of them stuck out before him, in shape like a man, that moved as he did in horrible mimicry. Baley had heard of shadows, of course, and he knew what they were, but in the pervasive indirect lighting of the Cities he had never been specifically aware of one.

Behind him, he knew, was the Solarian sun. He took care not to look at it, but he knew it was there.

Space was large, space was lonely, yet he found it drawing him. His mind pictured himself striding the surface of a world with thousands of miles and light-years of room all about him.

Why should he find attraction in this thought of loneliness? He didn't want loneliness. He wanted Earth and the warmth and companionship of the man-crammed Cities.

The picture failed him. He tried to conjure up New York in his mind, all the noise and fullness of it, and found he could remain conscious only of the quiet, air-moving chill of the surface of Solaria.

Without quite willing it Baley moved closer to Gladia until he was two feet away, then grew aware of her startled face.

"I beg your pardon," he said at once, and drew off.

She gasped, "It's all right. Won't you walk this way? We have some flower beds you might like."

The direction she indicated lay away from the sun. Baley followed silently.

Gladia said, "Later in the year, it will be wonderful. In the warm weather I can run down to the lake and swim, or just run across the fields, run as fast as I can until I'm just glad to fall down and lie still."

She looked down at herself. "But this is no costume for it. With all this on, I've *got* to walk. Sedately, you know."

"How would you prefer to dress?" asked Baley.

"Halter and shorts at the *most*," she cried, lifting her arms as though feeling the freedom of that in her imagination. "Sometimes less. Sometimes just sandals so you can feel the air with every inch—— Oh, I'm sorry. I've offended you."

Baley said, "No. It's all right. Was that your costume when you went walking with Dr. Leebig?"

"It varied. It depended on the weather. Sometimes I wore very little, but it was viewing, you know. You *do* understand, I hope."

"I understand. What about Dr. Leebig, though? Did he dress lightly too?"

"Jothan dress lightly?" Gladia smiled flashingly. "Oh no. He's very solemn, always." She twisted her face into a thin look of gravity and half winked, catching the very essence of Leebig and forcing a short grunt of appreciation out of Baley.

"This is the way he talks," she said. " 'My dear Gladia, in considering the effect of a first-order potential on positron flow——' "

"Is that what he talked to you about? Robotics?"

"Mostly. Oh, he takes it so seriously, you know. He was always trying to teach me about it. He never gave up."

"Did you learn anything?"

"Not one thing. Nothing. It's just all a complete mix-up to me. He'd get angry with me sometimes, but when he'd scold, I'd dive into the water, if we were anywhere near the lake, and splash him."

"*Splash* him? I thought you were viewing."

She laughed. "You're *such* an Earthman. I'd splash where he was standing in his own room or on his own estate. The water couldn't touch him, but he would duck just the same. Look at that."

Baley looked. They had circled a wooded patch and now came upon a clearing, centered about an ornamental pond. Small bricked walks penetrated the clearing and broke it up. Flowers grew in profusion and order. Baley knew them for flowers from book-films he had viewed.

In a way the flowers were like the light-patterns that Gladia constructed and Baley imagined that she constructed them in the spirit of flowers. He touched one cautiously, then looked about. Reds and yellows predominated.

In turning to look about Baley caught a glimpse of the sun.

He said uneasily, "The sun is low in the sky."

"It's late afternoon," called Gladia back to him. She had run toward the pond and was sitting on a stone bench at its edge. "Come here," she shouted, waving. "You can stand if you don't like to sit on stone."

Baley advanced slowly. "Does it get this low every day?" and at once he was sorry he asked. If the planet rotated, the sun must be low in the sky both mornings and afternoons. Only at midday could it be high.

Telling himself this couldn't change a lifetime of pictured thought. He knew there was such a thing as night and had even experienced it, with a planet's whole thickness interposing safely between a man and the sun. He knew there were clouds and a protective grayness hiding the worst of outdoors. And still, when he thought of planetary surfaces, it was always a picture of a blaze of light with a sun high in the sky.

He looked over his shoulder, just quickly enough to get a flash of sun, and wondered how far the house was if he should decide to return.

Gladia was pointing to the other end of the stone bench.

Baley said, "That's pretty close to you, isn't it?"

She spread out her little hands, palms up. "I'm getting used to it. Really."

He sat down, facing toward her to avoid the sun.

She leaned over backward toward the water and pulled a small cup-shaped flower, yellow without and white-streaked within, not at all flamboyant. She said, "This is a native plant. Most of the flowers here are from Earth originally."

Water dripped from its severed stem as she extended it gingerly toward Baley.

Baley reached for it as gingerly. "You killed it," he said.

"It's only a flower. There are thousands more." Suddenly, before his fingers more than touched the yellow cup, she snatched it away, her eyes kindling. "Or are you trying to imply I could kill a human being because I pulled a flower?"

Baley said in soft conciliation, "I wasn't implying anything. May I see it?"

Baley didn't really want to touch it. It had grown in wet soil and there was still the effluvium of mud about it. How could these people, who were so careful in contact with Earthmen and even with one another, be so careless in their contact with ordinary dirt?

But he held the stalk between thumb and forefinger and looked at it. The cup was formed of several thin pieces of papery tissue, curving up from a common center. Within it was a white convex swelling, damp with liquid and fringed with dark hairs that trembled lightly in the wind.

She said, "Can you smell it?"

At once Baley was aware of the odor that emanated from it. He leaned toward it and said, "It smells like a woman's perfume."

Gladia clapped her hands in delight. "How like an Earthman. What you really mean is that a woman's perfume smells like *that*."

Baley nodded ruefully. He was growing weary of the outdoors. The shadows were growing longer and the land was becoming somber. Yet he was determined not to give in. He wanted those gray walls of light that dimmed his portrait removed. It was quixotic, but there it was.

Gladia took the flower from Baley, who let it go without reluctance. Slowly she pulled its petals apart. She said, "I suppose every woman smells different."

"It depends on the perfume," said Baley indifferently.

"Imagine being close enough to tell. I don't wear perfume because no one is close enough. Except now. But I suppose you smell perfume often, all the time. On Earth, your wife is always with you, isn't she?" She was concentrating very hard on the flower, frowning as she plucked it carefully to pieces.

"She's not always with me," said Baley. "Not every minute."

"But most of the time. And whenever you want to——"

Baley said suddenly, "Why did Dr. Leebig try so hard to teach you robotics, do you suppose?"

The dismembered flower consisted now of a stalk and the inner swelling. Gladia twirled it between her fingers, then tossed it away, so that it floated for a moment on the surface of the pond. "I think he wanted me to be his assistant," she said.

"Did he tell you so, Gladia?"

"Toward the end, Elijah. I think he grew impatient. Anyway, he asked me if I didn't think it would be exciting to work in robotics. Naturally, I told him I could think of nothing duller. He was quite angry."

"And he never walked with you again after that."

She said, "You know, I think that may have been it. I suppose his feelings were hurt. Really, though, what could I do?"

"It was before that, though, that you told him about your quarrels with Dr. Delmarre."

Her hands became fists and held so in a tight spasm. Her body held stiffly to its position, head bent and a little to one side. Her voice was unnaturally high. "What quarrels?"

"Your quarrels with your husband. I understand you hated him."

Her face was distorted and blotched as she glared at him. "Who told you that? Jothan?"

"Dr. Leebig mentioned it. I think it's true."

She was shaken. "You're still trying to prove I killed him. I keep thinking you're my friend and you're only—only a detective."

She raised her fists and Baley waited.

He said, "You know you can't touch me."

Her hands dropped and she began crying without a sound. She turned her head away.

Baley bent his own head and closed his eyes, shutting out the disturbing long shadows. He said, "Dr. Delmarre was not a very affectionate man, was he?"

She said in a strangled way, "He was a very busy man."

Baley said, "You *are* affectionate, on the other hand. You find a man interesting. Do you understand?"

"I c-can't help it. I know it's disgusting, but I can't help it. It's even disgusting t-to talk about it."

"You did talk about it to Dr. Leebig, though?"

"I *had* to do something and Jothan was handy and he didn't seem to mind and it made me feel better."

"Was this the reason you quarreled with your husband? Was it that he was cold and unaffectionate and you resented it?"

"Sometimes I hated him." She shrugged her shoulders helplessly. "He was just a good Solarian and we weren't scheduled for ch—for ch——" She broke down.

Baley waited. His own stomach was cold and open air pressed down heavily upon him. When Gladia's sobs grew quieter, he asked, as gently as he could, "Did you kill him, Gladia?"

"N-no." Then, suddenly, as though all resistance had corroded within her: "I haven't told you everything."

"Well, then, please do so now."

"We were quarreling that time, the time he died. The old quarrel. I screamed at him but he never shouted back. He hardly ever even said anything and that just made it worse. I was so angry, so angry. I don't remember after that."

"Jehoshaphat!" Baley swayed slightly and his eyes sought the neutral stone of the bench. "What do you mean you don't remember?"

"I mean he was dead and I was screaming and the robots came——"

"Did you kill him?"

"I don't remember it, Elijah, and I would remember it if I did, wouldn't I? Only I don't remember anything else, either, and I've been so frightened, so frightened. Help me, please, Elijah."

"Don't worry, Gladia. I'll help you." Baley's reeling mind fastened on the murder weapon. What happened to it? It must have been removed. If so, only the murderer could have done it. Since Gladia was found immediately after the murder on the scene, she could not have done it. The murderer would have to be someone else. No matter how it looked to everyone on Solaria, it had to be someone else.

Baley thought sickly: I've got to get back to the house.

He said, "Gladia——"

Somehow he was staring at the sun. It was nearly at the horizon. He had to turn his head to look at it and his eyes locked with a morbid fascination. He had never seen it so. Fat, red, and dim somehow, so that one could look at it without blinding, and see the bleeding clouds above it in thin lines, with one crossing it in a bar of black.

Baley mumbled, "The sun is so red."

He heard Gladia's choked voice say drearily, "It's always red at sunset, red and dying."

Baley had a vision. The sun was moving down to the horizon because the planet's surface was moving away from it, a thousand miles an hour, spinning under that naked sun, spinning with nothing to guard the microbes called men that scurried over its spinning surface, spinning madly forever, spinning—spinning . . .

It was his head that was spinning and the stone bench that was slanting beneath him and the sky heaving, blue, dark blue, and the sun was gone, with the tops of trees and the ground rushing up and Gladia screaming thinly and another sound . . .

16

A Solution Is Offered

BALEY WAS aware first of enclosure, the absence of the open, and then of a face bending over him.

He stared for a moment without recognition. Then: *"Daneel!"*

The robot's face showed no sign of relief or of any other recognizable emotion at being addressed. He said, "It is well that you have recovered consciousness, Partner Elijah. I do not believe you have suffered physical injury."

"I'm all right," said Baley testily, struggling to his elbows. "Jehoshaphat, am I in bed? What for?"

"You have been exposed to the open a number of times today. The effects upon you have been cumulative and you need rest."

"I need a few answers first." Baley looked about and tried to deny to himself that his head was spinning just a little. He did not recognize the room. The curtains were drawn. Lights were comfortably artificial. He was feeling much better. "For instance, where am I?"

"In a room of Mrs. Delmarre's mansion."

"Next, let's get something straight. What are *you* doing here? How did you get away from the robots I set over you?"

Daneel said, "It had seemed to me that you would be displeased at this development and yet in the interests of your safety and of my orders, I felt that I had no choice but——"

"What did you *do*? Jehoshaphat!"

"It seems Mrs. Delmarre attempted to view you some hours ago."

"Yes." Baley remembered Gladia saying as much earlier in the day. "I know that."

"Your order to the robots that held me prisoner was, in your words: 'Do not allow him' (meaning myself) 'to establish contact with other humans or other robots, either by seeing or by viewing.' However, Partner Elijah, you said nothing about forbidding other humans or robots to contact me. You see the distinction?"

Baley groaned.

Daneel said, "No need for distress, Partner Elijah. The flaw in your orders was instrumental in saving your life, since it brought me to the scene. You see, when Mrs. Delmarre viewed me, being allowed to do so by my robot guardians, she asked after you and I answered, quite truthfully, that I did not know of your whereabouts, but that I could attempt to find out. She seemed anxious that I do so. I said I thought it possible you might have left the house temporarily and that I would check that matter and would she, in the meanwhile, order the robots in the room with me, to search the mansion for your presence."

"Wasn't she surprised that you didn't deliver the orders to the robots yourself?"

"I gave her the impression, I believe, that as an Auroran I was not as accustomed to robots as she was; that she might deliver the orders with greater authority and effect a more speedy consummation. Solarians, it is quite clear, are vain of their skill with robots and contemptuous of the ability of natives of other planets to handle them. Is that not your opinion as well, Partner Elijah?"

"And she ordered them away, then?"

"With difficulty. They protested previous orders but, of course, could not state the nature thereof since you had ordered them to tell no one of my own true identity. She overrode them, although the final orders had to be shrilled out in fury."

"And then you left."

"I did, Partner Elijah."

A pity, thought Baley, that Gladia did not consider that episode important enough to relay to him when he viewed her. He said, "It took you long enough to find me, Daneel."

"The robots on Solaria have a network of information through subetheric contact. A skilled Solarian could obtain information readily, but, mediated as it is through millions of individual machines, one such as myself, without experience in the matter, must take time to unearth a single datum. It was better than an hour before the information as to your whereabouts reached me. I lost further time by visiting Dr. Delmarre's place of business after you had departed."

"What were you doing there?"

"Pursuing researches of my own. I regret that this had to be done in your absence, but the exigencies of the investigation left me no choice."

Baley said, "Did you view Klorissa Cantoro, or see her?"

"I viewed her, but from another part of her building, not from our own estate. There were records at the farm I had to see. Ordinarily viewing would have been sufficient, but it might have been inconvenient to remain on our own estate since three robots knew my real nature and might easily have imprisoned me once more."

Baley felt almost well. He swung his legs out of bed and found himself in a kind of nightgown. He stared at it with distaste. "Get me my clothes."

Daneel did so.

As Baley dressed, he said, "Where's Mrs. Delmarre?"

"Under house arrest, Partner Elijah."

"What? By whose order?"

"By my order. She is confined to her bedroom under robotic guard and her right to give orders other than to meet personal needs has been neutralized."

"By yourself?"

"The robots on this estate are not aware of my identity."

Baley finished dressing. "I know the case against Gladia," he said. "She had the opportunity; more of it, in fact, than we thought at first. She did not rush to the scene at the sound of her husband's cry, as she first said. She was there all along."

"Does she claim to have witnessed the murder and seen the murderer?"

"No. She remembers nothing of the crucial moments. That happens sometimes. It turns out, also, that she has a motive."

"What was it, Partner Elijah?"

"One that I had suspected as a possibility from the first. I said to myself, if this were Earth, and Dr. Delmarre were as he was described to be and Gladia Delmarre as she seemed to be, I would say that she was in love with him, or had been, and that he was in love only with himself. The difficulty was to tell whether Solarians felt love or reacted to love in any Earthly sense. My judgment as to their emotions and reactions wasn't to be trusted. It was why I had to see a few. *Not* view them, but see them."

"I do not follow you, Partner Elijah."

"I don't know if I can explain it to you. These people have their gene possibilities carefully plotted before birth and the actual gene distribution tested after birth."

"I know that."

"But genes aren't everything. Environment counts too, and environment can bend into actual psychosis where genes indicate only a potentiality for a particular psychosis. Did you notice Gladia's interest in Earth?"

"I remarked upon it, Partner Elijah, and considered it an assumed interest designed to influence your opinions."

"Suppose it were a real interest, even a fascination. Suppose there were something about Earth's crowds that excited her. Suppose she were attracted against her will by something she had been taught to consider filthy. There was possible abnormality. I had to test it by seeing Solarians and noticing how they reacted to it, and seeing her and noticing how *she* reacted to it. It was why I had to get away from you, Daneel, at any cost. It was why I had to abandon viewing as a method for carrying on the investigation."

"You did not explain this, Partner Elijah."

"Would the explanation have helped against what you conceived your duty under First Law to be?"

Daneel was silent.

Baley said, "The experiment worked. I saw or tried to see several people. An old sociologist tried to see me and had to give up midway. A roboticist refused to see me at all even under terrific force. The bare possibility sent him into an almost infantile frenzy. He sucked his finger and wept. Dr. Delmarre's assistant was used to personal presence in the way of her profession and so she tolerated me, but at twenty feet only. Gladia, on the other hand——"

"Yes, Partner Elijah?"

"Gladia consented to see me without more than a slight hesitation. She tolerated my presence easily and actually showed signs of decreasing strain as time went on. It all fits into a pattern of psychosis. She didn't mind seeing me; she was interested in Earth; she might have felt an abnormal interest in her husband. All of it could be explained by a strong and, for this world, psychotic interest in the personal presence of members of the opposite sex. Dr. Delmarre, himself, was not the type to encourage such a feeling or co-operate with it. It must have been very frustrating for her."

Daneel nodded. "Frustrating enough for murder in a moment of passion."

"In spite of everything, I don't think so, Daneel."

"Are you perhaps being influenced by extraneous motives of your own, Partner Elijah? Mrs. Delmarre is an attractive woman and you are an Earthman in whom a preference for the personal presence of an attractive woman is not psychotic."

"I have better reasons," said Baley uneasily. (Daneel's cool glance was too penetrating and soul-dissecting by half. Jehoshaphat! The thing was only a machine.) He said, "If she were the murderess of her husband, she would also have to be the attempted murderess of Gruer." He had almost the impulse to explain the way murder could be manipulated through robots, but held back. He was not sure how Daneel would react to a theory that made unwitting murderers of robots.

Daneel said, "And the attempted murderess of yourself as well."

Baley frowned. He had had no intention of telling Daneel of the poisoned arrow that had missed; no intention of strengthening the other's already too strong protective complex vis-à-vis himself.

He said angrily, "What did Klorissa tell you?" He ought to have warned her to keep quiet, but then, how was he to know that Daneel would be about, asking questions?

Daneel said calmly, "Mrs. Cantoro had nothing to do with the matter. I witnessed the murder attempt myself."

Baley was thoroughly confused. "You were nowhere about."

Daneel said, "I caught you myself and brought you here an hour ago."

"What are you talking about?"

"Do you not remember, Partner Elijah? It was almost a perfect murder. Did not Mrs. Delmarre suggest that you go into the open? I was not a witness to that, but I feel certain she did."

"She did suggest it. Yes."

"She may even have enticed you to leave the house."

Baley thought of the "portrait" of himself, of the enclosing gray walls. Could it have been clever psychology? Could a Solarian have that much intuitive understanding of the psychology of an Earthman?"

"No," he said.

Daneel said, "Was it she who suggested you go down to the ornamental pond and sit on the bench?"

"Well, yes."

"Does it occur to you that she might have been watching you, noticing your gathering dizziness?"

"She asked once or twice if I wanted to go back."

"She might not have meant it seriously. She might have been watching you turn sicker on that bench. She might even have pushed you, or perhaps a push wasn't necessary. At the moment I reached you and caught you in my arms, you were in the process of falling backward off the stone bench and into three feet of water, in which you would surely have drowned."

For the first time Baley recalled those last fugitive sensations. "Jehoshaphat!"

"Moreover," said Daneel with calm relentlessness, "Mrs. Delmarre sat beside you, watching you fall, without a move to stop you. Nor would she have attempted to pull you out of the water. She would have let you drown. She might have called a robot, but the robot would surely have arrived too late. And afterward, she would explain merely that, of course, it was impossible for her to touch you even to save your life."

True enough, thought Baley. No one would question her inability to touch a human being. The surprise, if any, would come at her ability to be as close to one as she was.

Daneel said, "You see, then, Partner Elijah, that her guilt can scarcely be in question. You stated that she would have to be the attempted murderess of Agent Gruer as though this were an argument against her guilt. You see now that she must have been. Her only motive to murder you was the same as her motive for trying to murder Gruer; the necessity of getting rid of an embarrassingly persistent investigator of the first murder."

Baley said, "The whole sequence might have been an innocent one. She might never have realized how the outdoors would affect me."

"She studied Earth. She knew the peculiarities of Earthmen."

"I assured her I had been outdoors today and that I was growing used to it."

"She may have known better."

Baley pounded fist against palm. "You're making her too clever. It doesn't fit and I don't believe it. In any case, no murder accusation can stick unless and until the absence of the murder weapon can be accounted for."

Daneel looked steadily at the Earthman, "I can do that, too, Partner Elijah."

Baley looked at his robot partner with a stunned expression. "How?"

"Your reasoning, you will remember, Partner Elijah, was this. Were Mrs. Delmarre the murderess, then the weapon, whatever it was, must have remained at the scene of the murder. The robots, appearing almost at once, saw no sign of such a weapon, hence it must have been removed from the scene, hence the murderer must have removed it, hence the murderer could not be Mrs. Delmarre. Is all that correct?"

"Correct."

"Yet," continued the robot, "there is one place where the robots did not look for the weapon."

"Where?"

"Under Mrs. Delmarre. She was lying in a faint, brought on by the excitement and passion of the moment, whether murderess or not, and the weapon, whatever it was, lay under her and out of sight."

Baley said, "Then the weapon would have been discovered as soon as she was moved."

"Exactly," said Daneel, "but she was not moved by the robots. She herself told us yesterday at dinner that Dr. Thool ordered the robots to put a pillow under her head and leave her. She was first moved by Dr. Altim Thool, himself, when he arrived to examine her."

"So?"

"It follows, therefore, Partner Elijah, that a new possibility arises. Mrs. Delmarre was the murderess, the weapon was at the scene of the crime, but Dr. Thool carried it off and disposed of it to protect Mrs. Delmarre."

Baley felt contemptuous. He had almost been seduced into expecting something reasonable. He said, "Completely motiveless. Why should Dr. Thool do such a thing?"

"For a very good reason. You remember Mrs. Delmarre's remarks concerning him: 'He always treated me since I was a child and was always so friendly and kind.' I wondered if he might have some motive for being particularly concerned about her. It was for that reason that I visited the baby farm and inspected the records. What I had merely guessed at as a possibility turned out to be the truth."

"What?"

"Dr. Altim Thool was the father of Gladia Delmarre, and what is more, he knew of the relationship."

Baley had no thought of disbelieving the robot. He felt only a deep chagrin that it had been Robot Daneel Olivaw and not himself that had carried through the necessary piece of logical analysis. Even so, it was not complete.

He said, "Have you spoken to Dr. Thool?"

"Yes. I have placed him under house arrest, also."

"What does he say?"

"He admits that he is the father of Mrs. Delmarre. I confronted him with the records of the fact and the records of his inquiries into her health when she was a youngster. As a doctor, he was allowed more leeway in this respect than another Solarian might have been allowed."

"Why should he have inquired into her health?"

"I have considered that, too, Partner Elijah. He was an old man when he was given special permission to have an additional child and, what is more, he succeeded in producing one. He considers this a tribute to his genes and to his physical fitness. He is prouder of the result, perhaps, than is quite customary on this world. Moreover, his position as physician, a profession little regarded on Solaria because it involves personal presences, made it the more important to him to nurture this sense of pride. For that reason, he maintained unobtrusive contact with his offspring."

"Does Gladia know anything of it?"

"As far as Dr. Thool is aware, Partner Elijah, she does not."

Baley said, "Does Thool admit removing the weapon?"

"No. That he does not."

"Then you've got nothing, Daneel."

"Nothing?"

"Unless you can find the weapon and prove he took it, or at the very least induce him to confess, you have no evidence. A chain of deduction is pretty, but it isn't evidence."

"The man would scarcely confess without considerable questioning of a type I myself could not carry through. His daughter is dear to him."

"Not at all," said Baley. "His feeling for his daughter is not at all what you and I are accustomed to. Solaria is different!"

He strode the length of the room and back, letting himself cool. He said, "Daneel, you have worked out a perfect exercise in logic, but none of it is reasonable, just the same." (Logical but not reasonable. Wasn't that the definition of a robot?)

He went on, "Dr. Thool is an old man and past his best years, regardless of whether he was capable of siring a daughter thirty years or so ago. Even Spacers get senile. Picture him then examining his daughter in a faint and his son-in-law dead by violence. Can you imagine the unusual nature of the situation for him? Can you suppose he could have remained master of himself? So much the master of himself, in fact, as to carry out a series of amazing actions?

"Look! First, he would have had to notice a weapon under his daughter, one that must have been so well covered by her body that the robots never noticed it. Secondly, from whatever small scrap of object he noted, he must have deduced the presence of the weapon and seen at once that if he could but sneak off with that weapon, unseen, a murder accusation against his daughter would be hard to substantiate. That's pretty subtle thinking for an old man in a panic. Then, thirdly, he would have had to carry the plan through, also tough for an old man in a panic. And now, lastly, he would have to dare to compound the felony further by sticking to his lie. It all may be the result of logical thinking, but none of it is reasonable."

Daneel said, "Do you have an alternate solution to the crime, Partner Elijah?"

Baley had sat down during the course of his last speech and now he tried to rise again, but a combination of weariness and the depth of the chair defeated him. He held out his hand petulantly. "Give me a hand, will you, Daneel?"

Daneel stared at his own hand. "I beg your pardon, Partner Elijah?"

Baley silently swore at the other's literal mind and said, "Help me out of the chair."

Daneel's strong arm lifted him out of the chair effortlessly.

Baley said, "Thanks. No, I haven't an alternate solution. At least, I have, but the whole thing hinges on the location of the weapon."

He walked impatiently to the heavy curtains that lined most of one wall and lifted a corner without quite realizing what he was doing. He stared at the black patch of glass until he became aware of the fact that he was looking out into the early night, and then dropped the curtain just as Daneel, approaching quietly, took it out of his fingers.

In the split fraction of a moment in which Baley watched the robot's hand take the curtain away from him with the loving caution of a mother protecting her child from the fire, a revolution took place within him.

He snatched the curtain back, yanking it out of Daneel's grasp. Throwing his full weight against it, he tore it away from the window, leaving shreds behind.

"Partner Elijah!" said Daneel softly. "Surely you know now what the open will do to you."

"I know," said Baley, "what it will do *for* me."

He stared out the window. There was nothing to see, only blackness, but that blackness was open air. It was unbroken, unobstructed space, even if unlit, and he was facing it.

And for the first time he faced it freely. It was no longer bravado, or perverse curiosity, or the pathway to a solution of a murder. He faced it because he knew he wanted to and because he needed to. That made all the difference.

Walls were crutches! Darkness and crowds were crutches! He must have thought them so, unconsciously, and hated them even when he most thought he loved and needed them. Why else had he so resented Gladia's gray enclosure of his portrait?

He felt himself filling with a sense of victory, and, as though victory were contagious, a new thought came, bursting like an inner shout.

Baley turned dizzily to Daneel. "I know," he whispered. "Jehoshaphat! I know!"

"Know what, Partner Elijah?"

"I know what happened to the weapon; I know who is responsible. All at once, everything falls into place."

17

A Meeting Is Held

DANEEL WOULD allow no immediate action.

"Tomorrow!" he had said with respectful firmness. "That is my suggestion, Partner Elijah. It is late and you are in need of rest."

Baley had to admit the truth of it, and besides there was the need of preparation; a considerable quantity of it. He had the solution of the murder, he felt sure of that, but it rested on deduction, as much as had Daneel's theory, and it was worth as little as evidence. Solarians would have to help him.

And if he were to face them, one Earthman against half a dozen Spacers, he would have to be in full control. That meant rest and preparation.

Yet he would not sleep. He was certain he would not sleep. Not all the softness of the special bed set up for him by smoothly functioning robots nor all the soft perfume and softer music in the special room of Gladia's mansion would help. He was sure of it.

Daneel sat unobtrusively in one darkened corner.

Baley said, "Are you still afraid of Gladia?"

The robot said, "I do not think it wise to allow you to sleep alone and unprotected."

"Well, have your way. Are you clear as to what I want you to do, Daneel?"

"I am, Partner Elijah."

"You have no reservations under the First Law, I hope."

"I have some with respect to the conference you wish arranged. Will you be armed and careful of your own safety?"

"I assure you, I will."

Daneel delivered himself of a sigh that was somehow so human that for a moment Baley found himself trying to penetrate the darkness that he might study the machine-perfect face of the other.

Daneel said, "I have not always found human behavior logical."

"We need Three Laws of our own," said Baley, "but I'm glad we don't have them."

He stared at the ceiling. A great deal depended on Daneel and yet he could tell him very little of the whole truth. Robots were too involved. The planet, Aurora, had its reasons for sending a robot as representative of their interests, but it was a mistake. Robots had their limitations.

Still, if all went right, this could all be over in twelve hours. He could be heading back to Earth in twenty-four, bearing hope. A strange kind of hope. A kind he could scarcely believe himself, yet it was Earth's way out. It must be Earth's way out.

Earth! New York! Jessie and Ben! The comfort and familiarity and dearness of home!

He dwelled on it, half asleep, and the thought of Earth failed to conjure the comfort he expected. There was an estrangement between himself and the Cities.

And at some unknown point in time it all faded and he slept.

Baley, having slept and then wakened, showered and dressed. Physically he was quite prepared. Yet he was unsure. It was not that his reasoning seemed any less cogent to himself in the pallor of morning. It was rather the necessity of facing Solarians.

Could he be sure of their reactions after all? Or would he still be working blind?

Gladia was the first to appear. It was simple for her, of course. She was on an intramural circuit, since she was in the mansion itself. She was pale and expressionless, in a white gown that draped her into a cold statue.

She stared helplessly at Baley. Baley smiled back gently and she seemed to take comfort from that.

One by one, they appeared now. Attlebish, the Acting Head of Security, appeared next after Gladia, lean and haughty, his large chin set in disapproval. Then Leebig, the roboticist, impatient and angry, his weak eyelid fluttering periodically. Quemot, the sociologist, a little tired, but smiling at Baley out of deep-set eyes in a condescending way, as though to say: We have seen one another, we have been intimate.

Klorissa Cantoro, when she appeared, seemed uneasy in the presence of the others. She glanced at Gladia for a moment with an audible sniff, then stared at the floor. Dr. Thool, the physician, appeared last. He looked haggard, almost sick.

They were all there, all but Gruer, who was slowly recovering and for whom attendance was physically impossible. (Well, thought Baley, we'll do without him.) All were dressed formally; all sat in rooms that were well curtained into enclosure.

Daneel had arranged matters well. Baley hoped fervently that what remained for Daneel to do would work as well.

Baley looked from one Spacer to the other. His heart thudded. Each figure viewed him out of a different room and the clash of lighting, furniture, and wall decoration was dizzying.

Baley said, "I want to discuss the matter of the killing of Dr. Rikaine Delmarre under the heading of motive, opportunity, and means, in that order——"

Attlebish interrupted. "Will this be a long speech?"

Baley said sharply, "It may be. I have been called here to investigate a murder and such a job is my specialty and my profession. I know best how to go about it." (Take nothing from them now, he thought, or this whole thing won't work. Dominate! Dominate!)

He went on, making his words as sharp and incisive as he could. "Motive first. In a way, motive is the most unsatisfactory of the three items. Opportunity and means are objective. They can be investigated factually. Motive is subjective. It may be something that can be observed by others; revenge for a known humiliation, for instance. But it may also be completely unobservable; an irrational, homicidal hate on the part of a well-disciplined person who never lets it show.

"Now almost all of you have told me at one time or another that you believed Gladia Delmarre to have committed the crime. Certainly, no one has suggested an alternate suspect. Has Gladia a motive? Dr. Leebig suggested one. He said that Gladia quarreled frequently with her husband and Gladia later admitted this to me. The rage that can arise out of a quarrel can, conceivably, move a person to murder. Very well.

"The question remains, though, whether she is the only one with a motive. I wonder. Dr. Leebig, himself——"

The roboticist almost jumped. His hand extended rigidly in the direction of Baley. "Watch what you say, Earthman."

"I am only theorizing," said Baley coldly. "You, Dr. Leebig, were working with Dr. Delmarre on new robot models. You are the best man in Solaria as far as robotics is concerned. You say so and I believe it."

Leebig smiled with open condescension.

Baley went on. "But I have heard that Dr. Delmarre was about to break off relations with you for matters concerning yourself of which he disapproved."

"False! False!"

"Perhaps. But what if it were true? Wouldn't you have a motive to get rid of him before he humiliated you publicly by breaking with you? I have a feeling you could not easily bear such humiliation."

Baley went on rapidly to give Leebig no chance to retort. "And you, Mrs. Cantoro. Dr. Delmarre's death leaves you in charge of fetal engineering, a responsible position."

"Skies above, we talked about that before," cried Klorissa in anguish.

"I know we did, but it's a point that must be considered, anyway. As for Dr. Quemot, he played chess with Dr. Delmarre regularly. Perhaps he grew annoyed at losing too many games."

The sociologist interposed quietly. "Losing a chess game is insufficient motive surely, Plainclothesman."

"It depends on how seriously you take your chess. Motives can seem all the world to the murderer and completely insignificant to everyone else. Well, it doesn't matter. My point is that motive alone is insufficient. Anyone can have a motive, particularly for the murder of a man such as Dr. Delmarre."

"What do you mean by that remark," demanded Quemot in indignation.

"Why, only that Dr. Delmarre was a 'good Solarian.' You all described him as such. He rigidly fulfilled all the requirements of Solarian custom. He was an ideal man, almost an abstraction. Who could feel love, or even liking, for such a man? A man without weaknesses serves only to make everyone else conscious of his own imperfections. A primitive poet named Tennyson once wrote: 'He is all fault who has no fault at all.'"

"No one would kill a man for being too good," said Klorissa, frowning.

"You little know," said Baley, and went on without amplification. "Dr. Delmarre was aware of a conspiracy on Solaria, or thought he was; a conspiracy that was preparing an assault on the rest of the Galaxy for purposes of conquest. He was interested in preventing that. For that reason, those concerned in the conspiracy might find it necessary to do away with him. Anyone here could be a member of the conspiracy, including, to be sure, Mrs. Delmarre, but including even the Acting Head of Security, Corwin Attlebish."

"I?" said Attlebish, unmoved.

"You certainly attempted to end the investigation as soon as Gruer's mishap put you in charge."

Baley took a few slow sips at his drink (straight from its original container, untouched by human hands others than his own, or robotic hands, either) and gathered his strength. So far, this was a waiting game, and he was thankful the Solarians were sitting still for it. They hadn't the Earthman's experience of dealing with people at close quarters. They weren't in-fighters.

He said, "Opportunity next. It is the general opinion that only Mrs. Delmarre had opportunity since only she could approach her husband in actual personal presence.

"Are we sure of that? Suppose someone other than Mrs. Delmarre had made up his or her mind to kill Dr. Delmarre? Would not such a desperate resolution make the discomfort of personal presence secondary? If any of you were set on murder, wouldn't you bear personal presence just long enough to do the job? Couldn't you sneak into the Delmarre mansion——"

Attlebish interposed frigidly. "You are ignorant of the matter, Earthman. Whether we would or would not doesn't matter. The fact is that Dr. Delmarre himself would not allow seeing, I assure you. If anyone came into his personal presence, regardless of how valued and long-standing a friendship there was between them, Dr. Delmarre would order him away and, if necessary, call robots to help with the ejection."

"True," said Baley, "*if* Dr. Delmarre were aware that personal presence was involved."

"What do you mean by that?" demanded Dr. Thool in surprise, his voice quavering.

"When you treated Mrs. Delmarre at the scene of the murder," replied Baley, looking full at his questioner, "she assumed you were viewing her, until you actually touched her. So she told me and so I believe. I am, myself, accustomed only to seeing. When I arrived at Solaria and met Security Head Gruer, I assumed I was seeing him. When at the end of our interview, Gruer disappeared, I was taken completely by surprise.

"Now assume the reverse. Suppose that for all a man's adult life, he had been viewing only; never seeing anyone, except on rare occasions his wife. Now suppose someone other than his wife walked up to him in personal presence. Would he not automatically assume that it was a matter of viewing, particularly if a robot had been instructed to advise Delmarre that viewing contact was being set up?"

"Not for a minute," said Quemot. "The sameness of background would give it away."

"Maybe, but how many of you are aware of background now? There would be a minute or so, at least, before Dr. Delmarre would grow aware that something was wrong and in that time, his friend, whoever he was, could walk up to him, raise a club, and bring it down."

"Impossible," said Quemot stubbornly.

"I think not," said Baley. "I think opportunity must be canceled out as absolute proof that Mrs. Delmarre is the murderess. She had opportunity, but so might others."

Baley waited again. He felt perspiration on his forehead, but wiping it away would have made him look weak. He must maintain absolute charge of the proceedings. The person at whom he was aiming must be placed in self-convinced inferiority. It was hard for an Earthman to do that to a Spacer.

Baley looked from face to face and decided that matters were at least progressing satisfactorily. Even Attlebish looked quite humanly concerned.

"And so we come," he said, "to means, and that is the most puzzling factor of all. The weapon with which the murder was committed was never found."

"We know that," said Attlebish. "If it were not for that point, we would have considered the case against Mrs. Delmarre conclusive. We would never have required an investigation."

"Perhaps," said Baley. "Let's analyze the matter of means, then.

There are two possibilities. Either Mrs. Delmarre committed the murder, or someone else did. If Mrs. Delmarre committed the murder, the weapon would have had to remain at the scene of the crime, unless it were removed later. It has been suggested by my partner, Mr. Olivaw of Aurora, who is not present at the moment, that Dr. Thool had the opportunity to remove the weapon. I ask Dr. Thool now, in the presence of all of us, if he did this, if he removed a weapon while examining the unconscious Mrs. Delmarre?"

Dr. Thool was shaking. "No, no. I swear it. I'll abide any questioning. I swear I removed nothing."

Baley said, "Is there anyone who wishes to suggest at this point that Dr. Thool is lying?"

There was a silence, during which Leebig looked at an object outside of Baley's field of vision and muttered something about the time.

Baley said, "The second possibility is that someone else committed the crime and carried the weapon off with him. But if that were so, one must ask why. Carrying the weapon away is an advertisement of the fact that Mrs. Delmarre was not the murderess. If an outsider were the murderer, he would have to be a complete imbecile not to leave the weapon with the corpse to convict Mrs. Delmarre. Either way, then, *the weapon must be there!* Yet it was not seen."

Attlebish said, "Do you take us for fools or for blind men?"

"I take you for Solarians," said Baley calmly, "and therefore incapable of recognizing the particular weapon that was left at the scene of the crime as a weapon."

"I don't understand a word," muttered Klorissa in distress.

Even Gladia, who had scarcely moved a muscle during the course of the meeting, was staring at Baley in surprise.

Baley said, "Dead husband and unconscious wife were not the only individuals on the scene. There was also a disorganized robot."

"Well?" said Leebig angrily.

"Isn't it obvious, then, that, in having eliminated the impossible, what remains, however improbable, is the truth. The robot at the scene of the crime was the murder weapon, a murder weapon none of you could recognize by force of your training."

They all talked at once; all but Gladia, who simply stared.

Baley raised his arms. "Hold it. Quiet! Let me explain!" And once again he told the story of the attempt on Gruer's life and the method by which it could have been accomplished. This time he added the attempt on his own life at the baby farm.

Leebig said impatiently, "I suppose that was managed by having one robot poison an arrow without knowing it was using poison, and having a second robot hand the poisoned arrow to the boy after telling him that you were an Earthman, without its knowing that the arrow was poisoned."

"Something like that. Both robots would be completely instructed."

"Very farfetched," said Leebig.

Quemot was pale and looked as though he might be sick at any moment. "No Solarian could possibly use robots to harm a human."

"Maybe so," said Baley with a shrug, "but the point is that robots can be so manipulated. Ask Dr. Leebig. He is the roboticist."

Leebig said, "It does not apply to the murder of Dr. Delmarre. I told you that yesterday. How can anyone arrange to have a robot smash a man's skull?"

"Shall I explain how?"

"Do so if you can."

Baley said, "It was a new-model robot that Dr. Delmarre was testing. The significance of that wasn't plain to me until last evening, when I had occasion to say to a robot, in asking for his help in rising out of a chair, 'Give me a hand!' The robot looked at his own hand in confusion as though he thought he was expected to detach it and give it to me. I had to repeat my order less idiomatically. But it reminded me of something Dr. Leebig had told me earlier that day. There was experimentation among robots with replaceable limbs.

"Suppose this robot that Dr. Delmarre had been testing was one such, capable of using any of a number of interchangeable limbs of various shapes for different kinds of specialized tasks. Suppose the murderer knew this and suddenly said to the robot, 'Give me your arm.' The robot would detach its arm and give it to him. The detached arm would make a splendid weapon. With Dr. Delmarre dead, it could be snapped back into place."

Stunned horror gave way to a babble of objection as Baley talked. His last sentence had to be shouted, and, even so, was all but drowned out.

Attlebish, face flushed, raised himself from his chair and stepped forward. "Even if what you say is so, then Mrs. Delmarre is the murderess. She was there, she quarreled with him, she would be watching her husband working with the robot, and would know of the replaceable-limb situation—which I don't believe, by the way. No matter what you do, Earthman, everything points to her."

Gladia began to weep softly.

Baley did not look at her. He said, "On the contrary, it is easy to show that, whoever committed the murder, Mrs. Delmarre did not."

Jothan Leebig suddenly folded his arms and allowed an expression of contempt to settle on his face.

Baley caught that and said, "You'll help me do so, Dr. Leebig. As a roboticist, you know that maneuvering robots into actions such as indirect murder takes enormous skill. I had occasion yesterday to try to put an individual under house arrest. I gave three robots detailed instructions intended to keep this individual safe. It was a simple thing, but I am a clumsy man with robots. There were loopholes in my instructions and my prisoner escaped."

"Who was the prisoner?" demanded Attlebish.

"Beside the point," said Baley impatiently. "What *is* the point is the fact that amateurs can't handle robots well. And some Solarians may be pretty amateurish as Solarians go. For instance, what does Gladia Delmarre know about robotics? . . . Well, Dr. Leebig?"

"What?" The roboticist stared.

"You tried to teach Mrs. Delmarre robotics. What kind of a pupil was she? Did she learn anything?"

Leebig looked about uneasily. "She didn't . . ." and stalled.

"She was completely hopeless, wasn't she? Or would you prefer not to answer?"

Leebig said stiffly, "She might have pretended ignorance."

"Are you prepared to say, as a roboticist, that you think Mrs. Delmarre is sufficiently skilled to drive robots to indirect murder?"

"How can I answer that?"

"Let me put it another way. Whoever tried to have me killed at the baby farm must have had to locate me by using interrobot communications. After all, I told no human where I was going and only the robots who conveyed me from point to point knew of my whereabouts. My partner, Daneel Olivaw, managed to trace me later in the day, but only with considerable difficulty. The murderer, on the other hand, must have done it easily, since, in addition to locating me, he had to arrange for arrow poisoning and arrow shooting, all before I left the farm and moved on. Would Mrs. Delmarre have the skill to do that?"

Corwin Attlebish leaned forward. "Who do you suggest would have the necessary skill, Earthman?"

Baley said, "Dr. Jothan Leebig is self-admittedly the best robot man on the planet."

"Is that an accusation?" cried Leebig.

"Yes!" shouted Baley.

The fury in Leebig's eyes faded slowly. It was replaced not by calm, exactly, but by a kind of clamped-down tension. He said, "I studied the Delmarre robot after the murder. It had no detachable limbs. At least, they were detachable only in the usual sense of requiring special tools and expert handling. So the robot wasn't the weapon used in killing Delmarre and you have no argument."

Baley said, "Who else can vouch for the truth of your statement?"

"My word is not to be questioned."

"It is here. I'm accusing you, and your unsupported word concerning the robot is valueless. If someone else will bear you out, that would be different. Incidentally, you disposed of that robot quickly. Why?"

"There was no reason to keep it. It was completely disorganized. It was useless."

"Why?"

Leebig shook his finger at Baley and said violently, "You asked me that once before, Earthman, and I told you why. It had witnessed a murder which it had been powerless to stop."

"And you told me that that always brought about complete collapse; that that was a universal rule. Yet when Gruer was poisoned, the robot that had presented him with the poisoned drink was harmed only to the extent of a limp and a lisp. It had actually itself been the agent of what looked like murder at the moment, and not merely a witness, and yet it retained enough sanity to be questioned.

"This robot, the robot in the Delmarre case, must therefore have been still more intimately concerned with murder than the Gruer robot. This Delmarre robot must have had its own arm used as the murder weapon."

"All nonsense," gasped out Leebig. "You know nothing about robotics."

Baley said, "That's as may be. But I will suggest that Security Head Attlebish impound the records of your robot factory and maintenance shop. Perhaps we can find out whether you have built robots with detachable limbs and, if so, whether any were sent to Dr. Delmarre, and, if so, when."

"No one will tamper with my records," cried Leebig.

"Why? If you have nothing to hide, why?"

"But why on Solaria should I want to kill Delmarre? Tell me that. What's my motive?"

"I can think of two," said Baley. "You were friendly with Mrs. Delmarre. Overly friendly. Solarians are human, after a fashion. You never consorted with women, but that didn't keep you immune from, shall we say, animal urges. You saw Mrs. Delmarre—I beg your pardon, you viewed her—when she was dressed rather informally and——"

"No," cried Leebig in agony.

And Gladia whispered energetically, "No."

"Perhaps you didn't recognize the nature of your feelings yourself," said Baley, "or if you had a dim notion of it, you despised yourself for your weakness, and hated Mrs. Delmarre for inspiring it. And yet you might have hated Delmarre, too, for having her. You did ask Mrs. Delmarre to be your assistant. You compromised with your libido that far. She refused and your hatred was the keener for that. By killing Dr. Delmarre in such a way as to throw suspicion on Mrs. Delmarre, you could be avenged on both at once."

"Who would believe that cheap, melodramatic filth?" demanded Leebig in a hoarse whisper. "Another Earthman, another animal, maybe. No Solarian."

"I don't depend on that motive," said Baley. "I think it was there, unconsciously, but you had a plainer motive, too. Dr. Rikaine Delmarre was in the way of your plans, and had to be removed."

"What plans?" demanded Leebig.

"Your plans aiming at the conquest of the Galaxy, Dr. Leebig," said Baley.

18

A Question Is Answered

"THE EARTHMAN is mad," cried Leebig, turning to the others. "Isn't that obvious?"

Some stared at Leebig wordlessly, some at Baley.

Baley gave them no chance to come to decisions. He said, "You know better, Dr. Leebig. Dr. Delmarre was going to break off with you. Mrs. Delmarre thought it was because you wouldn't marry. I don't think so. Dr. Delmarre himself was planning a future in which ectogenesis would be possible and marriage unnecessary. But Dr. Delmarre was working with you; he would know, and guess, more about your work than anyone else. He would know if you were attempting dangerous experiments and he would try to stop you. He hinted about such matters to Agent Gruer, but gave no details, because he was not yet certain of the details. Obviously, you discovered his suspicions and killed him."

"Mad!" said Leebig again. "I will have nothing more to do with this."

But Attlebish interrupted. "Hear him out, Leebig!"

Baley bit his lip to keep from a premature display of satisfaction at the obvious lack of sympathy in the Security Head's voice. He said, "In the same discussion with me in which you mentioned robots with detachable limbs, Dr. Leebig, you mentioned spaceships with built-in positronic brains. You were definitely talking too much then. Was it that you thought I was only an Earthman and incapable of understanding the implications of robotics? Or was it that you had just been threatened with personal presence, had the threat lifted, and were a little delirious with relief? In any case, Dr.

Quemot had already told me that the secret weapon of Solaria against the Outer Worlds was the positronic robot."

Quemot, thus unexpectedly referred to, started violently, and cried, "I meant——"

"You meant it sociologically, I know. But it gives rise to thoughts. Consider a spaceship with a built-in positronic brain as compared to a manned spaceship. A manned spaceship could not use robots in active warfare. A robot could not destroy humans on enemy spaceships or on enemy worlds. It could not grasp the distinction between friendly humans and enemy humans.

"Of course, a robot could be told that the opposing spaceship had no humans aboard. It could be told that it was an uninhabited planet that was being bombarded. That would be difficult to manage. A robot could see that its own ship carried humans; it would know its own world held humans. It would assume that the same was true of enemy ships and worlds. It would take a real expert in robotics, such as you, Dr. Leebig, to handle them properly in that case, and there are very few such experts.

"But a spaceship that was equipped with its own positronic brain would cheerfully attack any ship it was directed to attack, it seems to me. It would naturally assume all other ships were unmanned. A positronic-brained ship could easily be made incapable of receiving messages from enemy ships that might undeceive it. With its weapons and defenses under the immediate control of a positronic brain, it would be more maneuverable than any manned ship. With no room necessary for crewmen, for supplies, for water or air purifiers, it could carry more armor, more weapons and be more invulnerable than any ordinary ship. One ship with a positronic brain could defeat fleets of ordinary ships. Am I wrong?"

The last question was shot at Dr. Leebig, who had risen from his seat and was standing, rigid, almost cataleptic with—what? Anger? Horror?

There was no answer. No answer could have been heard. Something tore loose and the others were yelling madly. Klorissa had the face of a Fury and even Gladia was on her feet, her small fist beating the air threateningly.

And all had turned on Leebig.

Baley relaxed and closed his eyes. He tried for just a few moments to unknot his muscles, unfreeze his tendons.

It had worked. He had pressed the right button at last. Quemot had made an analogy between the Solarian robots and the Spartan Helots. He said the robots could not revolt so that the Solarians could relax.

But what if some human threatened to teach the robots how to harm humans; to make them, in other words, capable of revolting?

Would that not be the ultimate crime? On a world such as Solaria would not every last inhabitant turn fiercely against anyone even suspected of making a robot capable of harming a human; on Solaria, where robots outnumbered humans by twenty thousand to one?

Attlebish cried, "You are under arrest. You are absolutely forbidden to touch your books or records until the government has a chance to inspect them——" He went on, almost incoherent, scarcely heard in the pandemonium.

A robot approached Baley. "A message, master, from the master Olivaw."

Baley took the message gravely, turned, and cried, "One moment."

His voice had an almost magical effect. All turned to look at him solemnly and in no face (outside Leebig's frozen glare) was there any sign of anything but the most painful attention to the Earthman.

Baley said, "It is foolish to expect Dr. Leebig to leave his records untouched while waiting for some official to reach them. So even before this interview began, my partner, Daneel Olivaw, left for Dr. Leebig's estate. I have just heard from him. He is on the grounds now and will be with Dr. Leebig in a moment in order that he may be put under restraint."

"*Restraint!*" howled Leebig in an almost animal terror. His eyes widened into staring holes in his head. "Someone coming here? Personal presence? No! No!" The second "No" was a shriek.

"You will not be harmed," said Baley coldly, "if you co-operate."

"But I won't see him. I can't see him." The roboticist fell to his knees without seeming aware of the motion. He put his hands together in a desperate clasped gesture of appeal. "What do you want? Do you want a confession? Delmarre's robot had detachable limbs. Yes. Yes. Yes. I arranged Gruer's poisoning. I arranged the arrow meant for you. I even planned the spaceships as you said. I haven't succeeded, but, yes, I planned it. Only keep the man away. Don't let him come. Keep him away!"

He was babbling.

Baley nodded. Another right button. The threat of personal presence would do more to induce confession than any physical torture.

But then, at some noise or movement outside the field of sound or vision of any of the others, Leebig's head twisted and his mouth opened. He lifted a pair of hands, holding something off.

"Away," he begged. "Go away. Don't come. Please don't come. Please——"

He scrambled away on hands and knees, then his hand went suddenly to a pocket in his jacket. It came out with something and moved rapidly to his mouth. Swaying twice, he fell prone.

Baley wanted to cry: You fool, it isn't a human that's approaching; only one of the robots you love.

Daneel Olivaw darted into the field of vision and for a moment stared down at the crumpled figure.

Baley held his breath. If Daneel should realize it was his own pseudo humanity that had killed Leebig, the effect on his First Law-enslaved brain might be drastic.

But Daneel only knelt and his delicate fingers touched Leebig here and there. Then he lifted Leebig's head as though it were infinitely precious to him, cradling it, caressing it.

His beautifully chiseled face stared out at the others and he whispered, "A human is dead!"

Baley was expecting her; she had asked for a last interview; but his eyes widened when she appeared.

He said, "I'm seeing you."

"Yes," said Gladia, "how can you tell?"

"You're wearing gloves."

"Oh." She looked at her hands in confusion. Then, softly, "Do you mind?"

"No, of course not. But why have you decided to see, rather than view?"

"Well"—she smiled weakly—"I've got to get used to it, don't I, Elijah? I mean, if I'm going to Aurora."

"Then it's all arranged?"

"Mr. Olivaw seems to have influence. It's all arranged. I'll never come back."

"Good. You'll be happier, Gladia. I know you will."

"I'm a little afraid."

"I know. It will mean seeing all the time and you won't have all the comforts you had on Solaria. But you'll get used to it and, what's more, you'll forget all the terror you've been through."

"I don't want to forget everything," said Gladia softly.

"You will." Baley looked at the slim girl who stood before him and said, not without a momentary pang, "And you will be married someday, too. Really married, I mean."

"Somehow," she said mournfully, "that doesn't seem so attractive to me—right now."

"You'll change your mind."

And they stood there, looking at each other for a wordless moment.

Gladia said, "I've never thanked you."

Baley said, "It was only my job."

"You'll be going back to Earth now, won't you?"

"Yes."

"I'll never see you again."

"Probably not. But don't feel badly about that. In forty years at most, I'll be dead and you won't look a bit different from the way you do now."

Her face twisted. "Don't say that."

"It's true."

She said rapidly, as though forced to change the subject, "It's all true about Jothan Leebig, you know."

"I know. Other roboticists went over his records and found experiments toward unmanned intelligent spaceships. They also found other robots with replaceable limbs."

Gladia shuddered, "Why did he do such a horrible thing, do you suppose?"

"He was afraid of people. He killed himself to avoid personal presence and he was ready to kill other worlds to make sure that Solaria and its personal-presence taboo would never be touched."

"How could he feel so," she murmured, "when personal presence can be so very——"

Again a silent moment while they faced each other at ten paces. Then Gladia cried suddenly, "Oh, Elijah, you'll think it abandoned of me."

"Think what abandoned?"

"May I touch you? I'll never see you again, Elijah."

"If you want to."

Step by step, she came closer, her eyes glowing, yet looking apprehensive, too. She stopped three feet away, then slowly, as though in a trance, she began to remove the glove on her right hand.

Baley started a restraining gesture. "Don't be foolish, Gladia."

"I'm not afraid," said Gladia.

Her hand was bare. It trembled as she extended it.

And so did Baley's as he took her hand in his. They remained so for one moment, her hand a shy thing, frightened as it rested in his. He opened his hand and hers escaped, darted suddenly and without warning toward his face until her fingertips rested feather-light upon his cheek for the barest moment.

She said, "Thank you, Elijah. Good-by."

He said, "Good-by, Gladia," and watched her leave.

Even the thought that a ship was waiting to take him back to Earth did not wipe out the sense of loss he felt at that moment.

Undersecretary Albert Minnim's look was intended to be one of prim welcome. "I am glad to see you back on Earth. Your report, of course, arrived before you did and is being studied. You did a good job. The matter will look well in your record."

"Thank you," said Baley. There was no room for further elation in him. Being back on Earth; being safe in the Caves; being in hearing of Jessie's voice (he had spoken to her already) had left him strangely empty.

"However," said Minnim, "your report concerned only the murder investigation. There was another matter we were interested in. May I have a report on that, verbally?"

Baley hesitated and his hand moved automatically toward the inner pocket where the warm comfort of his pipe could once more be found.

Minnim said at once, "You may smoke, Baley."

Baley made of the lighting process a rather drawn-out ritual. He said, "I am not a sociologist."

"Aren't you?" Minnim smiled briefly. "It seems to me we discussed that once. A successful detective must be a good rule-of-thumb sociologist even if he never heard of Hackett's Equation. I think, from your discomfort at the moment, that you have notions concerning the Outer Worlds but aren't sure how it will sound to me?"

"If you put it that way, sir . . . When you ordered me to Solaria, you asked a question; you asked what the weaknesses of the Outer Worlds were. Their strengths were their robots, their low population, their long lives, but what were their weaknesses?"

"Well?"

"I believe I know the weaknesses of the Solarians, sir."

"You can answer my question? Good. Go ahead."

"Their weaknesses, sir, are their robots, their low population, their long lives."

Minnim stared at Baley without any change of expression. His hands worked in jerky finger-drawn designs along the papers on his desk.

He said, "Why do you say that?"

Baley had spent hours organizing his thoughts on the way back from Solaria; had confronted officialdom, in imagination, with balanced, well-reasoned arguments. Now he felt at a loss.

He said, "I'm not sure I can put them clearly."

"No matter. Let me hear. This is first approximation only."

Baley said, "The Solarians have given up something mankind has had for a million years; something worth more than atomic power, cities, agriculture, tools, fire, everything; because it's something that made everything else possible."

"I don't want to guess, Baley. What is it?"

"The tribe, sir. Co-operation between individuals. Solaria has given it up entirely. It is a world of isolated individuals and the planet's only sociologist is delighted that this is so. That sociologist, by the way, never heard of sociomathematics, because he is inventing his own science. There is no one to teach him, no one to help him, no one to think of something he himself might miss. The only science that really flourishes on Solaria is robotics and there are only a handful of men involved in that, and when it came to an analysis of the interaction of robots and men, they had to call in an Earthman to help.

"Solarian art, sir, is abstract. We have abstract art on Earth as *one* form of art; but on Solaria it is the *only* form. The human touch is gone. The looked-for future is one of ectogenesis and complete isolation from birth."

Minnim said, "It all sounds horrible. But is it harmful?"

"I think so. Without the interplay of human against human, the chief interest in life is gone; most of the intellectual values are gone; most of the reason for living is gone. Viewing is no substitute for seeing. The Solarians, themselves, are conscious that viewing is a long-distance sense.

"And if isolation isn't enough to induce stagnation, there is the matter of their long lives. On Earth, we have a continuous influx of young people who are willing to change because they haven't had time to grow hard-set in their ways. I suppose there's some optimum. A life long enough for real accomplishment and short enough to make way for youth at a rate that's not too slow. On Solaria, the rate *is* too slow."

Minnim still drew patterns with his finger. "Interesting! Interesting!" He looked up, and it was as though a mask had fallen away. There was glee in his eyes. "Plainclothesman, you're a man of penetration."

"Thank you," said Baley stiffly.

"Do you know why I encouraged you to describe your views to me?" He was almost like a little boy, hugging his pleasure. He went on without waiting for an answer. "Your report has already undergone preliminary analysis by our sociologists and I was wondering if you had any idea yourself as to the excellent news for Earth you had brought with you. I see you have."

"But wait," said Baley. "There's more to this."

"There is, indeed," agreed Minnim jubilantly. "Solaria cannot possibly correct its stagnation. It has passed a critical point and their dependence on robots has gone too far. Individual robots can't discipline an individual child, even though discipline may do the child eventual good. The robot can't see past the immediate pain. And robots collectively cannot discipline a planet by allowing its institutions to collapse when the institutions have grown harmful. They can't see past the immediate chaos. So the only end for the Outer Worlds is perpetual stagnation and Earth will be freed of their domination. This new data changes everything. Physical revolt will not even be necessary. Freedom will come of itself."

"Wait," said Baley again, more loudly. "It's only Solaria we're discussing, not any other Outer World."

"It's the same thing. Your Solarian sociologist—Kimot——"

"Quemot, sir."

"Quemot, then. He said, did he not, that the other Outer Worlds were moving in the direction of Solaria?"

"He did, but he knew nothing about the other Outer Worlds first-hand, and he was no sociologist. Not really. I thought I made that clear."

"Our own men will check."

"They'll lack data too. We know nothing about the really big Outer Worlds. Aurora, for instance; Daneel's world. To me, it doesn't seem reasonable to expect them to be anything like Solaria. In fact, there's only one world in the Galaxy which resembles So-laria——"

Minnim was dismissing the subject with a small, happy wave of his neat hand. "Our men will check. I'm sure they will agree with Quemot."

Baley's stare grew somber. If Earth's sociologists were anxious enough for happy news, they would find themselves agreeing with Quemot, at that. Anything could be found in figures if the search were long enough and hard enough and if the proper pieces of information were ignored or overlooked.

He hesitated. Was it best now to speak while he had the ear of a man high in the government or——

He hesitated a trifle too long. Minnim was speaking again, shuffling a few papers and growing more matter-of-fact. "A few minor matters, Plainclothesman, concerning the Delmarre case itself and then you will be free to go. Did you intend to have Leebig commit suicide?"

"I intended to force a confession, sir. I had not anticipated suicide at the approach, ironically, of someone who was only a robot and who would not really be violating the taboo against personal presence. But, frankly, I don't regret his death. He was a dangerous man. It will be a long time before there will be another man who will combine his sickness and his brilliance."

"I agree with that," said Minnim dryly, "and consider his death fortunate, but didn't you consider your danger if the Solarians had stopped to realize that Leebig couldn't possibly have murdered Delmarre?"

Baley took his pipe out of his mouth and said nothing.

"Come, Plainclothesman," said Minnim. "You know he didn't.

The murder required personal presence and Leebig would die rather than allow that. He *did* die rather than allow it."

Baley said, "You're right, sir. I counted on the Solarians being too horrified at his misuse of robots to stop to think of that."

"Then who did kill Delmarre?"

Baley said slowly, "If you mean who struck the actual blow, it was the person everyone knew had done so. Gladia Delmarre, the man's wife."

"And you let her go?"

Baley said, "Morally, the responsibility wasn't hers. Leebig knew Gladia quarreled bitterly with her husband, and often. He must have known how furious she could grow in moments of anger. Leebig wanted the death of the husband under circumstances that would incriminate the wife. So he supplied Delmarre with a robot and, I imagine, instructed it with all the skill he possessed to hand Gladia one of its detachable limbs at the moment of her full fury. With a weapon in her hand at the crucial moment, she acted in a temporary black-out before either Delmarre or the robot could stop her. Gladia was as much Leebig's unwitting instrument as the robot itself."

Minnim said, "The robot's arm must have been smeared with blood and matted hair."

"It probably was," said Baley, "but it was Leebig who took the murder robot in charge. He could easily have instructed any other robots who might have noticed the fact to forget it. Dr. Thool might have noticed it, but he inspected only the dead man and the unconscious woman. Leebig's mistake was to think that guilt would rest so obviously on Gladia that the matter of the absence of an obvious weapon at the scene wouldn't save her. Nor could he anticipate that an Earthman would be called in to help with the investigation."

"So with Leebig dead, you arranged to have Gladia leave Solaria. Was that to save her in case any Solarians began thinking about the case?"

Baley shrugged. "She had suffered enough. She had been victimized by everyone; by her husband, by Leebig, by the world of Solaria."

Minnim said, "Weren't you bending the law to suit a personal whim?"

Baley's craggy face grew hard. "It was not a whim. I was not bound by Solarian law. Earth's interests were paramount, and for the sake of those interests, I had to see that Leebig, the dangerous one, was dealt with. As for Mrs. Delmarre." He faced Minnim now, and felt himself taking a crucial step. He *had* to say this. "As for Mrs. Delmarre, I made her the basis of an experiment."

"What experiment?"

"I wanted to know if she would consent to face a world where personal presence was permitted and expected. I was curious to know if she had the courage to face disruption of habits so deeply settled in her. I was afraid she might refuse to go; that she might insist on remaining on Solaria, which was purgatory to her, rather than bring herself to abandon her distorted Solarian way of life. But she chose change and I was glad she did, because to me it seemed symbolic. It seemed to open the gates of salvation for *us*."

"For *us*?" said Minnim with energy. "What the devil do you mean?"

"Not for you and me, particularly, sir," said Baley gravely, "but for all mankind. You're wrong about the other Outer Worlds. They have few robots; they permit personal presence; and they have been investigating Solaria. R. Daneel Olivaw was there with me, you know, and he'll bring back a report. There is a danger they may become Solarias someday, but they will probably recognize that danger and work to keep themselves in a reasonable balance and in that way remain the leaders of mankind."

"That is your opinion," said Minnim testily.

"And there's more to it. There *is* one world like Solaria and that's Earth."

"Plainclothesman Baley!"

"It's so, sir. We're Solaria inside out. They retreated into isolation from one another. We retreated into isolation from the Galaxy. They are at the dead end of their inviolable estates. We are at the dead end of underground Cities. They're leaders without followers, only robots who can't talk back. We're followers without leaders, only enclosing Cities to keep us safe." Baley's fists clenched.

Minnim disapproved. "Plainclothesman, you have been through an ordeal. You need a rest and you will have one. A month's vacation, full pay, and a promotion at the end of it."

"Thank you, but that's not all I want. I want you to listen. There's only one direction out of our dead end and that's outward, toward Space. There are a million worlds out there and the Spacers own only fifty. They are few and long-lived. We are many and short-lived. We are better suited than they for exploration and colonization. We have population pressure to push us and a rapid turnover of generation to keep us supplied with the young and reckless. It was our ancestors who colonized the Outer Worlds in the first place."

"Yes, I see—but I'm afraid our time is up."

Baley could feel the other's anxiety to be rid of him and he remained stolidly in place. He said, "When the original colonization established worlds superior to our own in technology, we escaped by building wombs beneath the ground for ourselves. The Spacers made us feel inferior and we hid from them. That's no answer. To avoid the destructive rhythm of rebellion and suppression, we must *compete* with them, follow them, if we must, lead them, if we can. To do that, we must face the open; we must teach ourselves to face the open. If it is too late to teach ourselves, then we must teach our children. It's vital!"

"You need a rest, Plainclothesman."

Baley said violently, "Listen to me, sir. If the Spacers are strong and we remain as we are, then Earth will be destroyed within a century. That has been computed, as you yourself told me. If the Spacers are really weak and are growing weaker, then we may escape, but who says the Spacers are weak? The Solarians, yes, but that's all we know."

"But——"

"I'm not through. One thing we *can* change, whether the Spacers are weak or strong. We can change the way we are. Let us face the open and we'll never need rebellion. We can spread out into our own crowd of worlds and become Spacers ourselves. If we stay here on Earth, cooped up, then useless and fatal rebellion can't be stopped. It will be all the worse if the people build any false hopes because of supposed Spacer weakness. Go ahead, ask the sociologists. Put my argument to them. And if they're still in doubt, find a way to send me to Aurora. Let me bring back a report on the *real* Spacers, and you'll see what Earth must do."

Minnim nodded. "Yes, yes. Good day, now, Plainclothesman Baley."

Baley left with a feeling of exaltation. He had not expected an open victory over Minnim. Victories over ingrained patterns of thought are not won in a day or a year. But he had seen the look of pensive uncertainty that had crossed Minnim's face and had blotted out, at least for a while, the earlier uncritical joy.

He felt he could see into the future. Minnim would ask the sociologists and one or two of them would be uncertain. They would wonder. They would consult Baley.

Give it one year, thought Baley, one year, and I'll be on my way to Aurora. One generation, and we'll be out in space once more.

Baley stepped onto the northbound Expressway. Soon he would see Jessie. Would *she* understand? And his son, Bentley, now seventeen. When Ben had a seventeen-year-old of his own, would he be standing on some empty world, building a spacious life?

It was a frightening thought. Baley still feared the open. But he no longer feared the fear! It was not something to run from, that fear, but something to fight.

Baley felt as though a touch of madness had come over him. From the very first the open had had its weird attraction over him; from the time in the ground-car when he had tricked Daneel in order to have the top lowered so that he might stand up in the open air.

He had failed to understand then. Daneel thought he was being perverse. Baley himself thought he was facing the open out of professional necessity, to solve a crime. Only on that last evening on Solaria, with the curtain tearing away from the window, did he realize his need to face the open for the open's own sake; for its attraction and its promise of freedom.

There must be millions on Earth who would feel that same urge, if the open were only brought to their attention, if they could be made to take the first step.

He looked about.

The Expressway was speeding on. All about him was artificial light and huge banks of apartments gliding backward and flashing signs and store windows and factories and lights and noise and crowds and more noise and people and people and people . . .

It was all he had loved, all he had hated and feared to leave, all he had thought he longed for on Solaria.

And it was all strange to him.

He couldn't make himself fit back in.

He had gone out to solve a murder and something had happened to him.

He had told Minnim the Cities were wombs, and so they were. And what was the first thing a man must do before he can be a man? He must be born. He must leave the womb. And once left, it could not be re-entered.

Baley had left the City and could not re-enter. The City was no longer his; the Caves of Steel were alien. This *had* to be. And it would be so for others and Earth would be born again and reach outward.

His heart beat madly and the noise of life about him sank to an unheard murmur.

He remembered his dream on Solaria and he understood it at last. He lifted his head and he could see through all the steel and concrete and humanity above him. He could see the beacon set in space to lure men outward. He could see it shining down. The naked sun!

130-82

FIC   Asimov, Isaac
ASI   The robot novels.
      The caves of steel
      The naked sun

                        $15.00

DATE DUE			